D0629580

Also by Emma Donoghue

Landing

Touch Subjects

Life Mask

The Woman Who Gave Birth to Rabbits

Slammerkin

Kissing the Witch

Hood

Stirfry

The Sealed Letter

The Sealed Letter

EMMA DONOGHUE

HarperCollins*PublishersLtd*

The Sealed Letter

Published by HarperCollins Publishers Ltd.

HarperCollins books may be purchased for educational, business, or sales promotional use through our Special Markets Department.

HarperCollins Publishers Ltd
2 Bloor Street East, 20th Floor
Toronto, Ontario, Canada
M4W 1A8

www.harpercollins.ca

Library and Archives Canada Cataloguing in Publication

Donoghue, Emma, 1969–
The sealed letter : a novel / Emma Donoghue. —1st ed.

ISBN: 978-1-55468-036-8

1. Codrington, John Henry, 1808–1877—Fiction.
2. Codrington, Helen, d. 1876—Fiction.
3. Faithfull, Emily, 1836?–1895—Fiction.
4. Divorce—Great Britain—Fiction.
I. Title.

PS8557.0559S39 2008 C813'.54 C2007-907035-3

RRD 9 8 7 6 5 4 3 2 1

Design by Sharon Kish.
Printed and bound in the United States.

Dedicated with love to my old friends
Gráinne Ní Dhúill and Debra Westgate

There are sealed pages in my heart,
Traced with illumined hand,
That none can see, and if they did,
Oh! who would understand?
But thou, by some strange sympathy,
Hast thrown a searching look,
And read at sight the hardest scroll
Indorsed within the book.

Eliza Cook,
"Stanzas, Addressed to Charlotte Cushman" (1851)

Contents

I

Prima Facie

(Latin, "at first sight" or "on the face of it":

evidence presumed to be true unless rebutted)

Every woman should be free
to support herself by the use of
whatever faculties God has given her.

Emily Faithfull,
Letter to the *English Woman's Journal*
(September 1862)

The last day of August, and the sky is the colour of hot ash. Something rancid wafts on the air from Smithfield Market; the air glitters with stone dust. She's swept down Farringdon Street in the slipstream of bowlers, top hats, baskets on porters' heads. A hand lights on her arm, a small, ungloved hand; the brown silk of her sleeve is caught between plump pink fingertips. She staggers, clamps her pocketbook to her ribs, but even as she's jerking away she can't help recognizing that hand.

"Fido?"

One syllable dipping down, the next swooping up, a familiar and jaunty music; the word skips across the years like a skimmed stone. Almost everyone calls her that now, but Helen was the first. Fido's eyes flick up to Helen's face: sharp cheekbones, chignon still copper. An acid lemon dress, white lace gloves scrunched in the other hand, the one that's not gripping Fido's sleeve. The human river has washed Fido sideways, now, into a scarlet-chested, brass-buttoned officer, who begs her pardon.

"I knew it was you," cries Helen, holding her emerald parasol up to block the terrible sun. "Did you take me for a pickpocket?" she asks, a giggle in her throat.

"Only for half a moment, Mrs. Codrington," she manages to say, licking her gritty lips.

A flicker of pain across the pointed face. "Oh, Fido. Has it come to that?"

"Helen, then," says Fido, and smiles despite herself. Despite the skin-tightening sensation of encountering a friend who is no longer one. Despite the memories that are billowing up like genii from smashed bottles. She wrenches a handkerchief from her jacket pocket and dabs at her forehead. The two women are blocking the traffic; an old man swerves around them, under a sandwich board that reads *No Home Should Be Without One.*

"But how you've grown," Helen is marvelling.

Fido looks down at the brown bulge of her bodice. "Too true."

Pink fingers clap to the coral mouth. "You monster! Still the same talent for mistaking my meaning, or letting on that you do. Of course I meant you've grown *up* so."

"It has been, what, seven years?" Her words are as stiff as tin soldiers. Checking her bonnet is straight, she becomes belatedly aware that the scarlet uniform she bumped into a minute ago is hovering, so she turns to see him off.

"Oh, my manners," says Helen. "Miss Emily Faithfull—if I may—Colonel David Anderson, a friend of the family's from Malta."

The colonel has dangling blond whiskers. Fido lets his fingers enclose hers. "Delighted," she says distractedly.

"*The* Miss Faithfull?"

She winces at the phrase. By his accent, he's a Scot.

"Printer and Publisher to the Queen?"

The man's well informed. Fido concedes a nod. "Her Majesty's been gracious enough to lend her name to our enterprise at the Victoria Press." She turns back to Helen. So much to say, and little of it speakable; words log-jam in her throat. "Are you and Captain Codrington home on leave, or—"

"Forever and ever, amen," says Helen.

That little twisted smile is so familiar to Fido that the years fall away like planks splintering under her feet. She feels dizzy; she fears she'll have to sink to her knees, right here in all the dusty clamour of London's City district.

"Matter of fact, it's Vice-Admiral Codrington now," remarks Colonel Anderson.

"Of course, of course, forgive me," Fido tells Helen. "I can't help thinking of him by the name he bore in the days . . ." *The days when I knew him? When I knew you?* But she's not that girl anymore. *It's 1864: I'm almost thirty years old*, she scolds herself.

"Harry's been immured in paperwork for weeks, ever since our vile crossing from Malta," complains Helen, "so I've press-ganged the colonel into service as my parcel carrier today."

"A keen volunteer, Mrs. C.," he corrects her, swinging two small packages on their strings. "I'll just pop across the road to pick up your whatsits, shall I?"

"Curtain tassels, a dozen of the magenta," she reminds him.

"That's the ticket."

Tactful of the officer to absent himself, Fido thinks. But once she and Helen are alone, the discomfort rises between them like a paper screen. "Such heat" is all she manages.

"It takes me back," says Helen pleasurably, twirling her fringed green parasol and tipping her chin up to catch the merciless light.

Watching that face, Fido finds it hard to believe that this woman must be—count the years—thirty-six. "To Italy? Or do you mean India?"

"Oh, both: my whole torrid youth!"

"Was it . . . was it generally hot in Malta?"

Helen's laugh comes out startlingly deep, like a sob. "So we're reduced to discussing the weather."

Irritation boils in Fido's veins. "As it happens, I'm pressed for time today—"

"Oh, yes, I was almost forgetting what a very important person you've become. *The* Miss Faithfull, philanthropist, pioneer!"

Fido wants to take her by the lemon-lace-edged shoulders and shake her like a doll. "I prefer to call myself a woman of business."

"I can quite see why I was dropped the moment I left the country," Helen rattles on, "considering how *pressed for time* you've been, what with all your valiant efforts on behalf of our downtrodden sex."

Her mouth, Fido finds, is hanging open. "Whatever can you mean, *dropped*?"

A pretty shrug. "It needn't have been done with such brutal efficiency, need it?" Helen's dropped the mocking tone. "Friendships have their seasons, that's understood. But you might have let me down rather more gently, I suppose, after all we'd been through."

Fido blinks dust out of her eyes.

"It wasn't kind, that's all I'll say. Or womanly. It wasn't like you, like what I knew of your heart, or thought I did."

"Stop." She holds up her white-gloved hand till it almost touches those rapid lips.

Helen only speeds up. "You'd had your fill of me and Harry by the time we embarked for Malta, was that it? All at once sick to death of us and our bickerings?" Her eyes have the wet blue sheen of rain. "I know, I know, I quite see that we'd worn you out between us. But I must confess, when I found myself tossed aside like yesterday's newspaper—"

"My dear." Fido almost barks it. "I find these accusations incongruous."

Helen stares at her like a baby.

"Must I remind you, I wrote twice to Admiralty House in Valetta and got not a word of reply to either?"

"Nonsense!"

Fido is bewildered. This is like one of those dreams in which one is caught up in an endless, illogical series of tasks.

"Of course I wrote back," cries Helen.

"From Malta?"

"Of course from Malta! I was a stranger in a strange land; I needed a bosom friend more than ever. Whyever would I have left off writing? I poured out all my worries—"

Fido breaks in. "When was this? What month?"

"How should I recall, all these years later?" asks Helen reasonably. "But I know I replied as soon as I got your letter—the one and only letter I received from you when I was in Malta. I sent several long screeds, but on your side the correspondence simply dried up. You can't imagine my nervous excitement when a packet of post would arrive from England, and I'd rip it open—"

Fido's chewing her lip; she tastes blood. "I did change my lodgings, that autumn," she concedes. "But still, your letters ought to have been sent on directly by the post office."

"Lost at sea?" suggests Helen, frowning.

"One of them, perhaps, but could the Continental mail really be so—"

"Things do go astray."

"What a very absurd—" Fido hears her voice rise pitifully, and breaks off. Scalding water behind her eyes. "I don't know what to say."

Helen's smile is miserable. "Oh heavens, I see it all now. I should have tried again; I should have kept on writing, despite my mortified feelings."

"No, *I* should! I thought—" She tries now to remember what she'd thought; what sense she'd made of it when Helen hadn't written back, that strange year when the Codringtons were posted abroad and Fido stayed alone in London, wondering what to make of herself. "I suppose I supposed . . . a chapter in your life had drawn to a close."

"Dearest Fido! You're not the stuff of a chapter," Helen protests. "Several volumes, at least."

Her brain's whirling under the hot, powdery sky. She doesn't want to cry, here on Farringdon Street, a matter of yards from her steam-printing office, where any passing clerk or hand might spot her. So Fido laughs instead. "Such an idiotic misunderstanding, like something out of Mozart. I couldn't be sorrier."

"Nor I. These seven years have been an eternity!"

What in another woman would strike Fido as hyperbole has in Helen Codrington always charmed her, somehow. The phrases are delivered with a sort of rueful merriment, as if by an actress who knows herself to be better than her part.

She seizes Fido's wrists, squeezing tight enough that her bones shift under the humid cotton gloves. "And what are the odds that I'd happen across you again, not a fortnight after my return? Like a rose in this urban wilderness," she cries, dropping Fido's wrists to gesture across the crowded City.

Fido catches sight of the straw-coloured curls of Colonel Anderson, making his way back across Farringdon Street, so she speaks fast. "I used to wonder if you had new, absorbing occupations—another child, even?"

Helen's giggle has half a shudder in it. "No, no, that's the one point on which Harry and I have always agreed."

"The little girls must be . . . what, ten or so?" The calculation discomfits her; she still pictures them spinning their tops on the nursery floorboards.

"Eleven and twelve. Oh, Nan and Nell are quite the sophisticated *demoiselles*. You won't know them."

Then the Scot is at her elbow. "Rather a nuisance, Mrs. C.," he reports. "They've only eight of the magenta in stock, so I've asked for them to be sent on to you in Eccleston Square when they're ready."

Fido's mind is suddenly filled with the tall white walls in Belgravia that she once called home. "The same house?" she asks Helen, under her breath. "Were you able to put the tenants out?"

"The same everything," she answers. "Harry and I have picked up our former life like some moth-eaten cloak from the floor of a wardrobe."

"Doesn't someone in Trollope tell a bride, 'Don't let him take you anywhere beyond Eccleston Square'?" asks Colonel Anderson.

Fido laughs. "Yes, it's still the last bastion of respectability."

"Are you a Belgravian too, Miss Faithfull?"

"Bloomsbury," she corrects him, with a touch of defiance. "I'm one of these 'new women'; they'd never have me in Eccleston Square."

"Even as '*Printer to Her Majesty*'?"

"Especially under that title, I suspect! No, I live snug and bachelor-style on Taviton Street. I read the *Times* over breakfast, which rather scandalizes my maid."

They all laugh at that.

"I was just setting off home after a morning at my steam-works, over there at Number 83," says Fido, gesturing up Farringdon Street. "The *Friend of the People*—a weekly paper—is in type, and goes to press tomorrow."

"How exciting," murmurs Helen.

"Hardly. Mulish apprentices, and paper curling in the heat!" Even as she's saying the words, this automatic disparagement irritates Fido. The fact is, it is exciting. Sometimes when she wakes in the morning, every muscle in her limbs tightens when she remembers that she's a publisher, and no longer just the youngest of Reverend Ferdinand Faithfull's enormous brood.

"I'll hail a cab at the stand, then, shall I," Anderson asks, "and drop you ladies home?"

"I have a better idea," cries Helen. "Ever since reading about the Underground Railway, I've been longing to descend into Hades."

Fido smiles, remembering what it's like to be sucked into this woman's orbit: the festive whims and whirls of it. "I don't mean to disappoint you, but it's quite respectable."

"You've tried it?"

"Not yet. But as it happens," she adds on impulse, "my physician believes it might be beneficial."

"My friend's a martyr to asthma," Helen tells the colonel.

My friend: two simple words that make Fido's head reel.

"The Underground's uncommon convenient," he says, "and certainly faster than inching through all this traffic."

"Onwards, then: a journey into the bowels of the earth!" says Helen. Her hand—the bare one—is a warm snake sliding through the crook of Fido's elbow.

Yet another building site has opened up like an abscess since Fido was last on this street. Anderson helps the ladies across the makeshift plank bridge, Helen's yellow skirt swinging like a bell. The wasteland is littered with wheelbarrows and spades, and the caked foreheads of the navvies remind Fido of some detail about face painting from a tedious lecture she recently attended by a South Sea missionary.

"I barely recognize London—the way it's thrown out tendrils in all directions," remarks Helen.

"Yes, and the government refuses to make the developers consider the poor," Fido tells her, "who're being evicted in their tens of thousands—"

But Helen has stopped to brush something off a flounce, and Fido feels jarred, as if she's walked into a wall. The old Fido—meaning, the young Fido—knew nothing more of the state of the nation than she'd picked up on parish visits with her mother in Surrey. That girl never spouted statistics; she talked of novels, balls, matches, who had *dash* and *go.* The long hiatus, the seven years during which Fido and Helen have been unknown to each other, seems to gape like a tear in a stocking.

In the station, a train is waiting, the hazy sunlight that comes through the roof catching its gilt name: *Locust.* "But we're not underground at all," complains Helen.

"Patience is a virtue," murmurs Colonel Anderson, handing the ladies into the first-class compartment.

White walls, mahogany and mirrors, a good carpet; the carriage is an impersonation of a drawing-room, thinks Fido. The gas globes hanging from the ceiling give off a light that's wan but bright enough to read by, and a peculiar fume.

Helen leans against Fido and shivers pleasurably. "I should think it must be fearfully hazardous to combine fumes and sparks in an enclosed tunnel."

The tone amuses Fido; Helen's always delighted in even a slim possibility of danger. "I suppose one must trust in the scientists."

"If there should be an explosion, I'll carry you out in a trice," Anderson tells Helen. "Both of you," he corrects himself, "under my arms, like twin battering rams!"

Fido can't stop her eyebrows shooting up.

"Beg pardon, my imagination rather ran away with me there." His whiskers look more like a spaniel's ears than ever.

"You must excuse the colonel," murmurs Helen, laughing in Fido's ear. "We're a dreadfully lax lot on Malta; the sun evaporates all our Anglo proprieties."

But Helen, after childhood in Calcutta and adolescence in Florence, is the most un-English of Englishwomen; she's always waltzed her way around the rules of womanhood. It's a quality that Fido relished even when she was young, long before she ever did any hard thinking about the arbitrariness of those rules.

Helen is staring at a label on the window that bears a picture of a heart, and inside it, in Gothic lettering, *The Dead Heart.*

"It's a play," Fido tells her.

"Ah." A sigh. "I've been gone so long, I'm quite behind the times."

"The whole city's pockmarked with these irksome labels," Anderson mutters. "Really, advertising has had its day; the public can't be fooled anymore."

"At the theatre, by the by, don't you hate women who're afraid to laugh?" Helen asks Fido.

"Awfully," she says, grinning back at her. It's the surges of familiarity that she's finding strangest: as if the friends haven't been apart for a moment.

A piercing whistle makes Fido jump, and the carriage sways into movement. All at once her dress feels soaked in the armpits and the small of the back. Her chest's a little tight; she makes herself take long breaths of the metallic air. The wheels start to thunder, the engine screams. The carriage is filling up with vapour, and she coughs violently; Anderson stands and wrestles with the window catch. "Breathe it in deeply," says Helen, one hand caressing Fido's shoulder blade.

The smoke feels poisonous, but then medicines often do; she does her best to fill her lungs and hold it in. The train's been swallowed up by darkness, and the gaslight flares up greenly. At this speed, there's a peculiar vibration, a sort of undulation of the thundering machine. Above them, she knows, there's more than twenty feet of packed London earth. How do the third-class passengers bear it in their open wagons? This isn't like a railway tunnel, because it shows no sign of coming to an end.

"More than a little oppressive, no?" she remarks, but the others show no sign of hearing her over the shrieking demons, and she shouldn't have spoken because now she's hacking so hard her lungs are on fire. Between the coughs, the wheezing is getting worse. She fumbles in her bag, claws the lining.

"Let me, let me," shouts Helen, taking the bag from her. "Is this little bottle—"

Fido undoes it with spasmodic fingers and puts it to her nose. The camphor and menthol make her eyes water, and she gasps. She takes a long drink that burns like vitriol. But already she can feel the laudanum calming her lungs a little. She finds a folded handkerchief and douses it in the mixture. Holding it to her face, she makes herself do nothing but breathe.

The train's stopped. Anderson is speaking in her ear, something about King's Cross, can she manage a little longer or should they alight here? She shakes her head, unable to speak. Her wretched lungs!

Another few minutes of jolting and shrieking, and then the train halts again: Euston. Anderson's helping her to her feet, and Helen's holding her other elbow. Up a long, twisting staircase—they all three stop whenever Fido's overtaken by a coughing fit. A male passenger's voice behind mutters a complaint, and Anderson turns to snap something about the lady's being unwell.

Finally they emerge on Gower Street. The sun's gone behind a thick veil of cloud, and it seems a little cooler. Fido's breathing has eased enough to let her speak: "I'm perfectly well now, really."

"All my fault," Helen is lamenting as they turn down Endsleigh Gardens. "My vagaries so often end in disaster . . ."

"Not at all," says Fido hoarsely; "my own doctor recommended the experiment."

Helen's face brightens. "It is rather a thrill, though, isn't it, to cross the capital in a matter of minutes?"

She nods, coughing explosively again.

At the entrance to Taviton Street, the top-hatted gatekeeper expresses such concern for Miss Faithfull's health that Anderson's obliged to tip him.

"If you please," says Fido, on her steps, loosening herself from her friends' arms, "I'm quite recovered now." Embarrassment makes her voice almost surly. "You've been awfully kind, Colonel."

"Fortunate to be of any assistance to such a celebrated lady," says Anderson with a neat bow.

"Will you solemnly swear to rest now?" breathes Helen in her ear. "And a line tomorrow."

"A paragraph, at the least."

They part laughing; their hot hands come away reluctantly, like ivy. It's all very strange, Fido thinks; seven years of silence cracked open like a windowpane.

She uses her own key; she's never seen the need for interrupting the servants' work to make them let her in.

It's these small, rational reforms that make the Reverend and Mrs. Faithfull shudder so, on their rare visits from Headley. Her father's a clergyman of the old, well-bred, moderate school; he preaches in tailored black, and has equal scorn for genuflecting Tractarians and Low ranters. Fido still feels bad about the enormous expense she put him to by her coming out: all those unflattering flounces, and for what? At twenty-two, finding herself alone in London after the Codringtons' departure, she had a quiet tussle with her parents that ended with her winning their cautious agreement that she was to be treated as a sensible spinster of thirty, with her own modest household, trying to make her way in the literary world. But two years later, when Fido broke it to them that she had taken up the cause of rights for women, and was setting up a printing house as a demonstration of female capacity for skilled labour, Mrs. Faithfull got two red spots very high in her cheeks and asked whether it wasn't generally held that a lady who engaged in trade, even with the highest of motives, lost caste. Fido countered with some sharp remarks about *idle femininity* that make her wince to remember, especially considering that her mother has never known an idle hour in her life.

What about these days? Do the Faithfulls consider the youngest daughter of their eight to be still a lady? Best not to ask. Officially they condone her life in the capital—*your mission*, her mother called it once, which must be how she describes it to her neighbours in Surrey—but Fido can sense the strain. They'd so much rather she were settled in some country town and producing a child a year, like her sisters.

Upstairs, in her bedroom, Fido catches sight of herself in the mirror. Intelligent eyes in the long, upholstered face of—well, there's no other way to put it—a well-fed dog. Her limp brown hair, cropped to her neck, is pulled back by a plain band. The flesh sags softly under her chin where white lace, grubby from her morning in the City, meets the brown cloth. No corsets, no crinoline: it cost her only a little pang to give them up, and she never misses them now. (They didn't make her look any prettier, only more conventional, another harmless frilled sheep drifting along with the herd.) Walking arm in arm with Helen this afternoon, it strikes her that the two of them must have looked like characters from quite different sorts of book. Well, Fido's as God made her. And as she's chosen to be. At least the way she dresses now is clear, uncompromising—and not eccentric enough to demand attention. It announces, *I have more pressing business than to wonder who's looking at me.*

She prises off her shoes before lying down. She hopes she isn't marking the counterpane. A shower-bath would be delicious, but the company only turns the water on in the mornings. Well, that's the last time she'll let herself be dragged through the vaporous sewers of the Underground. Some days this city is too much for her: a clanging machine that threatens to crush and swallow her. Some days she doubts her lungs will hold out till she's forty. But if she led the kind of quiet provincial days the Reverend and Mrs. Faithfull would prefer for their youngest daughter, it wouldn't be asthma that would choke off her life force in the end, but ennui. The fact is that for all its infinite varieties of filth, London is the thumping heart of everything that interests her, the only place she can imagine living.

She reaches into the bedside drawer for her tin of Sweet Threes and the little box of safety matches. (Fido has a standing order for her cigarettes; they're delivered straight from the factory in Peckham, so she doesn't have to push her way into a tobacconist's once a week, running the gauntlet of smirking men.) The Turkish tobacco in its tube of yellow tissue smells sweetly spiced and nutty—though when she first tried a cigarette, five years ago, it seemed to stink like used horse bedding. She draws the smoke deep into her raw lungs now, and feels her breathing ease at once.

Helen's back. Fido still can't quite believe it.

After her second cigarette she sleeps, a little, and then rings for Johnson to bring up some cold mutton and pickles. She always reads at meals, to make the most of her time and to keep her mental pistons firing. Over her dinner tray she skims the Social Science Association's latest pamphlet on *Friendless Girls and How to Help Them.* She clucks with irritation when she finds a misspelling she should have spotted in the galleys.

Her attention keeps wandering. What are the odds of running into someone in London? Three and a half million to one, according to the last census. It's not as if the two former friends ran into each other at one of their old Belgravia haunts, or the home of some mutual acquaintance. To happen to glimpse each other on Farringdon Street, in a mob of bankers and porters, only a fortnight after the Codringtons' return to England, with Helen in search of magenta tassels and Fido's head full of printing schedules—it can't be an accident. Such astonishing luck, after the awful mischance of the lost letters that ended their friendship so needlessly. Fido likes to think of her life as self-made, an ingenious machine held in her own two hands . . . but there's something so fortuitous about today's reunion, she can only attribute it to providence.

Friendless Girls has fallen onto the counterpane. She's back in Kent, all at once, at the spot on Walmer Beach where she first laid eyes on Helen Codrington in 1854. A lady with russet hair, perched like a mermaid on the rocks, those salty blue eyes staring out to sea. Fido was only nineteen, on a visit to help her sister Esther with the new baby, and green with inexperience. Green enough, for instance, to assume that a weeping wife must be grieving the lack of her brave captain (recently posted to the Crimea) rather than the fact of him.

The Reverend and Mrs. Faithfull's union was such a solid edifice, so proper in its manners and substantial in its comforts: what did Fido, at nineteen, understand of the darker games husbands and wives could play? How little she knew of marriage—of anything, she corrects herself now—before she became acquainted with the Codringtons. Before she found herself drawn into the absorbing misery of a principled man and a warm woman who had nothing in common. Nothing to bind them except two little daughters, and the full force of law.

The strange thing was, Fido liked them both. She felt drawn to Helen at once, by instinct, as a bloom opens to a bee. But to tall, bearded Captain Codrington too, as soon as he sailed home that November—when the Crimean winter shut down all possibility of what he called "decent action." She was drawn to his earnestness, his zeal for the Navy, his tenderness with the children; she found him manly in the best sense. And as for him, he took to his wife's new companion at once, paid her the compliment of serious conversation, as if she were something more interesting than a second-season debutante. Within a month she'd picked up his wife's un-English habit of calling him Harry. One afternoon, when Helen had had a tantrum over caraway cake and rushed off to her room, Harry confided in Fido how valuable he thought her influence; how much the children treasured their "Aunt Fido"; how he hoped she'd consider Eccleston Square as her home whenever her parents could spare her from the Rectory in Headley. And little by little, without it ever receiving any further discussion, Fido found herself one of the family.

She began with a fount of optimism, not just as Helen's friend but also as a friend to the marriage. Surely the fact that this man and this woman were by nature alien to each other needn't mean that happiness would always be beyond their grasp? If Harry only mellowed a little, approaching his fifties . . . if he came to appreciate that his young wife's qualities were those of the singing grasshopper more than the industrious ant . . . if Helen, for her part, could be persuaded to accept the real life she'd chosen, rather than hankering for those chimerical ones she found between yellow paper covers . . . That was how Fido used to think, in the first years at Eccleston Square.

It embarrasses her to realize that she pictured herself as a sort of Miss Nightingale, lifting her lamp in dark passages. She tried not to take sides, but it was a vain attempt, she sees that now. Harry was away serving his sovereign for long stretches of the mid-1850s, and even when home between campaigns, he couldn't help but stand awkwardly outside the magic circle of the women's intimacy. *I used to call her Madre,* she thinks now. *And sometimes, Little One.* It's quite mysterious to Fido, that electric chain of feeling that can link two women of different ages, backgrounds, temperaments; that throb of sympathetic mutuality, that chiming note outside the range of men's hearing. Without understanding it, she's always responded to it as a diviner to the call of water deep underground.

Setting her tray aside, on impulse she gets out of bed, and goes to unlock a little drawer in her bureau. At the very back, rolled up in a piece of linen, she finds the choker. A cheap thing, but nicely made: mother-of-pearl, shells, pebbles of amber, all the small treasures of the Kentish shore, sewn onto a band of black velvet. Helen gave it to her to mark the first anniversary of their meeting, and Fido wore it for the best part of three years. *The Codrington years*, as she's called them ever since, in the privacy of her head.

She blamed herself at the time; of course she did. The fact is that for all Fido's sensible advice, her loving counsel, the Codrington marriage disintegrated on her watch. She did her best, and her best did no good at all.

Worse than that: by stepping in as a wide-eyed go-between, she became an obstacle. That awful last year, 1857, when Helen shut her bedroom door against her husband, and finally—having wilfully misunderstood a paragraph in the *Telegraph* about the new Matrimonial Causes Act—made a wild demand for a separation on the basis of *incompatibility* (as if any such thing existed in law) . . . Fido still can't sort out the pieces of that puzzle. All she knows is that the more she tried to help, the more entangled she got, the more she tangled matters that she'd have been better off not meddling with in the first place.

All this remembering is hard work, like using a muscle that's gone stiff and sore. There are things she can't look at directly yet; passages in her long history with the Codringtons over which she skips. Those strange, terrible months of quarrels and illnesses towards the end, for instance.

It still makes her blush to the throat to remember that Harry had to ask her to move out. (She ought to have left months before that, but Helen needed her so desperately, and the wound-up, wailing little girls . . .) He did it in a gentlemanly manner; assured her, "No third party should be obliged to witness such scenes." But Fido stumbled away from Eccleston Square like a child with scorched fingers.

And then in a matter of months, news came that Captain Codrington was to be elevated to the rank of rear admiral and made superintendent of the dockyards at Valetta. His wife and children would accompany him on his first land posting, that was understood; Admiralty House had dozens of rooms, and Helen was one of these rare Englishwomen raised in the tropics for whom the heat held no dangers. So off they went, the whole Codrington ménage. "It'll be a fresh start," Fido remembers telling a tear-stained Helen that summer of '57. "A heaven-sent second chance." She wanted to believe it herself; she was holding out for something like a happy ending.

And now? she wonders, as she stands fingering the seashell choker. Helen sounded no worse than rueful today on Farringdon Street, when she mentioned Harry being buried in paperwork. Perhaps seven years have dulled her weapons, and his. Have the spouses somehow muddled through their old antipathies, Fido wonders, and reached an *entente cordiale*?

On the verge of their departure, in '57, Fido imagined herself writing twice a week, and going out to Malta for long visits. She was still wearing the choker then; she wore it till long after the letters stopped arriving. She wasn't to know that the friendship had slipped through her fingers, by what she's only learned today—it still chokes her to realize it—was the most trivial of happenstance. The inefficiency of the Maltese post!

Fido rolls up the velvet necklace and puts it back in the drawer. It probably wouldn't go around her throat anymore. She's solider, these days, not just in flesh but also in mind. Being stranded seven years ago, left to her own devices, did her good. It doesn't matter why; it doesn't matter that it was all a mistake. Fido had to grow up and make a life for herself: a full one, useful and satisfying, an important life (if she says so herself).

But to feel the grey ashes of friendship reddening to life again—

Enough. At this rate she won't sleep tonight.

Fido puts the tray outside her door for Johnson. She returns *Friendless Girls* to the pile of pamphlets on the bedside cabinet, and unlocks the lower drawer in which she keeps her fiction. Not that she has anything indecent; the spines all bear the Pegasus motif of Mudie's Library. Ridiculous things are said of Miss Braddon's novels, or Mr. Collins's—that they harrow the nervous system and drive readers to drink or insanity. Fido finds them enlivening, in the small doses she allows herself; as with any stimulus, it's a matter of moderate use. Appalling secrets, deaths, bigamies, doppelgangers: there's nothing like a taste of the sensational at the end of a hard day. She takes out *The Notting Hill Mystery* now, and finds her place.

Two pages on, she finds herself staring into space. This is ridiculous. For seven years, she's been getting along perfectly well on her own. *But we met again on Farringdon Street, by purest chance. In the multitudinous city, Helen laid her hand on mine.*

At any rate, these are pointless speculations, because it's too late to turn back. There's no one—has never been anyone—whose company Fido relishes as much as Helen Codrington's. Despite the woman's excesses and flaws; despite all the complications of their shared history. The grave is open and the dead friendship walks.

~

THE FOLLOWING AFTERNOON, Fido should be supervising the printing of the *Friend of the People,* one of the contracts on which she most relies. But she can't settle. Finally she leaves her most reliable clicker, young Mr. Head, in charge. She sends a boy to hail a growler from the stand and tells the driver, "Eccleston Square, if you please." That's one of the paradoxes of being a lady, it strikes her: it's more respectable for Fido to rattle along in one corner of this four-wheeled growler, which could bear a whole family, than if she took a low-slung hansom meant for two.

Outside the house on Eccleston Square, an aproned man is scattering fresh gravel and watering it to keep down the dust. When Fido steps down and looks up at the green railings, it's all so much the same as the day she packed her cases to leave that she's gripped by a subtle nausea, and almost wishes she hadn't come. So many things have come rushing back to her in the single day and night since she's found Helen again: they spill out of her memory like coins from a shaken box.

Mrs. Nichols, the sour-faced housekeeper, greets her by name as if it were only yesterday, and has a maid show her into the dim drawing-room. Apart from the dark panelling, everything looks brand new. Muslin curtains shift above the plant-crammed glass cases built into the windows; the grate is filled with a paper peacock. The wallpaper's green and pink, embossed with a creeping vine pattern. The room seems to Fido to hold three times as much furniture as in the old days, and every high-shelved whatnot or occasional table, every chair leg or handle, is bronzed or scalloped or carved with flowers and animals. She counts ormolu vases, photographs of unfamiliar garden parties, Bengal shawls, gilt-eyed wally dogs. Jardinières cascading with silk ferns, domes of polished wax fruit, a glass globe of silver fish, as well as cages of skylarks and parrots and cockatoos (some stuffed, one—startling her with a shriek—very much alive). "It's all different," she says, spinning round as Helen glides in, wearing a lilac wrapper.

Her friend grins as she unlocks one of the dozens of drawers on a marquetried chiffonier and produces a tea caddy and sugar basin. "I've only just begun. It'll take me at least a year to prettify this old barracks of a house, but I had to tackle the drawing-room the moment we unpacked. I've been roaming Whiteley's and Swan and Edgar's like a madwoman. Look at this cunning little iron casket, can you guess what it is?"

Fido opens it, and a glass inkstand pops out.

"And these are real leaves, electro-plated—whatever that means," says Helen with a giggle. "I'd have everything up-to-date if Harry would only loosen the purse-strings," she adds under her breath.

Oh dear, thinks Fido, recognizing an old theme.

The two of them settle against the plump crimson cushions as Mrs. Nichols brings in the tea tray. "I've been playing forfeits upstairs with the girls," Helen explains.

And here they come, in their white pinafores. Nan and Nell both have their mother's copper hair, brushed back smoothly under black bands, and their father's height, which makes them stand a little awkwardly on the scarlet and emerald Brussels carpet.

"*Darlingissimi*, I wonder do you remember Miss Faithfull, who used to live with us before we went to Malta?"

"I believe so," says one of the girls uncertainly.

"But we always called you Aunt Fido," says the other.

"Indeed you did," Fido tells the child with a surge of warmth, "and I'd be honoured if you'd do so again."

"Nan's a stupendous pianist these days," says Helen, beckoning to the older girl and sliding her arm round the narrow waist as if she's guessed that Fido has no idea which is which, "and very sensitive with a watercolour brush. As for Nell—"

"I'm much less accomplished," volunteers the younger girl.

"—but far more moral," adds her sister.

Fido laughs. "You share your sentences, the way you used to share your toys."

"Oh, they share everything, even their faults," Helen tells her. "They're a perfect conspiracy."

Fido scrabbles for a memory. "You both had a craze for spinning tops."

"We have a collection of thirty-four—" Nell confides.

"—but we don't play with them anymore, it's beneath our dignity," says Nan.

This makes their mother yelp with amusement. "These days it's all stereoscope, stereoscope," she says, gesturing to a mahogany and brass device on a tiny table. "Every time I turn around I find them attached to the contraption, which can't be good for their eyes."

"But it's marvellous, Mama. Things seem so very real."

"It's so much better than the old magic lantern at the Allens'."

"When I look at the *Stereo View from a Precipice*, I feel as though I'm going to topple in," adds Nan.

"Topple off to the schoolroom now, if you please, so Mama can talk to her friend."

Nan leans into the visitor's ear on her way out. "Are you going to live upstairs again, Aunt Fido?"

She jumps. "No, my dear," she says, too heartily, "but we'll see a great deal of each other, I hope."

The girls sketch a simultaneous curtsy, and the maid closes the doors behind them.

It's oddly difficult to be alone with Helen, Fido finds. She hears herself swallow.

Helen's smile is tight. "When I spotted you on Farringdon Street, yesterday, you looked so—so changed, I hardly dared hail you."

"Older and fatter, you mean."

"No, no. I believe it's that you don't curl your hair anymore, and it's cut to your shoulders. And the shorter skirts."

Dowdy, Fido translates. "Yes, we working women tend to follow the country style," she says. "Nothing that will catch in machinery or trail in the dirt."

"Harry would never stand for an uncorseted wife," remarks Helen.

Is there a little envy in her tone? A pause. It's harder to keep the conversational plates spinning here than it was on the street. The pouring of tea takes up half a minute, then Fido launches into an enthusiastic précis of *The Notting Hill Mystery*.

"Well," says Helen, leaning back on the cushions, "I'm relieved you still have at least two relaxing habits in your ever-so-strenuous way of life. Novels *and* cigarettes."

"How did you—"

A giggle. "Yesterday, when I held your hand in the Underground, my fingers smelled of Turkish tobacco afterward."

"Mock all you like," says Fido, sheepish. There's no rational reason why a woman shouldn't smoke, especially if she finds it beneficial to her health—but somehow Fido prefers to do it in the privacy of her bedroom. "As for my strenuous way of life, I must tell you, work has been a revelation to me. What is it Mrs. Browning says?" She strains to remember. "Yes, that work is worth more in itself than whatever we work to get."

One slim eyebrow soars. "Hadn't you ever worked hard before you started going in for your rights?"

"Oh, Latin lessons with my father, sewing clothes for parish children," says Fido with a wave of the hand, "but nothing meaningful. When I happened across a copy of the *English Woman's Journal* and discovered the Cause . . ." She pronounces the word with an odd bashfulness. "I marched into 19 Langham Place, introduced myself to Miss Bessie Parkes, said 'Put me to any use at all.' Oh, the thrill of spending one's energies on something that really matters—" She breaks off, belatedly aware of the insult.

Helen's smile is feline.

Fido almost stammers. "What I meant is—for those of us without pressing duties, children to educate, and households to run, and—"

"Come, come, don't we know each other too well for cant? Mrs. Lawless gives the girls their lessons, and I handed my keys to Mrs. Nichols years ago. I pass my days reading, shopping, and yawning," says Helen easily. "London's so dead, off-season." She scans the drawing-room. "I'm thinking of having gaslight put in; I believe I could talk Harry into it, in the spirit of scientific progress."

"Think again," Fido advises her. "I find it more trouble than it's worth. It leaks, stinks of sulphur, blackens the ceiling, and it's far too hot in the summer."

"Mm," says Helen, "but so marvellously bright! Move with the times, isn't that the watchword for you moderns?"

"Only real progress," says Fido, a little uncomfortable with the teasing, "not experiment for its own sake."

"I'd call running one's own publishing house *experimental.* It must feel peculiar, to earn one's bread."

Fido grins at her. "I'll tell you what, my dear—if one gets paid for one's work, one knows somebody wants it. And one gains a power to do real good in the world. The first time I ever brought a cheque to the bank, and saw it cashed into hard golden sovereigns . . . Perhaps you should try it," she adds slyly.

Helen only giggles. "I wonder, did you read about Madame Genviève last week?"

"I don't know the lady."

"Nor I: a tightrope walker, as well as wife and mother," she explains. "Madame Genviève was performing blindfolded at a fête in Birmingham when she toppled to her death. It turns out she was unbalanced—"

"Mentally?"

"Literally," Helen corrects her, "by being in the last month of a delicate condition."

Fido winces.

"So perhaps nature has set *some* bounds to female ambition?"

"That's a ghoulish anecdote, Helen, not a reasoned argument."

She cackles. "I always felt like a cow, in the final months. It was hard enough to walk upstairs, let alone along a high wire."

"Come, come," says Fido, straight-faced, "what of the pride of giving life to a new soul?"

"Speaks one who's never tried it," cries Helen, poking her in the arm. "All I remember is the smell of the chloroform, and the curious sensation of sky-rockets going off in my head. After that it's simply messy and confining," she tells Fido, "and I could never summon any *tendre* for them till the first few months were over. A newborn's frightful when undressed: swollen head, skinny limbs, and that terrible froglike action."

All Fido can do is laugh.

"But tell me more about this Reform Firm, isn't that what you call yourselves?"

"You're well informed." Fido is gratified that Helen would take such an interest in the Cause.

"Oh, the papers from home were full of you and your comrades at Langham Place: your *English Woman's Journal* and Married Women's Property Bill, your Victoria Press . . ."

"Then I'm sure you've read as much in the way of mockery as praise. The Reform Firm is what our enemies dubbed us—but like the Quakers, we've embraced the title, to take the sting out of it."

"So is this Miss Parkes the boss of the Firm?"

Fido shakes her head. "We're an informal knot of fellows," she explains, "each working on a variety of schemes to improve the lot of women. For instance, after that dreadful shipwreck last year in which all the female passengers drowned, we managed to persuade Marylebone Baths to open for women's classes one day a week."

Helen is clearly not interested in swimming classes. "Come, there's always a leader."

"Well, Madame Bodichon—Bar Smith, as was—could be called our guiding angel," says Fido, "as she ran and funded the first campaigns. But she's married a wild Algerian doctor and spends most of the year there."

"How sensible of her," says Helen wryly.

"Miss Bessie Parkes is Madame's chief acolyte and dearest friend, and set up the *English Woman's Journal*, and edited it till her health obliged her to resign the job to Miss Davies—a new comrade, but awfully capable—so yes, I dare say Miss Parkes could be considered *first among equals*," Fido admits. "My own efforts have focused on the press and SPEW—the Society for Promoting the Employment of Women—"

"What an unfortunate acronym," cries Helen.

"Isn't it! But five years ago, when we founded it in a surge of zeal, that seemed a trivial consideration."

"Tell me, which of these ladies—" Helen breaks off. "You're all ladies, I suppose?"

The question makes Fido uncomfortable. "By education, if not by birth. Miss Boucherett rides to hounds, whereas Miss Craig's a glover's daughter," she says a little defiantly.

"But what I want to know is, which of them is your real friend?"

Fido doesn't know how to answer.

"Who's supplanted me?"

For all its mocking tone, the question hits Fido like a crowbar. "Helen! You should know me better than to think I'd sacrifice old attachments for new."

Helen's face blooms, dazzles. "How it relieves me to hear you say that."

"There are certainly bonds of affection between us all at Langham Place, but—Isa Craig is very sympathetic, for instance, but I don't know that I could count her as a *real friend.* And since the death of Miss Procter—"

"You knew the poet, personally?" asks Helen, audibly impressed.

"Adelaide was our hardest worker, and our wittiest," says Fido sadly. "Since that loss, old ties have frayed somewhat, and differences loom larger. But our work still unites us," she adds, afraid she's giving the wrong impression. "There's a great spirit of love at bottom."

Helen snorts. "I've run charity bazaars with women I'd happily see dead at my feet. But *carina*," she laughs, resting her fingertips on the brown satin of Fido's skirt, "if you haven't found one true intimate among the whole coven—that's a crying shame. You've such a genius for friendship, such an adhesive disposition—"

When I was young, thinks Fido with a stab. *Perhaps it's rusted up*.

"I had a sort of friend, in Malta," volunteers Helen.

"A *sort of* friend?"

"Quite a bit older; the wife of a local clergyman. The Watsons had a French governess for their wards, you see, and invited Nell and Nan over there to share lessons, which seemed harmless," says Helen bleakly. "We were all great mates till she began to turn Harry against me."

Fido's eyebrows shoot up. "Surely he didn't—he wasn't—"

"Oh, her attractions weren't of that kind," says Helen, "but she gained a strange ascendancy over him. Prigs are the worst of women; all that prudery hides a lust for power."

It strikes Fido that this is her chance to enquire into the state of the Codrington marriage. She wonders if the admiral is downstairs in his study. Has Harry been told she's in the house, for the first time since the day he—regretfully, impeccably—asked her to leave?

But she's hesitated too long, and Helen's rattling on again. "Well, my dear, if you really haven't one kindred spirit among this gang of *black and midnight hags*—then I intend to reinstate myself at once."

They're both grinning at her cheek. "There are no hags at Langham Place," Fido tells her. "Bessie Parkes, for one, is so small-boned and lovely that I feel like a bull beside her. In fact, there was a comical incident last spring when some Swedish professor called and mistook me for Miss Parkes; he described her in his travel memoir as an independent, strapping female who went outside and called a cab for herself—much to Bessie's horror!"

When Helen has stopped laughing, she remarks, "Reading about your career, in Malta—I used to wonder if you might end up marrying some earnest reformer, a lecturer on hygiene or some such. Or a vicar perhaps, like your sisters."

Fido smiles slightly. "You know, the old maid of today is not an object of pity."

"I've never pitied you for an instant."

"Independence, a home of one's own, travel . . ." She marks them off on her fingers. "Liberty's been a better husband to many of us than love."

"I've not a word to say against the single life," Helen protests, "I just can't quite imagine how it's done. But you'll hear no hymns to matrimony from me," she adds darkly.

There, the subject's been laid squarely on the table. Fido speaks before she can lose her nerve. "Are you . . . may I ask, are you and your husband any happier, these days?"

A small grimace. "*Mi ritrovai per una selva oscura,*" recites Helen. "That's the only tag from Dante I can recall from all the Signora's lessons."

"You've . . . woken in a dark wood?" Fido translates.

"And once married folk have strayed into the dark wood, one doesn't hear that they generally find their way out."

"I'm so very sorry." Not surprised, though, she realizes; not surprised at all.

"Well at least Harry and I both behave rather better than in the era when you had to put up with scenes over the breakfast table," says Helen. "Somehow we've acquired the knack of getting through the days. The years, rather! Separate lives, separate rooms, separate friends . . ."

All Fido can think to say is, "I'm sure he still cares for you, in his stiff way."

"Huh! Everything you know about marriage comes out of a book."

Fido stares at her. "That's not true. I've talked to many wives. They often speak of marriage pragmatically, as an occupation with its own duties and satisfactions. Some tell me a husband can be managed quite easily, as he wants only to be treated with deference, as master in his own house."

"So I should pacify Harry, just as I'd soothe one of the girls if she had a stomachache, or nag a forgetful maid, or tot up a budget for coals and lamp oil?" Helen's tone is withering.

"It's nothing more than tact. Forbearance. A hidden power."

"You try it!" Helen rubs the back of her neck. Then, in a chastened tone, "Did living with us for all those years scare you off the whole business?"

"Oh no," Fido assures her. "I'm afraid I've simply never felt that interest in a man that the poet calls 'woman's whole existence.' Solitude suits me," she adds. *Is this true?* she wonders suddenly. She thinks of solitude within a marriage, like a hearth that gives off cold instead of light. "But it mustn't be thought that my views on the advancement of women mean that I've lost faith in marriage," she goes on confusedly.

"Well, that makes one of us."

"Helen!" In the silence, she scrabbles for an analogy. "One may have a single bad dinner on a Sunday, without deciding to scrap the whole institution of Sunday dinner."

"I've been choking down this particular dinner for fifteen years," says Helen under her breath.

"Marriage is still the bedrock of society," Fido tells her, almost pleadingly. "If founded on self-respect and freedom—"

"Aye, *if*," Helen interrupts. "There's the rub."

Fido sighs. "Well, yes, it needs reform, of course. The entire engulfing of the wife's identity in the husband's—her surrender of property—his almost unlimited rights over her person . . ." Does her friend even know her true position under British law, Fido wonders—classed with criminals, lunatics, and children? "And so often the wife's *I do* is neither truly informed nor free."

Helen is nodding eagerly.

"We of the Cause—we seek to open careers to women precisely to give them a choice," Fido explains, "so they won't be driven by monetary need into loveless marriage, as some sort of life raft."

"I thought I was choosing. I thought I loved him," says Helen in a shaking voice. "These December-May matches . . ."

"Hardly December. I see you're still absurdly prone to exaggeration," says Fido, trying to lighten the moment.

"Well, late October, at least. Harry was forty-one, and I barely twenty-one; he might have been my father! A handsome giant in blue and white, with gold lace cuffs," she says wistfully, "posted to shield us Anglo-Florentines from the rebel mob. And I, little Miss Helen Smith, a wide-eyed Desdemona, enchanted by his tales of adventure on the high seas."

Fido frowns. Helen as Shakespeare's heroine, perhaps, but anyone less like the jealous Moor than the sober, thoroughly English Harry Codrington . . . "My dear, haven't the years done anything to soften you two to each other?"

"Oh, you innocent," says Helen. "That's not what years do."

~

The early September morning's still cool. Fido stands in the shower-bath and pulls the lever decisively. The numbing deluge makes her hiss. Afterwards she rubs herself all over with the towel, coughing. So many of her sex spend a week in bed at the least sign of weakness, but in Fido's view, the body's tremendous engine must be kept running.

Outside, the distinctive clink-clink of the milkwoman's iron-shod boots. She'll be shifting her laden yoke on her shoulders, filling up a half-quart for Miss Faithfull and lowering it on a hook over the railings.

Fido's still brooding over the conversation at Eccleston Square two days ago. She made a hash of explaining her work, or rather, its contagious excitement. In an age when *the system* (that hackneyed phrase) is generally said to determine everything, when all social ills are *nobody's fault*, the women of the Reform Firm—with the men of the Social Science Association and a few other forward-thinking organizations—say, *not so!* Fido's seen change coming in a single generation; the icy chains of prejudice shaking loose. She toils hard and with pleasure, so that other women may be freed from their set grooves (whether of poverty or boredom, dependence or idleness), freed to toil hard and with pleasure in their turn. This is what gets Fido out of bed by six every morning. So why does she feel she left Helen with the impression that she sits around squabbling with other do-gooders?

The main office of the Victoria Press is at 9 Great Coram Street, five minutes' brisk walk from the house. (*Evacuation of Atlanta Ends Four Month Siege,* reads the newsboy's sign, and she considers stopping to recommend a hyphen between *four* and *month.*)

In the typos' room, she pauses to congratulate Gladys Jennings on her recovery from smallpox; the girl's still purple-tinged and marked with scabs that Fido pretends not to see. Then she stops by the desk of Flora Parsons. "This will take half the day to correct," she remarks, handing back the long slip she's marked up in red. "If you'd applied your mind the first time, as Miss Jennings always does—"

"Beg pardon, ma'am," mutters Flora Parsons, head down, still rapidly plucking sorts from the alphabetical cases.

"It's not a matter of my pardon," says Fido, exasperated. "I'm merely pointing out why Miss Jennings makes eighteen shillings to your ten. That's the very reason I pay by the piece rather than by the week: to put your earning power in your own hands."

"You're very good to us, ma'am."

Fido could hardly miss the sarcasm. This one's a hard case: a workhouse orphan with cream-coloured hair who's been here four years now and is as slapdash as ever. Engaged, already, to one of the junior clickers, Mr. Ned Dunstable, which Fido finds disheartening: young hands are more trainable than their elders, but most won't trouble to master a trade they expect to leave at any moment. "You underestimate yourself, Miss Parsons," she says now, on impulse.

That makes the blonde typo glance up.

"It's a marvel to me, for instance, that without any formal schooling, you've such a fine grasp of the language."

A shrug. "Down to all the copy I've set up, I dare say. What old Robert Owen would call the spread of education."

Fido stands closer to the desk. "What infuriates me—" She breaks off. "If you really applied your forces," she starts again, "you could be the quickest, most accurate typo here. Save some capital, go into your wedded life on terms at least approaching equality. In fact, I've never hired a married woman yet, but in your case I would consider—"

Flora Parsons interrupts with a peculiar half-smile. "Ned and I will do perfectly well, thank you, ma'am."

Without another word, Fido goes back to her office.

She still does her own correcting; it's hard to find the time. She'd be glad to find an educated lady to take it on—though she's not sure she could afford one, given that six of her apprentices become journeymen this year and will have to be paid half as much again.

Mr. Head comes in hangdog with the *Printer's Journal.* "You see here, Miss Faithfull, where the London Society of Compositors is debating a policy of making its members swear not to finish work set up by females?"

Fido winces. And to think she's had the impression the trade's hostility to her has been fading away, as the years prove that the Victoria Press is not going to depress wages . . . "*Women*, if you please, Mr. Head," she says, glancing through the article; "*females* smacks of the zoo. Do I refer to your sex as *males*, as if you were orangutans?"

He grins, but only briefly. "What if the society were to strike the press?"

Fido takes a long breath before she answers. "Have you received a direct order from your superiors?"

"No, no," he says, horrified. "They don't know I'm a clicker here."

It's as if she's running a gambling cellar or opium den. "Well, then, I suggest you put it out of your mind, Mr. Head. If that dark day comes, you'll be obliged to decide whether to let yourself be bullied out of a job that I think you've found both agreeable and profitable."

He nods unhappily. He makes no move towards the door. "Myself and Mr. Kettle were thinking, perhaps we could change names."

She blinks at him. "You would be known as Kettle, and he as Head?" (She doesn't like Kettle, as it happens; on occasion she's suspected something fishy about his figures, but she's never had proof.)

"No, no, we'd both assume false ones, aliases on paper, as it were. So that there'd be no record that it's we who supervise the girls."

She almost laughs at the atmosphere of skullduggery. "Very well, I'll pay my clickers under any *nom de guerre* of your choice. May I still address you as Mr. Head and Mr. Kettle, to save confusion?"

"Certainly, madam, it's just for the books," says Head, sheepish.

Don't fret, she tells herself when he's gone; she presses her fingers to her hot face. *It won't come to a strike. And if it does, well, I've survived worse.* Had Fido wanted a peaceful existence, she reminds herself, she could have stayed at home and helped her mother with the parish work.

With unnecessary violence she slits open some letters, including one from Matthew Arnold apologizing for the lateness of his review of a new translation of Marcus Aurelius. *My dear Faithfull* is how he addresses her, and she likes the style; in the world of letters, sex shouldn't matter. Emily Davies has forwarded a poem by Miss Rossetti; Fido finds it touching that these authors remain willing to write for the pittance the *English Woman's Journal* can offer them.

She spends the next half-hour proofreading an article for the enormous *Annual Proceedings of the Social Science Association*:

> **"Are Men Naturally Cleverer Than Women?"**
> **Men are superior to women because they know more, but they have this knowledge because they have three times the opportunities of acquiring it.**

She likes that line; it has a punch to it.

The boy's tapped three times before she looks up. "A Mrs. Coddleton and a Colonel Anderson, to pay their respects, ma'am."

"Codrington," a merry voice corrects him from behind the opaque glass of the door.

Taken aback, on her feet, Fido's all smiles. *Helen, here!*

"I badgered poor Anderson to bring me along, since my lord and master's still glued to his papers," Helen explains as she presses her cheek to Fido's in the Continental manner. She's in the tiniest of ivory bonnets today: it's a stray dove perched on her brilliant hair.

The officer's in mufti, a rather loud waistcoat: *the family tartan?* Fido wonders. "No badgering was required," he assures her.

"What fun, Fido, to glimpse you in character," cries Helen, tucking her arm through Fido's as they move through the workroom.

Fido flinches a little, because the typos will have heard the nickname then tells herself they must know it already. "That makes it sound as if I'm acting a role."

Helen's mouth twists. "Oh, don't we each have several selves?"

And indeed, even as Fido launches into the usual spiel about setting up the press four years ago, "as a practical demonstration to the world of the capacities of women's eyes, fingers, and brains," she's listening to herself with a strange self-consciousness, noting how cool and professional she sounds.

Helen sniffs the air.

"Ink," Fido tells her. She shows off the Wharfedale flatbed press, ornamented with brass eagles, "Capable of a thousand impressions an hour. Oh, and this is Miss Bridget Mulcahy: my first employee and right-hand woman."

The pallid Irishwoman smiles and bows, her hands skimming like dragonflies as she returns cleaned letters to their cases.

"Daughter of a Limerick printer, who took the unusual step of training her," Fido tells her visitors in a murmur. "After his death she saw my advertisement in a newspaper and headed straight for London."

"Isn't it an unhealthy occupation?" Anderson asks as they walk between the pew-like composing desks.

Fido's always glad when a visitor brings up this misconception. "Traditionally, but not necessarily. I remember the *Printer's Journal* claimed all my hands would sink under the strain! But you see, I make sure to provide good lighting, ventilation, breaks for lunch, and stools to sit on while they work."

"Mm, nothing *sinking* about these girls, by the looks of it," says Anderson with an appreciative scan of the room that Fido doesn't like.

"Your *hands*, is that what you call them?" asks Helen in amusement, wiggling her fingers. "As if you're some monstrous octopus!"

Fido grins, but uneasily; it's strange to have her old friend here in the workroom, cracking jokes. "I see myself in a maternal role, really," she says in a low voice. "Miss Jennings here, for instance, is only thirteen; apprenticed by the Asylum for the Deaf and Dumb."

"Awfully kind of you," remarks the colonel.

Fido shakes her head. "She's been rather more trouble to train, but wonderfully immune to distraction."

"Oh, but you have the coarser sex here too," Helen mutters, catching sight of Mr. Kettle chalking his hands.

"Well, of course there are tasks beyond the average girl's strength," says Fido a little defensively. "Carrying the type cases, feeding and striking off the sheets . . . So I hire one male clicker to oversee each company of five typos: he distributes copy, makes up the girls' work into columns and imposes the matter—puts the pages in the right order," she glosses. "But I'm proud to say I employ twenty-five girls here and fifteen at Farringdon Street."

Helen is hanging back, looking at the long racks covered with iron frames. "They're known as *chases*," says Fido, at her elbow, "but when they're filled with type and secured we call them *formes.*" It occurs to her that she's being a bore. "Miss Clark is setting up a line at a time on a composing stick—if I may, Miss Clark—it's adjustable in width, you see." She offers the stick to Helen.

She pulls back. "I mustn't get stained; Harry and I dine at the Beechams' tonight."

Anderson chuckles. "There's no ink on it yet, Mrs. C."

That name has jarred on Fido's ear each time he's used it. Too vulgar, or too presuming? It sounds like something a butcher might call his wife. She tells herself not to be such a snob; military circles have their own jargon. "Everything's thoroughly scrubbed after each print run," she assures Helen. "The trade absolutely depends on hygiene and order." *How pompous I sound, how elderly, at twenty-nine.*

"You'd never take me on, Fido," Helen remarks. "Far too disorderly, not to mention too plump in the fingers."

"Your fingers are irrelevant, but your character would be an obstacle," Fido agrees, loosening into laughter.

She offers them tea in her office.

"Aha, Tennyson, capital." Anderson points his cane's silver tip at a framed verse on the wall and recites:

Give every flying minute
Something to keep in store:
Work, for the night is coming,
When man works no more.

Fido smiles slightly. "In fact, the poet's a Miss Anna Walker."

Helen smiles at his discomfiture.

"Rather in the laureate's manner, though," ventures Anderson after a second.

Over shrimps and bread and butter, it emerges that some of Fido's Scottish connections are acquainted with some of the colonel's.

"This establishment is a great credit to you, Miss Faithfull," he tells her.

"Yet we've had our enemies," she says, theatrically.

Helen stops chewing a large shrimp.

Aha, that's hooked her. "Ceaseless sabotage, in the early days," says Fido. "Windows smashed, frames and stools daubed in ink to destroy the hands' dresses, sorts jumbled up in their cases or scattered like birdseed, machines prised apart with crowbars . . . the waste was simply ruinous, quite apart from the distress caused."

"My dear, how sensational," cries Helen.

Strange how a few years can reduce humiliation to an anecdote. "There were scurrilous attacks on me in the journals; I had to grow a rhinoceros's hide. But the Victoria Press was self-supporting in a year, I was honoured with Her Majesty's approval, and now we win medals for excellence from the International Exhibition." Well, one medal. In her attempt to impress her old friend, Fido's getting carried away.

"*Bravissima*," cries Helen, clapping her hands. "And to think, when I first knew you, it was four costumes a day and routs at Lady Morgan's."

Fido laughs. "I'm afraid we were a wild pair, my *soi-disant* chaperone and I," she tells Anderson.

"We had a policy of dancing with anything in trousers that asked us," contributes Helen.

"And made facile and impertinent remarks, in the name of youthful artlessness. You, as the married lady, should have reined me in."

"Ah, but Fido's always been my better self," Helen tells Anderson. "And look at her now, how she's transformed herself from deb to philanthropist . . ."

"Miss Faithfull, on that theme," he asks playfully, "wouldn't you admit that some of your woman-ist set want to go too far?"

Fido arranges her smile. (It's little by little that the world will be changed, she reminds herself, as mice nibble a hole in a wall.) "I assure you, Colonel, we don't mean to smash the social machine, only to readjust its workings."

"But one hears of calls for women judges, MPs, officers—"

"Oh, if any argument's pushed *ad absurdum* . . ." Fido controls her temper. "My own belief is that there should be no legal bars to our sex's progress—and certainly none are needed, because it's inconceivable that more than a handful would ever attempt to enter the professions you mention. Women naturally prefer the nobler spheres of education, medicine, and welfare."

"Nobler than your line, Anderson," Helen teases.

"Well, more conducive to human happiness than war is, shall we say?" suggests Fido.

He snorts. "I'll grant you that, Miss Faithfull. What those miserable Americans are suffering this year, on both sides . . ."

She likes him for that.

"But I'll confess, we soldiers are always panting for another dust-up."

"The colonel's glory days were in the Crimea," Helen says with a little yawn.

"And as for poor Navy men like Codrington," he adds, "the last real action he saw was at Acre, a quarter of a century ago!"

Rather a sneering remark to make about his friend, Fido thinks. "More tea?" she asks.

~

FIDO SHOULDN'T BE HERE THIS MORNING, strolling along the banks of the Serpentine; she should be at Langham Place, attending a meeting to discuss the draft of SPEW's quarterly report. But the sky's the blue of a vein, and the September breeze has cut the heat deliciously. And Helen asked her to come walking in Hyde Park, after all, and for the seven years in which she's done without her friend, it strikes Fido now, she's attended too many meetings.

"You must have read *The Woman in White?*" Helen asks.

"I got it twice from Mudie's, then bought my own," Fido admits. "The loyal, ugly Marion—she breaks my heart."

"I wore a white shawl all that summer."

"You're still a slave to fashion! What about Mrs. Norton's novels? Or Miss Braddon's?"

Helen nods eagerly. "My favourite title of hers is *Three Times Dead.*"

"Do you take *Temple Bar*? The current serial is by Miss Braddon," Fido tells her, "it's called *The Doctor's Wife*, but she's really just an Englished *Bovary*. Now, *Lady Audley* can be accused of stealing from *The Woman in White*—"

"But she's so elegant and audacious, I forgive her everything."

"There's that interesting passage," Fido recalls, "that suggests such crimes result from women being frustrated in their ambitions to enter the professions."

"My favourite is the scene in which she shoves her husband down the well."

Fido lets out a hoot. "Do you remember reading *Bleak House* to each other, all that first winter?"

"Of course. The death of Lady Dedlock—you made me shudder so, I couldn't sleep."

"Did you hear that Dickens put his wife aside, after she'd given him ten children?"

"My dear, *that* story must have reached Rangoon the day after it broke," says Helen. "What a dastard, to vilify her in the papers as incapable of maternal love!"

"It's said that he's entangled himself with an actress," Fido adds, automatically lowering her voice, even though there's no one close enough to hear them on the riverbank.

"Worse," says Helen with satisfaction. "His sister-in-law."

"No!"

"I'm sure it was she I saw buying galoshes on Regent Street last week. Mrs. Dickens, I mean, not her sister. She's let herself go, dreadfully."

"She lives with the eldest son, and the others rarely visit," says Fido. "I heard she still reads every word her husband publishes. How sad."

"And how exhausting."

It's Helen's delivery, as much as what she says, that makes Fido burst out laughing. She brings out a side of Fido, a flippant, frank, almost devil-may-care side, that's been in an enchanted sleep for seven years. "Do you miss Malta?" she asks her now.

"Well, Harry certainly does," says Helen, her eyes on a pair of haughty swans. "He was top man of the top brass—whereas now he's got nothing to do but go to the odd chamber concert, or a lecture on warship design. So many wives complain they can't lure their husbands home from the club," she adds darkly, "whereas mine mopes around the house all day! I do hope they find him some paper-shuffling job at the Admiralty, or he's going to drive me and the girls to distraction with all his fussing."

"It was you I asked about," Fido reminds her. "Do you miss it?"

A little shrug. "Places mean little to me; people are all that matter."

What does that mean? Fido turns to examine Helen's face.

It came to her, during a sleepless hour last night, that if they're to take up their friendship again, it must be on new terms. In the old days at Eccleston Square, Fido was very much the junior, the subordinate—a sort of female Horatio; she can see that now. She often suspected Helen of exaggerating, obscuring her real feelings behind a lot of hyperbolic verbiage. And at the time, Fido accepted it as *just Helen's way*; she was too dazzled by Helen's charm to challenge her. But now Fido's a grown-up, worldly and busy. This time the two women must meet eye to eye, heart to heart, if they're to call themselves by the sacred name of *friend.* So she asks the question that's been on her mind. "Lucky timing, wasn't it, that Colonel Anderson's leave coincided with your family's return?" She says it as lightly as she can, but it still sounds like a knife thrust.

Helen's eyes flick to hers, then away across the river. "He expects to be recalled to Valetta shortly."

"Which is his regiment?"

"He commands the second battalion of the Twenty-Second Cheshire. One of the old school, like Harry—iron discipline, and all that."

Fido's surprised. "He seems such an agreeable fellow."

"Oh, he's pukka. Very agreeable," adds Helen. Then, in a flat voice, eyes fixed on the opaque surface of the water, "Dangerously so."

Fido's pulse is getting louder. *You began this*, she reminds herself.

"Do you understand me?" asks Helen, turning to squint at her slightly in the afternoon sun.

Her breath escapes as if from a balloon. "I rather hope not."

"But you do," says Helen with a half-laugh.

You were fishing, Fido rebukes herself; *so don't complain if you've hooked something.*

Helen rolls her head to one side, and rubs her neck as if it aches. "The man's desperately in love with me."

Fido's face contracts as if she's bitten into something rotten.

"What, I mustn't put plain words on the thing, even where there's nobody but waterfowl to hear us? Very well, let's be ever so English and say Anderson's *confused*, then," snaps Helen, walking faster, so Fido has to hurry to keep up. "Let's not admit that it's possible for a single man to conceive a burning attachment to a superior officer's wife. That the mother of two half-grown girls could still excite passion, at thirty-six!"

Fido opens her mouth to tell her that she's no less beautiful than she ever was, then shuts it. Helen's always needed male attention—in the old days, Fido thought of this as a minor weakness, like a craving for sweets—but there's a new, unnerving fierceness in her voice today. "Oh, Madre," she says, "you have got yourself in a scrape!"

No reply.

Out of breath, she seizes Helen by the elbow. "Slow down, and tell me all. You sound almost proud of making this fellow unhappy," she says sharply.

Helen spins around; two scarlet spots on her cheeks make her look even prettier. "On the contrary. It's all a disastrous accident."

She's like a child who's smashed a trayful of china.

"You don't know how it's been, these past years," Helen wails. "Harry's such a blank, as a husband—such a stick-in-the-mud. *He* doesn't want my company. In Malta, he wouldn't stay more than an hour at parties, so I was obliged to dance with other officers and have them escort me home."

Fido's mind is whirling.

"So can I help it if I've made one of my husband's friends my own, in a sincere and ingenuous spirit, and the man's persuaded himself that more is meant by it?"

"Helen," she begins sternly, "you should have cut Anderson off at the first sign of infatuation."

A shrug, very Tuscan. "What's the first sign? By the time one notices the thing, it's grown like a mushroom in the dark."

"All the more reason to root it up at once."

"I don't give him any encouragement."

"You do, I've seen it with my own eyes! What do you call running round town *à deux*?"

"Hardly *running*," Helen protests. "A little shopping, a harmless visit to a printing press . . ."

Fido feels a little dizzy. Could the colonel have asked for a tour of the Victoria Press as a respectable cover for a morning with Helen?

All of a sudden, Helen stops in her tracks. "Oh Fido, I can't hide anything from you. The excitement of having a handsome, sparkling fellow hang on one's every word—you can't imagine!"

Actually, Fido would rate the admiral's black-bearded, tall good looks over Anderson's golden spanielish ones, but she supposes any scowling man is less appealing than a smiling one. Fido can understand the appeal of the other sex in the abstract, but there's something missing in her; the part of a woman's heart that, in the presence of the right man, melts and runs like a vein of ore from the rock.

"Really," says Helen, grabbing her wrist, "can you blame me if I've taken his devoted gaze, like a cordial, to refresh my spirits at gloomy moments?"

"For shame! You must have known this could only cause pain to both of you in the end," Fido snaps, pulling her hand away. "As a wife and mother—"

"Now for the lecture," Helen says under her breath.

And indeed, Fido's still enough of a Faithfull to have the whole speech by rote, every *principle* and *duty* in its place . . .

"Don't," says Helen, pressing one finger hard against Fido's lips.

"Don't what?" But she knows.

"Don't throw stones. Don't disappoint me with what every lady in Belgravia would offer, the usual pieties and pruderies! My friend, you've made something entirely new of yourself, these past years, and it awes me to see it; you've got quite out of the rut of convention," says Helen in marvelling tones. "What you were saying about marriage the other day at my house that a wife's whole identity is swallowed up—"

Fido tries to remember what bold statements she might have made. "Oh but my dear . . . I'm not being pious, nor a prude. It's a matter of . . ." She struggles for words. "Self-respect. Being true to oneself. You did take a vow."

"I didn't know what it meant," cries Helen, "how long a married life can be! And what other choice had a girl like me?"

"*Carina.*" She's trying to marshal her arguments, but compassion confuses her. "I do feel for you."

Helen's eyes glitter like sand. She throws herself on Fido.

Fido registers the hot weight of Helen's face against her collarbone, through the cotton, and smells some kind of floral water in her hair. Two ladies standing pressed against each other, skirt to billowing skirt, on the banks of the Serpentine at three in the afternoon: an incongruous sight perhaps, but Fido refuses to care. "Little One," she whispers.

"The relief of letting it out, you can't imagine," sobs Helen, muffled.

I'm the only one in the world she's told, Fido thinks, with a kind of vertigo. *We didn't exchange a word for seven years, but still, four days after meeting again, I'm the one she trusts.* This secret's weighing heavily on her already, but she's proud to bear it.

~

As Fido lets herself into 19 Langham Place, a middle-aged lady hurries up the steps behind her. "Please excuse me—is this the office of the Female Employment Register?"

"That's correct."

"Can you help me?"

Looking at the strained forehead, the soft white hands, Fido doubts it. "Do take a seat in our reading room," she says, showing her in.

The lady grasps Fido's sleeve. "I'm—I don't know you, madam, but I must tell you I'm in most urgent need of remunerative employment. My daughters and I—my husband's a physician," she goes on disjointedly.

Fido waits uncomfortably.

"His practice failed," says the stranger in her strangulated voice. "He has abandoned us. That was four months ago, and we have no other resources."

"My sympathies. I'll make sure someone upstairs will come and write down your details for our register," Fido tells her, gently taking back her sleeve.

As she goes up the stairs, she's remembering the first few such petitioners she met, when she came to work here six years ago, with her carpetbag full of essays and her boundless confidence. (*Our heartiest young worker*, she'd heard Bessie Parkes call her once, to a stranger.) How spring-like the atmosphere at Langham Place was back in '58: change like ripe fruit dangling almost within their gasp, fruit for which former, more fearful generations had never dared to reach.

Today Bessie Parkes, Jessie Boucherett, Isa Craig, and Sarah Lewin (their secretary) are poring over a portfolio of drawings at the big office table. "Hello, Fido," beams Isa Craig.

"We missed you yesterday," remarks Bessie Parkes.

"Yes, I am sorry. My lungs have been playing up," says Fido, startled by the lie even as she produces it; why couldn't she have simply said she was otherwise engaged? She turns to Miss Lewin to tell her about the doctor's wife downstairs.

"Quite unemployable," sighs the secretary, pushing back her chair.

"Every other day, these reduced gentlewomen turn up at my press," Fido remarks, "and I always redirect them here, to the Employment Register—"

"But their mistake's a natural one, as the Victoria Press is so much better known," says Isa Craig warmly.

"What do you believe becomes of these tragic cases, when we turn them away?" Fido wonders.

"Is this person . . . handsome?" asks Jessie Boucherett.

"Not unpleasant to the eye."

"Then she'll probably put herself under some man's protection, in the end, rather than starve," says Jessie Boucherett.

Protection, thinks Fido, disgusted by the customary euphemism.

"Which of us could throw the first stone?" asks Bessie Parkes. "The Magdalene was forgiven, we're told, because *she loved much*. Remember Adelaide's masterpiece, 'A Legend of Provence'?"

Fido doesn't meet any of her comrades' eyes, but she can tell what they're all thinking. They've noticed, without Bessie Parkes ever having announced it, that she no longer works on Sundays; they know she's on the brink of converting from the Unitarian Church to Adelaide Procter's: Rome.

Isa Craig has turned away to wipe her eyes.

"Isa, my dear, you mustn't keep dissolving into tears at the mention of the beloved name." Bessie Parkes speaks in exalted tones. "Adelaide doesn't want us to mourn. Wasn't I with her at the last, and didn't I tell you how she went willingly, radiantly, to her beloved Jesus?"

This strikes Fido as sanctimonious cant, but she says nothing.

"After retching up blood for two years," mutters Jessie Boucherett.

Religion is one of those topics on which the women of the Reform Firm will never agree, which is why they have a policy of keeping it out of the *English Woman's Journal.*

Bessie bites her lip. "The poem of Adelaide's I mentioned, for any of you who may not recall its details, is about a nun who nurses a handsome knight; he seduces her to run away with him. Years later, a broken beggar, she comes back to the convent, and finds that the Virgin has been impersonating her there all this time, *keeping her place.*"

"That's right," says Isa Craig, nodding. "The twist is that the nun can take up her old life again without fear of the holy sisters' judgement, because none of them ever knew she was gone."

Fido's lost in thoughts of Helen. She fears she may have been too hard on her yesterday. Who is Fido, who's never married a man nor been tempted by one, to stand in judgement on a platonic *affaire*, an unhappy wife's slim consolation? After all, these things die away on their own, like mayflies: the Channel and the Mediterranean will divide Helen from Anderson again in a matter of weeks.

"The infinite sympathy of the divine, the limitless mercy," marvels Bessie Parkes. She quotes from the poem: "*No star is ever lost we once have seen, We always may be what we might have been.*"

At that moment Fido realizes something with a sickening sensation in her chest, like a tendon snapping: *I'm jealous.* That's what lay behind all her stern words yesterday: not ethics, so much as hurt. With his spaniel curls and his flippancy, Anderson hardly seems worthy of Helen's burning attention. (But then, what man would?) Something glorious happened on the last day of August on Farringdon Street, a friendship that seemed extinct flared up red and phoenix-like—and what business has a blond puppy to be blundering into such a story?

"On a more practical note," says Sarah Lewin, breaking the silence with her throaty whisper, "I must announce that subscriptions to the *Journal* are down this month."

"Heavens!"

"Not again!"

"Mm, I'm afraid they've slipped below six hundred."

Bessie Parkes lets out a long sigh. "Would you be so good as to look into it?" she asks their secretary. "Sound out a few subscribers who've decided not to renew . . ."

"I hear from many sides that our serial novel's popular," puts in Isa Craig.

"Ah, but what has the novel to do with the advancement of women?" asks Bessie Parkes.

Fido shrugs, her mind still wandering. "Every pill needs a little sugar."

It's just at this point that Emily Davies glides in and takes her seat at the table. "I do apologize for my lateness, but I bring rather extraordinary news," she announces in her usual brisk staccato. The *Journal*'s editor is looking particularly doll-like today, Fido notices: bands of mouse-coloured hair framing her diminutive features. She slides a paper out of her thick pocketbook. "This morning I received a letter they call it a *memorial*, in their stiff way—from the University of Cambridge . . ."

The members of the Reform Firm are all agog.

" . . . approving, on a strictly once-off basis, our request to have girls admitted to its local examinations."

"After all this time," Fido whoops, seizing the document.

"Oh Miss Davies, felicitations. Laurels to the conqueress," cries Bessie Parkes, shaking her hand.

"Nonsense, it was teamwork," says Emily Davies. "Those breakfasts you hosted for influential men, Fido: I believe they were crucial. But the fact is, I'd almost given up on the dons."

Not that anyone in the room takes this literally, since in the short time since the vicar's daughter from Newcastle has come south to work among them, she's shown no signs of dropping any fight. Emily Davies is like a terrier who won't let go of the stick, Fido thinks, only calmer.

"Our long struggle is at flood tide," says Bessie Parkes in the thrilling voice with which she gives readings from her poetry. "Soon we sail into port!"

As always, Emily Davies ignores such outbursts. "The local exams will at least nudge open the door to university admission. I intend that our daughters—I speak metaphorically," she tells the group, very dry, "will be able to enroll in a women's college at Cambridge."

Fido is thinking back to her boarding school in Kensington, mornings memorizing a dozen pages at a stretch out of Woodhouselee's *Universal History* while four out-of-tune pianos banged away overhead. If as a tomboyish bookworm Fido had glimpsed the possibility of attending university, how different everything might have been. She'd never have wasted two seasons as a debutante, no matter how much her mother doted on the idea. Nor ever met Helen Codrington, perhaps: now there's a strange thought.

"Some of us may have literal daughters yet," remarks Bessie Parkes in a low voice.

Fido exchanges a covert grin with Isa Craig. The rest of them are spinsters by vocation, but not Bessie Parkes: she's spent seventeen years fretting over whether to accept her older, debt-ridden suitor. Jessie Boucherett claims that Bessie will say yes before her dreaded fortieth birthday; Fido argues that she'd have done it by now if she meant to at all.

Emily Davies is tapping the page. "Look at the date: the gracious dons have given us only a matter of weeks to prepare our candidates. What kept me late this morning was that I've set about hiring a hall, finding examiners, accommodation . . . In a postscript, you notice, we're urged to make *all necessary arrangements* for dealing with any candidate's *faints and hysterics.*"

Laughter all around.

~

THE NOTE JOHNSON THE MAID BRINGS into the study bears Fido's name in a familiar, sprawling hand. It has a green wax seal that Fido recognizes at once. *Semper Fidelis*, the motto of the Smiths, Helen's family: *always faithful.* The two of them used to joke that it should have been Fido's instead, given her surname. And when the letters never came from Malta, in those miserable months after the Codringtons' departure in '57, Fido had come to think of it as a hollow phrase. But Helen, for all her eccentricities, has turned out to be loyal after all. Fido cracks the verdigris wax between finger and thumb and reads the letter through in one rush.

Eccleston Square
September 6, 1864

My seelen-freund, my soul's mate,

I've brooded over everything you said by the Serpentine. You're a dark mirror but an accurate one. I see now that I've somehow stumbled into a dreadful story—the oldest kind. I haven't been able to find my way out of the maze by myself, but now you, my Ariadne, have offered me the thread.

Somehow it reminds me of what you were telling me the other day, that one should never buy silk flowers because (if I've recalled it aright?) the vapour rots the mouths of the girls who make them. You added something that struck me very much: "Knowledge brings responsibility." Well, you've opened my eyes, dearest Fido, and now I'll let myself delay no further in cutting the thing off at the root, at no matter what cost to my feelings or those of others.

You know what a wandering nature I've always had, and what a rebellious *heart. I've been so alone, these past years, without a single real confidante to keep me steady . . . But now I have you back, and I mean to mend. To be "true to myself," as you put it. If I can always have you near, for the rest of my life, I believe I'll grow a little better every day.*

May I come to you this afternoon?

Your
Helen

~

Fido's eyes rest on the framed photographs of her sisters and brothers and their infinite progeny, and they remind her of something; she jumps up to look in her writing desk. "Oh, I must give you my latest picture," she tells Helen, "in return for your lovely carte de visite."

Helen scrutinizes it. "It captures your majestic forehead, but it makes you look older than you are."

"Do you think?"

"Next time, some side lighting, perhaps."

A pause. Fido can't think of any subject of conversation except one.

"It must make such a difference," Helen remarks suddenly, "having an establishment of one's own."

Following Helen's gaze, Fido surveys the narrow drawing-room. *Establishment* seems a grand word for her skinny house on Taviton Street. The decor strikes her as shabbily old-fashioned, compared with Eccleston Square; how bare the little tables, how few bibelots for her visitor's eyes to rest on. "Such a difference?" she repeats, confused.

"To how one feels. You've such an independent spirit."

"If I do, you think I owe it to these four walls?" asks Fido, amused.

A graceful shrug. "Don't discount bricks and mortar. You can't imagine what it's like to live out one's days encompassed by a gloomy, ageing husband, my dear. I live between his four walls, wearing clothes he must pay for, obeying his minutest orders . . ."

"From what I recall, you ignore quite a few of Harry's *orders*," Fido can't resist saying.

Helen purses her coral lips. "Whether or no—they have a suffocating effect. I signed myself away at twenty-one," she adds, "as carelessly as a girl fills in her dance card at a ball!"

"Your letter—" Fido feels it's time to address the subject on both their minds, "it moved me very much."

Helen's smile irradiates her cheekbones, like a candle in a lantern.

"Is Anderson—" His name comes out rather gruff.

"He took the train to Scotland for a couple of nights; he's only just come back," Helen tells her.

"It's really not fair to leave any doubt in his mind—"

"That was my thought exactly; that's why I've invited him here."

Fido stares at her. "Here?"

But in comes Johnson, her narrow shoulders hunched over the tray that bears the steaming urn, pot, caddies and all. (More than once, over the years, Fido has had a quiet word with her maid about posture and health, but it does no good.) It takes several minutes for Johnson to unload everything

When they're alone, Fido brews the tea. "You might have asked me before making free with my house," she says under her breath.

"But I knew you'd say yes." Helen grins at her, rather wanly. "I can hardly speak to him at Eccleston Square, can I?"

Something occurs to Fido. "I thought you told me your husband didn't mind Anderson's squiring you all over town."

"I don't think I said that."

Fido tries to remember; perhaps she'd just assumed that the admiral, toiling away in his study, had no objections. "Don't tell me he . . . suspects the colonel of having feelings for you?"

"Feelings? I doubt it. Since Harry hasn't found me desirable in years, he can't imagine anyone else would," Helen says acidly. "But you see, I'd rather he didn't know that Anderson's back. It may seem rather coincidence, I mean," she says, rising to look out the window, "that the colonel's home leave should happen to overlap with the very month of our return."

Fido finds herself breathless. "Oh Helen! You mean to say that Anderson took leave in order to pursue you to London, and Harry believes him still in Malta, all this time?"

"I knew nothing of it myself till the man's letter turned up on my tray," mutters Helen, eyes on the glaring street.

"But—"

"Don't fuss and fret," she says mildly, "I'm going to set it all to rights. But now you see that I can't invite him into my own house, and I can hardly begin such a speech on the street, or in a carriage: what if he were to make a scene?"

Fido frowns. "Surely he's too much of a gentleman—"

"Yes, but he's a desperate man too." Helen turns, speaking in a thrilled murmur. "The things he's said, in the past few weeks—threats against his own life . . ."

Fido clamps her teeth together. *Vulgar, vulgar.* "Very well, let it be here: *if it were done when 'tis done, 'twere well it were done quickly*," she quotes. "On what day am I to expect the colonel?"

Helen glances at the clock on the mantel. "He should be here any minute."

Fido recoils.

"Four, I said in my note."

"I don't want to be a party to such a scene!"

"Dearest, I wouldn't ask that of you," Helen assures her, coming over to press Fido's hands between her own surprisingly cool ones. "Simply make some excuse and leave the room for half an hour."

"But—"

The doorbell chimes below. A pause, then Fido hears Johnson's heavy footsteps cross the hall. "You're a force of chaos," she growls. "My life has been infinitely calmer without you in it."

Helen's eyes are glittering. "Don't be hard on me just now; I don't believe I can bear it. I'll need all my courage for this interview."

"Bless you, then," says Fido, giving her a crushing hug, and a kiss on her bright hair.

"Won't you go to the top of the stairs to receive the poor man?" asks Helen. "He thinks such a great deal of you."

That's humbug, Fido knows: the officer's only met her twice. But yes, she does pity Anderson, despite her squeamishness; pities his state of enthralled fascination; pities his puppyish look as he hurries up the stairs, unaware of the coming blow. Falling in love with Helen has probably been the great drama of his life; it'll all be humdrum regimental routine from this point on. He should have kept his mouth shut, Fido decides; should have adored his beloved in manly silence, or consigned his feelings to bad verse and locked them up in his desk. But that kind of gallantry's dead and gone. And can Fido really blame him for speaking his love, when Helen—in her loneliness and, yes, vanity—has clearly been all too ready to hear it? (A prim old adage of her mother's runs through Fido's head as she's walking towards the stairs: *A gentleman is always a gentleman unless a lady forgets to be a lady.*)

So she greets the colonel kindly, and brews fresh coffee, as he doesn't care for tea; she even offers him a little chasse-café from the brandy decanter, to cushion his spirits. She remarks on the delicious cooling of the weather; she speaks highly of Mr. Gladstone's speech on the secret ballot. "Perhaps its time has come. After all, they've adopted it in France and Italy already."

"Exactly," says Anderson with a snort. "It's a Papist notion. A Briton casts his vote openly and without shame, in the sight of his neighbours."

"A man of independent means, may, certainly," Fido concedes, "but too many voters are under the influence of their squires, or employers, or rich customers, so come Election Day they act as so many timid sheep. Wouldn't the secret ballot give them protection from reprisal—and the courage of their convictions?"

Anderson makes a face. "To my mind there's something sneaking and unmanly about it."

"But that's the paradox, isn't it, Colonel? In the case of democracy, it may take secrecy to bring about sincerity. Behind the veil, the truth will out!"

His eyes are sliding away from her again, towards Helen, on the other sofa, pale as a marble.

It's time. Fido stands and says quietly, "I've promised Mrs. Codrington to allow her to speak to you tête-à-tête, because I know she has something very important to say."

Anderson blinks, jumps to his feet.

There, Fido thinks, giving Helen a look over her shoulder, that should screw her courage to the sticking-place.

Downstairs in her study, she can't settle to anything. She leafs through the September number of the *English Woman's Journal*, making a few desultory notes about what could be done to liven it up. (For years now she's been aware of the paradox that although all the members of the Reform Firm have a raging passion for the Cause, their *Journal* has the earnest, mildly querulous tone of the newsletter of some minor craft guild.) She finds a squashed piece of layout, and hisses with irritation: she's always reminding her typos at the press of the importance of maintaining the spaces between things. To pass a little more time, she brings her account book up to date, and replies to a short but affectionate note from her mother. *We've received permission from the University of Cambridge to put forward a few really superior candidates in the local examinations*, she writes, *an experiment which we do hope will contribute in some small way to raising standards in the proper education of girls, something that I know has always been dear to your heart, Mama.*

When Fido checks her watch, only sixteen minutes have passed. But really, how long can it take to tell a man to abandon hope?

She fiddles with the chain of her watch, which has developed a kink in it; she uses a paperweight of the Crystal Palace to press the two links back into line. Her father bought Fido this glass globe as a souvenir of their visit to the Great Exhibition when she was fifteen. (Out of the multitude of objects on display, for some reason the one she remembers is the gigantic pocket knife with eighty blades.) That was the same year she spent a month's pocket money on Longfellow's *Golden Legend*, and her brother George—too devout, even before he was ordained, to approve of poetry—burned it. She wept, and complained to her mother, but didn't dare buy another copy. These days Fido's so much her own person that she finds it hard to remember being that girl. How far she's come from the safe, enclosed world of the Rectory, where words were as solid as bricks: *brother, family, role, duty.*

Nineteen minutes. Almost twenty. *Such claptrap*, Fido thinks suddenly, *I'm not to be barred from my own drawing-room.* Besides, Anderson probably rushed off the moment Helen broke it to him; why would he stay for further humiliation? But then, Fido hasn't heard the front door shut, so he can't have left. Is the man distraught, barging back and forth across the carpet? Issuing denunciations? Threats? She imagines his hands (with their light pelt of golden hair) clenched on Helen's smooth arm.

It only takes Fido a moment to rush upstairs. She waits outside the door of the drawing-room, listening for any sounds of distress. If the two are talking quietly, she'll give them five more minutes; eavesdropping would be detestable. Dust motes dance in the shaft of afternoon light coming across the landing from a gap in the curtains. Oddly enough, Fido can't hear any voices at all, just a little sharp sound: a high-pitched rasping. A sob? Could Anderson have walked out of the house quietly, left Helen crying at the tea table? Or have the two of them reduced each other to speechless misery?

Suddenly, across the back of Fido's eyes, the image of a kiss: Helen's coral mouth, the officer's straw moustache. She feels something like rage. She's about to fling the door open when she registers that the little sound's getting louder and faster. It's not a sound she's ever heard before, which is perhaps why it takes her several more seconds to admit what she's hearing. It's not a gasp of grief or muffled protest, no, it's mechanical: the frantic squeak of the sofa springs as they're forced up and down, up and down.

Fido can't go into the drawing-room, not now, but she finds she can't drag herself away either. She sinks to her knees on the landing, and her brown skirt spreads around her like a puddle.

II

Feme Covert

(in law, a wife under the cover,
i.e., protection and authority, of her husband)

When we come home, we lay aside our mask and drop our tools, and are no longer lawyers, sailors, soldiers, statesmen, clergymen, but only men.

J. A. Froude,
The Nemesis of Faith (1848)

Almost time for the children's hour. Vice-Admiral Henry Codrington's reading the *Telegraph* in his lounging chair. His wife, playing solitaire at an occasional table, stares at the back of his greying, rectangular head. Even his hair seems tightly fastened on. White collar and shirt, black cravat, black waistcoat, black jacket: each fitted layer is buttoned up, despite the heat (which has come back in full force, after the first week of this dead month of September, when so many West End houses are shut up—their fortunate owners off fishing or shooting—that the sky's chronic haze has begun to clear). No sign of his balding, at least, Helen notes, without gratitude.

She watches her own short pink fingers lift a solitaire ball, then drop it back in its niche. She stands up and stretches her arms out to the sides, as much as her sleeves will let her. Sometimes Helen feels like a puppet, with no knowledge of who or what's pulling her strings.

She walks over to the mantelpiece and pretends to be examining a landscape Nan and Nell made out of dried leaves. All the time, she's reckoning yesterday's errors. It's like a blade lodged in her stomach: not guilt, only a dark astonishment at her own recklessness. On Fido's sofa, for God's sake, at four in the afternoon: whatever was she thinking? Really, Helen hasn't the self-preservation of a blind kitten. *Damn the man and his impetuosity*; her legs tighten with excitement at the memory of Anderson seizing her, on the bony brown sofa, as soon as their hostess left the room. Helen knew it was a mistake the minute it was over, as she sat smoothing down her skirts, cooling her cheeks with eau de toilette. Even before Fido's gnarled-looking maid came in with an unconvincing apology about her mistress being called away on sudden business.

But how did her old friend discover what she and Anderson were up to, Helen wonders now. Fido promised she'd give them half an hour, and Helen kept an eye on the grandfather clock all the time. Was it a flash of intuition that made Fido come upstairs early? Could she have listened at the door, flushed face pressed to the oak?

Then the sneak deserved a shock!

Helen bites her thumb hard. Why torment herself with speculations? She's already sent two notes this morning, the first cheery (a routine query about Fido's health), the second a little anxious: *Even though you're busy, my dear, surely you can find a moment to write.* No word back yet. She must be patient; it's only been a matter of hours. Fido's probably at her press, or Langham Place. Perhaps she knows nothing of the sofa business; perhaps she really was *called away.* She'll answer Helen's notes this afternoon, of course she will.

Helen walks to the piano and leafs through a passage of Mendelssohn, but doesn't lift the lid. Without turning her head, she knows her husband has lifted his eyes from the paper. In the early years, Harry used to ask her to play for him. They sang duets, she recalls as if from a distance of centuries. She can't remember now whether she stopped saying yes, or he stopped asking. What does it matter now? An ornately framed photograph on the embroidered piano-cloth shows the whole clan, assembled on the estate that General William Codrington—now governor of Gibraltar—inherited from Sir Edward, the hero of Trafalgar. *Their dearest Papa, the more famous admiral,* Helen comments spitefully in her head. His sons, Harry and William, sit like bristling bookends beside their long-faced sisters, who're stuck all about with sons and daughters. (The glacial Lady Bourchier is Harry's favourite; Helen can't abide the woman.) There's Helen in the back row, with the baby girls like two basset hounds propped up in her lap; she's looking sideways at something out of the frame, and her hair's drawn back smooth with a middle parting. (Ten years on, her hair is just as red, Helen decides, though her face is thinner, and she relies on discreet aids: face powders, eye drops, pink-tinted lip balm.) Her older sisters-in-law wear bonnets with big bows under their multiple chins. At what age will Helen be expected to adopt that dire costume?

The girls rush into the drawing-room, and the silence breaks like a biscuit.

"Whatever have you been doing to make yourselves so scarlet?" their father asks, folding up his paper.

"They've been running around in the square," supplies Helen.

"In this heat!"

"We couldn't keep on with geography, the crayons melted all over our hands," says Nell, arranging her gingham skirts as she perches on the padded arm of Harry's chair.

"So we persuaded Mrs. Lawless to let us release our animal spirits," says Nan, clearly proud of the phrase.

"Were the Atkins girls in the square?" Helen asks.

Both girls shake their heads. "Too hot for them."

"They'd faint."

"Like this," says Nell, dropping on the Brussels carpet.

Out of the corner of her eye Helen sees her husband's long nose turn her way; he's clearly waiting for her to make some show of maternal authority.

"Get up at once," he says at last.

"I was only demonstrating, Papa," says Nell, coming to life.

"Lucy Atkins faints on the least pretence," adds Nan in her sister's defence.

"Pretext," Harry corrects her gently. "You might have knocked your head on the fender, Nell."

"Then my brains would have spilled out and stained the hearth!"

Helen's mouth quivers with amusement.

"Where do you get your notions, child?" asks Harry.

"She read that bit about the hearth on a newsboy's sign," says Nan, older and wiser. "It was about a Horrible Murder in Islington."

"Were you out, earlier?" Harry asks his wife.

She blinks at him like a doll. "Why do you ask?"

"Simply expressing an interest in how you spent the day."

Now Helen rouses herself to be convincing. "I left a sheaf of cards—twenty-nine, I believe," she says with sardonic scrupulousness, "though I'm not sure of the wisdom of letting all our neighbours know, on their return from the country, that we've been unfashionable enough to have had nowhere to go, right through the dog days of the off-season."

He lets out a short sigh.

"But custom decrees," she says, "and I obey. It's very cruel of custom, I've always thought, to make wives deliver their husbands' cards as well as their own, and receive all the tedious calls too."

"Who's custom?" Nell wants to know.

"It's nobody, you nitwit."

"Don't abuse your little sister."

"Sorry, Papa."

"But you're quite right that custom is nobody, Nan," Helen goes on, yawning. "Or everybody, which comes to the same thing."

"Don't you think you're batting rather over their heads?" murmurs her husband.

"No harm, if I am."

"I'm not so sure about that. Custom, girls, is a civilizing force," says Harry, knobbly hands on his knees. "The rules of behaviour are tested and passed down by each generation."

"Who's batting over their heads now?" scoffs Helen. "Besides, if we go back more than a few generations, our ancestors bathed only once a year."

Cries of disgust from Nan and Nell.

Harry purses his chapped lips. "There's generally a great deal of sense behind the rules. Wives must pay and receive the calls, for instance, because husbands must attend to business."

Helen snorts mildly. "Not always."

A beat. "Do you have some particular meaning, my dear?"

When he calls her *my dear*, her hackles always rise. "No," she says, unable to stop herself, "I was only reflecting on the fact that lords are often idle between parliamentary sessions, and lawyers are at a loss between cases, and even quite high-ranking naval officers, say, find themselves stranded on shore for years at a time."

Harry keeps a pleasant expression on his face, but the lines around his eyes have deepened. "As I should have thought you'd appreciate by now, in peacetime the half-pay system allows the Royal Navy to keep a large, qualified force in constant readiness."

"Readiness for what?" she asks. "The last big battle was Trafalgar."

"1805," Nan puts in.

"Very good," Harry tells his daughter automatically.

"Britannia rules the waves," chirps Nell.

Not to be outdone, Nan launches into a shrill rendition of the naval anthem, "Heart of Oak."

Come, cheer up, my lads,
'Tis to glory we steer . . .

But her father shushes her and turns back to his wife. "You're rather parading your ignorance, I'm afraid. What of Navarino, Acre, Sweaborg?"

Ah yes, Navarino, Helen thinks with grim mirth, *as if we're ever to be allowed to forget the skirmish that left a shrapnel hole in Midshipman Harry's tender thigh, or the musket ball embedded in his calf the year before I was born!* "Oh, does Acre count as a battle?" she asks, deadpan. "I should have thought that for British artillery to bombard a Syrian town into dust was like pitting a bear against a mouse."

He huffs out a little laugh. "I don't know why it amuses your mother to spout such gibberish, girls."

"I'm only asking, what does the Navy really *do?* Aren't you less warriors than bobbies on the beat, these days?"

It amuses her that Harry would rather ignore her questions, but the pedant in him makes him answer. "One may as well ask, what do strong walls do?" he says coldly. "Her Majesty's Navy is a floating fortress around her Empire." He turns to the girls, a more sympathetic audience. "When we flex our muscle, slavers and pirates quail!"

The girls pretend to quiver and shrink.

"As do Indian mutineers, land-grabbing Turks, and even the Czar's colossal fleet," adds Harry. "It's a thing universally acknowledged that our patrolling of the world's oceans in unsinkable ironsides is a deterrent to war."

"What's the strongest ship there is?" Nell wants to know. (Nell, Helen would bet ten guineas, has no interest in warships. At such moments, listening to her girls ingratiate themselves with their papa, Helen really couldn't be said to like them.)

"Hm. HMS *Warrior* is probably the most feared, as she has firepower to blow any foreign fleet out of the water. Twenty-six sixty-eight-pounders, and ten 110-pounders . . ."

Helen allows herself a roll of the eyes. "You're not missing your arithmetic class, at least, girls . . ."

"But the old wooden vessels are handsomer," Nan objects.

"Well, many share your reservations," says Harry, "but to my own not inexperienced eye, *Warrior*'s sleek black lines have a modern sort of beauty. Uncle William tells me in his last that when she docked at Gibraltar, a crowd of six thousand turned out for her."

Tomorrow, Helen thinks with a fierce restlessness, *I could meet Anderson somewhere tomorrow, why not? The National Gallery? Too dark and dirty; shopgirls make assignations there. Somewhere outside, in a crowd?*

"So, to clear up your confusion, my dear—" says Harry, turning his large eyes on Helen again, "power held in reserve is the best weapon, because it involves no unnecessary bloodshed. Surveillance is the best defence."

She's sick of the subject, but can't stand to let him have the last word. She covers a ladylike yawn with her hand. "But surely the problem with deterrence is that it can only be inferred, not proved. It's like having some fat porter outside with a pistol in his greatcoat," she suggests, jerking her head towards Eccleston Square, "who shakes himself awake when you open the door, to assure you that since breakfast his presence has kept a dozen murderers from garrotting the whole family!"

Harry's face is a stone mask. After a moment he remarks to the girls, "Giddy-up! Mama's imagination appears to have run away with her again."

They giggle obediently.

"Silly Mama."

Her tongue feels thick with hatred. "Very well, I can tell the topic's a sensitive one, given your position."

His coal-black bushy eyebrows go up. "My—"

"Your current lack of one, I mean."

"My superiors consider me entitled to a restorative period after seven years of ceaseless application," he says, a muscle standing out on the side of his neck.

"No no, let's drop it. I'll read the paper, and you and the girls can entertain yourselves by practising faints on the rug."

Nan and Nell laugh, with the eyes of nervous fillies.

She reaches for the *Telegraph.*

"I haven't finished, as it happens," says Harry, moving it out of her reach and re-erecting it. "Here's an interesting fact for you, girls. Did you know there's a house in Bayswater that's only a false facade, constructed to cover a railway tunnel?"

"Why?" Nell wants to know.

"It looks more harmonious that way, I suppose. Otherwise people walking down that street would suddenly glimpse a train rushing past under their feet."

"That would be sensational!"

"Aunt Fido had a fit of asthma on the Underground Railway, didn't she, Mama?"

Helen's startled that Nell remembers. "That's right, after she and I ran into each other on the street."

"I still don't see what the two of you were thinking, travelling on the Underground, when we can afford to hire cabs," remarks her husband.

"My mistake," says Helen under her breath. "You blew so much steam when I asked about keeping a carriage, I had the impression we were on the brink of bankruptcy." Then she catches sight of the girls' faces, and regrets it. "Mama's joking, my sweets."

"Grown-up jokes aren't very funny," observes Nell.

"Indeed they aren't," says Harry, glaring.

"She gave me a tour of her famous press last week," Helen remarks, testing the waters.

A snort from her husband. "I wasn't aware that you took an interest in industry."

"Well, one must pass the days somehow; town will be quite moribund till January."

Today's cold silence from Taviton Street suggests that Helen's strayed across a line. If Fido was willing to counsel her friend through a thwarted romance with the handsome colonel, it appears she feels quite otherwise about a consummated one. *Hypocrite*, Helen snaps at Fido in her head. Sex looms so large in the pinched minds of spinsters. Do some snatched pleasures on a sofa really make all the difference between right and wrong?

"You could always spend time with the girls, improve their French and music," Harry remarks, crossing his long legs.

"Isn't that exactly what we pay Mrs. Lawless for?"

He quietly corrects the pronoun. "I hired her to teach them for certain hours of the day, yes, but surely it's their mother who should be preparing them for their future role in life."

"I do, as it happens," says Helen. "I take them out looking for wallpaper, let them sit in the cab when I'm paying calls . . ."

"I was thinking more of domestic duties."

"What, boiling a leg of mutton?"

"Now you're being silly again. Supervisory duties, I meant."

"Mrs. Nichols and her underlings boil mutton perfectly well, and wouldn't care for the three of us standing round the kitchen and goggling at them."

"My point is that there's no substitute, morally, for maternal care."

"If you mean to talk cant, I really must insist on reading the paper . . ." Helen holds out her hand for it.

"Don't, Mama," says Nan, hanging on her arm. "This press of Fido's, tell us why it's famous."

So young, and already expert in the feminine art of distraction. "For employing girls to set the type," Helen tells her.

What if Fido doesn't write back, not today, not next week? The buried friendship, which Helen's gone to considerable trouble to dig up and dust off, might have slipped through her fingers already.

Harry's smile is small. "Bourgeois female employment is a pure novelty, I'm afraid, as much as the stereoscope. These printers and nurses and telegraphists and bookkeepers, they'll die away like birds in winter."

"I'll be sure to pass on your encouragement the next time I see her." *I won't let her drop me*, Helen decides with a sudden fury. *I can fix this; I can make her remember how much she cares about me.*

"Speaking of our stereoscope, Papa, we've had all our views a very long time," Nell puts in.

"Meaning, a month," says Helen, sardonic.

"There's a set of photographs of Japan on tissue paper. That would be educational," Nan adds.

"Well, you may show me the catalogue," says their father.

"You encourage their addiction," Helen murmurs.

"May we come see Fido's press next time, Mama?"

"You may not," the parents chime simultaneously.

"You might get caught in a machine," says Harry, "and rolled out as flat as paper."

Nan mimes this, and she and her sister fall into ecstasies.

~

HELEN MEETS HER LOVER AT THE ZOO, at the north end of Regent's Park.

"Mm, I dare say we were rather rash the other day, at Taviton Street. I did like your virago," he says regretfully.

"Oh!" Helen pokes him hard in the ribs.

He seizes her cotton-gloved fingers. "Well, your strong-minded friend, then. She looks like a farmhand, but she seems a good soul, for all her radical notions. The thing is, how exactly is she going to be helpful to us now, if she's in high dudgeon?"

"Leave it to me," Helen tells him.

"You said she understood," he complains.

"She does, more than most women would." Besides, whom else can Helen rely on in this stiff-faced city?

"I still don't understand why you fed her that rigmarole about intending to give me the brush-off—"

"Men understand nothing about female friendship. These things take time; don't forget, she's a vicar's daughter. In a little while," says Helen, "I'm sure I can get her to pass on our letters, perhaps let us meet at her house again . . ."

"Time is just what we're short of," mutters Anderson.

Helen can't bear to ask whether he knows the date of his recall. Will her hold on her lover survive the distance? It strikes her that there are other lively, discontented wives in Valetta. The air carries a waft of reeking straw from the Carnivora Terrace, and she feels as if she might choke; she pulls her veil down. "You're a grumpy bear today." Entwining her gloved hand with his bare one.

"Am I?" asks Anderson, scratching one of his floppy side whiskers. "It's deuced hard on a fellow, all this hanging about for the post three times a day. Never knowing when he'll get a glimpse of his *inamorata*, not even allowed to write to her in case her husband sees the letter . . ."

She smiles silkily to hide her irritation: "Well, we're together now." They pace. "Remember what you whispered in my ear on the docks?"

A blank look.

"When I was about to get on the ship, in Valetta," she reminds him caressingly. "You told me that until you joined me in London, I'd be held in your thoughts like a jewel, all day and all night . . ."

His smile is boyish. "But now I'm here, thoughts aren't enough; I need to hold you in my arms."

She wants to snap, *it's only been four days since you got a lot more than that on Fido's sofa.* "Oh, for the balmy skies of our dear island," she sighs, instead.

In her mind, steel cogs are turning. She knows she holds this man by the thinnest of threads. In Malta, military society allowed a certain leeway, and Harry practically lived in his office; if there was gossip about his pretty wife and her constant escort, it never reached the pitch of accusation—that she knows of. But in England, Harry has too much time on his hands, which makes her nervous. He's beginning to poke his nose in: just think of his suggesting she instruct the girls in the supervision of servants! Here in the home country, Helen's never felt less safe, less at home.

Anderson, arms crossed, is considering the languid lions. "Apparently these poor beasts used to last only a year or two in their cages, but when the terrace was added, their life expectancy increased greatly."

"I sense a moral to this story."

"Well, yes: a little freedom does wonders." He grabs her hand, raises it to his hot mouth.

Helen snatches it back. "Don't."

"You think we'll be seen by someone who matters, in a herd of two thousand visitors?"

"The girls' governess sometimes brings them here."

"Your maternal side charms me," says Anderson. "It flashes out on occasion, like a comet."

Helen glares. "My daughters are everything to me."

"Sorry. You've teased me out of my manners," he tells her, turning his broad back to the odorous breeze to light one of his clove-scented cigarettes.

The Crimean left its thumbprint on the gentlemen of England, Helen thinks; they all went off smooth-cheeked, and came back grimly bearded and stinking of tobacco. "The least one can do, as a parent, is lie to one's children," she remarks. "I mean to protect mine from the truth till they marry, and discover it for themselves."

"Lucky girls," says Anderson wryly. "Would you care to see the rattlesnakes now?"

The last time she brought the girls here, they saw a boa constrictor seize a duck; Nell had nightmares for a week. "I believe you just want to get me in a dark room," she says, making herself loosen into a smile.

"Well, to bring me where every species can nuzzle or mount, and I mayn't so much as steal a kiss, seems peculiarly cruel."

Helen laughs.

His sigh is guttural. "Before my trip to Scotland, if we could only find somewhere to be at peace for an hour—"

"I'm perfectly at peace," she lies. He's going back to Scotland for his grandmother's hundredth birthday, when he could be staying in London to be near Helen.

"You witch! I can imagine you visiting convicts, tantalizing them, leaving a trace of perfume on the dungeon air . . ."

She smiles, peering into a cage where a large black cat appears to be sleeping.

"Couldn't I find a hansom and tell the man to go round and round the park?"

"London cabbies are notorious tattletales."

"I miss the admiralty gondola. Those moonlit nights, the sway of the waves . . ."

"You shocking man," she says pleasurably.

"My landlady's such a busybody," Anderson complains, "but I do happen to know a very nice, quiet hotel . . ."

Helen gives him a chilly look. "The notion has something soiled about it."

"Don't get your dander up."

Anderson sounds so crushed, she puts her mouth close up against his blond, rumpled head. "Patience," she breathes. "You know I'd risk my life for you and thank heaven for the chance."

"Darling brave girl," he groans. "Beautiful Helen, whose face launched the thousand ships . . ."

She moves away again, before he can kiss her. "When will your leave be up?" she asks, then wishes she hadn't.

His face flattens. "I expect to hear from my superiors any day now."

"You could always try to exchange into a home unit, couldn't you?" Oh, she shouldn't have started this; she's dashing across quicksand. "Officers do that, very often, I believe, if their regiments are sent to perform garrison duty in Canada, or the West Indies—"

"I rather like Malta, as you know."

She turns her head so he won't see the tears in her eyes.

"Officers often sell out, too," he points out. "Is that what you want of me?"

"Of course not," she says hoarsely. "I'd miss your scarlet regimentals."

Anderson manages a chuckle. After a short silence, he flicks open his watch. "The eagles are due to be fed, shall we watch?"

"I really had better be going," says Helen, to punish him.

~

In the next morning's note to Fido, Helen drops her pretence that nothing's wrong between them. After all, her old friend—with her radical notions and almost Bohemian way of life—is not like other women. The usual techniques of flattery, euphemism, and circumlocution won't work here. Helen's decided it's best to fling herself at Fido's feet.

I have no other ally in the world, she improvises,

and so in fear and trembling I beg you to hear the whole narrative from my own lips before you pass irrevocable judgement. Did you not tell me only the other day that sister-souls must stand by each other through all trials?

Hour after hour, she waits for a reply. The time for calls is almost over. Her husband, who's spent the day down at Deptford ogling some new armour-plated sloop or screw (Helen's always refused to learn these distinctions), comes in for a speechless cup of tea. He studies a report on naval reform; Helen reads the latest installment of *Our Mutual Friend*, but she keeps forgetting who's who. It feels as he and she are in a honeycomb; walls of wax keep them apart.

The bell, at last. The maid pops her head in to announce Miss Faithfull, and relief floods through Helen's veins like sugar.

Harry's face is neutral. "Show her up."

He's holding out his cup; she registers that he'd like more tea. Why won't the man make himself scarce?

Fido comes in looking tired. Helen's ribs feel bruised. She gives Fido an apologetic grimace, to say *if only we were alone!*—but Fido stares back like a stranger.

Harry stands up to greet the visitor, all unbending six foot five of him. Glimpsing him through Fido's eyes, Helen finds his height almost freakish. Not an aristocratic Norman, no, some older race: he rears up like some implacable, axe-wielding Hun.

They all sit down and pass round the rolled-up bread and butter. Harry asks after one of Fido's brothers, who's recently been promoted to the rank of captain. Soon they've moved on to her precious Cause. "But you see, Admiral, already a full fifty per cent of British women work for their bread,"

Fido is telling Harry, "and often at gruelling, repetitive tasks such as chain-making or mining at the pit brow."

"Ah, poor men's wives and daughters, that's quite another thing," says Harry. "But when it comes to women of the middling or upper orders—"

She interrupts him. "At our Employment Register, I'm constantly meeting the pathetic dependents of gentlemen whose fortunes have dwindled in the stocks, or who've otherwise failed to make provision."

"Girls like Nan and Nell?" asks Helen. She can see her husband's shoulders rise, and she almost giggles.

"Of course your daughters are charmingly accomplished," Fido says hastily. Then, after a moment, she goes on: "But to what profession could they turn their untrained hands if by any chance that dark day came? I suggest that it's no natural incapacity, but only custom and law that would prevent them from working in shops or offices, administering institutions or estates . . ."

Harry lets out a huff of breath. "I don't think I'll have much trouble finding my girls husbands."

My girls, says he, Helen thinks, fuming, *as if they sprang from his thigh!*

"Forty-three per cent of Englishwomen over the age of twenty are single," Fido announces.

The statistic makes him stare.

"I declare, Fido, you're a regular Blue Book," murmurs Helen.

"Ah," says Harry, holding up one massive finger, "but if you and your fellow Utopians were to train up well born girls, to render them independent of my sex—if you succeeded in turning single life into a pleasant highway, and marriage just one thorny path opening off it—then why would they marry at all?"

A pause. Fido chews her lip. "Matrimony is the special and honourable calling of most women, Admiral, but from lack of personal experience, I can hardly discourse on its allure."

Harry holds her gaze for a moment, then lets out a laugh.

Helen's been forgetting how much these two liked each other, in the old days. *He's always respected her mind more than mine*, she thinks, a little rueful.

"It's been a pleasure, Miss Faithfull. After all this time. Now I'm afraid I have letters to write," he says, rising.

As soon as the two women are alone, the silence clots like blood. Helen makes herself set down her cup and begin her speech. "The other day at your house, my dearest, in a moment of frailty for which I've been excoriating myself—"

"It was a long *moment*."

Helen's cheeks are flaming; she's lost control of this scene already.

"Your conscience is your own affair, I suppose." Fido speaks with a rigid throat. "But I'd have expected more of your manners."

Manners? Is this what it comes down to—an offence against English etiquette? Then she looks hard at Fido—the avèrted eyes, the compressed lips—and understands. The offence is against friendship. *She's hurt that I didn't tell her everything before*, she realizes; *she can't bear the fact that it was* her *sofa*. On impulse, she falls to her knees.

"Whatever are you doing?" Fido barks.

For a second, Helen doubts her strategy—and then decides that too much is better than too little. "Begging your pardon most humbly and sorrowfully," she answers, very low. Like some scolded dog, she lays her head on Fido's navy-blue skirt. "You do right to cast coals," she whispers. "But let me just say that the thing was not . . . premeditated."

A pause. "Really?"

Aha, thinks Helen: *she wants nothing more than to forgive me. She's been longing to let herself take me back!* She sits on her heels, wipes one dry eye.

"Get up, Little One. Come sit by me. I blame myself, in some ways," says Fido into her handkerchief.

Helen stares: whatever can she mean?

"After all, it was I who urged you to make the decisive break," says Fido in a low whisper. "Perhaps I was naïve; perhaps my ignorance of the other sex blinded me to the dangers. When a battle-hardened veteran sees all he longs for about to be snatched away—"

She thinks it was all Anderson. She's as gullible as a child, on certain subjects, Helen marvels. She starts nodding. "He was very fierce . . ."

Fido seizes her by the wrist. "And I was stupid enough to leave you alone with him, in my own drawing-room. My darling—did he hurt you?"

"No, no." Helen's gone too far. What, does Fido know so little of men that she thinks them all savages? Helen looks into her satin lap. How much can she risk admitting? "Perhaps it's not the male heart that's your blind spot, Fido, but the female." A pause. "When I said I meant to put a stop to this passion: it was not just *his* passion I meant."

A terrible silence. Her friend's plump cheeks cave in. Has Helen blundered? "I've always needed you to protect me from my weaker self," she pleads, "but never more than now."

"Oh my poor girl." Fido wraps her in a hard embrace.

Helen's head is crushed against her friend's ribs; she smells ink. She feels weirdly at peace.

"If you've surrendered your heart to this man . . . then I won't bother with stern platitudes, after the fact. But you must see that you've lost your way," says Fido, pulling back and fixing Helen with her doggish brown eyes. "It's not a question of conventional morality, so much as truth. Authenticity. Self-respect, as I've said before."

Helen isn't listening; she's preparing her next line. "Sometimes I fear my feelings for him will master me," she says in a tiny voice. "That he'll drag me from my husband, my children, even . . ."

"Don't say it! Don't even speak those terrible words. My love is as strong as his," says Fido, "and I mean to save you."

The woman looks magnificent, Helen observes curiously; those plain features are transfigured. "Oh Fido, you're all that stands between me and the pit!" The two are silent, for a few moments, and their hands knot together like the roots of trees.

Fido clears her throat. "On a horridly practical note . . . what if there were to be an accident?"

Thinking of crashed cabs or falls from balconies, Helen is bewildered, but then she understands her friend's awkward tone. She almost giggles. "Ah, no, set your mind at rest," she murmurs. *How revolted Fido would be to learn of my sponges and douches!*

"Well, at any rate, you mustn't see him again; don't you feel that?" asks Fido fondly. "I imagine it's like giving up opium; they say 'cold turkey' is best."

Helen sits bolt upright. This isn't how the conversation is meant to go; her elaborations have led her astray. "On the contrary," she improvises, "if I were to cut Anderson off now—that would be the most dangerous thing I could do. Why, it could make him desperate enough to tell my husband."

"He wouldn't dare!"

"Can I risk it?"

Fido writhes. "You could deny everything, if it came to that."

Oho, thinks Helen with silent mirth, *what price truth now?*

"What proof could Anderson—"

"Letters," Helen interrupts, squirming, "gifts: a locket of my hair."

Her friend covers her mouth. "Worse and worse."

"No, I must teach him how to give me up, step by step, little by little," insists Helen.

"But delay is so dangerous . . ."

"You mean we might be discovered?"

"Spiritually dangerous," snaps Fido. "Corroding your very self, day by day."

Helen resists the impulse to roll her eyes. "You must help me," she says. "Help us both."

"Both?" cries Fido, disgustedly.

"Anderson means me no harm."

"How can you say that? The blackguard's already treated you like a . . ." She doesn't say the word. "In my drawing-room!"

"Half the fault was mine," Helen reminds her. "You must be our friend now."

"Yours, only yours."

"His too, if you would be mine. Our confessor. Our saviour."

Fido's face twists like a sail in the wind. Helen, watching, can see the moment of surrender. "Anything I can do which is consistent with—"

"Bless you, bless you," Helen interrupts, pressing her mouth to Fido's fiery cheek.

~

September 15
Destroy after opening

Little One,

As promised I have forwarded yours of yesterday to the person in question, and enclose one in reply. You'll see I'm not using my own seal on the envelope, for discretion's sake.

I loathe these sneaking measures, but having weighed them in my heart I believe they can be justified for the sake of a greater good, i.e., preserving you—and your whole family—from disaster. For all that I've said in critique of marriage, the fact remains that when you accepted your husband fifteen years ago, you set sail in this particular vessel, and your whole future depends on averting a shipwreck.

It still seems to me that further encounters with the person in question will only lead him to maintain false hopes, but I give way: the breach is yours to accomplish, the safest way you can manage (and after all, what do I know of the opaque workings of the male heart?). His imminent departure from these shores will I trust ring down the curtain on this dangerous drama, and tho' I realize you will suffer, when he is gone, I can promise you all the consolation stored up in my heart.

I have not slept at all well since you entrusted your awful story to me, but sleep, my dearest, is the least I'd sacrifice to a friendship I thought extinct but which a merciful and mysterious providence has seen fit to return to us, like bread that was cast on the waters. I am at your back: remember that. Don't say you're "unworthy," my sweet girl; it brings tears to my eyes. Your heart is a wayward one, but there's no evil in it. Besides, when has "worthiness" ever been the criterion for friendship? The love of women is like the pull of magnets. Since the first day I met you on that beach in Kent, I've belonged to you, and always will.

If as you say it's absolutely imperative for you two to meet in a safe place, then I relent: I have told him to come to my house at half past five tomorrow (the sixteenth) and will *expect you half an hour earlier. I need hardly say that I will remain in the room throughout, and I trust you not to allow him to take any further advantage of my hospitality.*

Yours as ever—

~

In Fido's austere drawing-room at Taviton Street, Helen avoids the sofa's associations and picks an old straight-legged chair near the fire.

Fido draws her own chair closer. "Prepare yourself, my darling. You must be very strong."

"Oh yes?" says Helen, irked by Fido's sepulchral tone, and wondering why there's no cake on the tea table.

"You believe you know this man, for whom you've risked ruin?"

Ruin, echoes Helen scornfully in her head; *really, she's read too many potboilers.*

"Well. I took it on myself to make enquiries among my Scottish relations, for any insight into Anderson's character, and this morning I received some alarming information."

Helen smiles. "What have the detectives discovered, that he once lost a hundred pounds at cards?"

Fido's eyes rebuke her. "He's been linked to one of his cousins."

Helen waits. "Linked?"

"With a view to marriage."

The word makes her mouth curl up. "Whose *view*? Every eligible bachelor home on leave has the old hens of his family plotting to marry him off."

Fido shakes her head. "My informants were quite specific. This cousin, if you can believe it, has been linked formerly with the colonel's brother."

She's enjoying this, thinks Helen with a vast irritation, but she laughs. "That coda seems to explode the story entirely. So this girl makes eyes at his brother one summer, and Anderson the next, and means equally little on both occasions."

Fido sits back, sucking her lips. "Very well, if you don't tremble at having placed yourself in the shopsoiled hands of the kind of man who dallies with prospective brides—"

"I have no need to look as far as Scotland for imaginary bogeys," snaps Helen. "What makes me *tremble* is his imminent return to Malta, abandoning me to several more decades of misery with a corpse of a husband."

Water erupts in Fido's cocoa-brown eyes. "I didn't mean—" She puts a hand on Helen's magenta overskirt.

A distant doorbell: *thank God.*

Colonel Anderson is announced. He's only a little awkward. Fido, very much on her dignity, gives him a cup of coffee.

Helen considers various possible tones and plumps for light satire. "Well, Colonel, you're very good to spare us an afternoon before you take an express train north again. The Scotch climate must have special charms."

The gold moustache wobbles; a half-smile. "Not sure I catch your drift, Mrs. C."

"Oh, was I misinformed? Haven't the dowagers of the Anderson line taken to matchmaking?"

He relaxes into a laugh. (It's this face she loves, Helen realizes: a lad's loose grin.) "What can I say? It would be cruel to stop up their mouths."

Something in her unwinds. "But spare a thought for the poor coz who may be getting her hopes up."

"She's a very sensible sort, I wouldn't worry," says Anderson, leaving his chair and sitting down beside Helen, so close that his knee touches hers, through the layers of silk and linen and steel-framed crinoline.

Fido has moved to the round table and is looking through the *Times*. Her broad shoulders speak volumes.

"Look here, in all earnest," says Anderson under his breath, "I want to speak to you alone."

"You always want that," Helen murmurs silkily.

"Couldn't you persuade your faithful hound to allow us a momentary tête-à-tête?"

Helen raises her eyes to heaven. "I've had to swear to her that I'm cutting you off by degrees, like an opium habit."

Anderson tugs at his moustache. "How's Harry, these days?"

She makes a face. "An inert, brooding spider. He implies I'm a gadabout; complains I'm spending too much on modernizing the house."

"What a dashed bore." He slips his hand over hers. "But I suppose a husband must hold the reins."

Helen prickles. "You speak like my late mother. Must he hold the reins even when he's knuckleheadedly wrong?"

"That's neither here nor there, I'm afraid. A lieutenant may be wiser than his major, but the chain of command still applies," says Anderson.

She pulls her fingertips out of his grasp. She glances at the round table, and meets their hostess's reproachful eyes. Fido has pulled out her watch and taps it solemnly. Helen puts on a tragedy face, looks into her lap.

"This is absurd, we can't do anything here," says Anderson in a very low growl.

"We can talk."

"Not at ease. I'll tell you what: why don't I head off, and wait around the corner on Gordon Street, then in ten minutes you have a cab called and pick me up?"

"Because—" She hesitates. And changes her mind as quick as a blink, because why does the woman always have to be the careful one? And given the risks Helen's already run, is running now, for this man's sake, why hold back?

Anderson doesn't wait for her yes. "Miss Faithfull—" He rises to his feet.

"Look crushed," she breathes.

His face falls obediently. "I'm going to take my leave now," he says in hollow tones.

"Very well, Colonel," says Fido, rising like some stern but not ungentle schoolmistress.

"You've been immensely kind. I can't . . ." Anderson breaks off there, to Helen's relief. (He doesn't share her talents for invention.)

Fido rings for his coat, cane, and hat, and walks him to the stairs.

When she comes back into the room, Helen's arranged herself in a frail position on the sofa, face in one hand. Fido sits down beside her, very quietly, and asks "Is it—by any chance—over?"

"I tried," says Helen through her fingers. "I marshalled all my arguments. I gave him no hope. But the insane persistence of the man—"

"He must be eaten up with love for you," says Fido in a choked tone.

She nods. "I don't know why."

"Oh Helen . . ."

After a minute, she adds, "Little by little, he will realize I mean what I say. You must bear with me, Fido. Keep on being my rock."

The woman's solid arms wrap around her, and for a moment Helen feels dizzy, because both versions are true: in the back of her head she's laughing at the spinster's naïveté, and yet she'd like nothing better than for Fido to sort out her life for her, somehow. Helen's acting and she's sincere, at the very same moment; she wants to summon a cab and rush around the corner to join her lover, and she wants to stay here all evening, rocked like a baby in these strong arms. "I'd better go," she says at last, rousing herself, pressing the back of her hands to her eyes. "Harry likes dinner at seven on the dot," she adds. "He claims, a quarter-hour later and he's afflicted by heartburn!"

When Anderson climbs into the cab on Gordon Street, the warm September breeze rushes against their faces. He reaches out with one hand to draw the pleated leather curtains that close off the front of the hansom.

Helen restrains his arm. "What are you doing? On such a beautiful evening too—we may as well hang a banner from the roof."

He chuckles, and leaves the leather half-closed. "Where to?"

"Anywhere but home," she finds herself saying.

His grin is that of a child surprised with a present.

"I can't bear to go into that mausoleum and shut the door. Take me somewhere entertaining, won't you?"

"Somewhere *sensational*, as your girls are always saying?"

But she doesn't want to think about Nan and Nell, already putting on their white pantaloons and short crinolines for dinner with their parents. She'll have to send a telegram to explain her absence.

Anderson flips open the little trapdoor in the roof. "Driver, to the moon!"

"What's that, sir?" the man behind them calls over the clatter of hooves.

"Seems the lady doesn't want to go to Belgravia, after all," Anderson tells him.

"What about the Cremorne Pleasure Gardens?" Helen asks in a low voice. "I've never been. Unless it's not the thing?"

"No, no, this early in the evening it should be perfectly all right," says Anderson. "Chelsea, driver: the Cremorne, if you please."

Belatedly, Helen wonders whether the Cremorne has other associations for her lover. Has he gone before, with other ladies? She tells herself to stop fretting. If she's to risk Harry's temper by missing dinner, by God she means to enjoy the escapade.

~

There's a telegraph station in the Gardens, for receiving bookings. Helen sips a sherry while Anderson goes in with her message: *Miss F has begged me to stay and dine with Rev & Mrs F.* She congratulates herself on its brilliance and brevity: now Harry will picture her discussing the state of the Church with Fido's stout, unsmiling parents, up from their Surrey parish in all their tedious glory.

The day's generous light is cooling; the trees throw down long shadows. A steamboat emerges from Battersea Bridge and draws up at the landing station; Helen watches black coats, salmon skirts, turquoise wraps spill from its crammed decks. The Cremorne seems to attract all sorts: she notices some swells in evening capes, but also country families (the females in their red petticoats) and, of course, the clerk brigade. At the Chinese bandstand, the orchestra's playing *Tales from the Vienna Woods*, rather too fast for Helen's taste. Her eyes pick out Swiss chalets, miniature temples, and a marionette theatre scattered among the trees; even something marked *American Bowling Saloon.*

In a clearing, an aeronaut in form-fitting yellow leotards is checking her rigging while five men hold her basket to the ground; the gas flare roars like a monster, and high above, the vast silk balloon is swelling and rolling. Helen wonders what it must be like to trust yourself, night after night, to a sack of hot air. She thinks of the famous Madame Genviève, swollen in pregnancy, toppling from her tightrope.

Anderson, appearing at her shoulder, makes her jump. "I've managed to secure the last booth at the Crystal Platform," he says with that hint of sheepish pride common to gentlemen who've just had to hand over an outrageous tip.

"How marvellous." She slides her hand into the crook of his arm.

The orchestra's struck up a scottische, but no one's dancing yet; in the faint pre-dusk the Crystal Platform has the shoddy air of some Christmas decoration lost behind a sofa. But the booths are crowded with revellers. While Helen and Anderson are beginning supper at their tiny table, reminiscing about a masked party they once attended in Valetta, the "thousand lamps" come on all at once, to a general *oooh*, and Helen puts her chicken wing down so she can clap. Arches and festoons of gaslights; globes and cut-glass drops in garnet, topaz, emerald. However is it done? Spangled strings carry the radiance off in every direction through the trees, making the sky dark behind them. The Cremorne scintillates like some fairy fort sprung up on the banks of the Thames. For a moment Helen wishes her daughters were here to see this, then tells herself not to be a fool. (Perhaps she'll find them a slide of the scene, sometime.)

And now the firework display begins, and Helen can't eat a bite more, only sip her cold wine and grip Anderson's hand under the tablecloth. When there's a particularly loud crack or boom she digs her nails into his palm. The music is louder, now—a thumping polka, followed by a gallop—and the platform's come alive with couples. There are few families left in the Gardens, she notices; the crowd's changing, and young bucks roam the outskirts.

The orchestra strikes up a waltz. "One dance?" says Anderson in her ear. "Or had I better be taking you home?"

It only takes her a second to decide. "'Hung for a sheep,' as they say," she replies. "I feel as if I haven't danced in years." Not since that farewell ball in Valetta, when Harry stayed till the end, for once, and she and Anderson had to avoid each other's miserable eyes all evening.

She shakes off the memory and lets her lover lead her onto the polished floor. There's no one here who knows them, she tells herself. The colonel's an unobtrusively graceful dancer; it's like riding a horse who needs no signals. As she lets him spin her round, the gas lamps whirl and blur behind his halo of blond curls. This is a strange outdoor ballroom; many women are dancing in their summer capes, men with their hats on and canes in their hot fists. Anderson pulls her close; her skirt sways like a huge butterfly. She feels that at any moment their momentum may spin them up to orbit over the massive elms and sighing poplars; to whirl and float higher than balloons, birds, clouds, into the shiny night air. He presses his silky whiskers against her cheek, and she's laughing, and he is too. "Perhaps I'll never go home," she cries.

Anderson jerks as if he's been shot in the back.

Helen pulls away too, to look at his face, and now they've lost their rhythm, they've broken the line, and she stumbles, her heel caught in some hard-faced shopgirl's lacy hem. "I do beg your pardon," Anderson is saying in all directions, but Helen makes blindly for the booth. By the time she finds the right table he's at her side, begging her to finish the dance. Instead she gathers her cape and bag with shaking hands.

Only when they're well away from the platform, past the lavender bower and geranium beds, does Helen say a word. "It was a joke."

"I know that," he insists.

"Then why did you flinch?"

"I did no such thing."

"Don't take me for some green girl." Helen shakes off his arm as they take a path through the trees. "I've not the least intention of running away from my husband." She watches Anderson's face for the least flicker of grief, finds none. "I don't intend to make any claim on your protection," she growls, "for all the passion you've professed."

"Oh my darling," he groans.

"You needn't fear for the loss of your bachelor freedoms."

"Now that's too much." Anderson seizes her by the elbows, pinning her to the spot. It's dim here in the dark wood; the sounds of the pleasure gardens are hushed. "My only fear is for you, Helen, as you should know. It's because I treasure you that I've never once asked you to come away with me."

Helen looks away, licking her lips: tastes dye in the balm.

"Be sensible," says Anderson. "What could I offer you that could make up for such a . . . catastrophe?"

He means the question rhetorically, but there's one obvious answer. She considers, for the first time, the image of Anderson as a husband. Would he still wear that lazy, boyish smile? Would there be anything left of the man who once wooed her with his eyes across a crowd?

"All you'd lose—and the disgrace of it, besides—"

"Now you're being cruel," she says, very low.

"This snatched love is all we have," he says into her ear, "but by God, it's sweet. And to think that many die without a taste of it!"

All very stirring; Helen's mouth twists. She shivers. "It must be late. I ought to go home. What time is it?"

"Not very late," says Anderson. He tugs her by the hand, leads her step by step away from the path, into the darkest part of the wood where the aromatic trees grow close together.

She knows what he's up to. Men are so predictable: they can only think of one way to end a quarrel. "Take me home."

"I will, I promise. Just a little further, won't you, to show you've forgiven me?"

The cool part of her brain thinks, *Never mind your offended feelings, Helen; this is the best chance you'll have in weeks.* She's still frowning, but her feet follow him into the lush black vegetation, one step at a time.

~

HELEN LETS HERSELF IN WITH HER KEY at ten past eleven. She steps quietly through the darkened hall. She won't rouse her maid, even; she can undress herself when she must.

There's a light burning on the landing. As she tiptoes past the girls' door it suddenly opens. She prepares to shush them back to bed, but it's her husband.

Helen produces a marionette's smile. "You're still dressed."

His face is haggard. "Didn't you get my telegram?"

"Of course," she says automatically. Whatever does he mean? It was she who sent one, from the Cremorne. Did Harry shoot off a reply to the house on Taviton Street? A civil *Give my respects to the Faithfulls*? Or a sullen *Very well*? But neither would have needed an answer, so why is he asking whether she received it? Helen's always been a good bluffer; when she can be bothered to play cards, she usually wins. "I know I'm late, but I thought it might offend the reverend and his wife if I dashed off before dessert."

His lower lip has a raw patch, she notices now; it's dark with blood. "You're extraordinary. Not so much as a word in response, all these hours. Not a single word!"

Helen's stomach is a snake tightening round itself. "I'm awfully sorry—"

"She got worse after I sent for you," he tells her. "She was saying your name."

She looks away, so he won't read the shock in her eyes. *She*, which she? An accident? A sudden illness? And the worst of it is Helen must pretend she already knows all the facts. "Yes, the poor girl," she says hoarsely. "Has Doctor Mendelkirk—"

"He confirmed what I'd gathered from *Household Management*, when Mrs. Nichols and I finally found where you'd stuck it, in the middle of the atlases."

Oh get on with it, you petty despot!

"It's a dangerous cold on her chest," he tells her. "She's been burning up. She's had a dose of salicine but it hasn't broken the fever yet. Nan was in a state too, she kept refusing to go to bed."

It's Nell, then. *My baby*. "I'll go in to her right away," says Helen.

But Harry puts out his long arm. "The doctor gave her something to make her sleep."

"Then I won't be disturbing her, will I?" asks Helen, pushing past him.

In the girls' room, one of the little beds has been drawn close to the fire, and a screen arranged round it to enclose the steam puffing from a kettle. The air stinks of turpentine. A stranger's dozing in an easy chair; she must be a hired nurse. Helen sits on the very edge of the bed and watches her younger daughter's flushed face. The narrow chest under the lawn ruffles rises and falls regularly, but too fast, with a hoarse creak. Helen wants to scoop Nell up in her arms, but fears to wake her. Is Harry still out there on the landing?

Surely he can't mean to catch her as she emerges, and continue the interrogation? Why doesn't he come in and stand beside her, put his hand on her shoulder, even, like an ordinary husband and father, with an ordinary heart?

She waits, counts Nell's breaths for a quarter of an hour. There, surely Harry will have gone back to his own room by now. He'll be lying down in his nightshirt like some long marble effigy. Helen creeps to the door, puts her head out to scan the empty landing.

"Mama?"

She spins round, but Nell is still motionless. It's Nan who's sitting up, huge-eyed in her bed. Helen puts a finger to her lips and goes over to her elder daughter.

"You didn't come home."

All my accusers. "Mama had a social engagement," she says absurdly.

"Nell coughed and it was green," the girl confides.

Helen finds her eyes wet. "She'll be better in the morning."

"Will she?"

Helen has no idea. "Go to sleep now."

"May I kiss you goodnight?"

The request sounds oddly formal. "Of course, of course, my sweet girl." Helen leans down, offering one hot cheek. *Let her not smell my guilt.*

III

Reasonable Suspicion

(a suspicion that would convince an uninvolved, rational person when described to him)

No man should look for a wife
from among the tropics.

Anthony Trollope,
He Knew He Was Right (1868)

Harry takes off his tailcoat, his waistcoat, his cravat. It's some relief to detach his collar, with its two stiff, upward points, and turn his jaw from side to side. He removes his white shirt and vest. Empties his pockets in a neat pile on the dresser. There's his wife's telegram: *Miss F has begged me to stay and dine with Rev & Mrs F.* Harry steps out of his long linen drawers. *Like a beetle shedding its layers*: that was one of Helen's quips, back in the days when they still shared a room. When they were still capable of quips.

The reply he sent to Helen at Taviton Street was perfectly clear, wasn't it? No room for misinterpretation, even by an incompetent telegraphist: *Nell gravely ill, come home at once.* Most mothers, receiving such a message at a dinner party, would fall into hysterics, or at least ask for a cab to be called immediately. Only Helen could stay on for dessert, so as not to offend a rector and his wife! What can the Faithfulls have thought of such reptilian cold-bloodedness? Or perhaps, it occurs to Harry now, she didn't tell them what was in his telegram at all. He tries to picture her at the table, dithering between a candied walnut and a meringue. At the very least, she could have done him the courtesy of a reply to tell him she wasn't coming. But no, even that would have been too much trouble, too much of an interruption to the cataract of sparkling, self-dramatizing nonsense that pours from those lovely lips.

He's been rather mystified that she's taken up with Fido Faithfull again at all. When Helen first brought the girl home, all those years ago, in '54, it seemed handy for the whole family that moody Mama had a steady friend to keep her company while Papa was at sea. Fido Faithfull had more capacity for conversation than ninety-nine girls out of a hundred; at Eccleston Square, she'd listen to Harry discourse on such subjects as national education or the balance of trade for half an hour at a time, and ask some very intelligent questions. (He suddenly remembers a joke cracked by a fellow officer who lived with his wife and her sister: *the happiest marriages are made up of three parties.*) But then Harry came back from the Crimea, and a tide seemed to have turned: Fido the peacemaker looked more like a partisan, and there were rumblings of outright war. That hellishly hot summer of '57, when they'd all fallen ill one after another, and Helen had suddenly demanded a private separation—well, in all the chaos he'd no choice but to ask Fido to leave. Harry doesn't bear a grudge, though. He hasn't been surprised to learn that she's taken up reform, though he can only regret the extreme slant of her *woman-ism*, as the papers call it. No, all that puzzles him, now, is what interest his butterfly wife can hold for a woman of business such as Fido Faithfull has become.

But ever since the Codringtons landed at Portsmouth, Harry's been wasting too much time fretting over his wife's unaccountable whims. It comes of having too little to do, he recognizes that. It'll be better when he's got into a regular way of studying, dropping into Somerset House for his pay and gossip, perhaps a bit of yachting with old friends . . .

Harry chews on a frayed wooden skewer; rubs on some homemade tooth powder: it's bitter with quinine. *Nell, Nell.* She was teasing him only this afternoon, before the fever hit; she told him he ought to go to the barber to have his beard trimmed.

Helen's in the girls' bedroom now. Doting Mama rushes to her baby's side, only three hours late. For all her peculiarities, Nan and Nell prefer her to him, Harry knows that, has always known it. It's only natural; children lack discernment. He'd like to open the door quietly, so as not to disturb Nell, take his wife by the shoulder, and pull her onto the landing. Shake her so hard her neat little jaw bounces like a doll's, and the pins spring from her gaudy hair.

Instead he pulls his long, starched nightshirt over his head. He won't wear his nightcap, he's hot enough already.

This is a spare, masculine chamber, with nothing in it but a bed and dresser—both in the family for generations. A jug and basin where he stoops now to wash the last traces of medicated syrup from his fingers. (It didn't seem to bring Nell's chest the slightest relief.) He won't let Helen cram his room with whatnots and *objets d'art*; really, her taste is verging on vulgar these days. Harry keeps his bedchamber as shipshape as any of the cabins he occupied during his years at sea. When he was a young lieutenant on the *Briton*, six inches too tall for his bunk—Harry Longshanks, his shipmates called him, or the Giant Cod—he had the brilliant idea of hammering together a foot box that intruded into the next cabin, under that officer's pillow. He thinks of it now, as he lets himself down on the edge of his custom-made, long mahogany bed. Those nights with his sore feet jammed into the cabin wall, the young Harry knew he was happy—wrote to his family every week to assure them of the fact—but didn't know that it was the happiest he'd ever be.

He thinks of Nell's red cheeks, the terrible thumping sound when she coughs. But she's asleep now, and if she wakes the nurse will see to her, and if she gets worse . . . *She won't get worse*, he roars in the privacy of his head. *She'll be on the mend by morning.* Her constitution is strong. Both his girls have the Codrington sturdiness, and a certain resilience from the Smith side as well.

He doesn't mind having his own room; if anything, he rather prefers it. No capsized dresses litter the polished floorboards, not a cast-off stocking. Separate rooms is a point many marriages seem to reach, as far as Harry can gather from the hints other men drop. On the husband's side, familiarity breeds staleness; on the wife's, passion often proves to have been a fleeting phenomenon of the early years. Harry reads broadly in the sciences, and some years ago he came across a persuasive theory that once a woman has completed her childbearing, her redundant carnal urges fade away.

He sleeps rather better on his own, besides. (On the rare occasions when needs present themselves, he deals with them privately, which he doesn't believe—for all the superstition on the matter—poses any real risk to his health.) All Harry would ask of his wife is a daily, pleasant companionship. A domestic haven; a warm hearth. But he may as well demand a bite of the moon.

Nell gravely ill, come home at once. He's staggered that Helen could simply have ignored his telegram. If it were he who was ill, that would be one thing, but Nell, her youngest, her lastborn . . . Have the girls become pawns for Helen to hurl against him? Then this is a grim new era.

Harry puts his hand on the oil lamp, but doesn't extinguish it. His mind is too agitated; he won't be able to sleep. (This is how parents sometimes lose children, he thinks: between shutting their eyes in the night, and opening them again in the morning when the servant comes in with the news.)

He lies down on his back and tries an old trick of listing his vessels. His very first, the *Naiad*, a light frigate for hunting Corsairs during the Algerine war. Then the *Asia*, under his father, Sir Edward, in the Mediterranean. The *Briton*. The *Orestes*, nothing special as sloops went, but the first Harry commanded and dear to him for that. The *Talbot*, one of an abominable class of ships known in the service as jackass-frigates: very low between decks, with an armament of obsolete popguns. "I should very much like to set fire to that beast of yours, Codrington," Sir Robert Stopford once told him. The *St. Vincent*, as flag-captain to his father. Off to the Mediterranean again on the frigate *Thetis*, a useful man-of-war. Leghorn. Florence. Helen. No, he won't think about her.

Has she gone back to her own room by now? She's not the kind of mother to sit up by a sickbed when there's a nurse paid to do it. Is she stretched out on her bed in careless sleep? No, he must shut her out of his mind or he'll never sleep. Next, the *Royal George*, an old three-decker with an auxiliary screw to adapt her to steam. In '56, Harry was moved to the *Algiers*, as commodore of a flotilla of gunboats—but then peace forced him home. Malta in '57: an important position, though on shore. Then back to England.

What will his next ship be? If, that is, there'll be another.

This isn't helping.

Stretched out in bed as if on a rack, watching the flickering patterns the lamp makes on the ceiling, he listens out for any sound in the house. When he presses the repeater on his watch, it chimes a quarter to twelve.

Something's nibbling at the edge of his mind. He rears up again, and carries the lamp over to the dresser so he can reread Helen's telegram. *Miss F has begged me to stay and dine with Rev & Mrs F.* The boy brought it just after seven, when dinner was already on the table at Eccleston Square. Nell, scarlet-cheeked, was pushing her mutton round the plate; Harry, not realizing she had anything worse than a runny nose, snapped at her and made her cry. When he touched her forehead, it seemed to sizzle. Half an hour later he sent a corner boy off to the telegraph office with his own message: *Nell gravely ill, come home at once.* The bad news must surely have reached Helen by eight, he calculates. If Fido only belatedly asked her to stay to dinner at about seven—very odd behaviour in a hostess, by the by—could the guests really have got through all their savoury courses and reached the dessert by eight? And, granting that for a moment, even if Helen felt some inexplicable appetite for something sweet, while her child lay in the kind of fever that can snuff out a child's life in a night—what could have possessed her to sit there chit-chatting over coffee and cordials with the rector of Headley and his wife for a further three hours?

Harry turns out the lamp with a single twist of his thumb. He walks back to bed, but he can't lie down; his outrage will suffocate him. He sits bolt upright on the overstuffed edge of the mattress, staring out into the smoky darkness.

"Didn't you get my telegram?" That's what he'd asked her, a rhetorical question. "Of course," she said, in her musical voice. But all of a sudden he doesn't believe it. There's only one explanation that fits the facts. He has to admit this much: Helen loves her girls. She might sit cracking nuts while Harry was dying, but she wouldn't ignore a telegram about one of her daughters. So she never received it tonight—but she felt obliged to pretend she did. Because this evening she wasn't at Miss Emily Faithfull's, Number 10 Taviton Street. (Harry looked the address up in the directory earlier this evening, while the boy stood scratching one knee.)

Harry's mind is buzzing. Facts slide together like bolts. Helen was somewhere else tonight, then. With someone else.

A vast revulsion, growing. His eyes, wide open to the darkness, burn as if scales are peeling away.

~

OVER BREAKFAST, THE CODRINGTONS EAT ALMOST NOTHING, and talk only of Nell. How she seemed yesterday, at the onset; the signs they should have noticed; the infections that have been going around; the effect of dirty London air. The doctor's been again, and administered various doses, and assured them that the fever should break today.

Harry finds it surprisingly easy to maintain a normal tone while cutting his toast into smaller and smaller triangles. It strikes him that he and Helen must sound, and look, and seem, like an ordinary couple. Marriage is a habit much like any other, he supposes. He thinks of that house in Bayswater he was telling the girls about the other day: the facade perfectly correct, the trains roaring by beneath.

It's not that he's never considered the possibility of Helen and other men. In Malta, she quickly adopted the Continental style for wives, and was never without some idle army officer or other tagging along. But the very openness of her actions meant that they didn't alarm Harry. She was bored, she preferred the company of other (younger, jollier) men to his; what was noteworthy in any of this? There were petty improprieties that pressed themselves on his notice only now and then, in the intervals of business; generally he chose to overlook them, sometimes he mentioned them mildly to Helen if they seemed liable to cause talk, and though she rolled her eyes she corrected her behaviour accordingly. Flirtatiousness, that's all he ever suspected. Games and poses: he knew that to react to them with any heat would be to fall into her trap.

Their discussion of Nell's health over the breakfast table has lapsed into silence. Helen stretches out her hand for the *Telegraph*.

Harry shakes his head. "You never read anything but the advertisements."

"They're by far the most interesting part," murmurs Helen, snatching it up and opening it.

An automatic giggle from Nan, her mouth sticky with preserves.

Rage, like a swelling vein behind his eyes. Where was Helen last night? Who in the world was she with? She's only been back in London a matter of weeks; can that be long enough to form what they used in his youth to call a *criminal connection*?

"I can't be alone in my preference," says Helen, "as the first four pages are given over to advertisements. Listen to this, for instance," she goes on. "'The lady who travelled from Bedford to London by Midland train on the night of the fourth inst. is now in a position to meet the gentleman who shared the contents of his railway lunch basket.'"

"I don't know that this is the most suitable stuff for—for Nan," remarks Harry. He'd been going to say *the girls*, but Nell is still in bed, of course. Coming down the stairs, he heard her coughing like a wounded seal.

"Why, Papa? What was in his basket?" Nan is big-eyed.

"It's no worse than 'Orrible Murders, in my humble opinion," says Helen, and goes on to the next. "'MARY ANN do come home. You labour under an illusion.' Or here, Nan, listen to this: even more pathetic, but it must be a code. 'The one-winged DOVE must die unless the CRANE will be a shield against her enemies.'"

"What kind of code, Mama?"

"Murderers hatching their plots, perhaps?"

"Enough," barks Harry. "Do you want to give the girl nightmares again?" He holds out his hand for the paper, and watches it shake. Feminine evasions, equivocations, he's caught her out in those before, over the years. Never a barefaced lie. Never till last night: "Miss F has begged me to stay and dine with Rev & Mrs F."

"Perhaps I do. Nightmares are said to clean out the brain, like purgatives," says Helen, meeting his eyes for half a second. Like the glancing of fencers' foils.

"What's a purgative?" Nan asks.

"Now now, you know not to pay Mama any attention when she's in one of her nonsensical moods," says Harry, folding up the *Telegraph* so tightly the paper wrinkles.

~

UPSTAIRS, TO CHECK ON NELL. She asked for water half an hour ago, he learns, but fell back asleep before the nurse came back with it. Her cheeks are cotton stained with strawberry.

Into his study, to begin a letter to his brother.

Dear William,
Dear Will,

I would to God you were in London. I find myself in a position of peculiar discomfort and could do with your sound

I could do with your sympathetic yet objective counsel. Something seems to have

~~[illegible]~~ Something has occurred which has given rise in me

Something has occurred which has led me to form a suspicion of my wife behaving in a way

I suspect my wife.

No, it's impossible. The words "Dessert can't last three hours," set down in spidery lines of ink and posted to Gibraltar, would sound demented.

General William Codrington would write back from Gibraltar with uneasy warmth: *I rather believe you've got a little carried away, old boy. Too much time on your hands? These half-pay stints are the devil . . .*

Harry tears the draft into very small pieces before he throws it into the elephant's-foot basket.

His sisters? Equally impossible. Jane lives in London, so he could speak to her face to face, at least, but what could he tell her? She's never liked Helen, but that won't prepare her to listen to a mass of vague, outrageous allegations. Her face would turn pinched with distress.

No, broaching this subject to anyone in his family, without an iota of proof, would only cause embarrassment. It's not sympathy Harry wants, besides, but a thread to follow through this labyrinth. Someone who understands already; someone who can help him decide whether what he guessed, in the darkness of last night, is a paranoid invention or the rank truth.

~

"My dear Admiral, how it gladdens our hearts to see you again after so long," cries Mrs. Watson. "I was remarking to the reverend only the other day, how much we've missed your company—and that of your wife," she adds after a minuscule pause.

His old friend is looking rather older; she's more papery at the temples. At his wife's side, the snowy-bearded Reverend Watson nods like a jack-in-the-box.

"You're kind to say so," says Harry, dry-mouthed. Until they left Malta, several years before him, the Watsons were his closest intimates. Since then, a few civil, pedestrian letters on either side. He hadn't yet thought to look them up, since getting back to London; the friendship seemed like some thing folded away in tissue. But here he is sitting on a horsehair sofa in the Watsons' dull fawn drawing-room, in one of the less fashionable, but still genteel, parts of London.

"Are your charming children well?"

"Nan is," he says with difficulty, "but Nell's suffering from a very bad cold on the chest."

He listens to the expressions of sympathy, recommendations of liniments and plasters. He stirs himself. "Your wards, are they still with you?"

"Alas, no; residing with relatives in Northumberland," Mrs. Watson tells him. "The reverend and I are a lonely Darby and Joan, these days."

They have nothing to do, Harry realizes; any visit is a welcome one. He takes a long breath, and plunges in. "You were always so very good to my wife, Mrs. Watson, even at times when she tried your patience sorely."

"Oh—" she waves that away. "I was always glad to play my part. How is dear Helen, if I may still call her that?"

How to answer? "Good, as to her health. As to her character . . ."

The seconds go by. "It's always been a singular one," remarks Mrs. Watson, eyes on the faded blue carpet.

Harry forces himself on. "Over the years in Valetta, during those congenial Sunday visits—you and I often touched on her manner. Its . . . wildness, its irregularity."

"Alas, yes," says Mrs. Watson. "Hers is a constant struggle, and she's always had my sympathies."

From the reverend, an abstracted "Mm."

"I do hope there's been some amelioration, since your return to the bracing moral climate of the home country?" she suggests, her head on one side like a sparrow.

Harry shakes his head.

A little escape of breath from her thin lips, which are only slightly darker than her skin. "I feel sure—pardon the liberty, dear Admiral—I've always felt sure that Helen will reform, if you'll only tell her straight out what you expect of the mother of your children, without softening or prevarication. I'm afraid a free rein unleashes the worst in such a nature." She pauses. "If you were to entrust the task to me, I would accept it as my Christian duty to try to impress upon her—"

"It's too late for such conversations," interrupts Harry. "Recently—" That sounds slightly more considered than *last night.* "Recently, I must tell you in all confidence that I've come to suspect—"

Her gaze is owlish. *What big eyes you've got, grandmama,* he thinks irrelevantly, though Mrs. Watson can't be more than ten years older than his wife.

"That it's not only her manner," he goes on gruffly. "That here in London, her conduct itself—that she might possibly have actually stepped beyond the bounds of—beyond the bounds." He makes himself produce a brief account of last night.

Mrs. Watson's mouth forms a tiny circle. She turns to meet the reverend's watery eyes.

Harry's shocked them, he knows it. "But I have no proof," he winds up, "and I'm aware that jealousy's the besetting fault of older husbands."

"No!"

Her roar makes him jump.

"You, Admiral—the kindest, the least suspicious—" Mrs. Watson presses her fingers to her mouth, then takes them away. "The only wonder is that you've tolerated the intolerable for so long."

Harry stares at her. "You knew?" he asks in a boy's squeak.

"Not for sure. We only feared, didn't we, my dear?"

Another speechless nod from the reverend.

What shocks Harry is what lies behind the shock. Beneath the rage, beneath the mortification, he's feeling something he has to recognize as relief.

She's risen and crossed the room; she perches beside him on the horsehair sofa. "We never dared speak out. We hinted, we probed on occasion, but how could we put words to our dreadful deductions, when you were too gallant to hear a word against her? In conscience, we couldn't take it upon ourselves to be the first to accuse the mother of your children, without firm evidence—but I can tell you now, it seemed to us in Malta that Helen's dealings with various man-friends were consistent with the worst interpretation!"

Various man-friends? Harry's head suddenly weighs too much for him; he drops it into his hands. The points of his collar prick his jaw like knives. He tries to answer, but all that comes out is a sob. The tears stop up his mouth: slippery in his palms, soaking his beard, spilling into his collar and cravat. Salt as seawater but hot. He's weeping like a child, weeping for all the times over the years that he's shrugged instead, weeping for all he hoped when he stood up in that chapel in Florence beside his dazzling little bride and said so ringingly, *I do.*

Beside him, Mrs. Watson waits.

Finally he clears his throat with a sound like a rockfall. "I've been an utter idiot," he says into his wet fingers.

"Never that! Only the best of husbands." Her voice is as sweet as a mother's. "We considered you as a martyr among men, didn't we, Reverend?"

"We did," confides the old man.

Harry is mopping himself up with his handkerchief. "Well," he says through the folds of cotton. "No longer."

"No," agrees Mrs. Watson. "There comes an end to forbearance. For the little girls' sake—"

At the thought of Nan and Nell, he almost breaks down again.

"—not to mention your own. For the sake of religion, and, and decency itself," she goes on, "you must prove her guilt."

He balks at the word. "Or otherwise. It's still possible—"

"Of course, of course. It must be investigated, that's the word I was looking for," she assures him. "Enquiries must be made."

"How—" Harry breaks off. "It's all so tawdry."

"That's why it had much better be put on a professional footing at once, oughtn't it, Reverend?"

"Oh yes, at once, my dear."

"So that a man of your noble character needn't be embroiled in sordid details," she tells Harry.

"Professional?" he repeats dully.

"Why don't you let us play Good Samaritans—leave that in our hands?" says Mrs. Watson, giving him a light, careful pat on the sleeve.

IV

Engagement

(an agreement to enter into marriage;
the act of giving someone a job;
a hostile meeting of opposing forces)

The fast young lady and the strong-minded woman are twins, born on the same day, and nourished with the same food, but one chose scarlet and the other hodden gray; one took to woman's right to be dissipated and vulgar, the other to her right to be unwomanly and emancipated.

Eliza Lynn Linton,
"Modern English Women No. 11,"
London Review (December 15, 1860)

"Is it possible to silence that bird?" asks Fido, at Eccleston Square that same afternoon.

"Certainly," says Helen, rushing to throw a Bengal shawl over the large silver-plated cage. The parrot's squawkings are reduced to a mutter.

Fido turns her gaze to the bowl of fish; to the clock with its mother-of-pearl inlay; to the emerald and scarlet carpet. She looks everywhere but at Helen. Why does Fido feel so awkward, considering it's not she who's been caught out? She rouses herself to anger instead. "When the telegram arrived, yesterday evening, more than an hour after you'd left my house . . . I didn't know what to do."

Helen nods, eyes down.

"Since it was addressed to you, my first notion was to send it straight on here. But then I thought, who could know that you'd been at Taviton Street in the afternoon? Only—Anderson," she says, her voice dropping to a whisper as she names him. "So I could hardly take the risk of forwarding some urgent message from him, when it might be your husband who'd open it! I felt the best thing to do was to open it myself."

"Of course," murmurs Helen.

"I assumed at first that you and the telegram had crossed paths," says Fido, her voice hardening, "that Harry had sent it just before you'd got home for dinner, and its delivery had been delayed somehow. But in my experience the London telegraph office is entirely reliable." Not like the Maltese post, she thinks irrelevantly. "So I could only deduce that you hadn't gone home at all. Now your daughter was ill, but I had no way of telling you, having no idea where you were—though a pretty good idea *with whom.*"

"Oh, *carina*," Helen groans, "it seems hardly necessary to heap coals on my head. There's no punishment worse than the terror of losing a child."

Fido frowns at her. "But didn't the doctor say—"

"Doctors!" Helen says the word with scorn. "Can you imagine how long a night lasts, when a mother spends it by the bedside of her unconscious daughter, hanging on every strained breath? All the time cursing myself, and knowing that if she didn't live till morning, it would be my doing?"

"Oh, come now—"

"Yes, I went for a little drive with him, with the man whose heart I'm in the process of breaking," sobs Helen. "I was weak in the way of women. I took pity on him, and on myself. And for the sake of that single hour's drive on a warm evening, a vengeful providence has smited my child."

Fido lets out an exasperated breath. *Smited*, indeed! "Compose yourself," she says. "The fever will break soon, hasn't the doctor assured you of that? Nell should be perfectly well in a few days."

Helen, face buried in her handkerchief, shakes her head.

"I'm not accusing you of imperilling your daughter's life. I just don't like being put in such an uncomfortable position. Being misled. Told what's not true," Fido says bluntly.

No answer.

"You say you rely on me, Helen, you say I'm the only one you can trust—but then you go to these ridiculous lengths to obfuscate!" She drops her voice to a whisper. "Do you take me for a fool, I wonder? You tell me you're going home to dinner, but instead you sneak off to meet your—" She leaves the word unsaid. "You keep insisting you'll break off with him, but your actions suggest otherwise—that you're planning to keep it up to the sordid end."

"*Planning?*" repeats Helen, staring at her with wet eyes. A small, bitter laugh. "My dear, I'm not managing to *plan* anything: I'm running and leaping and tripping like some hunted rabbit!"

Fido sighs.

"How I wish you could inoculate me with even a fraction of your force, your coolness, your imperviousness . . ."

That pricks. *I sound like some statue.*

"If ever I give you . . . misleading impressions, it's because I don't know what I'm doing from one minute to the next, or I'm ashamed to admit even to myself how far I've slipped. When I love, I can't hold back. I can't help myself," says Helen in a choking voice. "You know that about me, don't you? You've always known."

Fido looks away, at the china-crammed shelves, the patterned walls of the drawing-room that seem to be closing in. She couldn't bear to live this life. Helen's had no job or cause to absorb her, to bear her up; passion has been her sole preoccupation, and look what damage it's done. If Fido can't find it in her heart to make allowances for Helen's frailties, and forgive the untruths Helen convinces herself it's necessary to tell then how can she call herself by the holy name of *friend*?

"Pity me!"

"I do," says Fido, finally meeting Helen's eyes, "I do. I don't condemn you for this affair. But I believe it's poisoning you by degrees." She gets to her feet, takes a long breath. "I won't aid and abet it any longer, I don't even want to hear about it."

"Oh, but—"

"Sh," she says, finger to her lips, looking at Helen with eyes that brim with scalding love.

~

THE REFORM FIRM'S BEEN SUMMONED to Langham Place by a mysterious message from Bessie Parkes, "to discuss matters of grave importance to the future of the *Journal*."

Rereading the note, Fido thinks, how strange: a month ago, she'd have been hard pressed to name anything of more importance to her than the future of the *English Woman's Journal*. Now she finds all her thoughts are of Helen Codrington. At moments, she catches herself wishing she hadn't run into her on Farringdon Street; that she'd been anywhere else in London on the last day of August, walking along, sufficient unto herself.

"This is a sorry mess," comments Emily Davies, taking her seat at the committee table.

Their secretary's all aquiver. "It has emerged—it seems that the *Journal*'s finances are in much worse shape than they seemed."

"Tell them what the subscribers said," says Bessie Parkes with a tragic empress's nod.

"I spoke in confidence to a dozen or so who've supported us for the past six years but don't mean to renew," says Sarah Lewin in her whispery voice. "In several cases, I was informed that the *Journal*, in their view, has never quite been able to shake off certain unsavoury associations."

"God knows we've tried," says Jessie Boucherett.

"Indeed," says Isa Craig sorrowfully. "Forcing poor Max to resign the editorship . . ."

Fido grimaces. She still feels obscurely guilty about the role she played in the purge of Matilda "Max" Hays, their fieriest campaigner, who was publishing demands for women's emancipation when the rest of them were still in short skirts.

"We didn't force her," Bessie Parkes protests.

"Obliged her, then," says Fido. "Induced."

"We had no choice: shadows clung about Max's name," says Bessie Parkes, looking into the distance. "Her reputation for Bloomerism, wild outbursts, that household of women in Rome . . ."

"But you were friends with her and Miss Cushman, you stayed there yourself," Jessie Boucherett points out.

"Yes, and Max will always be very dear to me," says Bessie Parkes in a shaking voice, "but reputation is such an insidiously lingering phenomenon. Desperate measures were called for."

Such a curious mixture of the soft and the diamond-hard about Bessie Parkes, Fido thinks. She finds herself gripping the bevelled edge of the table with her fingertips. A headache's started up behind her right eye. "I never saw her in bloomers," she bursts out, "only shirts and jackets of a tailored cut."

"Any eccentricity, even in dress, gives succour to our enemies," says Bessie Parkes.

"Besides," cries Fido, "it's so unfair that the *Journal* still has a reputation for laxity, when its content is of the tamest kind."

"You've put your finger on it," says Emily Davies, very crisp. "I believe this issue of reputation is a red herring; our readers have simply had enough of carrying a lame dog."

Isa Craig is looking distressed. "Now Miss Davies, you mustn't take things personally. Our readership was in decline from its peak of one thousand long before you took over the editorship."

"Oh I'm quite aware of that, and I believe I do a competent job with the resources available to me," says Emily Davies. "But the fact is that the *English Woman's Journal* has never been known for intellectual or literary excellence."

The women of the Reform Firm aren't meeting each other's eyes.

"Our friends buy it out of duty, and for the most part, I suspect, shelve it unread."

"Not so!"

"Surely—"

"Yes, yes, yes," says Fido, nodding at Emily Davies. "The problem is timidity. If we're too nervous to include any topic which could be considered remotely controversial, we're left with pedestrian exhortations to our readers to use their talents while making sure to fulfill their womanly duties!"

"May I ask," breathes Sarah Lewin, "what sort of topic—"

Jessie Boucherett interrupts her. "I rather agree with Fido. For instance, why have we never pointed out the many injustices to women that linger in the Matrimonial Causes Act?"

Bessie Parkes purses her lips. "Divorce is a dangerous subject. We could seem to be associating ourselves with women of doubtful reputation."

"But what about a blameless wife," asks Isa Craig, "whose husband takes half a dozen mistresses? As the law stands, she can only free herself of him if she proves him guilty of a compounding offence, such as desertion, cruelty—"

"Rape," contributes Fido, "incest—"

"Bestiality or buggery," finishes Emily Davies.

Bessie Parkes's lovely face is pale. "Words which will never be printed in the *English Woman's Journal* as long as I have any say in the matter."

"Oh come," Fido objects, "we're veteran journalists, we can raise these questions without verbal impropriety; there's always a way to say something without naming it."

"The divorce law is flawed and unequal, but I for one would not support liberalizing it further," Emily Davies puts in. "In my experience, divorce leaves women not merely ruined but penniless, and bereft of their children."

"Well, that's true. Without some legal barrier," jokes Jessie Boucherett, "I believe most men would roam like apes from female to female!"

"Divorce is only one example of the kind of subject we've been skirting for six years," says Fido. "Which reminds me of the chief who parted from his second wife at the recommendation of a missionary. When asked how he'd provided for the cast-off, he replied—" she waits till she has everyone's full attention "—'Me eat her.'"

Laughter eases the atmosphere in the room.

"What about married women's property, instead?" suggests Jessie Boucherett. "I agree with Miss Davies, that as marriage is the lot of the majority of women, our priority should be to ameliorate its conditions."

"Mm. On the property issue, it struck me the other night," says Fido, "that the possessions of the woman who commits murder, and those of the woman who commits matrimony, are both dealt with alike: by confiscation."

"You're in form today, Fido," says Isa Craig, grinning. "Oh, what about an article on the suffrage?"

"Come now, Miss Craig, you know Britain's not ready," Bessie Parkes scolds her gently. "I for one would rather dismantle that wall gradually, brick by brick, than smash our hearts—and my beloved Bar's money, may I add!—against it."

Emily Davies is nodding. "We need to get access to higher education first, to prove we're intelligent enough to vote. Let's fight one fight at a time, so that the tainting associations of one don't rub off on the others."

"But getting back to the *Journal*—" says Fido.

"I know it's very dear to all of us here," says Bessie Parkes. "It's the beating heart at the centre of all our endeavours to uplift our sex, the moral engine that powers the whole Cause."

Emily Davies plays a silent piano on the table. "But given the state of accounts, it seems unlikely to limp on till Christmas."

"Defeatist thinking," says Bessie Parkes in awful tones, "and from the editor too!"

"I don't think I'm known for giving up easily," says Emily Davies with a mildness that snaps like a whip. "But I have grave doubts about carrying on editing a small-scale publication that speaks only—and not eloquently—to the converted. In six years, what laws has it changed?"

"You know," says Fido, "perhaps what's needed is an altogether different kind of magazine." She's surprised herself; these are only half-formed notions.

Bessie Parkes looks at her hard. "A radical diatribe that won't be let into respectable houses even as kindling?"

Fido takes a long breath, to keep her temper. "In fact, I was thinking of a well-funded periodical of general interest, written by the most talented male and female authors, which discusses the Cause among a broad range of other topics. One that looks outward, not inward. A magazine that readers actually want to read!"

Emily Davies has her head on one side, like a curious squirrel.

"My own view," snaps Bessie Parkes, "is that if a change must come, the *Journal* should become more practical, less theoretical. Cheaper, for instance, to appeal to the masses of working women."

This raises a few eyebrows.

"But at any rate, none of you need fear its demise by Christmas. What I should perhaps have announced before this interesting discussion ran away with itself is that the immediate pecuniary crisis has been averted by our guardian angel: Bar has sent a cheque for the rent from Algiers."

Little cries of relief and gratitude go round the circle. Fido, teeth set, tries to look pleased.

"As she's the major shareholder of the *Journal*, you understand that I'd prefer not to make any dramatic changes until I've had a chance to consult her."

No one can do anything but agree with Bessie Parkes.

First among equals, thinks Fido bitterly, on her way down the stairs. *We are divided.* The machine rolls on but squeals, the little screws are starting to loosen and pop out.

~

THE BLUE WAX SEAL IS UNFAMILIAR TO FIDO, when she cracks it at her desk at Taviton Street, but she's guessed from the Scottish postmark that the letter's from Colonel David Anderson. She's bristling already. Let him make his own assignations: she won't play gullible hostess and go-between any more.

Two lines into the note, she starts to wheeze.

Dear Miss F.,

You can imagine, I believe, with what difficulty I write today to inform you that I am engaged to be married.

She gasps for breath. *Oh Helen.* The scoundrel, the blackguard, the brute! Not content with destroying one woman's peace of mind, he takes a whim, a mere fortnight later, to marry another.

Let me begin by assuring you that at your house on the sixteenth, where you were kind enough to allow me to meet our friend for a private discussion, this was not yet the case. As your correspondents rightly informed you, a cousin of mine, who cares for me with a devotion that I cannot claim to deserve, has had reason to believe that I would make her an offer, but I did not in fact commit myself until I reached Scotland on the eighteenth, when I was lucky enough to be accepted by that young lady.

I am aware that my recent behaviour towards our mutual friend has been in certain respects unbecoming to a gentleman as well as to an officer of Her Majesty's armed forces. All I can say to mitigate if not excuse my offence is that the situation has become intolerable and seems to offer no prospect of ease on either side. As I know you disapprove in the sternest terms of the connection, and rightly so, I hope it will be with some measure of relief admixed with concern for the lady that you will hear now that it is at an end.

It's true: behind her outrage, Fido's aware of a surge of gladness. This will be a blade to hack through the coils in which Helen's tangled, as perhaps nothing else could. But how dare Anderson offer that as an excuse! For him not to give the woman who's compromised herself for him as much as a moment's warning of this cataclysm—

Despite the short period of our acquaintance, Miss F., my respect for your intellectual as well as sympathetic capacities has grown to the point that in my current state of discomfort I can see no better—less cruel, rather—way to break the news to our friend than by asking you to do it as my proxy. At such times man is but a blunt instrument, and I feel sure that you will be better able than I to offer comfort and counsel to a lady of whose unhappiness I confess I took advantage, and whose future life can only be improved by the voluntary though sorrowful departure from it of

D. A.

(I will count it as the last of your many kindnesses to me if you'll destroy this letter and any other record of an episode that should never have been begun.)

Fido folds it up with shaking fingers. The blue wax is breaking into fragments: cheap stuff.

~

THE NEXT DAY, as soon as she can get away from the press (and a tiresome mix-up about the reprinting of a miscellany celebrating last year's marriage of the Prince of Wales to Princess Alexandra), Fido hails a cab to Eccleston Square. But instead of going in, she sends the driver to ask if Mrs. Codrington would be so good as to come down for a few minutes. It's occurred to her that this news should be broken where none of the family or servants could possibly overhear a word of it.

"Fido! What's all this hugger-mugger?" Helen, leaning in the cab window, is looking very stylish in flamingo silk.

"Climb in, won't you? I've something very particular to say."

She waits till her friend is sitting down beside her, and then she tells her. Helen's eyes shut and her head sags back against the greasy upholstery. Fido takes her by the shoulders and pushes her face down onto her skirt. Helen, doubled up, lets out a moan. Fido uncorks a small bottle of salts and holds it close to the sharp little nose; the pungency makes Helen rear up. "Oh you poor creature," cries Fido, "if I could have thought of any kinder means—"

Helen blinks at her like some small, stunned animal.

Fido hesitates. "But his letter does contain one truth, and in time I hope you'll come to see it: this awful blow is for the best."

Helen pulls back so hard, she bangs her shoulder against the window frame. "How dare you!"

Fido presses on. "Anderson's been a brute, yes, but perhaps . . . a rational one. Whatever could you have hoped for, what future could there have been, in your connection with this man?"

She speaks through closed teeth. "It's been keeping me alive."

"But tainting your relation to your husband, your children, your own heart," says Fido pleadingly. "This way it's over with one sharp cut, and you're saved."

"Saved?" Helen's eyes narrow.

Fido starts to stammer. "It's my, I wouldn't speak this way if I didn't feel it to be my duty—"

"Damn your duty," says Helen in a voice that comes out as deep as a man's. "Are you my vicar or my friend? I can't bear preaching, today of all days."

"My dearest, I'm only fearful for your welfare. For your—"

"My what? My soul, or my reputation?" asks Helen, sardonic.

"All of you!"

They lapse into a fraught silence. Fido, desperate to turn Helen's anger back towards its rightful object, says, "It's the cowardice of it I can't forgive. To think, Anderson fled like a rat to Scotland, and proposed to this cousin, just two days after your last rendezvous!"

"Two days." Helen speaks so hoarsely Fido can hardly hear her. "After two years."

Fido stares at her. "I beg your pardon?" she says after a few seconds.

Helen's watching her own hand scrunch her pink skirt into a thousand creases. "Am I so easy to forget?"

"What was it you said about two years?"

Helen finally meets her eyes with a look of irritation. "What?"

"You said two years. You don't mean to tell me—" Fido pulls in a long breath of stale, hot air, and speaks with as much control as she can muster. "It was my understanding that you and Anderson—that it was only a fortnight ago that matters came to—that consummation—" She silently curses her tied tongue: why is it so difficult, after a genteel education, to put plain words on things? "Two weeks since he took you on my sofa!" That comes out far too loud.

Helen's looking into her upturned hands, as if to read the lines.

What's she going to tell me, Fido wonders? That she misspoke, that what she meant was that Anderson's been yearning for her from afar for the past two years, like some medieval troubadour? That until he followed her to England, he never dared speak a word of it, or ask the least favour? *But I don't believe that.*

"Two weeks, I meant. Of course I meant two weeks," Helen repeats. "Right now I don't know one word from another."

"Oh, I think you meant two years," says Fido, her tongue like a stone in her mouth. So that afternoon, in her drawing-room, those terrible sounds behind the door: they weren't the beginning. How stupid Fido can be about the dim world of the relations between men and women. She's the fool who's stumbled late and oblivious into this play, the butt of the joke.

"Two weeks, two years," mutters Helen, "what's the difference?"

"Get out," says Fido, leaning across her to grab the handle and thrust open the door.

V

Surveillance

(watch or guard kept over
a suspected person or prisoner)

So far as the anxieties of the outer life penetrate into it, and the inconsistently-minded, unknown, unloved or hostile society is allowed by either husband or wife to cross the threshold, it ceases to be home; it is then only a part of that outer world which you have roofed over and lighted fire in.

John Ruskin,
Sesame and Lilies (1865)

At thirty-five a Captain and the "hero of Trafalgar," now at fifty-seven, and a Rear-Admiral, Sir Edward Codrington was raised to the august position of Commander-in-Chief of the Mediterranean Fleet, with his flag on the Asia.

In his study, Harry straightens in his chair, mulls over the grammar of his sentence, then bends to his pen again. Jane, working interminably on the memoirs of their late father, keeps asking her brother for an account of the naval side of things, and now, at last—to keep his mind from gnawing on itself like a rat—he's writing it. Harry will be fifty-seven himself next year, and a vice-admiral is one rung above a rear, so to an outsider his career may seem to be advancing faster than his father's, but the fact is that Sir Edward Codrington is remembered by a grateful nation, and his younger son is the hero of nothing in particular.

The front door. That'll be Nan, going to the museum with Mrs. Lawless. Her hair's held back with a sky-blue ribbon today. Nell is still frail and confined to bed; when Harry went up to see her half an hour ago, she was half-asleep over *The Thousand and One Nights,* her toast-and-water barely touched on its tray. She jolted when her father put his head around the door. He knows his smile has a ghastly, painted quality these days.

The spy is out there on Eccleston Square. Not that Harry's seen him; the fellow wouldn't be much of a spy if he were visible, after all. (*Enquiry agent* is the term the Watsons prefer.) He's been posted there for four days now, according to Mrs. Watson. *These things take time, Admiral.*

Harry bites the edge of his thumb, then stops himself: it's a filthy, schoolboy habit. He consults his notes, and stabs his pen into the inkwell.

In order to protect from enslavement the beleaguered inhabitants of the Greek provinces and islands, who were at that point resorting for nourishment to boiled herbage, Sir Edward found it his duty to destroy the Turko-Egyptian Fleet at Navarino on October 20, 1827. This victory over the Ottoman Porte is so justly celebrated, it is sufficient to record here that the Allied Fleet, amounting altogether to eleven sail of the line, nine frigates, and four brigs, suffered a loss of just 172 men killed and 481 wounded, among which the present writer (Sir Edward's third son, a midshipman at the time) counted himself honoured to count himself.

Irritated when he spots the repetition, he scores it out.

. . . judged himself honoured to be counted.

Automatically Harry's fingers move to a hand-span above his right knee; through the cloth he can find the ragged scar. (Nan and Nell used to clamour to do this, like little Doubting Thomases.) Just as well he'd got blooded at nineteen. Heaven knows, Harry has enough gumption in him to shed any amount of blood for his Queen—if only an occasion for bloodshed would present itself. But in these peaceful times he's been obliged to loiter in *private life* (as the euphemism has it) for four years in his twenties, another five in his thirties, another five in his forties. Now he waits for another posting, or even a pen-pusher's job at the Admiralty, to fill a few years. At the ready, at all times, he waits.

His wife's upstairs in her boudoir (newly papered with birds of paradise, at inordinate expense), trimming an old bonnet, or at least that's what she announced at lunchtime that she'd be doing. Harry realizes now that he has no idea what *trimming* involves. To readjust the bonnet for use somehow, as in trimming a sail? To make it smaller, as one trims a beard? And does Helen really have the skill to do any of these things, given that she needs the maid to undo her buttons at the end of the day? Helen's a sort of engine of idleness; all she does is consume. Like the unseen spy outside, Harry's been keeping his wife in his sights: covertly focusing on her an intense observation that reminds him, strangely, of the days of their courtship. (The sight of Helen Smith's young wrist emerging from her glove once distracted him so much from his task of defending Florence from hypothetical mobs, it's a wonder the Grand Duchy didn't fall.)

What happens if the spy finds something to report? It's still unreal to Harry. His wife is upstairs doing something to a bonnet. How could she be having carnal relations with a stranger? And what stranger? Harry quite agrees with Mrs. Watson that it's imperative he should know the truth—but they haven't yet spoken of what he'll do with that knowledge. What if the spy manages to come up with proof, hard and indisputable proof, that Helen has . . . Harry's mind reels from the various phrases. *Dishonoured him? Betrayed him?* That she's *fallen, ruined, lost*?

Or, of course, the spy may discover nothing at all. Perhaps his wife really did linger over syllabub with the Reverend and Mrs. Faithfull, five nights ago;

perhaps she's a slapdash mother, nothing worse. Will Harry be relieved to have her guiltlessness proved, even if he's had to hire a spy to do it? (How very modern, he thinks scathingly; what a model of a husband, in the mode of 1864.) What then? Will he be able to meet his own eyes in the mirror every morning?

He stares at the page under his hand, and forces out another sentence.

Although loaded with laurels in immediate consequence by his own Sovereign and those of France and Russia, the gallant Commander was afterwards recalled by the Admiralty as a result of political machinations to which, it is generally agreed, he was made a scapegoat.

A loud knock makes Harry jump. It suddenly strikes him as absurd that one keeps a servant to open the front door in order to save one from interruption, and yet one's work is in fact interrupted, since one always sits motionless, listening to deduce who's at the door; it would be almost simpler to stamp down the hall (in defiance of custom) and open it oneself.

The housekeeper, Mrs. Nichols, brings in the telegram herself. Heart thumping, Harry finds he's assuming the worst: critical illness in one or other branch of the family, the death of his elderly father-in-law in Florence . . . Or could it possibly be from top brass? But no word of a posting would be urgent enough for a telegram. He slices the envelope with his knife.

Messrs GABRIEL, dentists, Harley-street, Cavendish-Square. Messrs Gabriel's professional attendance at 27, Harley-street, will be 10 till 5 daily.

Harry blinks at it. Why, it's nothing but an attempt to drum up business. The nerve of these fellows, clogging up the telegraph wires and wasting the time of important men with unsolicited messages! As if Harry would dream of having his teeth drilled by such upstarts as Messrs Gabriel. Why, he has a good mind to write to the *Telegraph*.

He pauses, then screws up the paper and tosses it in the basket. Letters to the *Telegraph* may be exactly what Messrs Gabriel are counting on. That's the devil of publicity: an airing of any kind only feeds the flame.

Harry rereads the few stiff paragraphs he's produced about his father. This is much like hanging about for a wind, at sea, when the canvas is limp; one begins to imagine malign forces conspiring to stop anything from happening. One prays for wind, as if the Lord has no more important business on His mind. *The weather must break by Sunday, surely*, one remarks—when of course nothing is sure, and any day can be still as easily as windy. There's a malady peculiar to becalmed crews, called *calenture*: in the end the sun turns the men delirious and they imagine the sea is land and step out onto it . . .

The door, again. Harry listens hard. Only the maid's feet in the hall. Who could it be, this time? On impulse, to stretch his long legs, he goes to the front of the house, and looks out the drawing-room window. The winter curtains—red velvet, heavily swagged—have been hung up; Harry stands behind them, peering through a narrow gap. He sees a rough-looking man going back to a hansom cab and climbing up into the seat on the dickey. Then more footsteps in the house: what sounds like someone hurrying downstairs. His wife? Harry's left his spectacles in his study; he rubs his eyes, strains to make out the details of the scene outside. The driver's whip doesn't stir; the reins lie in his lap. From this high angle, the interior of the cab is in darkness. Here comes Helen out of the house, now, in flamingo pink, her bright head bare. (Every other adult female in England has learned to cover her head when she steps outdoors, but not his wife.) She leans over the cab's folding door, talking to the unseen occupant.

Rage blooms inside Harry's eyeballs. Is the man in there, in the shadowy recesses? (What man?) Would they dare, in broad daylight?

Helen turns and glances up at the house; Henry shrinks into the shadow of the curtain. Is she sensitive enough to feel his gaze?

Then the door of the cab folds back and he braces himself to see the face of the passenger. But instead Helen climbs in, lifting her brilliant skirts out of the September mud. Harry stands in the window like some pillar of salt. A strange lightness clouds inside his chest. All he can see is a piece of his wife's sleeve. He watches the silent conversation, his face against the glass, which smells of something vinegary.

Suddenly Helen bends at the waist, doubles over. What the devil can be happening in there?

She sits up again. She's turned away from him, in intense conversation with the other passenger. Her hands move in sharp, mysterious gesticulations.

Harry could rush downstairs right now, catch the pair red-handed. But what if the fellow shoots off in the cab, leaving Harry on the curb? Yes, he feels suddenly sure that Helen's about to go off with this stranger, whoever he is. That would be like her: to drive off, after fifteen years, without so much as a bonnet or a handbag. *Go, then*, Harry barks in his head. He's paralyzed: all he can do is watch and wait.

But the cab isn't moving. The driver picks at something on the back of his hand. Then he leans down, opens the little hatch, and seems to exchange a few words with his passengers before he closes it.

A minute later, the cab door swings open so suddenly, Harry recoils. Helen climbs out, stumbles on the step. Her face is as unreadable as some Egyptian mummy's as she walks towards the house.

Harry thinks his skull is going to explode. He lurches out of the room.

~

The public house is almost empty, at noon. While Crocker licks his finger and flicks through his notebook, Harry looks him up and down. About thirty, Harry reckons, with the bad skin characteristic of his class, and an uncomfortable way of clearing his throat.

The fellow begins to read in a monotone. "I began my observations of Mrs. Codrington's home in Eccleston Square on September the eighteenth, 1864."

"Could you keep your voice down a little, if you please?"

"Certainly."

Harry glances round at the scattered drinkers. "And perhaps . . . there's no need to use names, is there?"

"Whatever you like, sir." Crocker is about to resume his report when the barman arrives with his tray: beer for the enquiry agent, brandy for the admiral. Harry likes beer himself, but it seems an occasion for marking the distinctions.

"On the eighteenth inst.," Crocker goes on in a low voice, "I did not see any movements from the house in question except those of servants, and that of Admiral Cod—pardon me, sir, the husband of the party in question—who left at twelve and returned at ten past five."

Harry's seeing his life through the wrong end of the telescope. Well, he supposes one can't set a watch on one's wife without being oneself the object of surveillance. "I know my own comings and goings," he says in a tone that aims for lightness, "so you may leave them out. How do you . . . do you crouch behind a cart, Crocker, or something of that sort?"

The man looks mildly offended. "I've made an arrangement with your neighbour Mrs. Hartley across the street, to pose as a painter."

"What, you paint the same railings over and over?"

"Exactly, sir, the regulation green: then I clean them off." Crocker returns to his notes. "On the night of the eighteenth I watched the house until just after eleven when, as the agreed signal that the family were all accounted for, the husband of the party turned out all the lamps downstairs."

Harry finds himself wondering how the fellow manages about food, or the calls of nature.

Crocker's finger inches down the page. "On the nineteenth of September at ten in the morning I observed Mrs.—the party in question—leaving the house. I knew her from a photograph given me. She had with her two children, both female, I knew she was their mother from one of them calling her Mama."

"How is this germane? I'm well aware that my daughters are the children of my wife."

"Correct, sir, but Mrs. Watson says I'm always to note down why I believe something to be a fact. Assume nothing, you see."

Harry makes himself nod.

"On that day, the nineteenth inst., I followed her to the following establishments: Gambel's, Doughty's, Lock's. I saw her purchase two children's mackintoshes, some goldfish food, and a decanter for spirits. Also she was measured for a pair of shoes."

"You can leave out her purchases too."

"Very good, sir." A hint of sullenness this time. "Though it's hard to give a full account if all these things are cut out—"

Harry drums on the table beside his untouched brandy, and wonders whether the Watsons couldn't have found him a more competent, or at least laconic, spy. They're being terribly kind, but perhaps they've exceeded their expertise. (He says *they,* because Mrs. Watson says *we*, but of course it's a linguistic fiction: the Reverend Watson is a man of straw.) "Have you done much of this sort of thing before, Crocker?"

"What, watching? Oh no, sir. I have four horses, I'm a cabman," he says, and it's the first time his face has shown any enthusiasm. "I'm just doing Mrs. Watson a favour on account of my mother being in service in her family. On the twentieth of September," he goes on, sober again, "no movements observed all morning."

What an impeccable blank this domestic record is: like a strip of paper dolls. It occurs to Harry that perhaps Mrs. Watson should have sent a maid instead, to worm her way into Helen's trust, but he supposes that would take too long. Time was, in Malta, Mrs. Watson herself had been Helen's confidante, her—what's the phrase women like?—*bosom friend.* Such strange reversals, everywhere Harry turns.

"On the twenty-first, after lunch, one of the female children was seen—"

"Yes, yes, Nan went to the British Museum with Mrs. Lawless yesterday. Get on to the cab," Harry says eagerly. "Yesterday afternoon I happened to see my wife go outside and get into a hansom."

Crocker looks peeved: the client's overstepping his bounds. "That's correct, sir. The party remained in the vehicle for approximately ten minutes, then went back into the house."

"She seemed agitated, when she got down. Didn't you think?"

Crocker purses his lips.

"From where I was standing at the window, at least," says Harry, "I conceived the impression . . ."

"Impressions are one thing, sir. Facts quite another."

"Yes," says Harry, abashed. Then something occurs to him. "If you were watching from the other side of the street—you must have seen his face?"

"Whose face would that be?"

"The passenger's!"

"The person in the cab was a female," Crocker explains. "A lady, I should say."

Harry stares at him. "What kind of lady?"

"Somewhat stout. Hair cut above the shoulders."

"Oh. Never mind her, she's a friend of my wife's," says Harry.

And then dark thoughts swarm across his mind like clouds staining the sun. If it was only Fido—why didn't she come into the house? Whatever could have been the subject of such an intense conversation?

She knows, he thinks, shutting his eyes. *Women tell each other everything.*

And then something else occurs to him. When his telegram about Nell's illness was delivered to Fido's house last week, surely, if Helen wasn't there, Fido should have forwarded it to Eccleston Square? The fact that Harry received nothing from Taviton Street that night can mean only one of two things: that Helen was indeed there, staying to dine with the Faithfulls—or that she was elsewhere, and Fido was in on the fraud.

Is it possible? A pandering woman, who in her cool collusion is almost more disgusting than the one who gives way to desire. Can Fido Faithfull really be conspiring so malevolently against a man who once gave her the protection of his home?

The she-devil!

The enquiry agent shuts his notebook with a snap. "That's all for now, sir."

Harry's sunk in gloom. It depresses him even more to realize that he was hoping for some meaty bit of evidence. "There's nothing to the point in all this, Crocker, is there?"

An uneasy shrug.

"I don't mean to cast any aspersions on your work—"

"Thank you, sir."

"All I'm trying to ascertain is whether the trivial, daily movements you report contain in them any evidence to back a charge of . . ." Harry doesn't want to say the word aloud in a public house.

"That's out of my sphere," Crocker assures him. "Say, I may see a certain party and a certain other party of the contrary sex enter a house together, and I note it down carefully with circumstances appertaining? Though 999 out of a thousand may call that a sign of the parties being up to no good at all, as to whether it's proof that would satisfy a jury, sir, I couldn't dare to say." Tapping his nose, one two, as if he's learned the gesture from a play.

Harry's pulse hammers in his head. "You're telling me that you saw my wife go into a house with a man? What house?"

"Oh no, sir, these are hypotheticals. I'm just explaining the limits of my employment. Though I can't say as how I like it."

Harry stares. It hasn't occurred to him to wonder whether such a man enjoys his work, any more than to ask it of a barber or footman.

"I told Mrs. Watson," says Crocker confidentially, "it seems rather mean, watching a lady's movements on the sly, but she says go on with you, it's an honourable occupation, being as how it's for the sake of freeing a worthy gentleman from the yoke of matrimonial bondage to a—" Crocker hesitates. "Bondage, at any rate."

Harry nods, speechless.

"Also that it's a matter of bringing truth to light, as it were, which can never be wrong. Airing out a stink."

Bile rises in the back of Harry's throat.

Surely there was a time when he'd have been cheered by proof—if only the negative kind—that Helen was true to him? But the mind, it seems, is a warren of occluded passageways. He hadn't thought he suspected his wife of anything worse than coquetry—but it seems now as if, all along, in some dark mental cloister, he's been condemning her.

The fact is, he doesn't want Helen, now, on any terms. How has it come to this, he wonders, that the girl who made him weep by presenting him with the most beautiful babies, *the most charming wife in the Navy* as one admiral of the fleet dubbed her—that all Harry wants now is to cast her off like a monkey from his back, and be justified in the eyes of the world?

~

THE CHAMBERS IN LINCOLN'S INN are small, oppressive. Mr. Bird's desk is thick with piles of tape-tied papers. The leather chair is comfortable, but Harry shifts from side to side. "Of course, no evidence has been uncovered, nothing of substance at any rate," he repeats.

"That's all right," murmurs Bird. "Early days yet." The solicitor—an old acquaintance of the Watsons'—has bushy salt-and-pepper whiskers, and is hung all around with watch chains and seals.

"It was really just a matter of her not replying to the telegram, the night our daughter was ill." Even to himself, he's sounding delusional, a jealous old husband out of a pantomime.

The solicitor makes a tent of his black-haired fingers and speaks soothingly. "Proof of adultery is generally constructed of many isolated facts, Admiral—each of which could seem insubstantial on its own."

"My wife may still be innocent," Harry insists. The word seems an incongruous choice. *Virtuous*, in the technical sense? *Faithful?*

A muffled snort from Mrs. Watson.

"Unlikely," says Bird. "In my experience the injured party's suspicions can generally be trusted."

Mrs. Watson bursts out in musical tones. "We've watched over your marriage as over an invalid clinging to life, Admiral, but the nadir is eventually reached when all hope must be surrendered."

"Now," asks the solicitor, "any idea of the identity of the other?"

Harry blinks at him.

"The other party; the co-respondent, as we say?"

"I have no notion." Something seems expected of him by the ring of faces. "In Malta, over the past few years," Harry says unwillingly, "my wife did have a friend—a regular escort—"

"Oh yes?"

"A colonel, David Anderson by name—" his mind flits around the golden-haired officer "—not that his presence caused me any real concern. A very clubbable sort, with a harmless manner, that's the only way I can put it." Now Harry's not sounding paranoid anymore, but gullible. He shakes his head as if banishing a wasp. "But that was in Malta. Here in London . . . well, I'm at a loss to think of a single name."

"That's all right."

"All I can guess is that she's meeting him—whoever the other party is—with the connivance of an old friend of hers, a Miss Emily Faithfull."

"Proprietress of that female printing press?" Bird nods, making notes.

Mrs. Watson speaks up. "If it's not taking too much upon myself, Admiral—I must tell Mr. Bird that my husband and I left Valetta before the arrival of this Colonel Anderson, but there was during our time a Lieutenant Mildmay, of the third battalion of the Rifle Brigade—"

"Mildmay," Bird mutters, scribbling it down.

Mildmay? thinks Harry, remembering pleasant chats with the fellow about meteorological patterns. *This is ridiculous.*

"And I wouldn't be very much surprised if there were other *spiantati.*"

The solicitor looks up, puzzled.

"Cast-offs," translates the reverend in a whisper.

Harry studies the grain of the desk.

"If and when this Crocker comes up with the goods, Admiral," asks Bird—"I'm assuming, from your doing me the honour of this visit, that you do want some action to be taken?"

"Of course," he says, rubbing his beard where it itches. "Need you ask?"

"It may shock you to learn in how many grand London mansions adultery—even on the distaff side—is an open secret," says Bird with an air of satisfaction. "Sometimes husbands simply cease to communicate with their spouses except by way of the servants."

"Then I don't know how they can bear their lives."

Reverend Watson reaches out one knobbly hand and pats Harry on the knee.

"You could always come to some discreet arrangement—send her abroad, *for reasons of health*, don't you know." Bird taps his nose the same way Crocker did in the public house, and Harry feels a surge of dislike. "Or perhaps you'd like me to negotiate a private separation?"

"I believe, in the case where I were presented with convincing evidence, I would—" He tries again, more firmly. "I want a divorce."

The word comes out as sharp as a fishbone, and he expects it to shake the Watsons. But the reverend only nods, and Mrs. Watson wears a ghostly, radiant smile. *She's never liked Helen*, Harry realizes, *not from the start.* Not that it matters. He needs allies, and their motives are irrelevant.

Bird is unruffled. "Is it that you wish to marry again, if I may ask?"

This hasn't occurred to Harry.

"The Church, alas, turns an obdurate eye," begins Reverend Watson faintly, "but a civil ceremony . . ."

"You'd like a son, perhaps?" suggests the solicitor.

"No," says Harry, decisive. William's sons will carry on the Codrington name and keep up the estate; Harry's girls are quite enough for him.

Bird presses the point. "Then why, exactly—"

I want to be rid of the whore. The words, even in the silence of his head, heat Harry's face. "To end it," he says haltingly, instead. "To draw a line."

"So you can steel yourself to face the public scrutiny of a trial? I feel it my duty to caution you that your domestic troubles will be closely dissected," says Bird, "not only in court but all over again in the press—with the attendant risks to other parties, such as your daughters."

The prospect makes him swallow hard.

"If you're at all familiar with the admiral's record in his sovereign's service," Mrs. Watson is telling the solicitor rather frostily, "you'll know that nothing daunts him."

"Very good," says Bird, leaning back and crossing his legs.

The atmosphere in the chambers eases; Harry feels as if he's passed some test.

"Certainly, the Matrimonial Causes Act has made the business infinitely easier," Bird concedes. "Currently, petitions for divorce stand at an average of two hundred and twenty-five per annum, of which approximately one hundred and fifty are granted."

Harry's head is buzzing with these figures.

"Plenty of military men in that list, by the by," comments Bird. "Foreign service is evidently hard on marriage, whether the wife goes or stays behind."

Harry reflects on the fact that he left Helen in London when he was at sea, but he brought her to Malta. Was it there that the real damage was done? Between one squabble and another, a chilly breakfast and a late dinner?

"Is Mrs. Codrington likely to defend herself, in your view, Admiral?"

"Defend herself, in open court?" gasps Mrs. Watson.

"You mistake me, madam," says Bird with a touch of irritation, "I only mean, is she likely to have her counsel deny the charge?"

Harry shrugs, then says "I should have thought so. She doesn't . . . she never turns away from a fight."

"My reason for enquiring is that an undefended petition costs only about forty pounds, whereas to argue a case can go up to five hundred or so."

Harry doesn't have the money to hand, but it can be raised: he nods mutely. This interview is one of the most peculiarly mortifying he's ever had.

"Now," says Bird with enthusiasm, "let's consider your case, Admiral. The burden of proof will lie on you. Hard evidence must be put forward that Mrs. Codrington has been guilty with one or more partners."

"Would several, a whole series, be best?" Mrs. Watson is asking with a zest that makes Harry's gorge rise. "Because I really think that Lieutenant Mildmay, for one—"

"That all depends," says Bird, his lips pursed. "It'll blacken her nicely—but we mustn't give her counsel room to argue that for years on end, the admiral turned a blind eye."

Something else is troubling Harry. He clears his throat. "By hard evidence . . . Must I actually catch her *in medias res*?"

"Oh no, that won't do at all," says Bird, tut-tutting as he readjusts one of the piles of papers in front of him. "If the good lady will excuse my frankness," with a nod to Mrs. Watson, "I'm afraid that even if you, sir, walked in on your wife and another, unclothed on a bed together, it wouldn't be the slightest bit to the purpose."

Harry stares at him.

"One peculiarity of the law, you see, is that the petitioner and the respondent are assumed to be biased, and so mayn't speak for themselves. Everything must be testified to by other witnesses."

He scratches his side-whiskers. "So I can do nothing?"

"Far from it, Admiral, you'll be our chief fount of information. Every detail of your marriage you recall, however private or apparently irrelevant, must be laid on the table."

The solicitor has the smug air of a torturer, it seems to Harry. "Very well," he says, very low. "Whatever's necessary."

Mrs. Watson throws up her hands. "If any man ever deserved to be happy . . ."

"Ah, but divorce has nothing to do with happiness," says Bird, wagging his finger almost humorously. "Lay persons often make the mistake of believing it a legal remedy for the purpose of relieving miserable couples. In fact, divorce frees a good spouse from a wicked one."

The Watsons nod in perfect unison.

"It's not only requisite for one of you to be guilty, you see," Bird tells his client, "but for the other to be guiltless."

"Of adultery, you mean?" asks Harry, frowning. "I assure you—"

"Of all wrongdoing and negligence," the solicitor clarifies, steepling his fingers on the desk. "I very much fear it will be alleged, in this case, that you've been guilty of allowing Mrs. Codrington improper freedoms."

"Are you married, Mr. Bird?" Harry demands.

"I am not, Admiral; I've seen that craft founder in too many storms to ever trust myself to its timbers," says Bird, obviously pleased with his nautical metaphor.

"For fifteen years I've done my best to maintain the domestic peace," Harry growls, "and that meant keeping my wife on rather a long leash. If it's true that she's been . . . that she's formed a, a *criminal connection*, then I can only say that I knew nothing about it."

"Nothing at all?"

"Do you doubt the admiral's word, Mr. Bird?"

"Not at all, madam—"

Acid burns in Harry's oesophagus. *What a double-dyed buffoon I've been.* "I was preoccupied with work."

"It's just that there's a danger they'll argue *remissio injuriae.* Meaning that you must have guessed and forgiven her years ago, you see," explains Bird. "In which case the jury will probably consider you to have made your bed, et cetera."

"Forgiveness—" begins the reverend.

"Oh, it's considered very estimable at the bar of Heaven," Bird interrupts with a grin, "but down here, in court, quite the contrary, I'm afraid. It's not so inexcusable if a wife forgives—especially if she has children, and nowhere else to go—but a husband . . ." He shakes his head.

"I assure you, Mr. Bird, I was unaware that there was anything to forgive," says Harry, his voice tight as a rope. "I believed my wife to be flawed, yes, but not . . . I was labouring under the misapprehension that she wasn't a passionate person." They're all staring at him now. Of course Helen's a passionate person, given to whimsical notions and impetuous demands. But how, especially in mixed company, can he explain his long-held view that, after two babies, all her yearnings were . . . north of the equator?

Bird nods kindly. "And our counsel will portray you as a loving husband who, though noticing certain signs of lightness in his wife, refused to believe the worst until the occasion of the unanswered telegram."

The Unanswered Telegram: it sounds like a ghost story from one of the popular magazines. "If you knew her . . ." Harry's head is in his hands. "She's still such a girl; always striking some arch pose from one of her yellow-jacketed French novels. Once, after a chance meeting at a party, she talked a lot of rodomontade about the Prince of Wales being infatuated with her, do you remember, Mrs. Watson?"

She nods, her face puckered.

"Early on, I formed a policy of discounting at least half of what Helen said. We've led such separate lives . . ."

"Ah, but that smacks of negligence," says Bird, holding up one finger in warning.

"Would it help if the admiral now began laying down the law in earnest, at home?" asks Mrs. Watson. "Enquiring into or forbidding her excursions?"

Bird smiles. "Paradoxically, that would make it impossible for—what's the agent's name?"

"Crocker," she supplies.

"Crocker, yes, to collect any evidence. No, your dilemma," turning to Harry, "is that of a policeman who notices a dubious character loitering in an alley. Should you chase him off, thus preventing a crime, or linger silently till the ruffian breaks a window, which allows you to make an arrest?"

Harry's head is beginning to thump dully.

"No, you must act a subtle role, Admiral," says Bird. "By all means, throw out the odd animadversion on her neglect of you and the children, but do nothing to thwart her meeting her paramour."

None of this sounds real to him: *her paramour*, a faceless bogey, a slavering silhouette on a magic lantern.

"Restrain your feelings, and remember that in all likelihood there's no virtue in her left to save."

Harry swallows. "How long will all this drag on?"

"That depends on what Crocker can gather here, and what my own agents can dig up in Malta," says Bird.

"Strike not till thy sword be sharpened," Mrs. Watson puts in, in biblical tones.

~

HIS FAITH IS LITTLE COMFORT to Harry, these days. He sends up brief thanksgivings for Nell's recovery, that's about all. With regard to Helen, he doesn't know what to ask.

Since the family's return, he's taken the girls to the church in Eccleston Square on several Sundays; he recognizes only a couple of neighbours' faces, and the sermons are dry investigations of certain controversies in church reform. Today, he leaves Nan at home to amuse her convalescent sister. (Yesterday, he caught them noisily practising *chassée-croisée* up and down the schoolroom: thank God for the blindness of children.) He sets out on foot to his childhood parish in Eaton Square, "for a change," he remarks to Helen on his way out, in an unconvincingly festive tone, but the fact is that he has to get away from this house before he begins to roar and kick little tables over. He's spent months on end on sloops that never felt so cramped.

At fifty-six, he still walks like a sportsman. (People often look up in astonishment as Harry marches by; he's too tall to blend into a crowd.) Today he reaches Eaton Square far too early for the service. He kills some time strolling among the graves, visiting the tomb that his parents share with his eldest brother and William's eldest son. Both boys drowned; it strikes Harry now as a toll the sea takes of the Codringtons, once per generation.

Harry was just fifteen, writing poetry in the dorm at Harrow, when the message came: his handsome brother Edward's boat had capsized off Hydra. When the mourning was over (nobody said, but everybody was aware), there'd be a vacancy as a midshipman in their father's gift: Sir Edward's nominee to replace his lost son would be accepted without question. Though fifteen was late to start, and Harry knew little Euclid or trig—the twin poles of a Naval Academy education—he immediately decided to seize this chance. He knew a life at sea would be a dangerous one, but active and absorbing.

Only now, leaning on the Codrington tomb around the corner from his childhood home, does it strike Harry as disturbing that he stepped into a dead boy's shoes. On what arbitrary pivots our lives turn.

The bells, calling the congregation: Harry goes into the narrow church and finds a verger to pay for a pew. The hangings are more faded and dustier than he remembers. The liturgy's familiar, and mildly comforting; he can shut his eyes and pretend he's a boy again. But the sermon text, by some perverse chance, is from Proverbs:

> *Strength and honour are her clothing . . . She looketh well to the ways of her household; and eateth not the bread of idleness. Her children arise up, and call her blessed; her husband also, and he praiseth her.*

Harry tries not to listen, but the vicar's insipid pieties on the subject of marriage creep into his head. He finds himself picturing the wide-eyed, petrified face of his drowning brother. All at once Harry fears he's going to vomit, here and now in the pew.

He pushes his way out, making his excuses in a strained whisper. How coldly the parishioners of Eaton Square stare.

On the street, he's shivering; the late September breeze infiltrates his summer coat at the neck and wrists. Sweat going clammy on his forehead, and under his black beard. *What have I become?* A creeping, plotting, spy-hiring man. A skeletal puppet of a husband. And what if he's wrong, after all, it occurs to Harry like a knife between the ribs: what if Helen really did get that telegram the other night, but decided out of misguided politeness to stay for dessert? What if all her crimes are his diseased inventions? What if she's never been any worse than an artless, restless young woman who likes a little flattery? What kind of monster would set a deadly trap for the mother of his children?

He keeps on walking. His stomach is feeling somewhat settled by the time he turns the corner onto Eccleston Square; the pain in his head has eased.

But there's a hansom parked outside his house. The driver's leaning down to the little hatch in the roof, collecting his coins. And then the door folds back, and a blond head emerges. Unmistakable. A man who should be in Malta but somehow is here instead, on the path outside Harry's house, tucking his watch back into his pocket with easy grace. Colonel David Anderson.

I have her.

Or rather, *I've lost her.*

Harry's knees give; his cane scrapes across the stone. *Pull yourself together, Codrington.* A quick glance across the road: no Crocker painting the glossy green railings. *Damn the man.* Of course, it's Sunday; the painting alibi would look very suspicious, and scandalize Mrs. Hartley's neighbours. Harry's shaking so much he has to lean against the garden wall of the corner house.

As the horse moves off, Anderson stands looking up at the Codringtons' house. Harry mustn't take a single step forward. Bird's warnings ring in his ears: his only chance of doing anything useful is to do nothing. He edges back around the wall, but it only comes up to his chest. He crouches down, then realizes that makes him look like a housebreaker, so he straightens up again. *Let Anderson not look my way.* It's a sort of terror.

In Sir Edward Codrington's day, a gentleman in this predicament knew exactly what to do: call the cur out. It was the age of heroes, and what did it matter if a little more blood got spilled? But nowadays a duel brings the parties nothing but reproach and ridicule. Harry was born too late: this is the age of correct form and due process. This is what comes of the long peace Harry's toiled to preserve.

He'll have to stand here like some tailor's dummy while Anderson goes into the house—then wait till he comes out again, some time later. The thought of this man with Helen chokes Harry. Behind closed doors, no witnesses. *Crocker, where in the devil's name have you got to?* Could the spy possibly be watching from some other nook? Or has he gone off for a bag of shrimp? It occurs to Harry to grab the nearest pedestrian and demand, "Will you testify on oath that you saw that person there going into and coming out of my house?" *Calm yourself, man, the servants can do that much.*

A dreadful plan occurs to Harry. He'll give Anderson five minutes. Ten, let's say. How long do these things take? (Harry has never had an intrigue. His few premarital experiences were strictly commercial.) Then he'll let himself into the hall with his key, very softly, and find a maid. No, the footman; a man will be more credible in court. "Be so good as to come with me to my wife's room," he'll say, "as quietly as possible."

All this shoots through his mind like a train, in the few moments Anderson is looking up at the house. But then the golden silhouette turns, and the handsome mouth opens in a very wide smile. Or a rictus of shock?

A hearty roar: "Codrington, the very man!"

Harry jerks as if he's been shot. Anderson's walking towards the corner with his hand out; Harry lurches towards him. "Good morning to you," he manages.

"I was just about to ring your bell."

"Oh yes?" Like a ventriloquist's doll. "What are you doing on these shores?"

"Ah, well, that's the nub of it. I got some leave for a rather particular purpose. This is a farewell call, I'm afraid."

Harry sucks the soft inside of his lip. "But you've only just arrived."

"Farewell to single life, I meant," says Anderson with a gulping sort of laugh.

Harry's mouth goes slack.

"Yes, I'm just down from Scotland, and dropping cards all round town to announce that my cousin Gwen's consented to make an honest man of me at last."

Could Harry have misread the whole story? Has he been so bored and dull, in the purgatory of half-pay, that he's made up nightmares to scare himself? "Well! Congratulations, old fellow," he says in a strangled voice.

"Thanks, thanks. My ship's come in, that's a fact," beams Anderson. "She's a very dear girl, and quite a beauty. She's heard all my tales, over the years; she'll be thrilled to meet you, when we come to town."

"I very much look forward to it." Harry struggles to find some harmless truism. "Marriage . . ." he begins.

"Nothing like it, so all the chaps tell me," supplies Anderson after a second.

"Quite so."

"Well," with a stretch and a grin, "mustn't dally. I've still got most of Belgravia to cover, and all of Mayfair."

Harry's heart starts pounding, worse than ever it did during a bombardment at sea. *Liars always say too much.* What gave it away was the cab: Anderson sent the cab away before walking up to the house on Eccleston Square. Who ever heard of delivering a sheaf of cards on foot, all over Belgravia and Mayfair? And on a Sunday morning too? Now Harry knows for sure. It may not count as *hard proof*, but it's enough to still the nagging doubts in his mind. "Oh," he says mechanically, "won't you come up for a moment?"

"No, no, I don't think so. Time's winged chariot, and all. Give my respects to Mrs. C.?" The colonel pronounces this without a quaver.

"Indeed. Dine with us this week, won't you?"

"Ah, a shame, I'll be back in Scotland."

"Of course." Harry starts up the steps to his front door. Then an idea shoots through his head like an electric shock. He turns, fumbling in one of his pockets. "I say, have a copy of my latest photograph."

"Awfully kind of you, Codrington. Now I can prepare the future Mrs. A. for your fearsome beard!"

"Have you got one on you?"

The man blinks at him. "I—yes, I believe so," he says, leafing through his pocketbook, "though it's not kind to the old Anderson chin. Here you go."

"Well done, again." Harry waves, and watches the officer walk round the corner.

Now he has a picture to give to Crocker: *This is the man. The other party; paramour; co-respondent.* He looks down at the matt image, grips it so hard that the serene face buckles under his thumbnail.

VI

Actus Reus

(Latin, "guilty act": the legal maxim,

Actus non facit reum, nisi mens sit rea,

means "The guilty mind and guilty act are

both needed to constitute a crime")

Women are greater dissemblers than men when they wish to conceal their own emotions. By habit, moral training, and modern education, they are obliged to do so.

Jane Vaughan Pinkney,
Tacita Tacit (1860)

Sunday, September 23

It has taken me two days to compose this letter.

Surely, before you formed an engagement you were bound in all honour to tell me of the changed state of your heart. What, in heaven's name, could have led you to take such a sudden and terrible step? I cannot believe that in a matter of days the tender recollection of the past two years can be obliterated so utterly, leading you to spurn one who up to that time (you've claimed) has been constantly in your thoughts day and night. But I will say no more of my own pain; there are certain crushing sorrows wherein the heart alone knows its own bitterness.

Believe me, I am writing today not

in reproachful or jealous wrath, but out of the most tender concern for your welfare. You gave our friend no explanation for your extraordinary decision except your cousin's affection for you. Let me beg of you solemnly, think well before you bind yourself for life. Self-sacrifice may be all very well under certain circumstances, but not when the happiness of two souls (say rather, three) is at stake. Unless you can feel for this cousin what a husband ought to feel, it were far better that you should give her the immediate pain of breaking off, than that you should leave her to find it out after the wedding. As I know all too well, it takes a profound devotion to stand the wear and tear of married life.

I wish to see you once more; there are certain documents and mementos that I must return to you with my own hands. I believe you were intending to return to London yesterday; if this note reaches you at your lodgings this morning (Sunday), I ask that you come to me at home at eleven. (H. never returns from church before noon.) Don't dread the meeting; rest assured that if it truly must be, I will let the past be forever past and never more think of what we have been to each other. You who know me well can tell what it costs me to beg this last favour.

I need hardly remind you to burn this.

Ever yours
faithfully—

~

Ten past eleven, already, by the ormolu clock in Helen's drawing-room. Almost a quarter past. Her ears strain for the sound of the doorbell. This morning Helen put on her loveliest dress, the emerald and magenta satin, then ripped it off again in case Harry asked what the occasion was. She's in plain lilac now; she regrets its insipidity. Her eyes in the mirror over the mantelpiece are red-rimmed, and the skin beneath is faintly brown. *Discarded*, she mouths in the glass. *Cast-off.*

"What has an eye but can't see?" asks Nan.

"That's easy. A needle," croaks Nell, still wrapped up in flannel on the sofa.

"A face, but no mouth?"

"Ask Mama."

"What's that?" says Helen.

"It's a riddle, Mama," says Nan. "What has a face but no mouth?"

Helen grimaces. "What monstrous images you conjure up."

Almost a quarter past. Her ears crave the bell. There's a risk, of course, that one of the servants might mention Anderson's visit to their master—but Helen's beyond such petty calculations. She can't think of anywhere else to ask him to meet her on a Sunday morning, now that Taviton Street is out of bounds. (Fido, having almost pushed Helen out of the cab Friday afternoon, is evidently still in a fury. She won't even answer Helen's notes, let alone be of any practical assistance.)

"Guess, do."

"Guess, Mama," Nell orders in her ragged voice.

When the maid comes to announce Anderson, should Helen let the girls stay for a few minutes, to greet their old playmate from Malta? That might fill him with nostalgia for summer days on the hills above Valetta. Or, of course, remind him that his Mrs. C. is a mother and a wife, past her prime. (*My marriage didn't stand in our way*, she argues in her head, *why should yours? Husbands take mistresses every day.*) But then the girls are sure to mention Anderson to their papa. Besides, there's not enough time; he must at all costs be gone by the time Harry gets home from church. "A face but no mouth," mutters Helen. "A mouthless face. Sewn shut?"

"It's a clock, of course," crows Nan, and Nell giggles. "Another?"

"Really, I—"

"Another for Mama!"

Twenty past. If Anderson comes now, they'll barely have half an hour. Was there a line in her letter that scared him off? Helen made it as high-minded and persuasive as she possibly could; she tried to write it in the voice of another kind of woman altogether. Damn him, he owes her a meeting; he owes her one more chance.

Fido would no doubt advise Helen not to *lower herself any further.* She'd urge *self-respect.* But she's not here, is she? So much for loyalty. So much for the friendship of women.

"What has hands, but no fingers?"

Helen makes a small exasperated sound. "Are all your riddles on the theme of mutilation?"

"You're prevaricating," sings Nan, proud of the new word.

The man's not coming at all. Behind that shining, bluff face, what cruelty.

"Guess! Guess!"

"You'd never treat your father like this," says Helen. "Let me see, no fingers. Has it thumbs?"

"*No* fingers, *no* thumbs, only hands," says Nell, holding up clenched fists.

"May I have a clue?"

Her daughters exchange serious looks. "You've already had one," says Nan.

"Hands with no fingers or thumbs . . ."

"She'll never get it. The clock, again," squeals Nell, and Helen, horrified, looks where her daughter's pointing. "A clock has hands, just as it has a face."

"You're rather stupid today, Mama," observes Nan.

"Yes, I am," says Helen, and her voice comes out tragic.

"Mama, I didn't mean it!"

"It's just that we've had more practice at riddles than you," Nell assures her. "Let's try a different game."

"I'm tired of riddles, anyway," says Nan. She picks up a pack of cards. "Shall we play All Fall Down?"

"I rather think I'm still too shaky," says Nell, holding out her hand and watching it tremble.

"Oh, I'll build the house," says Nan, already forming cards into precarious triangles on the table. "You and Mama may shout when it falls."

Speechless, Helen's turned her face to the window. The streets are quiet on Sundays. No sound for several minutes but the faint contact of card on card. Then a flutter, and Nell yelps, "All Fall Down!"

But Helen's heard the scrape of the front door opening, and she whirls around. "I believe we may have a visitor," she cries, too excited. "Whoever could it be? Come, let's tidy these games away."

Nan shakes her head at her. "Nobody rang or knocked, silly Mama. That means it's only Papa, home from church."

"Let's play Old Maid," suggests Nell.

"Happy Families," Nan countermands.

When Harry comes into the drawing-room, Helen's sitting quite still, beside her daughters, like some tableau of domesticity. "You're early," she murmurs without looking up. "Nell, I'm looking for . . . Mrs. Bones the butcher's wife."

"Not at home!"

"Who's winning?" he asks.

"I am," crows Nan. "Mama keeps forgetting the rules."

~

The following day, late in the afternoon, Helen walks out the door of her house, to a waiting cab.

Rattling along, she takes out one of the large buff cards that say *Mrs. Henry J. Codrington.* She stares at the four corners—*Felicitation, Visite, Condolence, Congé*—but none of them seems appropriate to fold down, and she can't think of anything to write on it. Blank will have to do.

She's never been to Anderson's lodgings before; she's never let herself risk it. Today she gets the driver to stop outside Number 28 Pall Mall—as a measure of discretion—but asks him to take her card in to Number 24.

"Twenty-four, you said?" He glances up at the house number.

"That's right," she says coldly.

It's nearly six; her stomach rumbles. If she's not there for dinner at seven, will Harry have a fit? Heartburn, at least. At best, a choking, fatal apoplexy on the hearthrug.

After a few endless minutes, Anderson comes out the front door, and looks where the driver's pointing, to the cab parked outside Number 28. Helen takes a long breath.

He's unsmiling. He gets into the cab and pulls the door shut; he sits beside her, rather than opposite.

That means he wants to be near me. Or, of course, that he can't look me in the eye.

"I did call at Eccleston Square yesterday morning," he starts abruptly, "but of all the confounded luck, I ran into Harry on the doorstep."

"I knew something must have happened!" No response from Anderson. "Yes, he left church early; he wasn't well. Was he—did he seem surprised to learn that you were in London?"

Anderson shrugs.

"Was he . . . unfriendly?"

"No. We exchanged photographs."

Photographs? Men are bizarre creatures. Helen examines her small pink nails. *Don't go on the attack*, she reminds herself. "Have you nothing more to say to me," she asks quietly, "after I poured out my very soul in that letter?"

Anderson clears his throat. "You shouldn't have come here." A silence grows between them; she waits. "You look very lovely today," he adds glumly.

Her mouth twists. Does he think she's a girl, to be fobbed off with compliments? And yet it does gladden her to hear.

"I know I've wounded you," he says.

"Do you, though?"

Anderson takes a small packet out of his pocket, and sets it in her lap.

"What's this?" she asks.

"Some remembrances."

She doesn't need to open it to know what's there. A fob chain she worked herself, rather amateurishly, the Christmas before last; also, cufflinks in the form of stars; also, a coppery coil of her hair.

"The letters are burned already."

"Then burn these too." She shifts her leg, letting the packet drop to the floor of the cab. She thinks of the smell of singed hair.

Anderson bends to pick it up as if humouring a child. "Did you bring the items you wanted to return to me?"

She shakes her head.

"Helen!"

"It flew out of my mind."

"I thought that was the very purpose of this meeting."

"Yours, perhaps," she says through a swollen throat. "Mine was to make you look me in the eye and tell me you no longer feel anything for me."

Anderson lets out a grunt, and then, as she tilts up her face, he seizes it and kisses her, as she knew he would.

Helen presses herself against him. This is her moment: power like sugar on her tongue. After a few minutes she breaks away an inch or two, enough to say, "Can we go inside?"

Anderson shakes his head. "My landlady."

Her stomach sinks.

But he rears up to slide the trapdoor, and calls to the cabman. "The Grosvenor Hotel, if you please."

She flushes to think of how that sounds. *Why is it*, she wonders, *that we care what faceless strangers think of us?*

The growler gets held up in a jam at Hyde Park Corner, behind a horse who's collapsed in his traces. The two passengers don't speak; Helen bites her tongue so she won't say anything to make Anderson change his mind. *Come on, quickly . . .*

At the hotel, he registers in the names of Lieutenant and Mrs. Smith. The clerk gives them a dubious tilt of the eyebrow, but it is Helen's maiden name, after all, and she stares right through him.

"No luggage, Lieutenant?"

"I only require accommodation for my wife to rest before an evening engagement," says Anderson frostily.

The room is strikingly ugly. Helen was right, all those times, to refuse this; better a seized embrace in the dim woods of the Cremorne Gardens. In the glass, in her lilac bodice, she looks raddled; there are harsh lines around the corners of her mouth. How far she's come from Miss Helen Webb Smith of Florence.

Anderson makes no move to lead her to the bed. He paces. *This is how it could end*, thinks Helen, *with silence in a nasty rented room.* "You may smoke," she tells him. "These curtains aren't worth saving."

"You don't mind?"

She almost laughs. "How considerate you are of my feelings!"

Anderson lights his cigarette before he answers. "Darling girl, I couldn't be sorrier."

Oh, but you could, you will.

"The best thing you can do is forget me."

She breathes in the spicy scent of tobacco. "That's the advice an executioner gives his victim: don't flinch, don't swerve, so the axe will make a clean stroke."

"Oh, Helen."

"Was it all a chimera? People are always telling me I have an overactive imagination," she says in a voice that comes out high and uneven. "Was our whole story one of my *imaginings*?"

Anderson shakes his heavy lion's head. "Fact is, there comes a time in every fellow's life when he begins to think of settling down."

"What for?"

"A home," he offers uneasily, "an heir. My cousin Gwen's a splendid girl—"

She holds up her hand. "I didn't come to this establishment, at considerable risk, to hear you sing the praises of your brand-new *fiancée*." She pronounces the word like a curl of sulphurous fumes.

"All I wanted to say was, I don't deceive myself that she'll ever be to me what you've been."

A small pleasure, a wild strawberry swallowed as the cliff crumbles under her. Helen makes her mind up: she's not here to punish this man—satisfying though that would be—but to keep hold of him. "Marry her, then, but save your secret heart for me." She meant to say it in a seductive whisper, but it comes out like a command.

He looks away, and it strikes her like a brick to the head that she's lost the game.

"You and I," says Anderson, "—it started to go awry the day you left Malta."

What, if you can't have me twice a week, in a comfortable gondola, is it too much bother? But she keeps her mouth clamped shut.

"You know we'd have been found out sooner or later. People notice things. Even your numbskull husband couldn't have kept his head in the sand forever."

This is an argument that won't be won with words, it strikes Helen. But she has other weapons.

"Give me a cigarette," stretching out her hand. "Have I shocked you?" she asks, when he doesn't move. "Do you think me *fast*?"

The absurdity strikes him too, and they both smile. He lights a cigarette and she draws on it without coughing; the smoke leaves a bitter scrape in her throat.

"I've never seen a woman do that before."

"Really? Fido smokes like a longshoreman."

He blinks. "Your friend Fido?"

"Oh, I'm not sure she'd answer to that name," says Helen, as flippantly as she can. "She's cast me off for the *egregious falsehoods* I told her for your sake. No, I've not a friend in the world anymore."

Anderson kisses her, more roughly this time, with his tongue. "Do you like the taste?" she asks, when she can catch a breath.

"Hm. Rather like kissing a longshoreman."

She laughs.

Anderson's eyes widen, and he plunges his face into the curve of her bodice, his arms thrashing about in her layers of diaphanous silk. Some women find this animal quality in men off-putting, Helen reflects as she slides down the slippery upholstered sofa. *But we're all beasts of the field, after all.*

Oh, how could she have ever learned to do without the hot weight of this man, his strong movements on her, inside her? She finds herself thinking of her husband, his long white limbs, their torpor; Harry never seized her this way, even on their wedding night; never looked into her eyes with such desperation. She feels a choking rage, now, at the admiral in Eccleston Square, newspaper erect like a shield, swallowing his heartburn as he waits for her to come home.

But no, she mustn't spoil this moment by letting herself think of dried-out cutlets and old arguments. Helen banishes everything else from her head, brings herself back to this squeaking sofa, this glorious, writhing conjunction. *It will be all right*, she tells herself, shouting into the void, *everything will be well now, because this man wants me, will always want me: no marriage can put a stop to this. Not mine, not his.* Bone and scalding flesh, the grapple of muscle, every thrust a pledge, signed and sealed.

VII

Desertion

(abandonment; withdrawing support or help despite allegiance or responsibility)

If a lady be pressed by her friend to remove her shawl and bonnet, it can be done if it will not interfere with subsequent arrangements . . . During these visits, the manners should be easy and cheerful, and the subjects of conversation such as may be readily terminated.

Isabella Beeton,
Household Management (1861)

"It's an animal that eats up gold," groans Emily Davies, sitting in Fido's office at the Victoria Press the next day. "I so long to be done with it, I'd be happy to pay the costs of winding it up myself."

"Miss Parkes is always complaining the *Journal*'s destroyed her health," says Fido, "yet she won't surrender the reins to anyone with fresh ideas. Surely Madame Bodichon won't be willing to supply the gold forever?"

"I doubt it," says Emily Davies. "In her last, she tells me that Miss Parkes has always had an exaggerated view of the *Journal*'s influence. But you know their long friendship . . ."

There is a pause, now, which stretches into awkwardness. It's up to Fido to speak. "I asked you to call on me this afternoon, Miss Davies, because— well, perhaps you've guessed." She finds this woman's small face unreadable. "The other day at the meeting, when I spoke of a first-class magazine which would combine the progress of women with other vital topics of the day, you seemed . . . interested. Was I mistaken?"

"You weren't." Emily Davies's eyes narrow. "But if it's not to be a new format for the *English Woman's Journal*, wouldn't such a magazine constitute a rival publication?"

"No," Fido insists, her voice shaking with excitement, "because it would appeal to quite a different, broader audience. What I'm thinking of is an entertaining monthly, on the *Fraser's* or *Macmillan's* model, which will inoculate readers—without their feeling so much as a prick!—with advanced ideas on the relations between the sexes." (She's spent the weekend mulling over this plan, in an attempt—only partly successful—to keep her mind off Helen.)

"Would you be the publisher?"

"Indeed I would. I have some capital, and a good chance of securing an investment partner, a Mr. Gunning; you must meet him. You'd be the sole editor—unencumbered by a committee," she adds wryly, remembering how Emily Davies once painstakingly cut down a rambling article of Arnold's from thirty pages to twenty, before Bessie Parkes could inform her of the *Journal*'s policy of never editing the prose of a distinguished man. "How do you like the sound of the *Victoria Magazine*?"

"Very much indeed," says Emily Davies, with a precise, doll-like smile.

For a quarter of an hour they throw themselves into the details: topics, writers, artists, rates per page. They'll save money on an office by using the premises of the Victoria Press. "What ought our motto to be?" asks Emily Davies.

"Liberty! Let every woman do that which is right in her own eyes," Fido improvises.

"I must insist on a contract; there's too much slapdash informality in the Woman Movement."

"What would you say to one hundred pounds per annum?"

"Payment in addition for any articles I write?"

"Five shillings a page," offers Fido.

They're grinning at each other like children when the boy knocks to say Mrs. Codrington is asking for the proprietor.

Fido's throat locks. Without a word she stands and goes to the door of her office.

"If you have another visitor—"

"No no, do excuse me, if you please, Miss Davies, I'll only be a—"

Helen's rushing across the workroom to seize her by both wrists. "Fido!"

Flora Parsons, for one, is smirking over her composing desk.

Abstractions and judgements fall to dust: this is Helen. "My dear," whispers Fido, trying to steer her away from the office where Emily Davies sits, "this is neither the time nor the place . . ."

Helen won't move a step. There's something askew about her jacket. "He—" she chokes. The tears are coursing in sheets down her face, into her lace collar.

Fido hisses in her ear. "Whatever the colonel might have—"

"Not him," Helen wails.

Before Fido can stop her, she's swept through the door marked *Proprietor*. Fido hurries after. Emily Davies is on her feet, sliding her notes into her pocketbook. Fido makes a rapid calculation of status; Helen, for all her dishevelment, comes out ahead by a nose. "Mrs. Codrington—may I present Miss Davies?"

"Delighted," says Emily Davies, holding out her hand, but Helen stands like Niobe, her face eroded with tears.

Wildly, Fido says, "My colleague and I were just discussing the possibility of a collaborative venture."

Helen tries to speak, makes a dreadful gulping.

"Another time," Emily Davies murmurs, edging towards the door.

"He's taken Nan and Nell," Helen bursts out. "And my desk, he's smashed open my writing desk."

The visitor's tiny eyebrows shoot up.

Fido sucks in her lips, gives Emily Davies a shake of the head.

"Ladies, good day." And Emily Davies is gone, shutting the door quietly behind her, thinking God knows what about the kind of lunatics Fido Faithfull harbours among her intimates.

But through her fog of mortification, Fido has registered something. "Anderson's abducted the *girls*?"

A violent shake of the head. "Their father has. I came home, I was shopping," she sobs, "when I walked in the door the house was empty. He's sent all the servants away too."

"Where's he taken them? Not the servants: Nan and Nell," she clarifies.

"If I knew, do you think I'd be here?" shrieks Helen. "I'd crawl to China on my knees for my babies."

"Sh," hisses Fido, casting a desperate glance at the door that separates them from her typos. "Sit down, won't you? A glass of water—"

"I'll never sit down again!"

Exasperation, like a wave engulfing Fido. *This kind of behaviour is why no one wants to employ women*, she finds herself thinking nastily. "What was that about your desk?" she asks after a moment.

"It's broken open, it's in splinters. Everything's gone."

"Everything, what everything?" She waits. "Don't tell me there were letters."

"I—"

"Helen!"

"Nothing from Anderson, I burn them all as soon as I read them, or nearly," Helen assures her.

"What then? Not a diary?"

The beautiful cheeks are sunken. "Just an appointment book."

Fido clenches her fists.

"And there might have been . . . scribbles. A few drafts of letters."

"This is dreadful."

"Do you think I need you to tell me that?"

Fido tries to gather her thoughts. "So all the staff are gone?"

"Except for Mrs. Nichols. She claims to know nothing," says Helen, scrabbling in her bag, "but this wasn't sealed, so I'd lay money she's read it." She slaps down a piece of paper.

Fido picks it up warily. "*Eau de toilette*," she reads aloud, "*gateleg table, chintz samples, nerve tonic . . .*"

Helen snatches it back from her and digs in her bag again. "Here."

The note is unsigned; the admiral must know his wife will recognize his hand. Dated today, Tuesday the twenty-fifth. A single line: *You will be hearing from a Mr. Bird, my solicitor, with respect to a petition for divorce.* Fido covers her mouth.

~

At Taviton Square, after some laudanum, Helen's a little calmer. She lies stretched out on Fido's bed, staring at the gaudy sunset that fills the window. "To think," she marvels, "all these years, ever since I made that rash request for a private separation, he's been plotting to punish me."

"You can't be sure of that," says Fido. "It could be a sudden impulse on Harry's part."

"He must have guessed the whole story, on Sunday when he bumped into Anderson on Eccleston Square. Funny," says Helen, her voice cracking, "the price of a single carelessness. I only asked Anderson to come to me at home because you'd barred the door to yours."

Fido feels a stab. "I was acting in accordance with my conscience," she says in a small voice.

"Oh, I know," wails Helen. "I've no right to come here after all the tarradiddles I told you. Why didn't I trust you with the whole truth from the start? I've no right to ask you to have a woman's heart towards me—and yet I do."

Fido puts her finger against Helen's lips to hush her.

"Divorce would rob me of everything. Reputation, name, my daily bread . . ." Helen lists them bleakly.

The girls, thinks Fido, but doesn't dare say so. "I'm only glad you didn't run to Anderson," she says softly. "So often, I believe, a woman in this kind of *débâcle* sees no other way out. She throws herself on the man's mercy—and what once was romance slips into squalor, as he learns to rate her on the world's polluted terms."

Helen's smile is a distorted one. "I saw him yesterday evening, at a hotel."

Fido stiffens. "I don't want to hear anything said or done in any hotel." For the first time, it hits her that a divorce may mean a trial, in open court, with witnesses saying appalling things out loud.

"He gave me the impression that his feelings for me were quite . . . unquenched," says Helen. "But then, it seems I'm the worst judge of men's hearts. This morning he sent a little note to say he was returning to Scotland and we wouldn't be meeting again."

"Oh, my darling girl!"

"*Regrets*, it said. *Regrets, D.A.*"

Fido doesn't say anything for a moment, because if she tries she'll be in tears, and one of the two women must be strong. One of them must remember the way through this nightmarish maze. Finally she speaks, decisive. "You must put this scoundrel out of your mind, Helen. You've wasted quite enough of your time and spirit on him."

Helen shuts her eyes. Her hair, half out of its chignon, looks like blood spilled across the pillow.

"You were right to come to me." Fido's voice vibrates very low, like a cello. "You must have known you'd find safe haven here."

Eyes flicker open, almost turquoise in this strange evening light. "I couldn't be sure. After the way you flew into a rage in the cab—"

"That's all in the past. There must be no more evasions between us, no more falsehoods," she says, seizing one of Helen's hands.

Helen squeezes back. "I've nothing left to hide from you. My heart's split open as if on the vivisector's table!"

Fido winces at the image. She bends over Helen. "Lean on me, my own one. I'll stand by you."

"Through everything?"

"Everything!"

"I can stay?"

"For as long as you need." *Forever*, Fido's thinking, though she doesn't dare say it, not yet.

"Oh Fido, how did I ever manage without you, all those lonely years!"

Her mind is leaping into the future. Why not? Women do live together, sometimes, if they have the means and are free from other obligations. It's eccentric, but not improper. She's known several examples in the Reform movement: Miss Power Cobbe and her "partner" Miss Lloyd, for instance. It can be done. It would be a change of life for Helen—but hasn't her life been utterly changed, without her consent, already? Can't the caterpillar shrug off its cramped case and emerge with tremulous wings?

As if reading Fido's mind, Helen clings to her hand like a drowning woman. "If you cast me off or betray me like these men have, I'll perish."

"I never will." There'll be some discomfort, some embarrassment consequent on setting up house with a divorcee, but nothing Fido can't weather for her friend's sake.

"Swear."

"There's no need—"

"Swear it!"

"I swear, then." In the ragged silence, Fido plants a hot kiss on that smooth face.

Later that night, when darkness has drawn a merciful cloak over the lurid sky, Helen's fast asleep, on her front, as still as a baby. Beside her, Fido, propped up on four pillows, strains for breath and represses a nagging cough. Emotion always goes to her lungs.

How long does a divorce take? she wonders. The thing is rare in English fiction. In *East Lynne*, she recalls with effort, the husband seems to obtain one without much trouble—but by then, the deluded Lady Isabel has already eloped to France, which makes the case clearer. Abandoned by her seducer, unrecognizably scarred, Lady Isabel comes home and takes a position as governess to her own children. Doesn't one of them then die in her arms? *Wake up. This is real life*, Fido reminds herself sternly.

If Helen were to admit the charges—casting the lion's share of blame on Anderson, for his ceaseless solicitations and threats that induced her to break her vows—then perhaps the thing needn't take very long at all. It could all be resolved before the winter, thinks Fido giddily. She pictures Helen and herself celebrating Christmas in the drawing-room below.

In the faint gaslight from the street that comes through the crack in the curtains, she watches the infinitesimal rise and fall of Helen's shoulder blades under the white muslin of the borrowed nightdress. Some lines from Lord Tennyson repeat themselves in her head.

Strange friend, past, present, and to be,
Loved deeplier, darker understood.

It's too late for qualms. In one turn of the planet, everything has changed. While Helen was out shopping today, she was, all unknowing, robbed of everything. The whole establishment of her life has fluttered to the ground like a pack of cards. At a moment like this, Fido can only follow her nature, which is to hold, to save, to love.

The grandfather clock on the landing chimes two. If she'd known what a storm was brewing just over the horizon, Fido wonders, would she have turned away, that parched afternoon on Farringdon Street, on the last day of August?

Fido?

You're mistaken.

But you're my long-lost friend, my faithful Fido!

Not I.

The very thought of it makes her despise herself, for lack of nerve, parsimony of heart. No, she can't wish that day—not the whole last chaotic month—undone. In the past, Fido's never come quite first for Helen; she's always known that. But now Helen's been shaken awake; she's learned that men's flattery isn't enough to live on. She's come to treasure the one true friend she possesses, the one soul that speaks to her soul. Helen's going to survive these horrors, somehow, and it's Fido who will pull her through. There could be long years of happiness ahead, waiting for them just around the corner.

On impulse she gets out of bed, very softly so as not to disturb the sleeper, and searches in the back of her bureau drawer. She doesn't need a light to find the roll of linen. There's the choker Helen gave her all those years ago, in memory of the beach in Kent where they met in the year 1854: shells, amber drops, mother-of-pearl scattered along the velvet. Fido puts it round her throat now and fastens the clasp. It's tighter than it used to be, but not too tight to bear.

Wheezing a little, she stands beside the bed and pulls the blankets up to Helen's nape, to where the dark hair breaks over pale skin.

~

SHE WAKES TO FIND HELEN STANDING at the window in the grey morning, fully dressed. "My dear—"

"The girls are terrified, I can feel it," says Helen, without turning. "We must find where he's hidden them."

Fido rubs dust from her eyes. "You're in no fit state, my dear. Why not wait till tomorrow, at least?"

"Tomorrow means one more day without my darlings," says Helen in a guttural voice.

She struggles up on the pillows, suppressing a sigh. She's known Helen to travel for weeks—months—without her children. But she supposes it's different when they've been snatched away. After all, what does Fido know of a mother's feelings?

For the best part of the morning, they hunt Nan and Nell all over town. It's a peculiarly mortifying sort of business.

Helen begins by leaving a pleading note for Harry (drafted by Fido, on a writing tablet on her knee in the waiting cab) at his club. The Rag Club—properly, the Army and Navy Club—stands on Pall Mall, a modern, impregnable fortress, with a crossed sword and anchor over the great arch, and the motto, *Unitate Fortior.* The doorkeeper's face is marble; he won't give the ladies any clue as to whether Admiral Codrington is in residence.

Then they try the houses of several of the Codringtons' long-time acquaintances. They're met with soaring eyebrows, startled denials. How can any decent mother possibly mislay two daughters, eleven and twelve? There's nothing like a little mysteriousness to make word spread. Really, thinks Fido with a private groan, Helen may as well put a small advertisement in the *Times* to announce the eruption of her domestic hearth.

At the marble-fronted townhouse of the Bourchiers, Helen sends the driver in with her card bearing a scribbled message, and receives a curt reply that her Ladyship has nothing to communicate to her brother's wife.

Helen falls back into the corner of the growler. "He must have told her. He's probably told everyone by now," she snarls. "Do you think she has my girls locked up in there?"

"It's possible."

"You try, won't you, and this time don't ask for her, just find out from the footman whether the Misses Codrington are staying with their aunt."

"Helen, I—"

"Please! You have a winning face."

Fido burst out laughing. (It must be the strain.) "I've never heard it called that before."

"Strangers like it at once."

"Especially the lower orders, you mean?"

"They assume the worst of mine," says Helen instead of answering.

It's true, Fido thinks; Helen's brand of ostentatious loveliness puts people's backs up. She gets down and goes up to the door; it's starting to rain. By wearing her most benign, parish-visitor expression she manages to extract from the boy in livery the information that the admiral's daughters haven't visited in some weeks.

"Well, at least we know that much," she tells Helen, wiping wet hair out of her eyes.

"We know nothing," Helen corrects her with a groan. "They could be floating in the Thames, as we speak!"

Fido shuts her eyes for a moment, then opens them. "Don't let's give way to melodrama," she says lightly. "No doubt I'm very stupid, but . . . what possible motive could Harry have for throwing the girls in the river?"

A silence, and Fido holds her breath: is Helen going to fly into hysterics again?

No: a small, grudging smile. "Their resemblance to their mother?"

"Ah, but they have the Codrington stature. No, it would surely be simpler for him to hire some thug to throw *you* in the river."

Helen giggles. "Harry would hate to spend the money."

"When he could do the job himself, you mean? An excellent point."

"Of course, you may be driven to such lengths yourself, Fido, before he gets a chance."

"Very likely. If you annoy me, I dare say these arms have force enough to manhandle you over Westminster Bridge," says Fido, holding them out to examine them in their tight brown sleeves. "If we're to live together, no doubt you'll discover all sorts of brutish qualities in me."

But the moment of humour has gone by; Helen's staring out the window at the Bourchiers' house again. Fido pulls out her watch, and tuts. "I really ought to be at the press by now," she tells Helen. "I must arrange a meeting with Mr. Gunning, about the finances of my new magazine."

Helen's face falls. "You wouldn't leave me, today of all days?"

"My dear, it would only be for an hour, two at most—"

But Helen clings to Fido's brown skirt, her face contorted, and Fido gives in; pats her hand.

The rain's heavier now, so she has the cabman rein in his horse by a London Umbrella Company stand so she can hire one for the afternoon. Then she gives him the next address on Helen's list of acquaintances.

After two more dead-ends, Helen turns from the streaky window and says, "I'm a fool not to think of it before: he must have tracked down the Watsons!"

At first the name means nothing to Fido. Then she says, "Your friends in Malta?"

"*His*," says Helen, scathing. "When the reverend lost his post, they came back to London. I can just see Harry turning to them for this kind of trick. The husband's a cipher, but the wife would be capable of anything."

In the directory Fido's been carrying around in her bag, she does find a Reverend Joshua Watson in the farthest fringes of Bayswater.

At the house, Helen sends in her card, and after a moment a greying middle-aged lady comes out to the carriage, under a faded umbrella.

"Is that her?" Fido asks, and in response Helen squeezes her wrist tight enough to hurt.

Helen leans out the window and begins without preamble. "You have them, don't you? Give them to me!"

Fido's cheeks go hot. "Please excuse my friend—" she begins.

But then she registers the minute smile on the face of the clergyman's wife, and a tiny glance up at the house. *They're here!*

"Mrs. Codrington. The girls' father—their sole legal guardian," Mrs. Watson spells out, a word at a time, "has indeed honoured my husband and self by entrusting them to our care for the moment. In the admittedly unlikely case that you have any true feeling for them—"

"How dare you," cries Helen.

"For the sake of little Anne and Ellen, I suggest you give over making a scene in the public street."

"Nan," she spits, "they're called Nan and Nell."

The little smile broadens. "My husband and I have formed a policy of using their proper Christian names, to help them make a fresh start."

"They're mine!"

"As a point of law," says Mrs. Watson with her head on one side, "it's only a woman's virtue that induces her husband to leave his children in her custody.

Technically speaking, children are a sort of gift a man gives his wife, you see, which he can withdraw at any time."

"Lying hag!"

Fido is shaken by the statement, but she knows the facts are true.

"You've gone astray, Mrs. Codrington," remarks Mrs. Watson in a sort of joyful sing-song. "You've done dreadful things."

"I'll do something worse, you bitch, if you don't bring down my children," says Helen, lunging at her through the open window. The older woman jerks away from the cab.

"For shame!" Fido's appalled by the language as much as the violence.

But Helen's scanning the upper storey. What comes out of her mouth is like the cry of a gull. "There they are!"

Mrs. Watson turns to look up at the rain-smeared window; frowning, she makes a banishing gesture. But two blank faces stare down at the scene.

"Nell! Nan! Mama is here," Helen shrieks out the window.

Fido pulls Helen back onto the seat. "This is doing no good," she pleads in her ear.

"I don't know you, madam," Mrs. Watson remarks to Fido.

"Emily Faithfull," she says reluctantly, after a second.

"Ah yes, I'm familiar with the name." Very knowing.

Fido stares at her. Familiar with it from the press? From Helen's reminiscences, while she was in Malta?

"I wonder that you continue to associate with this person."

"That is the nature of friendship," she says thickly.

"I, too, was taken in by her, for a little while, Miss Faithfull," says Mrs. Watson with a ghastly benevolence. "You're clearly still caught in her coils."

While Fido's been distracted, Helen has got the door open and jumped down into the street. "Open the window, darlings," she roars up at the white faces. But they don't seem to hear her.

"Won't you be Christian enough to let her have just a moment with her children?" Fido asks Mrs. Watson. "If you please, she's terribly distressed."

"Indeed she is, and it might do the girls incalculable harm to be put through such an encounter with a foul-mouthed hysteric."

"One moment," says Fido furiously, "one embrace."

"The time for embracing is over," intones Mrs. Watson.

Then the faces are gone from the window, and Helen lets out a long, shrill wail.

Fido steps out into the rain, to take Helen by the wet sleeves and pull her back into the cab. "Taviton Street," she calls to the driver.

~

THE SOLICITOR'S NAME IS FEW, "But my clients are many," he mentions. The ladies stare at him. "Just a little joke," he says regretfully. Another pause. He smoothes down his chalk-white hair. "Now, to the purpose, Mrs. Codrington. The admiral will of course be liable for an allowance to maintain you until the trial—and for my fees, should you win."

Helen holds up her hand. "Let's not get ahead of ourselves, Mr. Few," she says with a self-possession that staggers Fido. "It's been two days now since my husband walked out; his temper must have cooled. Why don't you propose to this Mr. Bird that the two of you draw up a deed of private separation? I could live very quietly and economically with the girls, or even on my own, so long as I was allowed to see a good deal of them."

The elderly solicitor blinks at her.

Live quietly and economically with me at Taviton Street, says Fido loudly in her head. She's glimpsing new possibilities: *We could both be mothers to Nell and Nan.*

"I'm afraid it's too late for any such measure," says Few, shaking his head as if marvelling at female ignorance. "The admiral wants a divorce not simply *à mensâ et thoro*, that is, a separation from bed and board, but *à vinculo matrimonii*, from the bond of wedlock itself. Had he simply wanted to reside apart from you, he'd hardly have filed a petition yesterday stating that he believes you *guilty of misconduct with—*" he puts on his glasses to read it "*—one Colonel David Anderson.*"

Helen's cheeks are pink. Fido wonders suddenly: is she imagining herself and Anderson as Lancelot and Guinevere, accused before the world? But such cases aren't decided by single combat in these civilized times. It's not the man's prowess that will save the lady or fail to, but the facts, the arguments, the oiled machine of the law. *So Harry's filed his petition already*, thinks Fido with dread. What does that mean? She wishes she knew more of the law. Does Few mean that it's too late for Helen to make a full confession of adultery and come to some arrangement with Harry as to her future?

"*That in Malta Anderson frequently and habitually did visit her and commit the act in question with her during the years 1862, 1863, and 1864,*" Few recites, eyes on the page. "*Also that in Malta, one Lieutenant Herbert Alexander St. John Mildmay frequently and habitually did visit her and commit the act in question with her during the years 1860, 1861, and 1862.*"

Fido sits bolt upright. Who on earth is this Lieutenant Mildmay?

Helen doesn't meet her eyes. Fido answers her own question. So the golden colonel wasn't the first man to whom Helen succumbed, then. *Later: I'll get the whole story from her later.* Fido feels sick to her stomach, and looks at the floor.

"Unlike Mildmay," Few remarks, "Anderson is a named co-respondent to the petition, and as such the admiral's entitled to ask damages of him, though so far he's not done so. Anderson's solicitor tells me his client is presently in Scotland, and that the intended plea is not guilty."

"As is mine," says Helen hastily. "That—" she gestures at the statement of charges as if at a brimming sewer, "that can all be demolished."

"I'm relieved to hear it." The old solicitor's tone is so habitually dry, Fido can't tell if he's being sardonic. He looks back at his client.

"Mr. Few—I'm in a dreadful state today."

"I understand, and I hate to press a lady. But some hints, some beginnings—"

Helen stares out the window as if for inspiration, then takes a long breath. "Things are so very different beyond these shores! I was raised in India, you see. And in Florence, where I spent the last years of girlhood, it's quite acceptable for a married lady to have an acknowledged escort, don't you know: a *cicisbeo.*"

She's fudging a point, Fido wants to say: quite acceptable for the *signore,* yes; not for the Anglo ladies.

"Lax but harmless foreign mores," murmurs Few, writing it down.

"I admit I've been foolish," says Helen with an infectious smile, "rather frivolous in my pastimes, unwise in some of my friendships. I shouldn't have allowed either Mildmay or Anderson so much of my company if I'd imagined that it would provoke malicious tongues."

Fido finds herself almost admiring the sheer gall of her friend. Perhaps Helen should have been a woman of business; she has powers that Fido's never noticed before.

"Admits to lacking the decorum of a British wife," says Few under his breath. "No hard evidence, then?" He looks over his glasses.

Helen hesitates. "What exactly—"

"For instance," says Few, "statements by servants, friends, letters of yours, or received by you, letters of others referring to you, entries in this appointment book your husband took from your desk, testimony by cabmen . . ."

Helen is sinking back in the leather chair.

And Fido melts into compassion, again, the way a wave at its height collapses into froth. "Helen, would you care for a glass of water? Mr. Few, perhaps—"

He pours each of the ladies a glass, from a decanter on his sideboard. "Mrs. Codrington," he asks, "I wonder would you like to reconsider your plea?"

"My thoughts exactly," says Fido firmly.

Helen's eyes look bruised. Instead of answering, she begins, "My girls—"

The solicitor nods, his face creased with sympathy. "Don't let that be a consideration. I very much fear that, in any case, they won't be coming home."

Helen's salt-blue eyes bulge.

"As long as a paternal parent has not been proved insane," Few explains, "sole guardianship lies with him."

Helen burst out. "There must be exceptions."

"Some," he says dubiously. "Any mother, even if proved adulterous, may petition for access or custody of offspring up to the age of sixteen . . . but in practice, the court won't give children above age seven to a mother unless her reputation is unblemished, *and* the father's brutal, drunken, ah, diseased—you take my meaning," he says awkwardly. "Oh, and the poet Shelley, of course, he lost his children for atheism."

"The law's a blockhead," says Fido between her teeth.

He gives her an owlish look. "Whenever the point's come up for discussion in Parliament, Miss Faithfull, there's a lot of sanctimonious talk about the hallowed rights of fatherhood—but many of us suspect that the real reason's a more pragmatic one. If women could shed their husbands without risk of losing their children too, it's feared that an alarming proportion of them would do so!"

Still not a word from Helen: her face is a blank page.

Fido speaks up. "Say for the sake of argument that my friend were to alter her plea to guilty, Mr. Few—might it simplify things, speed them along?"

The solicitor holds up one skeletal finger. "Ah, there's an interesting novelty in the 1857 Act: a wife may admit the charges, but then countercharge. If we could prove that the admiral was in any way culpable in the adultery, he'd have to settle for a separation, and pay her full maintenance."

Fido frowns. "But if you failed to implicate Admiral Codrington, Mr. Few, and my friend had already confessed—"

"You've an acute mind, Miss Faithfull," says Few in that patronizing tone she's often heard from men with whom she's had dealings. "There's a little twist I propose to use: Mrs. Codrington could deny all the acts—to cover her back, as it were—but add that *if they did occur*, her husband was to blame."

Helen yelps with laughter, then covers her mouth. "Excuse me. Isn't that an absurdity?"

"Perhaps in logic, but not in law."

Fido rubs her eyes. *What is this looking-glass world into which we've stepped?*

"So, Mrs. Codrington, of what could you accuse your husband? The easiest is mutual guilt," Few points out dryly. "Have you reason to believe that the admiral has, like so many husbands, especially military ones, alas . . ."

"No," she says with audible reluctance.

"Maids, letters from ladies, that sort of thing?"

Helen shakes her head.

"In that case, what we're looking for are the seas."

Fido stares at him.

"The Five C's, we call them," the old man explains. "Did the admiral *conduce* to misconduct by leaving you lonely and unprotected? Did he *condone* it by tacit forgiveness?"

"Definitely conducement," says Helen crisply before he can go on, "and quite possibly condonement."

"Condonation," Fido corrects her automatically, head spinning.

"So you believe he knew all along, Mrs. Codrington?"

Helen hesitates, pouts elegantly. "He must have done."

But Helen's always assured Fido that Harry hasn't had the least suspicion. Now, it seems, she's picking up every hint the solicitor drops, and telling him exactly what he wants to hear.

Few only nods. "And the more evidence against you his counsel may dig up, the more our side will make the case that any husband of reasonable intelligence must have understood the situation. Did he *connive* with you or Anderson or Mildmay by turning a blind eye?" he asks. "Or even *collude* in the hopes of obtaining an easy divorce?"

Helen's mouth twists.

Fido finds all this sickening. "What's the fifth C?" she snaps, to get it over with.

"Cruelty," says the solicitor.

"How's that defined?" asks Helen.

"Not as broadly here as across the Atlantic—the Americans count anything that makes a wife unhappy," says Few with one of his flashes of wintry wit. "But Judge Wilde generally extends it to include any behaviour that causes the lady illness."

"Mrs. Codrington enjoys very good health," says Fido meanly.

~

IN THE CAB, FIDO'S ANGER struggles with her mercy, and by the time they're on the dusty outskirts of Euston, anger has the upper hand. She clears her throat. "May I ask, who is Lieutenant Mildmay?"

Helen's slumped in the far corner.

"Another *friend of the family's*?"

Helen says, barely audible, "If you like."

"I don't." Fido rubs at a scrape on the back of her hand. "I don't like any of this. It seems to me we've left the truth far behind, and we're adrift in open seas."

"I dare say you're in a huff because I didn't mention Mildmay before."

"A *huff*?" Fido's voice rises to a shriek.

The small trapdoor in the roof opens with a thud. "All right in there, ladies?"

"Perfectly," she barks.

A second passes. "Very good," says the driver, shutting the hatch.

Fido's got her voice under control. "What, may I ask, is the point of play-acting at friendship?" She waits. "I urge you to lean on me, I offer you my—all I have, all I am—and in return you keep shutting me out with your fibs and frauds!"

"Oh, Fido," says Helen exhaustedly, "you make it sound so simple."

"Isn't it? Open yourself to me, I say; tell me everything, so I can help you."

Helen's face, when she lifts it, is like a caved-in cliff. "There are limits to your love, like everyone else's."

"You wrong me," says Fido furiously.

"When I glimpsed you on Farringdon Street, last month—what ought I to have said?" Helen's eyes are huge. "That, since the last time we met, unhappiness had changed me in ways that would appall you? That not one, but two successive men had managed to dupe me into trusting them with my heart and drag me into the dirt?"

Fido struggles for words.

"Your life is such a clean, upright thing. You know nothing of getting into disastrous messes." Helen rests her forehead on one fist. "If I'd told you all that, on Farringdon Street—how could you have resisted casting the first stone?"

Fido is blinded so fast she thinks something has struck her, but it's only tears. "Helen!" She moves to the other side of the vehicle and takes Helen by the shoulders. "I don't mean to pontificate, or play the prude. I want nothing more than to stand by your side, and support you through this terrible passage in your life. To lead you to the other side as fast as possible," she adds, "which is why I wanted you to plead guilty."

Helen's nostrils flare.

"Why not drop all this legalistic feinting, simply admit your mistakes, and beg Harry on your knees to let you see something of the girls?"

"Wasn't it you who told me the law belongs to men?" Helen demands. "What about the double standard? A man's reputation can survive a string of mistresses, but if I admit to one intrigue, let alone two, I'll lose everything. My name, my children, every penny of income . . ."

"Share mine." That comes out very hoarse. She tries again. "As long as I have a home, so do you."

"Oh, Fido." Helen subsides: shuts her eyes, rests her head on Fido's shoulder as simply as a child.

Fido can feel Helen's hot breath against her throat. "Sh," she says, putting one hand up to the vivid hair. They ride in silence, right to Taviton Street.

~

THE NEXT DAY, FRIDAY, FIDO GOES STRAIGHT FROM THE PRESS to meet Helen at Few's chambers for another gruelling session. The solicitor keeps harping on his Five C's.

"Harry wouldn't bring me to parties," offers Helen, "could that count as cruelty?"

Fido has to repress a smile at the idea.

The solicitor pulls at his grey whiskers. "Ah—neglect, perhaps."

"Or if he did come, he'd stand around in a sulk, and go home early on the pretext of having papers to read—abandoning me to whatever escort I could muster," Helen goes on. "Sometimes he wouldn't speak to me for days at a time—thwarted my management of the girls, and the house—confiscated my keys once."

Fido recognizes that as a story from the old days, at Eccleston Square; to the best of her recollection, what actually happened was that Helen hurled the whole bunch of keys at her husband's feet. This rewriting of the past leaves a bad taste in Fido's mouth. But the law is unjust to women, she reminds herself. Helen's a reluctant player, after all, in a game in which the odds are stacked against her.

"Oh, and of course the detestable Mrs. Watson, in Malta," says Helen, brightening. "He cruelly neglected me for her."

Few prompts her. "You suspected—"

"Nothing of that sort; I believe the aged reverend was always in the room, though perhaps not always fully conscious," quips Helen. "But Harry certainly let himself be turned against me; she poured all manner of poison in his ear."

"Hm, possible alienation of affections," mutters Few, scribbling. "Now, Mrs. Codrington—as to nocturnal arrangements, if I may?"

She looks at him blankly, then at Fido.

"Has your husband ever been, shall we say, inconsiderate?" asks the solicitor with a fatherly expression. "While you were in a delicate condition, perhaps? Or even . . . I hate to ask, but juries look very sympathetically on wives who've been subjected to anything, ah, degrading. In military circles, it's not entirely unknown—"

Fido can't stand much more of this; she interrupts him huskily. "The Codringtons have kept separate rooms for many years. Before leaving for Malta, in fact."

A pause. Surely Helen's not going to deny this? Then she nods.

"At the admiral's behest?" Few asks.

"Well, mine, originally," concedes Helen. "But on various occasions I've done my best to be reconciled to him."

That's the first Fido's heard of it.

"Once after a party I went into his room, and he grabbed my arm and thrust me out!"

This story rings true, somehow; Fido can just imagine Helen, tipsy and giggling, tiptoeing into her husband's austere bedroom.

"Excellent," murmurs Few, "refusal of marital rights, coupled with a degree of violence. So it's the admiral's fault, then, that you haven't been blessed with any more children?"

Helen examines her smooth fingernails. "Harry certainly feels no sorrow on the subject," she says, instead of answering the question. "I've heard him joking to friends that two is an ample sufficiency. But the feelings of a woman, and a mother . . ." She lets the sentence trail away.

Fido is longing for this interview to be over.

"Mr. Few," Helen asks suddenly, "what if a husband, simply to exercise his tyranny, casts his wife's dearest friend out of the house?"

His eyes swivel to Fido, whose cheeks are scalding. "This is many, many years ago," Fido murmurs to the solicitor. "I was more or less residing with the family here in London from '54 to '57, at which point . . ."

"That last summer," says Helen with a shudder.

"There was a crisis—between the spouses," says Fido, too loudly, her voice reverberating in the narrow chambers, "and the upshot was that Ha—the admiral suggested I leave. The reason he gave was one I considered perfectly proper: that no third party ought to be obliged to witness such scenes." She adds this stonily, not looking at Helen. She won't be a party to this fantasy of Harry as some vicious, arbitrary Nero.

"Promising," murmurs Few over his notes.

Helen leans towards her. "Fido dear," she objects in a whisper, "how can you report it with such Christian mildness when he—while you were living under our very roof—" she pauses, staring at her.

Fido raises her eyebrows.

"Mr. Few, perhaps that's enough for today?" Helen asks abruptly.

The old man blinks. "Certainly, Mrs. Codrington, I do apologize for tiring you." He rings for their wraps.

There's a branch of the Aerated Bread Company just across the street. "I was quite desperate for some tiffin," remarks Helen, leaning over the little table towards Fido. "I do like these new tea shops; however did we manage in the days when there was nowhere ladies could go for a bite to eat without a breach of etiquette?" She stirs another lump of sugar into her cup. "Have you ever lunched at Verey's in the Strand?"

Fido shakes her head. She feels as limp as if the meeting in the law chambers lasted a week.

"Have an iced fancy."

She ignores the plate. This woman bewilders her. One moment howling like a banshee at being separated from her babies, the next, nibbling cakes.

Helen is fallen: that odd word always makes Fido think of a wormy apple. But where are the hollow eyes, creeping walk, feverish delirium of fallen women in novels? (The women that other women such as Fido, in their strength and wisdom and passionate sisterhood, are described as bending down to lift from the gutter.) Clearly adultery need not be a fatal condition. Helen sits here as pertly elegant as ever, sipping her tea.

"You talked a lot of balderdash in there," Fido remarks. "The idea of Harry cruelly thwarting your longing to have more children!"

She purses her lips. "He's said far worse about me."

Well, there's no denying that. "And what was all that mysteriousness about his treatment of me?"

Helen's fork freezes, mid-air. Her eyes have a guarded expression. "Never mind," she says after a moment.

"But—"

"I'm sorry I brought it up, in Few's office. We needn't speak of it if you'd rather not." She makes a show of going on with her cake.

"I'm perfectly willing," says Fido in exasperation.

"Really? You've never spoken of it in all these years. I've had the impression you hid it away in the deepest folds of your memory."

Fido stares at her. "We seem to be talking at cross purposes, now. What *it* have I hidden away?"

"Dearest, let's drop the subject," says Helen, pushing away her plate so suddenly the fork clatters. "Trust me, I wouldn't dream of using it to strengthen my case."

Fido's pulse starts to hammer.

"I only—in there, in the law chambers," says Helen with shiny eyes, "I couldn't quite believe I heard you defending my husband as *perfectly proper*! It breaks my heart to think that you—so independent, so undaunted—that you're the kind of woman who'd blame herself for such an incident."

Fido swallows hard. "My dear," she says, very low, putting her hand over Helen's on the tablecloth, "let's be quite clear: of what incident are we speaking?"

"*The* incident. The unspeakable one."

A hard pebble in Fido's throat, spots before her eyes. The tea shop seems too full, all at once, though there is only a scattering of customers. "Something involving Harry?"

The blue eyes widen. "You aren't going to claim you don't remember *anything*?"

"Tell me exactly what you mean," she snaps.

"Wouldn't you rather wait until we can be private?" Seeing Fido's face, she rushes on. "Very well. If you really can't recall it . . . cast your mind back to the autumn before Harry evicted you."

Fido bridles at the word.

"I'm talking about the night you woke up beside me, and he was there."

"Harry, you mean?" Fido frowns in concentration. "I know he used to come into my bedroom sometimes. On occasions when you were sharing it," she adds.

"That's right, and you didn't like it at all. But that particular night . . ."

"I woke up and saw a white figure, at the door," she says, nodding, and Helen clasps her hands. "I remember you told me afterwards it was Harry in his nightshirt."

"Of course it was him; who else?"

"That's all I saw: a white figure. I'd had bad asthma, I'd taken my medicine."

"That explains it," cries Helen under her breath. "You were in a stupor from the laudanum."

"That explains *what?*"

"Why you've forgotten."

Fido strains. A spectral figure, in the doorway: it's a troubling memory, somehow, like a scene of obscure distress from childhood. "I woke up rather agitated."

"I should say you were!"

"I suppose he'd come into my room to ask you something, and found us both asleep?"

Helen taps her fingernails on the edge of the table, and whispers something.

"I beg your pardon?"

Words in her ear, hot breath that makes her jump: "He got in."

"No," says Fido flatly.

"In between us. He clambered over me," Helen whispers.

"I can't believe that."

"Oh, my dear," wails Helen, "I witnessed the whole thing; it's burned on my mind. But if I'd realized how utterly you've managed to erase it from yours, I wouldn't have said a word today. Sometimes it's better to forget."

Fido's chest is tight; her throat makes a high creaking sound. "He climbed into the bed, you say." Very low. "Is there . . . worse?"

Helen's face is contorted.

A pair of ladies at the next table is looking at them with frank curiosity. "You may as well lift the veil, now," says Fido.

"Oh, but—"

"Go on."

A rapid whisper: "You were dead to the world. I tried to thrust him out, but I hadn't the force; I think he was the worse for drink. He made a joke about it being a cold bed with two women alone in it. And something coarse about the fire needing poking. He grabbed your nightgown and—"

Fido puts a finger against Helen's lips, quite hard. "No."

"It didn't happen," Helen hisses, "I mean, not the final outrage. He only tried—clumsily attempted—you cried out in pain, and then woke up."

She's dizzy with shock. She tugs at her velvet choker, to stretch it slightly. Harry Codrington, rummaging in her nightdress while she lay comatose? No man's ever laid hands on her before. The very thought—

"When you began to struggle, he lost his nerve—thank heavens—kicked his way out of the bedclothes, and fled from the room."

Fido can see the new version, now, like a ghostly image overlaying the old memory. She's so shaken she can hardly speak. "What kind of animal—to try to, to *violate*, his guest, his wife's—friend."

"One of the family," says Helen in a half-sob.

"But why ever—what possible motive—" Fido presses her knuckles against her lips, very hard. "I'm not the kind of woman that men find irresistibly attractive," she makes herself remark in a tone that would almost pass for humour.

"It was my fault; that's the conclusion I've come to after brooding over it, all these years. I'd maddened him by refusing him his rights for so long," says Helen. "He was drunk, and furious with you for taking my side, I suppose, for being my only succour. I believe it was meant as a punishment of the pair of us. Oh Fido, I'm so very sorry."

Their hands knot like rope on the white tablecloth. All Fido can do is shake her head.

"The truth is, that's why I didn't dare contact you again, from Malta," Helen admitted. "When you didn't write back, I thought you must have cut me off. What kind of a friend had I been, after all? I'd offered you a home, and brought down horror on your head."

"Don't say that." The silence stretches out like a dark pool. "It's you who must forgive me," says Fido hoarsely. "I haven't understood the nature of the beast, not till this moment. What you've had to bear, for so long!"

Helen smiles unevenly; puts Fido's hand to her hot cheek.

Fido makes herself say it: "I shall tell Mr. Few at once."

Her friend jerks upright. "Impossible."

"It's my duty."

"But to stand up in open court, and recount such a narrative—I'd never ask that of you, dearest."

Fido hasn't thought that far ahead; she shrinks at the prospect. "Oh, I didn't mean—I couldn't go into the witness box." Her head's in a sickening whirl. "If only there were a way . . ."

Helen shakes her head vehemently. "I couldn't put you through that, not though my whole future were to depend on it."

"I wonder—" Fido hesitates. "Few needs to know what he's dealing with; what kind of monster you married. Perhaps the information could be useful, somehow."

"But what—"

"Oh, how little I know of the law," Fido frets. "What if Few—if he were to warn his opposite number, your husband's solicitor—"

"Mr. Bird," Helen supplies.

"If he told Bird that he has knowledge of an attempted rape." Her voice drops; she barely mouths the word. "Surely, if Bird passed this on to his client—Harry would quail at the possibility of the story getting out? He'd realize that although we are women," she goes on, her voice strengthening, "we're ready to put a name to evil, when our backs are to the wall."

"Yes," marvels Helen, "yes. It could work. He'll be shamed into dropping this wretched petition," she goes on, "and he might even send the girls home!"

Fido doubts that very much, but she can't bear to be the one to strip Helen's illusions away: time will do it for her.

~

They lie as tight as spoons, that night, in Fido's hard bed, and talk in whispers till very late. "It's not too early to begin to consider your future," says Fido.

"My future?"

"If worse comes to worst."

"I thought . . . you said I could stay here," says Helen like a frightened child.

"Of course you can!" Fido squeezes her, plants a kiss on the back of Helen's hair. "No matter what happens, we'll be together." She waits a moment; Helen doesn't contradict her. "But it'll be a rather different sphere of life," she goes on. No grand rooms to stuff with trinkets, she wants to say; no girls to prepare for presentation at court. But she doesn't spell out any of that, not yet. "Time might hang heavy on your hands at first, without an occupation." Especially as Fido's always hard at work, from six in the morning—but she doesn't say that either. It strikes her, for the first time, that Helen might require constant companionship, at home or out shopping; might raise objections to Fido's commitment to the Cause. The thought gives her a kind of vertigo. *Don't borrow trouble*, she tells herself; *haven't we more than enough on our plates?* She hurries on: "You do have one real asset, Helen: a fine grasp of the English language."

A little giggle, in the dark. "I hope you don't propose I'm to take on Miss Braddon?"

"No no, not writing for publication, but correcting for it, perhaps. For some time now, as it happens," says Fido with a kind of shyness, "I've been looking out for an educated lady, to check proofs at the press."

No answer.

"You could do the work at home, if you preferred—"

"Don't be silly, Fido."

She opens her mouth, and shuts it again.

"I'm not that kind of woman."

Fido stiffens. "You know, for a lady to find respectable employment doesn't lower her to the rank of a fishwife; in fact, it raises her to that of her father or brothers."

"It's a matter of temperament, that's all. The leopard can't change her spots," says Helen, laughing.

"I dare say that's true," says Fido, loosening. *What an odd couple we'll make*, it occurs to her. The divorcee and the spinster. The adulteress and the woman's rights-ist. The leopardess and the . . . house cat?

"I'd better let you sleep," says Helen.

Fido snorts. "No chance of that. Every time I think of speaking to Few tomorrow, my stomach bucks like a mule."

"Oh my dear. If only I could take this cup from your lips!"

"No," says Fido, "the truth must out. It's only an absurd sort of squeamishness, on my part; the thought of telling such a story to a man, a virtual stranger."

Helen holds her closer, puts her feet against Fido's cold ones. "I wonder—"

"Yes?"

"Would it help at all if I were to go in first, and give Few the gist of it?"

"Would you really?" Relief floods her veins.

"It's the least I can do. Besides, I'm a married woman," says Helen. "Such language comes rather easier to us."

"Yes, then, yes: it would be so much easier, if you prepared the ground."

"But you have to promise to sleep a little, now," says Helen in motherly tones, "or you'll be in no fit state for anything."

"I promise," says Fido, shutting her eyes, letting out a long breath.

~

TAKING FIDO'S KASHMIR SHAWL, the aged solicitor clears his throat in a melancholy way. "The Codringtons' is a very sad case," he observes. "Well, as the Bard put it, marriage has many pains but celibacy has no pleasures."

"I believe that was Dr. Johnson."

"Was it? Ah, well, you're the woman of letters, Miss Faithfull."

Silence, broken only by the creaking of her lungs.

"I can't say I was entirely surprised by what Mrs. Codrington told me this morning," says Few, eyes on his desk. "I suspected she was hiding something, yesterday, when she spoke of her husband. These military men—whited sepulchres, more often than not—"

Fido traces the seam of her glove.

"I needn't take up much of your time this morning; I already have a statement of the facts from Mrs. Codrington. This is really a formality, Miss Faithfull—and believe me, I wish I didn't have to offend your modesty in the least degree—"

"Whatever's necessary to help my friend."

"Your loyalty does you credit. And it will indeed be immensely helpful. Perhaps the strongest weapon in our arsenal." Few glances down at the topmost paper of his stack and clears his throat. "One night in the autumn of 1856, then, you were occupying the same room and in the same bed as Mrs. Codrington in Eccleston Square, both being asleep, when the petitioner came in—that's the admiral—"

"He was only a captain at the time," Fido says.

"Never mind that."

And in fact Helen was awake. Fido doesn't suppose that matters either, though it's odd that he formed the impression they were both asleep. Perhaps he assumed it, since it was night? Or perhaps Helen thought it would simplify the story to leave herself out, since she's not permitted to testify; after all, she played no part in events that night, or none that made any real difference.

Few goes on, eyes on the page. "He got in between the two of you, and attempted to behave improperly to you, Miss Faithfull—to treat you, ah, as if you were his wife—but your resistance frightened him and he rushed away. Correct?"

She wheezes; she turns towards the window, but it's shut tight against the late September damp. It's only the difference between her having woken during the attack and her having woken just after it ended: a matter of seconds. When one's taken laudanum, the border between those states of consciousness is never clear. But she doesn't want to sound like an unreliable witness; that would be of no use to Helen's case. Need she mention the laudanum at all, if it would only undermine her account?

"Are you feeling quite well, Miss Faithfull?"

"Habitual asthma," she whispers. "If we could possibly complete this interview at another time—" She's longing for a cigarette. A little time to puzzle this out. On that night—almost eight years ago now—did she half-wake, fight Harry off in her dulled state, and manage to blot the whole thing out of her mind afterwards? Can one be said to have had an experience, if one has only the most fragmentary, uneasy recollection of it?

"I'm afraid it must be done today, as tomorrow is Sunday."

If she tries hard enough, she can almost summon up the scene, feel the bed shudder as Harry clambers in between the women; almost see his gigantic silhouette blotting out the candlelight.

"No need to speak, if you'd prefer: simply nod," adds Few after a second. "Was it as Mrs. Codrington told me?"

He seems to understand. There's no objective way to tell a story. But this is the terrible truth of that night, as best as she and Helen can muster it between them. A sort of joint testimony. Helen could witness to it herself were it not for the absurdity of the law that gags the participants in a divorce. Fido makes herself nod.

"Very good. I regret, again, that this is necessary. I can hardly imagine your distress."

At twenty-one, on that autumn night, is that what he means? Or at twenty-nine, sitting in his chambers?

"Now if you'll be so good as to look over the affidavit, I'll sign it." Few slides the crisp page across the desk.

But Fido has broken out in a sweat, her eyes are swimming. *The affidavit*: that sounds alarmingly official. She's not sure she can bear to see this story written down in black ink on the long, tombstone shape of a legal document.

"Would you prefer me to read it to you in full?"

"Oh no." That would be worse. Fido glances through the paragraphs, but they make no sense to her. Her eyes catch on jagged phrases: *separate but adjoining, in a nightdress, attempted to have connection, resistance of the said Miss Faithfull.*

"I wonder, have you any sense of the date of the incident?"

Fido shuts her eyes. She can barely think of her own name. "I really don't . . . October. Around the eleventh?" she hazards, just to put an end to it.

"Very good." Few takes the paper back and scratches a few words in.

He walks her to the door and uses a cab whistle to call a growler to take her home.

VIII

Mutatis Mutandis

(Latin, "the necessary changes having been made"; in law, this refers to the application of an implied, mutually understood set of changes)

What should we think of a community of slaves, who betrayed each other's interest? Of a little band of shipwrecked mariners upon a friendless shore, who were false to each other?

Sarah Ellis,
The Daughters of England (1845)

In Few's chambers on Monday morning, Helen sits fiddling with the coral-beaded fringe of her bag.

The solicitor shuffles his papers and looks up over his tiny glasses. "I must observe that for a woman of business—that's what they call themselves, I believe?—your friend's not very businesslike."

Helen stares at him.

"First thing this morning I received a rather absurd note from Miss Faithfull at her press, asking for the affidavit to be returned to her for burning as soon as I've shown it to your husband's solicitor. How can she have thought that was its purpose?"

"Perhaps she took you up wrongly," Helen mutters, her mind scurrying.

"As if detailed evidence were to be handed over to the opposition in advance of the trial!"

"I suppose . . . I have the impression she hoped Harry would withdraw his petition if he were warned of such a damaging countercharge. He must have been trusting to feminine timidity to prevent Fido and myself from mentioning the attack," Helen argues.

Few frowns. "After fifteen years of wedlock, Mrs. Codrington, you ought to have known the masculine mind better. To be charged with a crime of virility—if I may put it so bluntly—is something many men take in their stride."

"Not Harry, the pillar of virtue," she says, sullen.

"Well, whatever his private mortification at being accused of such an attempt, it can hardly match your friend's at being its victim. And judging by today's note, she doesn't seem to have grasped that she'll have to attest to it in court." He takes off his glasses, scowls as he swabs them on his neckerchief. "It is just a matter of maidenly modesty, I hope?"

"How do you mean? My friend is modest, certainly."

"Well, I don't like to doubt a lady's word, but . . . I don't suppose her reluctance to repeat her story means that there's something less than reliable about it?"

Helen draws herself up. "She's the daughter of the rector of Headley, and a noted philanthropist. If you knew her as I do, you'd never suggest such a thing."

"No offence intended." Few scowls at the rolls of documents covering his desk. "Well, I wrote back to Miss Faithfull at once to clarify that she'll be called into court; the affidavit will be worse than useless unless she backs it up."

"I'm sure I can persuade her to muster her courage," says Helen. Her mind goes through its calculations. No doubt Fido will huff and puff and make a scene, but when it comes to it—when she sees that Helen needs her to be brave, that it's a matter of friendship (Fido's sacred cow) . . .

"Certainly you have some time. The court is overbooked, as ever," he remarks. "The Dickenses have renewed their endless squabble about his non-payment of maintenance."

Helen is diverted by this piece of gossip. "And to think what his books and magazines must make him!"

"No no, this is the bankrupt brother, Frederick. All three brothers left their wives in '57, a curious coincidence—or sign of the times, one might say." Few is searching through the pile of papers again; his white straggling hair almost touches it.

Helen finds herself wondering how old he is, and the odds of his dropping dead while her case is still in preparation.

"Lieutenant Mildmay," he says, meeting her eyes, and she can't stop herself twitching at the name. "Petitioner's counsel have applied to make him another co-respondent, which of course would seal his mouth like yours and Anderson's, and prevent us from calling him in your defence."

"That's outrageous," she says, as it seems expected.

"We'll oppose that application—unless of course you've any reason to fear the lieutenant's evidence might tell against you?"

Helen's mind races. "I'm sure he'll deny any wrongdoing."

"We'll have our man in India examine him, then, and bring back a deposition."

India? She didn't know Mildmay was stationed there. Disconcerted, she pictures him in a bright sash, riding on a howdah, like the dashing officers she used to wave at when she was a little girl in Calcutta. They haven't corresponded since he left Malta. (Helen finds writing to faraway friends a chore.) But there was never any falling out, only a mild falling away. Gradually it came about that she saw more of Anderson and rather less of Mildmay; neither man was ever so crass as to press her about her choice.

Few goes on. "I must ask—have you seen the *Times* this morning?"

"I've had no leisure for reading the paper," says Helen. The truth is that she can't bear the prospect of seeing her surname leaping in capitals all over the Legal Notices column. *Codrington*: she's never liked the stuffy, provincial ring of it, but she dreads the prospect of losing it too.

"There's an article. You may wish to—at your leisure." He slides a copy of the paper across the desk, and she accepts it, but doesn't unfold it. "Vis-à-vis Colonel Anderson. On page nine there's a notice of his marriage," says Few, frowning. "Perhaps the colonel feels that taking this step at the eleventh hour dissociates him from the charges—as if any jury would be so credulous."

"A . . . a notice that it's forthcoming?" she says, hating the way her voice shakes.

"Rather, an announcement that it's taken place." Few waits. "I felt I ought to draw your attention to it; it's best to face these things."

Her voice cracks. "You're not paid to lecture me, Few. I'm already *facing* the loss of my whole world."

He nods, priestly. "You have my sympathies."

Helen snatches her coral-fringed bag and gets to her feet. "I don't want your sympathies, or your homilies. I want your professional expertise. Block this damned divorce and get my daughters back."

She expected her language to stun the old man, but he only shakes his head. "I really must impress upon you that the two aims are mutually inconsistent.

My hope is to win you a separation with a comfortable settlement—but as to your daughters . . ."

She watches a dying fly stumble along the window sill.

"Are you listening, Mrs. Codrington?"

"I made them, didn't I? In my—in me." Her voice is so guttural she hardly recognizes it.

Few sighs. "Your being permitted to set eyes on them ever again, even from a distance, depends entirely on the admiral's goodwill. And the fact is, every day you resist this divorce—not to mention accusing him of cruelties and depravities—you sacrifice more of that goodwill."

She staggers towards the door.

"My dear madam—"

Outside on the street, Helen lurches along like a madwoman. *Nell*, she says in her head, *Nan*, trying to conjure them up. But their tiny, warped images stay locked up in the bottle. It's only been six days, but their faces are blurring already. What was the last thing they said to her? Or she to them? Some snapped criticism, no doubt. She clings to the thought of Nan asking her for a kiss, that night in the sickroom. The final game of Happy Families.

There's something awry in Helen. She's coming to see that she was born with something missing. She has talents, she even has virtues, but something's lacking that would bind them all together.

She shudders, she sobs. *I'll never see my girls again.* Still gripping the rolled newspaper like a club, she drops to her knees on the chilly pavement, retching. *They'll never see their Mama again.* Shiny bile runs from her lips to the stone like spider's silk.

~

Codrington v. Codrington & Anderson

Among the many elevating qualities that have made marriage the central institution of modern (as of ancient) society, it is a marvellous instrument of education. By yoking one woman to one man, it imparts strength to the weaker, softness and moral beauty to the stronger. The blessed companionship of two complementary natures, whose most

potent bond lies in the very fact of their difference, enlarges the social sympathies and quickens the spiritual instincts of both.

It is a fact to be lamented, then, and not merely by the individuals involved, when a marriage is dissolved—and generally the less said about it the better. When the Matrimonial Causes Act opened the floodgates in 1857, the Divorce Court's first President, Sir Cresswell Cresswell, expressed the hope that the attendant publicity would be on the whole beneficial; that a calm consideration of marital strife and the disgrace which must attach to it would have a deterrent effect. But since then, many commentators have argued that the Court's influence is rather corrupting than otherwise. Unhappy couples are known to attend sessions of this "School for Divorce" to learn the sordid tricks necessary to throw off a burdensome yoke. The public now turns to the Law Reports for a succession of sensational narratives that air details so filthy they put cheeks to blush and make ears ring. Any journal that reports the Court's proceedings at length, then, risks stooping below the level of a French novel.

That being noted—the petition for divorce of Vice-Admiral Henry CODRINGTON, on the grounds of his wife's misconduct with Colonel David ANDERSON, arguably represents an exception to the rule. The Petitioner, son of the late lamented Admiral Edward Codrington, hero of Trafalgar, and younger brother of General William Codrington, Governor of Gibraltar, has won considerable distinction in his own right, most recently as Admiral-Superintendent of the Docklands at Malta, the principal scene of much of the alleged criminality. The Respondent, née Helen Jane Webb SMITH, is the sole progeny of Christopher Webb Smith of Florence, late of the East India Company and author of those modestly invaluable works *Oriental Ornithology* and *The Feathered Life of Hindostan*. As is so shamefully often the case, especially in cases that originate in the lax circles of colonial outposts, the Co-Respondent, Colonel ANDERSON (for whose recent marriage, interested readers should turn to page 9, below) is an officer in Her Majesty's Army.

The Admiral's petition has appended to it a strikingly diverse list of locations in which Mrs. Codrington is accused of having committed the offence in question with either Anderson or another paramour (Lieutenant Herbert Alexander St. John MILDMAY): Admiralty House in Valetta, the Admiralty gondola, Mildmay's lodgings in Valetta, the resort of Cormayeur, the Grosvenor Hotel (London), and, perhaps most intriguingly, the Bloomsbury residence of Miss Emily FAITHFULL, the petticoat philanthropist whose founding of the VICTORIA PRESS has made our readers familiar with her name.

The questions raised when this petition comes to trial will involve the most momentous interests of the parties concerned: the honour of

two gentlemen who have served their Sovereign with honour, and the fair fame of two well nurtured and educated ladies. The Codrington trial, in addition, will, according to our sources at the Bar, offer legal novelty in the form of a particularly shocking counterclaim against her husband by the Respondent, and may be considered a test case of the Matrimonial Causes Act's procedural workings.

If the Divorce Court is a necessary evil, then, on such occasions as these, to report on it seems a necessary evil too. When large questions are involved, or the character of those who have achieved celebrity, the organs of opinion are bound to speak, or the public will be left to form their views without guidance. With these high purposes, then, this newspaper will from the first day of the trial embark on the most minute diurnal reportage of the case of Codrington v. Codrington & Anderson.

~

There's a wet, autumnal quality in the air already. Helen shivers in the growler as it brings her back to Taviton Street, and forces herself to read the article through one more time.

Instead of hot tea and buttered muffins, there's an envelope waiting for her on a silver tray, with Fido's familiar red seal on it.

October 1, 1864

Helen,

I have asked Johnson to give you this in my absence, as I feel unable to speak to you with any self-possession. This morning all peace of mind was robbed from me by two things I read.

The first was the piece in the Times, which named my house as one of the places in which you and A. had your trysts. I can't imagine how your husband's solicitor found this out—by means of a spy, perhaps?—and I'm filled with horror to find myself named in print as some kind of knowing procuress, when the truth is so much more complicated. When I think of my parents catching sight of the family name in the paper this morning, a name on which through untold generations no shadow has been cast—well, you can imagine how I blanch.

The second shock was Mr. Few's note, explaining that the document he signed in my presence, describing the incident of 1856, irrevocably commits me to testify against your husband. In the teashop, I remember, you said that you'd never ask that of me, not even if your whole future were to depend on it; I can still hear you saying those words. I can't bear to think that you have misled me yet again, Helen, after all your assurances. I can only tell myself that in your present state of *distress, you didn't make yourself quite understood to Mr. Few when you were telling him of the incident, and that he must bear some responsibility for having failed to spell out what would follow from committing it to paper in the form of an affidavit. But the fact remains that I find myself faced with the prospect of standing up to describe, in a public courtroom, an obscene and violent attack of which, as you know, I have no clear recollection.*

Shame, then; anger at the confusion and passivity I have displayed over the course of the past month; guilt at the part I have (partly unwittingly) played in the dissolution of a family; terror of the consequences both personal and professional, and of the damage perhaps already done to my most beloved Cause . . . I am wracked with all these feelings. And also, I hardly need say, an overwhelming sympathy for your plight; a wish to stand by you in burning affection to the end, like the knights of old; a longing for something I was just beginning to glimpse, a future together. As I write this, these forces are pulling me a dozen different ways, like wild dogs.

I don't know what to do. Truth is the principle I hold most dear, but I seem to have wandered far from its shining beacon. I owe it to myself, I believe, to take stock before going one more step.

Under the present circumstances you'll understand, I hope, that you can't stay at Taviton Street just now. I live in the public eye, and you (as of this morning) have had notoriety thrust upon you; for us to be known to live under the same roof would do nothing but harm to both. Please believe that through these and all trials I remain

Your friend,
Fido

When Helen looks up from the page, the maid's wearing an insolent expression. Can she have read it? No, the red seal was unbroken.

"I've packed your things, Mrs. Codrington." Holding up a small valise.

Helen ignores that. "Where's your mistress? Is she in her room?"

"Not at home," comes the answer, a beat too late to be persuasive.

Helen heads for the stairs to the second floor.

Johnson scuttles after her. "She's gone out, I tell you." On the landing she puts a reddened hand on Helen's arm.

Helen regards it as if it were a spider. "I'd advise you not to touch me." The hand withdraws. "Fido?" She rattles the knob of the bedroom door. "Open up this minute."

Not a sound from within.

"She's at the press," says the maid belatedly.

"Fido, how can you abandon me so?" cries Helen, mouth to the wood. "Such a cold, analytical note, like something a man would write!" She waits for an answer. "Haven't you anything useful to do, Johnson?" she snarls out of the corner of her mouth, but the maid doesn't move. Helen turns back to the door. "Fido! You accuse me of exposing you to the winds of scandal, but none of it's been my doing. And what about me? I'm losing everything I treasure. I'm stripped bare to those winds."

A listening sort of silence, from behind the door; Helen just knows Fido is in there, blinking at the window or hunched on her bed, making her little irritating wheeze. (If she didn't devote so much morbid attention to her lungs, Helen believes they might work better.)

"You call this friendship?" she demands. "A door slammed in my face? Well, if you twit me with my words, I can do the same: *As long as I have a home, so do you*—that's what you told me, two days ago!" She slams her fist on the smooth oak. Rage fills her like a gas; she parts her lips and hisses. "You're all for truth, are you? You canting hypocrite! You dare to sit in judgement, when for all your starched manner, you're made of the same stuff as me and the rest of our misbegotten sex." Out of the corner of her eye Helen can see the maid; she wonders how much to let out. "Can you look into your own heart, Fido," she demands in a ragged whisper, "into its shrouded crevices, the secrets you've managed to mislay in the darkness, with your trick of *forgetting*—can you do that, and then condemn me?"

A stiff, high voice comes from inside the room. "Johnson, show the lady out at once."

The maid's skinny fingers close around Helen's arm.

~

October 2, 1864

Dear Hew,

I write from Eccleston Square, where I have taken up my solitary residence again in obedience to your insistence that it would sound bad in court if I'd moved to a hotel. I attach the list of particulars you asked for, which runs to some dozen pages. I have tried to be as precise as possible, eschewing what you're pleased to call "feminine vagueness." At the distance of (in some cases) many years I can hardly be expected to recall chapter and verse, especially considering that many of the alleged incidents never took place and that others, though now given a sinister prominence by my husband's counsel, seemed to me too harmless to be committed to memory.

I include also, at your request, my suggestions as to witnesses who may be willing to contradict those of my husband, or speak in more general detraction of his character. NB: To summon my father from Italy would *do no good, as he is old and frail (and, I must add in confidence, rather more a supporter of his distinguished son-in-law than of his own unfortunate daughter).*

I would appreciate it if you could advance me a sum of five pounds on the maintenance that my husband's solicitor has so far failed to furnish.

Yours sincerely,
Helen Codrington

~

October 2, 1864
Eccleston Square

My still dear Fido—or Madre, as I used to be allowed to call you, in happier times. May I begin with a fervent apology for the abuse I heaped upon you at your house yesterday? It was my rage at a harsh world that spoke, not I, your Little One.

From the address above, you'll see that—having not a soul in the world to harbour me, and caring not at all where I lay my splitting head—I've returned to the empty mausoleum. As Mrs. Nichols is dead set against taking on any of the duties of a lady's maid, I'm reduced to doing everything for myself, to the best of my ability. In any other year, at this turn in the season, I would be seeing to the girls' winter clothes—but no, I must not think of them or I will break down entirely. It strikes me that I resemble some female Crusoe, picking through the detritus of my former life.

Your letter implied that you need time to examine your conscience. It's at this address that you'll find me, then, should that conscience incline you to reach out to one who's always been proud to call herself

Your carina,
Helen

~

October 3

From their mother, for the eyes of Miss Nan Codrington and Miss Nell Codrington only.

Nellikins, Nanling, my sweetest and bestest girls, I write to you every day but I've had no reply. I can't believe that you sweet girls would fail to write back to your poor frantic Mama, who though she might sometimes have been a little snappish, will always love you above all else in the world. So I must conclude that the woman in whose house you're presently confined is playing the censor. (And if you've dared to read thus far, Emily Watson, then know this: God will not let such a trespass on the holy soil of motherhood go unpunished.)

I drive past the house of your imprisonment very often in a growler, girls, hoping for a glimpse of you. If you come to the front and look out the window you might see me waving.

I hope you're bearing up valiantly. You must cling to each other like the pair in "Goblin Market" who saved each other from the goblin men. Remember, "there is no friend like a sister."

Does your Papa visit often? Why don't you ask him, very prettily, if he might let you see your Mama for half an hour, at a place of his choosing? Five minutes, even, would be of immeasurable comfort to one who went through so many hours (rather days) of agony to bring you both into the world. Do beg him, letting him see how distressed you both are, but without mentioning that the request came from me.

Don't fear for the future, my precious girlies, Mama will be with you very soon. Close your eyes now and feel me wrapping you up in my arms, squeezing so tight that you squeal!

~

Anderson—

I've torn the scales from my eyes. In refusing to so much as acknowledge *my communications, you show not the slightest compunction. What a poor specimen of manhood you are!*

Sometimes these nights I fear I'm going mad, but perhaps it's the other way round, and only now am I waking from delusion. Evidently you never cared for me; it was all my invention. I was nothing but an object of your carnal whims, to while away the convenient hour.

My curse on you, and on your line. First cousins ought not to marry, it's said; the crop often goes wrong. Perhaps the new Mrs. Anderson will look elsewhere, the first time you're posted away from her. It would seem only fitting if you ended up wearing the horns yourself. I wish you all the pain I can imagine: disgrace, the terror of poverty, the agony of losing children. When misfortune crushes you, perhaps then you will remember

Helen

~

Fido, where are you? Why won't you answer my letter?

Nobody does. My words seem to evaporate from the page. I've become quite insubstantial, a woman of glass. An untouchable, like those creatures we walked past on street corners in Calcutta. (I read today that a cyclone there has killed seventy thousand; it's a measure of my state that I can feel nothing but a numb blankness.) Sanity seems to give way under my feet like a frayed rope.

This will be my last attempt. If ever you loved me —

IX

Counterclaim

(a claim made by a respondent

to offset a petitioner's claim)

The Pope he leads a happy life,
He has no care nor wedded strife . . .
Yet, his is not a family house,
He has no cheery, loving spouse.

Anonymous
"The Pope"

He wakes in his rooms at the Rag Club, his head throbbing like a wound. It reminds him of something. Harry hasn't had too much to drink since he was a very young man, but he still recalls that sensation of his veins being clogged with poison. Not that he took anything last night except half a glass of claret with some arid chops. His brother William tried to drag him off to the Haymarket for *Orpheus in the Underworld*—"take your mind off things for a few hours"—but Harry went to bed instead.

On the bedside table sits a red leather case containing his medals. Apart from clothing, this was all he thought to put in his valise when he left Eccleston Square. Harry opens the case now and examines their worn sheen: the Cross of St. Vladimir, the Legion d'Honneur, the Order of the Redeemer of Greece. And it occurs to him, with a surge of pain in his jaw, that the Allied sovereigns didn't really mean to decorate Midshipman Codrington for his gallantry against the Turks, or for the injuries he suffered at Navarino three days after his nineteenth birthday, but merely as a compliment to Sir Edward. So the most glorious laurels of Harry's career are nothing but his father's leavings.

Perhaps I'll never get another posting.

Enough of that. He snaps the case shut and gets out of bed. In the mirror he considers his beard-shrouded face. Perhaps a trim today, so he won't frighten the girls. *But was alarmed by the resistance of the said Miss Faithfull.* Just one of many phrases from Helen's so-called counterclaim that keep ringing in his head, making him stiff with outrage.

The last eight days have rained down on him like blows from a club. Mrs. Watson's turning up at Eccleston Square, eyes glittering, to present Crocker. The spy's meticulous account of following Helen and *the male party* to the Grosvenor Hotel. The prizing open of Helen's cherry-wood desk; oddly enough, that's the part that still fills Harry with shame to remember, despite all the evidence that spilled from the shattered marquetry: the drafted letter to Anderson, the appointment book. His brief, mortified interview with the girls; their eyes, as stunned as those of rabbits the moment the gun goes off. (*Mama isn't well*, that's the only euphemism that came to mind. *You remember dear Mrs. Watson*, he kept repeating inanely; *you'll be quite comfortable at her house until matters are settled.*) How rapidly he'd packed his case, scuttling out of the house like a cockroach before Helen came home from shopping; he was almost afraid to face the woman who's blighted his life. Then the endless interviews with Bird; the debating of strategy (like some obscure Mediterranean war). Visits to the girls every few days, to play Spillikins or the Ball of Wool. (They've stopped asking whether Mama is better yet.) The shock of reading Helen's counterclaim: neglect, cruelty, *attempted to have connection with the said Miss Faithfull.*

A rap at his door. "Nothing just now, thank you," says Harry.

But it opens anyway and his brother puts his face in. William's salt-and-pepper beard is glossy white now; Harry still isn't used to it. "Aren't you dressed yet?"

"Give me ten minutes." He's grateful, of course, he's immensely grateful to William for dropping his duties in Gibraltar the moment he got the telegram to catch a fast packet and stand shoulder to shoulder with Harry through *this ghastly business,* as William keeps calling it—but he finds his brother's company exhausting all the same.

"Thought we'd take the girls to the zoo, what do you say?"

William has the boundless energy of a tourist. They've already brought Nan and Nell to the Museum of Practical Geology and the East India Company Museum (where the Hindu idols in silver and gold reminded Harry of Helen, somehow) and they heard the thousand-strong choir of the Foundling Hospital.

All Harry manages now is a shrug. Each day must be passed, somehow, until the trial finally comes to court. It's not as if any of his former pursuits have the least appeal: reading, taking notes on innovations in warship design, attending lectures on military hygiene, going for long tramps on Hampstead Heath . . . These days Harry watches busy people with dyspeptic envy. The silliest bride leaving cards all over town has a momentum to her hours for which he'd pay any money.

An hour later, he's staring into the infinitely weary eyes of a lion. He wishes they hadn't come; the zoo is entirely too public a stage, and he's convinced that every second passerby is giving him a look of sharp recognition. *Those poor mites. What could their father be thinking of, dragging himself and his family through the dirt?* Harry can guess these thoughts, because he would have had them himself, a month ago.

"Papa," says Nell, tugging at his sleeve, "I wish you'd bring us to the zoo *every* week."

Something in the child's tone pricks him; the show of happiness, the insistence on what a delightful father he is. Do she and Nan fear that they might lose him too, at a moment's notice, as they have their mother, without so much as a farewell kiss? They haven't asked whether she's dead, it occurs to him now.

"That's slang," Nan corrects her little sister. "It's the Zoological Gardens."

Harry read once—where?—that nymphomania is a congenital trait. These girls seem wholesome in every pore, and yet he watches the pair of coppery heads closely, alert to every vocal echo, every charming turn of the chin that reminds him of their mother.

A chill breeze blows across Regent's Park. William sniffs, makes a face, and suggests moving on to somewhere less odoriferous. Nell is delighted by this new word.

An elephant comes lumbering across the grass towards them, beside its keeper; William buys the girls some bags of buns to feed it. They scream with pleasure as the creature nuzzles their palms with its trunk. It's a bizarre limb, up close, Harry thinks; it has the rude look of a hairy snake.

When he turns his head, he sees his brother regarding him curiously. "D'you suppose you'll miss her, at all, when it's over?" William asks under his breath.

He manages a huff of laughter. "You can still ask that, after all you've learned in Bird's office? The gondola, the pier, the hotels . . ."

"Well, the details were exotic," concedes William.

"The details?" Harry stares at his brother. "You mean to say you'd guessed the main point?"

"What, that the woman's . . . that she doesn't play by the rules?" murmurs William, his eyes on his nieces as they pat the elephant. "It's been known in the family for years, my dear fellow."

This idea staggers Harry. "So my humiliation's been the stuff of sneers and gossip?"

"Steady on. No one's broached the subject; that's not our way. It's just an atmosphere I'm describing, and I could be wrong," says William unconvincingly. "But there's always been something in our sisters' tone, when they use her name."

"You knew it yourself. However did—"

A slight shrug. "Always easier to spot these things from a distance. The way Helen carries herself, perhaps. The way she treats you."

Harry wouldn't have thought it was possible to feel even more of an idiot, but he does. "Why, may I ask, did no one say a word to me?"

"Speaking for myself—I had no facts," says William gruffly, "only a general impression. I dare say I assumed you didn't want to hear it. That you two had come to some sort of terms."

Nan, letting the elephant pluck a bun from her palm, casts an anxious glance over her shoulder at her father, who manages a wave and a rictus of cheer. When she's turned back to the animal, he lets his jaw drop into his hand. The edges the barber shaved two days ago are as rough as limestone. "Is it possible that I knew, without knowing I knew?"

"Now you're splitting hairs, old boy," says William.

"A moment ago," says Harry, puzzling it out—"why did you ask me if I'll miss her?"

An odd little smile. "I fear I might, if I were you."

The governor's wife, social sovereign of Gibraltar, is a plump, serene matron who's never given William a moment's worry. Harry speaks bleakly. "The best of Helen—her youthfulness, her merriment—was lost to me a long time ago. Living with her in recent years has been a penitential exercise. What's there to miss?"

A slight shrug. "I dare say you'll find out."

Pacing down the Bird Walk ten minutes later, looking for parrots in the trees, Harry asks the girls, "Are you enjoying yourselves at Mrs. Watson's?" Then instantly regrets it.

His daughters look at each other like mute conspirators.

"I know, of course, that things must feel rather up in the air . . ."

Nan waits for him to trail off before she speaks. "She is a kind lady."

"I still don't see why they aren't with Jane," mutters his brother by his side. "Surely these things are best kept within the family?"

Harry waves that away. It was all done in such a hurry, after the smashed desk gave up its secrets; he can barely remember his reasoning, and it would only upset the girls to change their lodging at this point, besides.

"We were wondering . . ." starts Nell.

Nan's eyes fix on hers. "Might we come home? When . . ."

"When the divorce is over," finishes Nell.

Harry stares at her. "Where did you pick up that word?"

"Steady on, old boy," says William.

"Is it a bad word?" Nan gnaws her lip.

He struggles to find an answer.

"Is it slang?"

"It's the sort of grown-up trouble that little heads don't need to fuss about," their uncle tells them.

Harry sets his teeth together, hard.

"It was on a sign," Nell confesses. "A newsboy's sign. It said *Codrington Divorce, Four Full Pages.*"

"It was the *Telegraph,* she wanted to buy a copy," says Nan, looking at her patent shoes.

"To look at those funny little messages Mama used to read aloud. I thought she might have written us a message," Nell admits, "but Nan said I was a nincompoop."

He can tell she's on the brink of tears. *There's that brute Codrington making his children cry in the park! Neglect. Cruelty. Attempted violation of a . . .*

"Oh my sweet girlies," he says, squatting down and crushing them both to his chest. "You're cold. Are you cold? Hail a cab, won't you?" he asks William, "the girls are freezing."

On impulse, he stops the cab at a toy shop on Marylebone High Street. The first few things his daughters pick out are so cheap they irritate him: a cardboard castle, a tiny jointed doll. "That's childish," Nan scolds Nell.

"What's this splendid instrument?" says William like some showman, laying his hand on a brass machine that calls itself, in elaborate script, *The Zoetrope, Wheel of Life.*

"The very latest thing, General," the clerk tells him, rushing to wind up the handle. "No home without a zoetrope!"

"What, you're claiming every house in England has one?" asks William.

The clerk falters. "It's just a slogan, sir."

As Harry peers through the slot, a red devil somersaults through a hoop. Unnerved, Harry jerks away, then puts his face back to the cold brass eyepiece. A series of images on a rotating drum, that's all, but how it tricks the eye. Persistence of vision, that's the scientific phrase. "Look, girls," he orders. "Watch the fellow jump."

They bend, taking turns; they are enthusiastic, but not quite as much as he would have hoped. Always something forced about the girls' smiles, these days. "We'll take it," he proclaims.

"Really, Papa?"

"It's for us?"

"Yes indeed. You can wrap up half a dozen of those image drums—" he tells the clerk.

"Lucky, lucky girls," says the fellow fawningly.

But they seem loath to choose. William suggests a couple waltzing round a dance floor and a waiter falling downstairs. Harry picks a stork beating its wings, a tree shaking in the wind, monkeys exchanging top hats in an endless loop.

"May we bring it home?" asks Nell in a small voice, as they stand waiting for another cab.

Harry realizes he never did answer the original question. "Best to keep it at the Watsons' for now, darling. But very soon we'll be back at Eccleston Square."

"Yes, but . . . will it be like before?" asks Nan.

William looks away. "No," Harry tells her as gently as he can, "not like before. You'll understand when you're older." But he doubts that.

~

It happens the moment Harry stops the cab on Pall Mall. He's alone, at least, having dropped the girls at Mrs. Watson's and William at his tailor's on Jermyn Street: that's a small mercy. He's distracted, fumbling for a third shilling. When she comes running at the cab he doesn't recognize her at first.

His wife, in black like a widow; like some chalk-faced, brass-headed simulacrum of the girl he fell in love with all those years ago in the Tuscan spring. "Drive on," he calls to the cabman, but his voice comes out as faint as a mouse's. Helen seizes the door handle. He holds it shut from the inside, averting his eyes. "Drive on, I say!" That's better, louder, but Helen's clinging to the door, pressing her face to the window: her sea-glass eyes, her pointed nose and distorted lips. *Making a public spectacle*, he thinks with a surge of loathing so pure it reminds him of desire.

He lets go of the handle, so the door swings open taking Helen with it; she staggers backwards, her skirt flapping like some great bloated raven.

When Harry steps out she speaks, one word, but it comes out so strangely he doesn't understand her. "I beg your pardon?" Then the politeness strikes him as absurd. He has nothing to say to this stranger, this lurid character from a spy's reports. He veers away from her, towards the pillars of the Rag Club.

"Mercy." That's what she's saying, mumbling it over and over.

"Oi! My fare," roars the driver, from the cab roof.

Harry turns back, hot-faced with confusion, rooting in his pocket.

"Ask anything of me," demands Helen, grabbing his arm.

"Well, I like that trick," broadcasts the driver. "Scarpering into his club, with his lady-friend!"

"Anything I can do, anything I can say—" she sobs.

He knows there's a third shilling somewhere in the handful of coins, but his eyes can't pick it out, and his fingers are trembling. His wife hangs on his elbow like a terrier; he tries to shake her off.

"Don't let on you don't have it," calls the driver, rolling his eyes for the benefit of the gathering audience.

Harry grabs the first gold coin he can find—a half-sovereign—and hurls it in the man's direction. But it hits the shiny paintwork of the cab and bounces into the gutter.

"All I beg of you is, let me see my babies!"

"Hold your tongue for one moment," he barks in her face. He stoops, claws the half-sovereign out of the mud and holds it up for the driver. She's still clinging to his other arm.

The driver beams at him. "Well, now, that's what I call handsome . . ."

Harry turns away, towards the club's entrance, then—changing his mind—in the opposite direction. He walks a few steps, Helen a leaden shackle on his arm. What must they look like—a military lecher and his cast-off? "What can you possibly hope to gain by this, this *exhibition*?" he asks her, very low.

"They wouldn't let me into your club. They say you won't receive my letters. I'm at the brink of utter distraction!"

Something in her tone rings false to Harry. Is it just that he can no longer believe a word she says, since so much of what she's said to him over fifteen years of marriage has turned out to be claptrap?

"I'll take back everything my solicitor's said of you, all the, what are they called, countercharges," she promises with a gulp so violent it sounds as if she's retching up a stone. "I'll bow to your will in everything, Harry—if only you and the girls will come home."

He stares at her.

"What's done is done, but let's put it behind us, and try to be content in the years that remain to us. Come home, my love!" And she stretches up, on tiptoe, and twines her arms around his neck, and moves to kiss him. On Pall Mall, at ten past noon.

Harry's about to hurl her from him. He can feel it in his hands already, the satisfaction it will give him to rip Helen's arms (like coils of strangling ivy) away from his neck, to shove her away and see her drop into the gutter, revealed for all to see as the broken whore she is.

But something freezes his hands. The not-quite-convincing delivery of her lines? Something guarded, even calculating, in the back of her wide blue eyes? Whatever the hint is, it's enough to make him stand very still—*hold hard, old boy, hold hard*—while Helen hangs around his neck, planting desperate, muffled kisses on his beard. *Everything my solicitor's said of you*: he repeats her words to himself. *All the, what are they called, countercharges.* (As if she wouldn't recall the term!) Cruelty, yes. Husbandly brutality. That must be what she's hoping to provoke with her coarse effusions, with her humid lips: one public act of violence from Harry that just may be enough to sway a jury.

So he stands very still, instead, and takes a long breath. It doesn't matter who's gawking at this strange pair, on Pall Mall; what is vital is for Harry to stay out of this woman's trap. With the infinite delicacy of a policeman dismantling a bomb, he reaches behind his neck to unknot Helen's hands. "I know your game," he whispers in her ear, "and I'm not playing."

She looks back at him, eyes burning, unblinking.

It takes him considerable effort to undo her plump pink fingers, but he does it so carefully, with such apparent tenderness, that it strikes him that passersby must take them for lovers oblivious to the world.

X

Subpoena

(Latin, "under penalty":
a writ commanding the presence of
a witness in court to give testimony)

The "old maid" of 1861 is an exceedingly cheery personage, running about untrammelled by husband or children; now visiting her relatives' country houses, now taking her month in town, now off to a favourite pension on Lake Geneva, now scaling Vesuvius or the Pyramids . . .

Frances Power Cobbe,
"What Shall We Do with Our Old Maids?" (1862)

"More men than women in the first few issues, until our audience is established," suggests Emily Davies, biting on the end of her pen.

"Quite," says Fido. Her mind is not on business, as she sits in her office at the press, but she hopes she's hiding it. Fido can't breathe properly; ever since Helen slammed the door of Taviton Street behind her, there's been a rigidity in all the passages of her lungs, like old India rubber gone brittle. At the office she keeps all the windows closed, to shut out the black smuts of the London autumn. At home she does the same, and smokes her Sweet Threes for hours, but they don't bring her any relief; nor does the kettle in her bedroom that sends out its ribbon of mentholated steam all night.

"I've already sent out requests to Arnold, a couple of fine young essayists . . ." Emily Davies puts her small head on one side. "I thought a travel series on the Far East, perhaps."

"So you believe the *Victoria Magazine* can burst onto the scene in November?" asks Fido with forced enthusiasm.

"I don't see why not, if your typos can set it that fast," says Emily Davies.

"Some of them are careless and slow enough to make anybody swear," Fido admits. (Unless, as she's sometimes suspected lately, one or two of the clickers—Kettle? Dunstable?—are cooking the figures, boosting their wages by exaggerating the percentage of the girls' work the men end up having to do over. She won't worry about that now; her head's already crammed to bursting.) "But I can answer for the press meeting this deadline."

"Capital."

"Well, how splendid! I dare say we'll have to break the news to the rest of the Reform Firm now . . ."

"Oh, I've already submitted my resignation as editor of the *Journal.*" Emily Davies sighs. "Its demise, whether immediate or protracted, will be a blow to Miss Parkes, at first, but ultimately I hope a relief."

"Some people cling to their burdens."

"How true. There's a peculiar streak of self-glorifying sacrifice in many of the women drawn to our Cause," comments Emily Davies, flicking through her notes.

Fido's been fretting over whether to discuss what happened at their last meeting. "By the by—you must have wondered at the extraordinary behaviour of my visitor last Tuesday."

"No need for an apology."

She could leave it at that, but she finds she needs to press on. "You'll have gathered the whole story from the papers since then, or at least one version of it. I must beg you not to credit everything—"

Her colleague interrupts wryly. "As one vicar's daughter to another, I must tell you, I'm not as easily shocked as you imagine. At the age of twelve I was going round the slums of Gateshead, where I saw deformed babies born to girls molested by their fathers."

Fido is speechless.

"I am sorry for your friend. The law is a blunt instrument."

"She was staying at my house, just at first," says Fido miserably, "but I felt I had to ask her to leave."

A nod. "Shall we get on with our plans?"

"Of course," says Fido, and launches into an analysis of the *Victoria Magazine*'s budget.

It's the kind of day that seems to last a week: one obstacle after another to surmount or demolish. After lunch Fido has the particularly distasteful duty of calling Flora Parsons into her office.

"You were seen last night, on the Strand," she says, wheezing a little.

Flora Parsons wears a faint air of amusement.

"You don't deny it, then?"

"No use, is there?" answers the girl. Then, "Who was it saw me, may I ask?"

Fido hesitates. "One of the clickers."

"Head?"

A good guess; Fido blinks.

"What was he doing there at that time of the evening, is what I'd like to know," says Flora Parsons pleasantly.

"Waiting for his omnibus," she snaps. From the day she hired her, she should have recognized a certain set to the girl's lips. Fido leans over her desk; she means to seem impressive but the pose strikes her as desperate. "Miss Parsons, haven't you been happy in your position at the Victoria Press?"

"I dare say."

"Don't I pay you fairly?"

"That's what the job pays."

The impudence makes Fido's teeth ache. "Isn't it enough for your needs?"

A twist of the mouth. "Not for extras."

"You're one of my most talented hands," Fido tells her. "You have a natural quickness of mind."

"Thank you, Miss Faithfull."

The slut, she takes it as homage! "Which makes it all the more inexplicable that you'd jeopardize your position by stooping to the very lowest trade your sex can make."

Our sex, the girl's eyes seem to correct her. "Oh, you've got it roundabouts," says Flora Parsons. "I didn't take it up to make more cash just now; I've been at it since I was fifteen."

Fido flinches.

"I'm just a mot who does some typographing on the side, see?"

"Quite." She tries to gather her thoughts. "What about your engagement—what about Mr. Dunstable?" she asks, with a stern nod towards the workroom.

"That's all off," says the girl with a toss of the head.

"You don't care that I am obliged to turn you off without a reference?"

"It's not like I'll starve." The girl gives her a lingering smile, before turning towards the door.

Fido knows she ought to give this creature the most impassioned of lectures, but she can't summon her energies. *No use, is there?*—as the girl said. Flora Parsons has chosen her path, it's just a shame that Fido failed to see it years ago, and wasted the training.

Alone in her office, she leans back in her chair, entirely limp. Like some stain spreading across the buttoned leather. She's been trying to lose herself in work, in the three days since she turned Helen out of the house, but it's impossible: she can't sleep, she can barely eat. She doesn't know herself. How could she have done that to the woman she—despite everything—loves? And yet how could Helen have dragged her into this stinking quagmire?

People are never what they seem, not even to themselves. Harry Codrington tried to rape her, after all, she reminds herself—and all these years she's managed to deny it. How murky the human mind can be. What other terrible things has Fido managed to forget? What else lies occluded in the back of her thoughts? Her mind's a graveyard where the ground has started buckling; bones heave out of the grass.

The boy puts his head round the door. "Madam? Miss Parkes."

Oh dear God, today of all days. Fido jumps up, a wide-eyed jack-in-the-box, to offer her visitor a chair.

Bessie Parkes is looking particularly smart this afternoon, for all her plain blue costume; there's a healthy colour to her cheeks. "I must begin by congratulating you."

Fido is winded. And then she understands. "Oh, the *Victoria Magazine*, yes, thank you."

"I've already offered Miss Davies my felicitations on the new enterprise," says Bessie Parkes, "since it was she who had the courtesy to tell me about it."

Fido shrinks at that.

"And now that she's resigning the editorship of the *English Woman's Journal*, I mean to take the helm again myself, as in the early days."

"Marvellous," says Fido feebly.

"As it happens," remarks Bessie Parkes, "I've recently come into a legacy which will allow me to become the principal shareholder, and bear the *Journal*'s entire management on my shoulders."

"How fortunate," says Fido, startled. Not that she'll miss those interminable committee meetings—but she can't help feeling there's been a *coup d'état.*

"I want to transform it into a more practical vehicle, to uplift working women. The *Alexandra Magazine and English Woman's Journal*, I was thinking of renaming it," says Bessie Parkes.

Fido represses a smile. To borrow the princess's name is such an obvious echo of the *Victoria.* "How exciting!"

"I'm afraid I'll be obliged to end our printing contract with your press. I'll need lower rates, you see, and a more reliable schedule."

She nods, reckoning the financial loss. "We'll be fighting the good fight on two fronts, then. As sister publications," she adds.

Bessie Parkes's smile is distinctly sour. "Miss Faithfull—are you being wilfully naïve?"

"I don't believe I understand you," says Fido.

"The Codrington case—"

"Yes," she gabbles, "I'm really uncommonly sorry that I didn't tell all of you about it beforehand, but you see, there was a misunderstanding."

One tapered eyebrow goes up.

"The solicitor—he gave me the fallacious impression that my name was to be quite kept out of it."

"Miss Faithfull," says Bessie Parkes as if to a child, "you're all over the papers as the woman's chief intimate, and worse."

Her cheeks are on fire. "Much of what they say is pure libel. And I've already taken steps to dissociate myself from Mrs. Codrington somewhat—" She finds herself listening out for a cock crow.

Bessie Parkes brushes that away. "We of the Cause must keep quite clear of anyone who has publicly violated the cardinal rules of morality. It's a thing understood; at least I thought so. One can't touch pitch and not be defiled."

"My friend hasn't been found guilty of anything yet," says Fido, too loudly. Something occurs to her. "And what of Miss Evans? Ten years ago, you and Madame Bodichon made a point of standing by her when she eloped with a married man."

Bessie Parkes's mouth purses. "Marian's circumstances were highly particular; Lewes was only prevented by a legal technicality from getting a divorce so he could marry her. And she's famous not only for her novels but for acting on the highest principle, which is why she's been accepted in society again since. Your Helen Codrington, on the other hand—"

It's the sneering tone that forces Fido to interrupt. "I still owe her something. What of loyalty? What of sisterhood, if you will?"

"Oh, but I won't. Were you thinking of us, of your comrades in the Reform Firm, when you got yourself entangled in this notorious case? Where was your precious *loyalty* and *sisterhood* then?"

Fido clings to the edge of her desk and strains to take a breath. "I deeply regret the publicity. But it should die away soon, as I've no intention of going into the witness box."

Bessie Parkes tilts her small head. "Haven't you been served with a subpoena yet?"

Fido shakes her head.

"Did you or did you not approve that affidavit?"

"Yes, but—"

"Then you'll be obliged to appear, on pain of fine or imprisonment."

Fido sucks her lips in panic. "I mean to write to Mrs. Codrington's solicitor again. There's still time; the case won't come up for several weeks, I understand—"

"Monday, according to my father," says Bessie Parkes crisply.

She's been forgetting that Joseph Parkes is a lawyer. "Monday?" She can hardly form the word. This is Thursday.

"An unexpected reconciliation between the parties in another case has created a sudden opening in the court's schedule."

Fido blanches, gets to her feet. "I—I'm not well."

"Oh, you're hoping a doctor's note will let you off? I doubt that very much, Miss Faithfull." Bessie flips open her watch.

"The Cause means everything to me," sobs Fido, "and I won't be forced into anything that will do it the slightest harm."

"I wonder, have you the slightest grasp of what harm you've done already?" And she sweeps out of the office.

Fido just needs to get home and lie down. A little steam, a few cigarettes, and surely her lungs will loosen a little. *Monday, Monday.* She won't think that far; she can't spare the breath. Four days to live through, and then whatever comes after. She'll have to take these appalling hours one at a time. The fearlessness of the reformer, the world-changer, has dropped away; she's plain Miss Faithfull of the rectory again, wheezing with fright.

"A clerk was here, from a Mr. Few's chambers," Johnson tells her as soon as she steps through the front door.

Fido stares at her maid. "Did he—did he say what it concerns?"

Johnson shakes her head, neutral as ever. "He has something to put into your own hands, that's all he said. He'll call again this afternoon."

Her pulse stops for a second. *The subpoena.*

She can't; she simply can't. It's not just the mortification of standing up in court, in four days' time; Fido believes she could muster the strength for that, if conscience required it. No, it's the choice that lies before her: to damn a man by swearing on oath to what she really can't remember, for all her efforts—or to admit that she can't remember, and has perjured herself, and so destroy her friend's whole case.

Impossible.

She's been putting off answering a note from her favourite sister. She scribbles a reply now, standing at her desk, afraid to sit down in case she loses momentum.

October 4

My dear Esther,

I can't express how ashamed I am that our parents have learned from the newspapers of my reluctant association with this Codrington case. Please assure them that I hoped to spare them and all the family this distress by keeping my name clear of the business—but in vain.

How sweet of you, Esther, to offer to accompany me to the Matrimonial Causes Court. But I must tell you that I will not be appearing as a witness. I go abroad today and will stay away until the trial's conclusion. If you please, if you hear what's said of me, don't believe any real evil of

Your sister,
Emily

In flight Fido finds a kind of steely strength. She's packed in half an hour. She picks up her velvet choker, studded with all the small treasures of the Kent shore, holds it in her palm for a moment, wraps it in its linen strip, and puts it back in the bureau drawer. She leaves instructions with Johnson to tell the others to say, if anyone asks, that their mistress is gone abroad on private business. "Accept no documents in my name, on any consideration, remember."

"Yes, madam." The maid's sallow face is as blank as ever.

The servants read the newspapers too, Fido remembers; *they must see right through me.*

If she never receives the wretched summons, surely she can't be found guilty of having defied it? She wishes she knew more about the law. Not for the first time, she curses the sporadic, gappy nature of even the best female education. It occurs to her to consult a solicitor of her own—there's Mr. Markby, who represented the press in that ridiculous plagiarism case about the rules of bridge—but no, she can't bear to explain to him that she approved (without reading it) an affidavit about an incident during which she was asleep.

The maid follows her down the passage and asks, "But where are you going, really, madam?"

Is that concern in the low voice? Disapproval? Affection? Fido can't decide. "I'm truly sorry, Johnson. But if you don't know, no one can oblige you to tell." She takes the valise and lets herself out the front door. She looks down Taviton Street, and the city opens like a chasm.

XI

Trial

(a test; a frustrating or catastrophic event;
an examination of a case by a competent tribunal)

Women should not make love their profession.

Barbara Leigh Smith (later Bodichon),
Women and Work (1857)

"Do sit down," Helen tells Few on Friday evening, leading him into the dusty drawing-room. In the ten days since the staff—all but the taciturn Mrs. Nichols—were discharged, the house has taken on a derelict air. "A sherry?" Helen asks. The formulae of politeness are stiff in her mouth. The cockatoo shrieks.

"Nothing, thank you," says Few, taking a small chair. "My family will be expecting me."

That startles Helen; the solicitor seems too much of a dried-up bachelor to have a family. "To business, then," she says, as briskly as she can manage, sitting down. "Judge Wilde: what can you tell me about him?"

Few shrugs. "He breeds roses."

Helen wonders what bearing this trait may have on her case. An intolerance for anyone who poses a threat to the laws of lineage—or a sympathy for the frail flowers of womanhood? She notices that the three silver fish are floating motionless at the top of their bowl. Mrs. Nichols must have remembered to feed the noisy birds, but not the fish.

"Mrs. Codrington? I've come in person, to give you some bad news."

"My girls?" Her voice is strangled.

"No, no. Your friend, the inaptly named Miss Faithfull," he says dryly. "She's disappeared."

Helen stares.

"Yesterday, the very afternoon my clerk attempted to serve her with the subpoena—he found that she'd gone abroad."

"I don't believe it."

"That's all her servants will say—no forwarding address. And the same goes for her employees at the press; my clerk's talked to several of the girls, as well as the men who supervise them."

Helen sets her teeth.

Few releases an old man's sigh. "I need hardly point out that without her testimony as to the attempted rape . . . her flight at the eleventh hour may strike the jury as giving the lie to the whole story."

Damn the woman.

"Now, the petitioner's case will take several days to present, which gives our side a little time. If you have the least notion where Miss Faithfull might be skulking, with a particular relative perhaps . . ."

She shakes her head.

"I thought you were very old friends."

"Well, I thought many things," hisses Helen. "I thought I knew her, and it appears I was mistaken."

"Hm," says Few. "Well. I must take my leave. I'll send over a full report on Monday evening on the first day's business . . ."

When she's shown him out she stands there, in the dim hall, unable to decide what to do next. Should she go to bed, in the faint hope of sleep? Ask Mrs. Nichols to send up something to eat? Sit in the dim drawing-room, contemplating the putrefying fish in their bowl?

She doesn't move. She looks out the glass panel in the front door, as if the answer she seeks might be out there on the silent pavements of Eccleston Square.

Fido, Fido, where are you?

Helen's imagination roams all over London. England. Europe. The railway's reached Nice this year. Squeezing her eyes shut, Helen pictures Fido wheezing as she walks along the Promenade des Anglais, under a hard Riviera sun.

How could you abandon me in my hour of need? The woman's only lost her nerve, Helen's sure of that. But it amounts to the same thing: betrayal. *After all these years. After all we've lived through, all we've been to each other. She owes me!*

It's much later, tossing around in bed, entangled in her hot nightgown, that Helen comes to a more painful conclusion.

Yes, she used Fido. She took advantage of her old friend's innocence and idealism from the start. Much as Anderson took advantage of Helen's boredom and vanity, it occurs to her now. It's the way of the world, she supposes: everyone uses everyone. The trick is to know how much a given person can bear. No doubt Fido would have stood by her side throughout this ghastly trial, if Helen hadn't pushed her a step too far by obliging her to testify about Harry's attack. *My fault, my own stupid fault!*

Now Helen's lost everyone. Husband, daughters, lover, friend, like sand trickling through her fingers.

~

Helen finds a seat near the back. She's as calm as fifteen drops of laudanum can make her. Despite the protection of her veil, her heart judders with dread that she'll be spotted and pointed out. The court's crammed with visitors, as they're officially known, though Helen finds it a curious choice of word: as if they're paying some courtesy call. *Watchers* might be better, *carrion feeders*. It seems as if everyone in London who can muster a coat and hat has been allowed in; here comes one of the under-sheriffs, finding a place for a dodgy character in a battered topper. Some of the crowd standing at the back smell so mouldy, Helen suspects they just want to get out of the autumn rain. She's never come, herself, but a couple of her acquaintances queued up last year to hear the octogenarian Viscount Palmerston defend himself against a charge of adultery with the wife of a dissolute Irishman. How irritated they were when it was announced that the Irish marriage was not legally valid, so the case was dismissed! Helen thought it an amusing anecdote, at the time.

She tries to steady herself and make some sense of what her eyes are taking in through the irksome layer of black lace covering her head. There's the judge's high, empty seat. Newspapermen are on its left, squeezed into the first of the visitors' benches. To its right, what Helen recognizes from illustrations as the witness box—as if witnesses must be caged like lions or else they'll flee. And a larger panelled enclosure where miscellaneous men are already filing in and taking their seats: they must be the jury. Some have a pompous manner, some more hangdog, some a curious combination of the two. They'll sit there for long hours, for no pay, but at least there's a thrilling case in their hands. *Who are these strangers to judge whether Harry should have the right to cast me off?* Three gentlemen, perhaps four, she reckons; the others bourgeois. A military fellow who smirks through a thick moustache at a lady in the audience: he just might favour Helen's side.

No sign of Anderson in the audience, of course. Off on honeymoon, or hurrying back to his regiment in Malta, little Scotch bride in tow? Will Helen's last note have given him nightmares, she wonders? It's all that's left to her to hope. How she's come to despise her persuadable heart.

Now Helen sees her solicitor plodding up the aisle. "Mr. Few," she hisses as he passes her elbow.

He peers at her, then his expression turns to a frown.

"I found I couldn't stay away."

Few tuts. "It will only upset you, and if you're recognized it'll cause talk."

Talk? Helen laughs under her breath. What else is this mob gathered for but to hear *talk* about the most private details of her history? "It's only your beetling brows that will make anyone give me a second glance," she tells him, almost flirtatiously. "Which is my barrister?"

"The tall gentleman at the table on the left," he says, pointing discreetly with a thumb towards the middle of the courtroom. "Hawkins is a very brilliant advocate."

The man looks suave in his wig and gloves; half Few's age, which is some comfort. The one with his head in some legal tome has a more dusty air about him, and his bands are crumpled. "Is the other . . ."

"Bovill, counsel for the petitioner," says Few shortly, before he moves on.

A few minutes later her husband stalks up the aisle, his huge silhouette passing within inches of Helen's skirt. She flinches, but he doesn't notice her. *Insensate frog!* He's looking much as he did last Wednesday outside his club, when with maddening mildness he peeled her arms away from him, holding her at a distance as one would a yowling kitten. (So all that grovelling was for nothing: Helen's jaws tighten at the memory.) Harry takes his place beside his barrister and they exchange a few words. Helen squeezes her eyes shut for a moment.

When Judge Wilde sweeps in—all jowls and bushy white eyebrows—the back doors are forced shut, and the under-sheriffs can be heard announcing "No room, no room within."

The petition's read aloud by a clerk with a nasal voice, and the audience starts to stir like a beehive. There's something intoxicating, Helen's surprised to find, about such words being released into the air. This court is the one place in England, it occurs to her—except perhaps a doctor's office—where one's encouraged to speak bluntly about the carnal.

"I wish to express my sympathy with you on what must be an uncongenial duty," Judge Wilde is saying to the jury. "The evidence which will be laid before you is extensive, and contains much that is peculiarly sordid." An anticipatory giggle from somewhere in the courtroom makes him frown. "But I trust that the members of the public permitted to observe these proceedings will refrain from loud or vulgar reactions."

When Bovill stands up to speak for her husband, Helen revises her estimate of the enemy; though the barrister's robes could do with pressing, his manner is intelligent and precise. "Some have found fault with the relative facility with which divorces can be obtained, nowadays," he begins quietly, "but when you have heard the evidence, gentlemen, you will feel no small satisfaction in releasing the petitioner, a battle-scarred servant of Her Majesty's, from the onerous chains that bind him to an immoral woman."

Helen licks her numb lips. Behind her veil, it's as if she has no face. She might have overdone her dose by a few drops.

"A wife who has been no real wife—who has neglected her household and maternal duties, thwarted and opposed her husband, and repeatedly dishonoured him with other men."

Perhaps it's the laudanum that's giving Helen this strange detachment: she listens to the harangue as if it concerns some other woman altogether. As Bovill starts recounting the admiral's distinguished early career and choice of a younger, foreign-bred bride, she can't shake off a sense of unreality; this isn't her being described, this isn't Harry, these are tiny puppets on a faraway stage. Does her husband feel the same way?

"Until some time after the birth of their two daughters, that illusory happiness was uninterrupted. If I may enter into the record a letter the respondent wrote the petitioner in April 1856, when he had received orders to proceed to the Crimea—" Bovill reads it as dryly as a laundry list.

Merely one line with everything that's dear to you, my own Harry, on this our seventh anniversary. How rare the woman is who can say she's never experienced anything but kindness from her spouse. God ever bless you and keep you! Addio alma di mia vita.

Helen

"The Italian can be translated as *Goodbye, love of my life*," Bovill says in an aside to the jury.

Helen has no memory of writing this, but it doesn't surprise her: is there a wife who can't drum up an affectionate note on occasion? Now she comes to think of it—yes, she must have scribbled it to smooth Harry's feathers after a petty squabble they'd had while he was packing his trunks. How strange, to see all this flotsam of their private life wash up again. She's beginning to grasp Bovill's strategy. It wasn't that the couple was incompatible from the start; no, no, it was the wife whose heart cooled while her gallant lord and master was off fighting the Russians.

Her ears prick up at Fido's name.

"The situation was exacerbated by the presence in the household of the respondent's companion, Miss Emily Faithfull, with whom Mrs. Codrington generally slept. That same Miss Faithfull who has claimed, in a bizarre and libellous affidavit appended to the respondent's countercharge, that in October 1856, the petitioner attempted her virtue. An allegation that I almost shrink from repeating," intones Bovill, "so foul it is—and so ludicrous. The very idea that a respectable gentleman would clamber into bed between his unconscious wife and her unconscious friend—a maiden of twenty-one, and, I feel obliged to add, not reputed to be of conspicuous beauty—"

This raises a few guffaws.

"—and there attempt a violation of the latter! I have just learned, and am eager to inform the court," he says with relish, "that Miss Faithfull has mysteriously absented herself and gone abroad before she could be served with a summons to testify. The gentlemen of the jury may draw the logical conclusion."

It suddenly occurs to Helen that Harry might have hired some thug to abduct Fido. She peers through the sea of heads to catch a glimpse of his. The bearded face is grim and familiar. But how could the hypothetical thug have persuaded every one of the woman's servants and employees to say she'd gone abroad? *This isn't a sensation novel*, she scolds herself.

"Things came to a head in the spring of 1857," Bovill goes on, "when Mrs. Codrington took the extraordinary step of positively declining *ever again* to enter the petitioner's bed. From that time forward, if the court will pardon my frankness, all conjugal intercourse was at an end." He pauses to underline the gravity.

The story's convincing, Helen grants the barrister that; it has a simple thrust to it, like a sermon. The truth is more bitty, harder to explain. She feels a sudden temptation to stand up and say, *There was no key in my door. Don't tell me he was burning for me, because I won't believe it.*

"The respondent made a wild demand for a separation on grounds of incompatibility—though there are of course no such grounds in British law," Bovill adds. "The petitioner very correctly invited his wife's parents, and his own brother, General Codrington, to mediate. The conclusion was that the respondent agreed to resume at least the appearance of married life."

The house was in chaos, Helen remembers. Quarrels in corners, scenes in the hall, lukewarm soup . . . One of the girls hurled a wooden block through a stained glass window.

When she manages to turn her attention back to Bovill, he's describing their way of life in Malta. "The respondent's behaviour became increasingly erratic: in private, moody, flippant, and self-aggrandizing; in public, spendthrift, loquacious, and coquettish." The barrister's tone darkens. "In the year 1860 she began to be seen constantly in the company of Lieutenant Mildmay—who we learn from Bombay has refused, on advisement, to submit to an examination."

The cur! To think Mildmay once sobbed into her lap, kissed her ankle. How hard would it have been for him, at the safe distance of a few thousand miles, to answer *No, not so, nothing of the sort, an impeccable lady*?

"I look forward to my learned friend's explanation," remarks Bovill with a lifted eyebrow.

My learned friend, that must mean Hawkins. It's as bad as the House of Commons.

"In the meantime I will leave it to the jury's discernment to deduce why Mildmay, this former confidential friend of the respondent's, might be unwilling to enlighten the court with regard to his relations with her."

A few gruff laughs from men in the crowd. Helen stiffens: two women on the bench in front are looking over their shoulders at her. One mutters something to the other. Helen worries her lip, wishes her veil were thicker. She's not the only lady wearing one, but the others all seem too old or dowdy to be *the notorious Mrs. Codrington*, as the *Spectator* called her on Saturday. Yes, for lack of anyone to talk to at Eccleston Square she's been reading the papers again, with a painful hunger.

"The petitioner, being an early riser, had to be in bed by midnight," Bovill explains, "whereas Mrs. Codrington would insist on staying at parties to dance, only coming home in the Admiralty gondola at two, three, or even four o'clock, escorted by an officer—usually either Lieutenant Mildmay, or the co-respondent named in this case, Colonel David Anderson."

The barrister holds up what Helen takes for a toy. When it turns out to be a scale model of the gondola, she almost laughs aloud. It's the kind of ingenious little device her daughters love. The audience cranes to see the jury examine the roofed-in cabin. This is verging on a sideshow: what magic will the mountebank produce from his pocket next?

A little dark man steps into the box as the first witness and swears his oath. Helen's sure she's never seen him before, but he turns out to be one of the boatmen.

"Signor Scichma, how long is the passage across the harbour at Valetta, from the town centre to Admiralty House?" asks Bovill.

"One quarter of one hour, sir," articulates the Italian. He sounds coached, to Helen.

"Does the door have a pane of glass?" Bovill holds up the model again, tapping the cabin.

"*Si*, but nobody see inside if the light out in there."

"In the cabin."

"*Si.*"

"In English, if you please. Your answer is yes?"

"Yes, sir."

"On the nights when Colonel Anderson or Lieutenant Mildmay happened to be in the cabin with Mrs. Codrington, was the light on inside, generally?"

"No, no. Only a light in the bow of the boat."

"Did you notice anything else in particular, on those nights?"

An obedient nod. "The gondola get, how you say it, out of trim."

A gasp of satisfaction goes up from the audience, and Judge Wilde raps his gavel, but lightly.

Behind her veil, Helen's face is hot and tight. How can she ever have thought of a gondola as a romantic setting? This beetle's-eye perspective on her past turns everything to mud.

"Can you explain what you mean, Signor Scichma?" asks Bovill.

"It sway on one side, so we have trouble rowing," says the boatman, with an expressive movement of his hand.

"It swayed such that it was evident the two persons inside were sitting close together on the same bench, rather than on opposite benches?"

"I object, my Lord." Her barrister, Hawkins, has risen to his full height, suddenly fiery. "Unwarranted conclusions!"

Judge Wilde scratches one white, rampant eyebrow. "Mr. Bovill, if you'd care to rephrase your question?"

"Certainly, my Lord. Signor Scichma, what did you believe was the cause?"

"Just how you said. The two of them sit together."

Helen rolls her eyes; these are merely word games.

"It make me think of bad things," the boatman adds, like a schoolboy currying favour with the master. "I laugh with the other men about it."

Helen can hardly believe her future's going to hinge on the movement of a boat in a choppy harbour.

Hawkins rises elegantly to cross-examine the witness about what he derides as this "tale of a tub." Apart from insisting that it's in a boat's nature to sway, he seems to Helen to achieve nothing in particular.

Here comes the second witness, and Helen's stomach knots, because she knows him all too well: George Duff, that loathsome footman with the greasy hair. How did she put up with him for five whole years?

Duff's grudge gives him fluency. "Well, sometimes on landing, he'd wish her good night, Mildmay would, but sometimes he'd go with her into Admiralty House."

"And remain there?" Bovill prompts.

"Yes, sir, for twenty minutes. Or an hour even," Duff adds, less plausibly. "In a little sitting room that had a sofa in it. With the lights out."

Lying hound, thinks Helen. The lights were hardly ever out.

The woman sitting in front of Helen squeezes her companion's arm with glee. Helen has noticed that a lot of these females have come along in pairs, for mutual encouragement.

"Where would the petitioner be, while this was going on?" asks Bovill.

"Retired for the night, sir. Or sitting up writing in his office, not to be disturbed."

"Did you ever go into this sitting room while your mistress was there with Mildmay?"

"No, sir," says Duff with mild regret, shaking his hair out of his eyes, "but once I went into the passage leading into it—"

"When was this?"

"Late in 1860. Or perhaps early in 1861," he says, eyes flicking from side to side. "I saw Mildmay standing with his arm round her neck." He mimes it, slinging his arm lecherously around an invisible woman.

Helen's troubled by a sudden sense of the warm weight of Alex Mildmay's arm. He was a sweet fellow—or at least she thought so till today, when she learned that he wouldn't so much as sign his name to save her. These men! Do they all hate women, or is it some knack they have of putting the past behind them as if on the other side of a thick pane of glass?

"And what did you do?" Bovill asks.

"I went away to the servants' quarters," says Duff virtuously.

On and on he testifies. Sounds on the dark staircase at Admiralty House; whisperings and rustling of dresses, exclamations, and the drawing of breath. A scrap of fabric found on the stairs after a visit by Colonel Anderson that Duff claims matched a certain rip in Mrs. Codrington's bodice that he noticed another day. This is beginning to sound like the kind of smut gentlemen keep in a locked bookcase, thinks Helen. Bovill produces a little model of the staircase, which prompts some satiric applause. Who makes these models, she wonders? Deft, slim-fingered children in some sweatshop in Soho?

Perhaps a third of Duff's allegations correspond to vague memories of Helen's. But of course the jury won't know the difference between his half-truths and his pure fictions. Nor does he mention all the wearisome days Helen spent fulfilling the duties of consort to the admiral-superintendent of the dockyards. Nor all the time with her girls, when she wasn't a bad mother, not by any reckoning.

She feels a little relieved when Hawkins stands up to cross-examine the witness. "Mr. Duff," he drawls, "would you agree that you displayed antipathy towards your mistress?"

The footman squirms, and tucks an oily strand of hair behind his ear. "Well. She frequently made complaints of me without cause."

"For instance?"

"That I wouldn't take my hat off when the host was carried by in a procession."

Actually, Helen had forgotten that piece of insolence.

"You're not insinuating that Mrs. Codrington is a Roman Catholic," says Hawkins sternly.

"No, but she said it showed discourtesy to neighbours who were."

Hawkins glances down at his notes. "Is it not true that you were turned out by the admiral after you made an indecent attempt on Teresa Borg, a maid?"

Duff's face contracts, which pleases Helen. "I discharged myself voluntarily. There was no truth in it; the Borg woman called me into her room herself and only accused me afterwards. She's a Maltese," he says, appealing to the jury.

Hawkins makes another of his lightning changes of tack. "Can you specify the time, or date, or year, even, of any of the alleged incidents involving Mildmay or Anderson?"

A shrug. "I had no reason to make a note."

"But you claim you were disturbed by them. Surely it was a dereliction of duty, then, not to inform the admiral?"

"I—" Duff pauses, blinking, like a burglar interrupted on the job. "I didn't think it was my place."

"How so?"

"Well, he must have known how often those two officers came to his house."

Hawkins's patrician face brightens. "Ah. You believed the admiral turned a blind eye to his wife's friendships with these men, or encouraged them even? Perhaps in order to furnish grounds for a divorce?"

Condonation, connivance, Helen lists in her head. Her barrister's not just a highly attractive man but also something of a genius.

Bovill's glaring at his witness: Duff scrambles to recover. "I never said any of that."

"No, your lips were sealed tight until petitioner's agents tracked you down in France a few weeks ago. May I ask, what compensation did they offer you in exchange for your spontaneous recollections?" Hawkins asks witheringly.

"Just the expenses of the voyage. Steerage," he insists.

"One final question, Duff. Did you ever, with your own eyes, see any actual misconduct take place between Mrs. Codrington and any male person?" Hawkins speaks one word at a time, as if to an imbecile.

"I suppose not."

"A simple no will suffice."

Once Duff's stood down, Bovill gets up again. "Thus matters went on." Helen's beginning to recognize it as his catchphrase, intoned a touch more grimly every time. He now reads the depositions of a number of witnesses taken under a commission in Malta. The accumulation of suggestive detail depresses Helen. The two women in front have clearly found her out; they keep turning to glance at her, whispering to each other. This wretched veil is like a sign over her head, marking her out as the one with something to hide. But she'll hear this out, as long as it takes.

She can't believe her eyes when the next witness turns out to be none other than Mrs. Nichols, the housekeeper who served Helen a late, singed breakfast this morning. The double-dyed treachery!

"Would you describe it as a Christian household?" Bovill is asking.

"Well." A small sigh. "The admiral reads prayers with the children every morning, but the mistress doesn't attend. And she doesn't go to church above twice a year."

To think I've kept her on all these years, though she boils the meat to leather . . .

"During summer months, on Malta, where did the family sleep?"

"Oh yes," Mrs. Nichols says, nodding eagerly. "Admiralty House was in a pestilential spot, so the admiral took the girls and us staff to sleep on board the *Azoff*, but the mistress insisted on going home every night. Said she slept better there." A sardonic curl of the mouth.

"Now, please tell the court about the trip to Cormayeur, a resort on the Franco-Italian border, in August of 1860."

Helen's stomach tightens; she forgot this had to be coming.

"The party was composed of Mrs. Codrington, her parents, the two girls, myself, and a maid," lists Mrs. Nichols, like a schoolgirl repeating her lesson. "After a few days, Lieutenant Mildmay turned up to stay at the same hotel, as if by accident. I heard the mistress introduce him to a new acquaintance as her cousin!"

"Did she ask you to take a letter to his room?"

A nod. "And when I objected she said, 'Well, Mary will take it, then, silly.'"

Did Helen really say that? She might have done.

"Back in Valetta, did you ever see the respondent and the lieutenant together in private?" asks Bovill.

"Once he was in her room for ten minutes while she was in bed," says Mrs. Nichols with relish. "I was going in and out all the while."

"She was wearing what, a nightgown?"

"With a jacket over it," she concedes reluctantly. "She had purchases from Naples and Leghorn spread all over the counterpane. She was asking him to take the handkerchiefs to England to get them embroidered."

A simple conversation; Helen vaguely recalls it. Neither she nor Mildmay would have thought there was anything to hide, just then.

"Oh, and another day the mistress had a blister on her foot from walking and he opened it with his pocket knife."

The mention of this intimacy causes quite a stir in the crowd. Helen smiles a little, under her veil. He did it so deftly, it barely stung.

Mrs. Nichols is well warmed up now. "One night," she volunteers, "I found him sitting on the staircase."

"Mildmay?"

"No, beg pardon, I mean Colonel Anderson, that time. I said, 'How you frightened me, sir,' and he laughed."

He and Mildmay have that in common, Helen acknowledges; they're both ready laughers. She used to love that about them. She can't quite remember what else there was. Did she sell herself twice over for a bit of merriment?

"Also, going along a dark passage another night, after ten," says Mrs. Nichols, switching to Gothic tones, "I almost walked into them—her and him, Anderson, I mean, again—they were close together. I ran back to the bedroom."

"What was she wearing, at that hour?"

"A loose red skirt and a flannel jacket," the housekeeper reports.

"So," says Bovill crisply. "By the year 1862, Mrs. Nichols, was the co-respondent, Colonel Anderson, beginning to take Lieutenant Mildmay's place as the respondent's regular escort?"

"That's right, we all noticed the change. A regular relay, one of the boys called it."

This raises such a laugh that Judge Wilde resorts to his gavel.

Hawkins stands to cross-examine the housekeeper. Helen sits forward in anticipation, her stomach tight.

"When my colleague Mr. Few interviewed you, some weeks ago, didn't you acknowledge that you never saw anything even approaching actual impropriety between your mistress and any man?"

Mrs. Nichols purses her dry lips. "I might have said that."

The look he gives the jury—sweeping, magnanimous—is a marvel to watch. "No further questions, my Lord."

The housekeeper's face crumples. "But Few took me unawares in front of my husband, so he did, when it would have put me out of countenance to say all I knew," she gabbles, "and besides I wasn't on oath then as I am now."

"Oh, so you only speak the truth on special occasions?"

For a moment it looks as if Mrs. Nichols will burst into tears.

"You may step down," the judge tells her.

By God, thinks Helen, *I'll discharge the bitch tonight if it means I have to toast my own bread.*

A stranger gets into the box, in the tall varnished hat of a policeman, with a truncheon looped onto his belt.

(This is like dying, Helen decides. Faces familiar and forgotten move in a spectral parade before her eyes.)

"John Rowe," says the man, identifying himself gruffly. "Employed in the Dockland Police at Valetta."

"Can you tell the court what happened on July the tenth of this year?" asks Bovill. "That is, some four weeks before the Codringtons' departure for England."

"Yes, sir." Rowe keeps his eyes on the floor, but somehow the effect is to make him look shy rather than shifty. "I remember that night because there was a band playing; there were illuminations in town for some Romanist festival."

Helen's cheeks heat up under her veil, as she remembers.

"I approached the gate of the victualling yard and I saw her—"

"The respondent?"

"She was walking towards me, and Colonel Anderson—the co-respondent," he corrects himself, "was behind her at the waterside arranging his costume."

Scattershot sniggers from the benches.

"Could I trouble you to be more particular?" asks Bovill in his scholarly way.

"He was buttoning up his trousers," says John Rowe to the floor.

Bovill always waits a beat or two after some shocking detail, Helen notices, to give it a dreadful weight.

"Did Mrs. Codrington speak to you?" he asks at last.

"She engaged me with some questions about pigeons."

More laughter. Yes, Helen remembers a pleasant conversation about the use of carrier pigeons in police work. All these perfectly commonplace moments in her past, now re-enacted in harsh limelight like scenes from *Othello.*

When her barrister stands up, irritation is breaking through his suave manner. "This extraordinary tale of dropped trousers," Hawkins snaps. "Was there really light enough, Rowe, for you to see every detail of the gentleman's clothing?"

"It was a full moon, because of the festival. I mean to say," the policeman corrects himself, "they hold the festival at the full moon."

"If you saw such a shocking sight, why did you not report the matter to your superiors at once?"

"I dare say I put it out of my mind."

"Are you a logician, sir?"

The policeman's jaw tightens.

"In logic there's a principle known as parsimony, meaning, in layman's terms," Hawkins tells the jury, "that the simplest of two explanations is usually correct. Now, given that the co-respondent was standing by the waterside, don't you agree that he might very well have loosened his clothing in order to perform a natural function? If the court will permit—is micturition not a simpler, and therefore more likely, cause than adultery?"

A female laugh, very shrill, just behind Helen's head.

Rowe shakes his head. "I can't see an officer doing something like that in front of a fellow officer's wife."

This provokes gales of merriment.

I'll never be quite English, thinks Helen. This stuffy idiot truly believes that to make water in front of a woman is worse than to have her.

The judge calls a recess, now, and most of the crowd rear up and shuffle out the back doors. Some keep their seats, Helen notices, and pull out packages of sandwiches. Few pauses beside her. "May I offer you some refreshment?" he asks tiredly.

She shakes her head. "It's going rather badly, isn't it?" she asks in as brave a tone as she can muster.

"Oh, early yet."

Helen drifts out into Westminster Hall with the dregs of the crowd. Through her thick veil, she cranes up at the bare, gigantic timbers, hung with faded banners, like something out of a Nordic saga. But instead of massive heroes, the hall is crammed with bewigged lawyers and their clients, and always the shuffling, chattering crowd that spills from one or other of the courts.

She has a pie from a stall. She can always eat, no matter what troubles beset her. Once, in the days of courtship, Harry told her that the life force sprang up very strong in her. She wonders what he'd call it now: vulgarity?

The first witness after the recess is the one Helen's been dreading: Emily Watson. It occurs to Helen that every friend one makes in life is a liability: one has let her past the walls, allowed her to matter, and one must keep her as a friend forever or she'll become an enemy.

Oh Fido, Fido.

The grey-haired lady makes quite a production of unpeeling her glove so her skin can touch the Book as she takes the oath; Helen's fingers tighten with rage. "My name is Emily Watson, wife to the Reverend Joshua Watson," says the witness with modest satisfaction. She aims a sudden, quick smile into the crowd: *that must be for her beloved Harry*, thinks Helen.

"When did you first meet the respondent in Malta?" asks Bovill.

"In July 1861. For several nights Helen and I—forgive me, that's what I always called her—were in attendance on an invalid in pecuniary distress, a Mrs. Coxon."

"What estimate did you form of the respondent's character on that occasion?"

Here Mrs. Watson makes a show of hesitating. "A touch too free in her manners, I dare say. A certain spirit of wildness about her."

"Subsequently you became friends with Mrs. Codrington, despite your reservations?" asks Bovill.

"Very good friends. I pride myself on believing the best of people, even if sometimes I suffer for it," she remarks, smoothing her iron chignon.

Helen nibbles her thumb through her cotton glove. *How could I ever have harboured this snake in my bosom?*

"And how did the couple live together at this time?"

"Outwardly contentedly—but privately, quite otherwise." The sigh of a tragedy queen. "We—the reverend and I—took it as our mission to bring about a better state of feeling between them. The admiral confided his sorrows to us, as in a brother and sister, and I did my utmost to counsel his wife."

Bovill is nodding. "How did the admiral treat her at this time?"

"With exemplary attention and kindness. Admixed with the occasional silent reproof," Mrs. Watson tells him. "He was anxious about dear Helen's debts; her gay demeanour; her carelessness of the world's opinion."

"The impropriety of her behaviour with men?"

She throws up her wrinkled hands. "That's a strong term."

The woman's coyness makes Helen want to scream.

"I would prefer frivolity," she says squeamishly. "The admiral assumed—all three of us did at first—that she was only foolish, not wicked. Dear Helen had not found in motherhood the normal womanly fulfillment, and I formed the belief that she was . . . well, taking refuge in flights of fantasy."

"How do you mean, fantasy?" asks Bovill.

"Exaggerating her own charms, you see," says Mrs. Watson with compassion, "and imagining herself an object of fascination to every bachelor on the island."

Jealous hag!

"And indeed, to others in the home country: she spoke very foolishly of attentions she claimed the Prince of Wales had paid her once at a party."

Helen's hands are knotted together in her lap. Can't the jurymen see through this woman?

Bovill's voice takes on a deeper bass note. "When did you first suspect that the respondent's friendships might border on the criminal?"

"In October 1861," says Mrs. Watson in a throbbing tone. "Helen confided in me that she'd discovered Lieutenant Mildmay in her sitting room, his head in his hands, quite wretched with passion for her."

Yes, Helen had been unable to resist dropping little hints; the round-eyed Mrs. Watson had responded with a titillated astonishment.

"He'd rushed at her, and in resisting him . . . she'd bitten his cheek."

The audience likes this; there's a lot of muttering. *I never said that*, thinks Helen, appalled. *I never bit anyone's cheek.*

"Did you and she have a quarrel in consequence?"

"Not a quarrel," she demurs. "I reproved and cautioned her, but had not the slightest idea of actual guilt on her part. Then later that evening I was amazed to see her going out in a loose gown. 'Mildmay is frantic,' she told me, 'I must see him.' Well, as her intimate friend I couldn't stand by; I said, 'Think how it could be misconstrued if you're seen meeting him alone; I'm determined to go with you!' Then she promised to stay in, and assured me she'd only meant to soothe his savage bosom, as it were."

Helen's head is spinning. It's as if Emily Watson is reading from some novel in which she's the pious heroine—or at least the confidante.

Under his calm manner, Bovill's clearly delighted by all this. "At what subsequent period did you come to believe your friend guilty of actual misconduct with Lieutenant Mildmay?"

The witness puts her hand across her eyes.

"Mrs. Watson?" asks the judge. "Do you need a moment's respite?"

She shakes her head. "Perhaps . . . a glass of water?"

"Certainly."

She's laying it on thick, thinks Helen venomously. *Did she and Bovill work this up together, for effect?*

Emily Watson waits till a clerk rushes in with some water. She takes a ladylike sip. "I blame myself," she wails suddenly, "for an innocence that prevented me from acting in time to save my friend."

"Shall I repeat the question?" asks Bovill.

A fragile nod.

"At what subsequent period did you come to believe your friend guilty of actual misconduct with Lieutenant Mildmay?"

"I did not realize that the seal of infamy was set until . . . until the night she made a full confession."

The word acts like a thunderclap.

What confession? Through her own confusion and panic, Helen registers that Bovill's staring at his witness: *he didn't know this was coming.*

But the barrister makes a good recovery. "When was this?"

"December the thirteenth, 1861," says Mrs. Watson fluently. "Helen Codrington made a communication to me which has never yet passed my lips, because she demanded of me a promise of secrecy before she spoke. But now I have been put on oath, I consider myself released, and in fact bound, to speak the whole truth."

What in all the seven hells is she talking about?

Mrs. Watson puts her hand to her temple for a moment. "I expected Helen to tea at seven o'clock, but she did not knock at the door till half past eight, and my husband let her in. Instead of coming at once to the drawing-room, she went to my bedroom and sent down a message saying she begged to speak to me in private. She had the servant bring her a bowl of hot water. When I went up I found that she was trying—" a long pause, another birdlike sip from the glass "—she appeared to be attempting to sponge out a spot on her skirt."

A snort of laughter, from a fellow picking his nails just a few feet from Helen. She shuts her eyes. The only time she ever scrubbed her skirts at the Watsons' was to get some mud off.

"What kind of dress was it?"

"Yellow nankin, as I recall."

"Can you describe the stain?"

"Not its colour, or consistency, as she'd already put water on it," says Mrs. Watson regretfully. "But it was on the front of her skirt, about as large as the top of a finger."

"A fingertip?"

"The whole upper phalange of a finger," says the witness, holding up her own.

Bovill bends to exchange a few words with his client—Harry, entirely impassive by his side—then scribbles something in his notes.

They haven't heard a word of this fiction before, Helen guesses. *The witch saved it all for the witness box.*

Harry's barrister clears his throat. "What exactly did Mrs. Codrington say to you?"

"She burst out in violent agitation," says Mrs. Watson, "and told me that the climax of evil had been reached."

The audience stirs with loud enjoyment.

The judge glares down at them. "Is it going to be necessary for me to clear this courtroom?"

They settle down like cowed schoolchildren.

"The climax of evil," indeed! Helen knows she sometimes puts things strongly, but she'd never resort to such a penny-dreadful phrase.

"Were those her very words?" asks Bovill, as if struck by the same doubt.

"I cannot recall precisely how she put it," admits Mrs. Watson, "as the fact of the matter was so shocking to my sensibilities."

"Naturally. Did she give you any . . . details?"

"Oh yes. She told me that Mildmay had escorted her to my house half an hour before, but instead of bringing her in, he'd persuaded her to go up the lane at the back, where the dreadful deed was accomplished."

Bovill's mouth opens but nothing comes out.

"I was paralyzed with horror," Mrs. Watson rushes on. "Helen put her head between her hands and said, 'Do you scorn me, Emily? Do you shrink from me? I am lost.'"

"And did you in fact shrink from her?"

Mrs. Watson hesitates. *Deciding on a politic reply*, thinks Helen. "At first, yes," she assures the barrister. "But then I asked myself who was I that I should cast her out into the darkness? She was weeping at my feet, scrubbing at her dress like a lunatic. So I said, 'Helen, if you are truly penitent—as the Lord said to the Magdalen—go and sin no more.'" Her eyes are shining.

Could she possibly believe her own rigmarole? Helen wonders. Memory is unreliable, especially as one ages. Could it be that Emily Watson mistakes these grand scenes for how it was? No, the explanation must be simpler: a courtroom turns nobodies to tyrants for an hour, giving them a stage on which to spin their most inventive lies.

Mrs. Watson rushes on. "I made her promise to break off this unholy connection with Mildmay, and send back the rings and lockets he'd given her. Then the tea was ready and we went down," she finishes, anticlimactically.

Bovill seems at a loss as to what to ask his witness, for a moment. "Did you tell Reverend Watson about her confession?"

"Not at the time, because his doctor had instructed me to shield him from anything conducive to anxiety. Of course this made my trial all the heavier." She puts her handkerchief to her eye.

"Did she, to your knowledge, return Mildmay's gifts?"

"I thought she had," says Mrs. Watson grimly, "but she'd only locked them up in her bureau. Gradually, over the months that followed, little hints told me that she'd not broken off her intrigue with him at all!"

"And you quarrelled?"

Again, Mrs. Watson squirms at the word. "Not openly. Excessive loyalty is my weakness."

Helen wants to take her by the shoulders and shake her till something cracks.

"But I had withdrawn my heart from her, in private," Mrs. Watson assures Bovill. "We had one painful discussion, early the following year. I heard a rumour that she'd been calling Admiral Codrington's visits to my house *too frequent*; claiming there was an *undue intimacy* between us. Well, I broached the subject candidly; I reminded her that my friendship with the admiral had been formed with her full compliance and for her good. She accused me of having a *Jesuitical influence* over her children, of attempting to usurp her position as mother and as wife!"

Yes, Helen does remember that row; she allows herself a narrow smile.

"I asked her to deny the rumour in writing," says Mrs. Watson, "but she retorted that an honest woman didn't need a ticket of virtue! And when I made a delicate allusion to her own tarnished honour, she began to shriek in a frenzy: 'Send for my husband! You may as well tell him my secret and ruin me at once!' Then she flung herself on her knees and begged me to forgive her. I parted the hair on her brow and said, 'Oh Helen, darling, is this my return for all my love to you?'"

Helen is bewildered by this woman's gall; stray facts and purest fiction are mixed fluently in every sentence. What she's describing is their real, prickly friendship, but as if recalled in a delirium. Something occurs to Helen now: *I'm the most exciting thing that's ever happened to her.*

Bovill has been taking rapid notes with a scratchy pen. Now he peers at them. "Did the respondent ever write this letter you asked for—the letter denying she'd meant to accuse you and her husband of undue intimacy?"

Complacent: "She did, and I showed it to several acquaintances, to clear my name in Valetta before I left."

"The following question is of vital importance, Mrs. Watson." He gives her a hard look. "Before you and your husband departed from Malta in July 1862, did you ever breathe a word to Admiral Codrington of his wife's secret?"

"I did not."

"Or afterwards, in correspondence? Not even a hint, to put him on his guard?"

Go on, make up some scene in which you played the wise sybil, Helen urges her silently. Even a little hint could prove him guilty of condonation . . .

"Not one."

Unfortunately, she's not a fool.

The older woman's cheekbones are suddenly mottled with scarlet. "Some will blame me for this omission, though I know the admiral does not," she adds, with a grateful nod towards Harry. "I considered my silence a sacrifice on the altar of a dead friendship. My motive was womanly compassion."

As Bovill thanks his witness, and reminds her to stay in the box for cross-examination, Helen remembers something she's been trying to keep in the very back of her mind all day: *this woman has my children.*

Her own barrister, Hawkins, has been in intense, whispered discussions with Few. He rises now, unfolding his slim length, and glides towards the witness.

Save me, Helen tells him silently; *do your worst.*

"Now, Mrs. Watson," begins Hawkins, "from the time when the respondent ceased to accompany the petitioner to hear your husband's sermons, his Sunday visits to your home were of necessity paid alone. I must ask whether, from first to last, he ever took any liberty with you, or did or said anything inconsistent with your position as a married lady?"

An intake of breath. "Never."

Bovill jumps up. "My Lord, does my learned friend dare to imply what I think he is implying?"

"Only what is in the countercharge," says Hawkins mildly, "that the petitioner neglected his wife's company for that of another man's wife."

"The wording is ambiguous," protests Bovill, "and calculated to cause obscure damage to an impeccable lady's reputation."

Helen smiles, behind the clammy lace.

"I'm happy to let this point drop, if it causes so much offence, and move on," says Hawkins. "Though I must confess I hardly know where to begin, in responding to this *impeccable lady*'s almost . . . unbelievable testimony."

Emily Watson bristles visibly.

"To take just one instance. This lane behind your house in Malta, madam—are there houses on this lane?" asks Hawkins.

"There are."

"And people continually passing by?"

"I don't know about that."

"What puzzles me is, how could any two persons commit the act in question in such a lane undisturbed, around eight o'clock in the evening?"

A small shrug. "I gave it verbatim, as my friend—as was—confessed it."

Hawkins turns towards the jury. "What my client is barred from telling you herself, gentlemen, is that Mrs. Watson's statement is utterly false." He's allowed his voice to heat up now. "This *impeccable lady* has told us of a private dialogue between herself and the respondent—a *confession,* so-called—knowing full well that the mouth of the respondent is sealed."

Judge Wilde, nodding, clears his throat with a roar. "This is one instance of the many evils that flow from forbidding the parties in a divorce case to testify—a flaw in British law which I hope one day to see reformed."

"An admirable aim, my Lord," says Hawkins, with a broad smile. Then his mouth turns hard again as he glances at his notes, and looks up at Mrs. Watson. "You claim that you had 'withdrawn your heart' from the respondent by the early months of 1862, because by then you thought her engaged in a lasting intrigue with Lieutenant Mildmay. Yet I have here a letter dated June the fifteenth, a full six months after the alleged confession. Is this your hand?"

Fumbling, she puts her glasses on to look at it. "I believe so."

"I will now read a passage to the court."

My dearest Helen,

I am sorry you should feel annoyed with me on account of my leaving hurriedly the other day. Since I am customarily admitted to your room at all times, your dressing seemed no reason for not seeing me. But enough of this; life is too short to spend in vain squabbles, and true friends are too rare to lose. Let this be but an April shower, the sun must now shine again.

Believe me always
lovingly yours,
Emily Watson

The witness sucks her lips.

"Would you not agree that this letter implies an ongoing intercourse of the most cordial kind?"

Her eyes flick between the judge and jury. "The outward skin of that intimacy survived," she says, stammering, "even when it was dead within."

"The rankest hypocrisy!"

"I was anxious not to distress the admiral by any open scandal—"

Hawkins narrows his eyes. "Logic will suggest to the gentlemen of the jury that either you were lying in this letter, with its warm declarations of sisterly love, or that you're lying now: that there *was* no breach, because you did ***not*** in 1862 believe the woman you addressed so dotingly to be adulterous, since the alleged *confession* never took place."

"Not so, not so." Mrs. Watson takes a drink of water, swallows as if it's ground glass.

Hawkins leaps on. "How is it, I wonder, that you can recall with such precision the date of the alleged confession?"

"I noted it down in my memorandum book."

His slim eyebrows shoot up. "With what intention?"

"None. I hardly know. On a sort of impulse—"

"An impulse, a plan, a plot, in fact, someday to destroy your *dearest Helen's* marriage?"

Bovill stumbles to his feet. "I object, my Lord, in the strongest—"

"I should be happy to rephrase that," concedes Hawkins. "Mrs. Watson, were you anticipating that you would one day give evidence against her in a divorce case?"

"No!"

"A divorce case, in fact, of which you are the origin, the prime mover. It was you, was it not, a clergyman's wife," Hawkins barks before she can answer, "who when the petitioner called on you last month, lost not a moment in encouraging his jealous imaginings. Far from attempting to pour Christian unction on the troubled waters of that marriage, you immediately hired a spy for the purposes of surveillance on his wife. Pretty sharp work, if I may say so!"

"The admiral was in great distress," Mrs. Watson protests.

"So you found him a solicitor for the purpose of obtaining a divorce—in direct defiance of the teachings of your husband's church, by the way. You egged him on to cast off a lady you'd always envied for her personal charms, her lovely children, her lofty position in Maltese society. A lady on whom you'd privately vowed to have vengeance, ever since she'd complained of your fawning over her husband."

"Come, come," begins Bovill, half-rising.

But Hawkins has already spun to address the jury. "It will be for you, gentlemen, to decide where there is any grain of truth in all this tarradiddle.

Whether this false friend turned open enemy can be trusted to report on private conversations with the respondent, who, as Mrs. Watson knows, is barred from defending herself. Whether perhaps some talk on the subject of Lieutenant Mildmay's unreciprocated infatuation with the respondent did pass between the two ladies, but Mrs. Watson has distorted and exaggerated it. Or whether in fact the tale of the stained dress and the confession, brought out today like a rabbit from a hat, is the most egregious *coup de théâtre.*"

Strangely enough, Helen's enjoying herself.

"I am not well," whimpers Mrs. Watson. "May I be granted a rest?"

"Hm. You were inexhaustible in answering my learned friend's questions," remarks Hawkins. "But I have just one more."

"Will you carry on?" Judge Wilde asks her.

"If I must."

"On September the twenty-fifth of this year, the day the admiral deserted his wife and home, did you take away their two daughters?"

"He was gracious enough to consign them to my care," Mrs. Watson says faintly. "Mine and my husband's."

"And have these girls—at the tender ages of eleven and twelve—been allowed to meet, correspond with, or even glimpse their mother since that date?"

"They have not."

She steps down, looking older.

Was that antidote enough to the woman's poison? Helen wonders. Hawkins is a superb performer, but the story of the so-called confession still seems to linger on the courtroom's stifling air. It will be a sad twist if what damns Helen is not the truth but these lies.

She's suddenly bone-tired. She barely listens as Bovill continues his narrative: the departure of the Watsons, the transfer of the respondent's affections from Mildmay to Anderson, then Admiral Codrington's receiving orders to return to England in the summer of 1864, and Colonel Anderson's *fortuitously coincidental* request for home leave. She only comes to attention when Bovill remarks, "Her old friend Miss Faithfull, as we will prove, aided and abetted the sordid affair."

Fido, Fido, Helen thinks giddily, *you may run to the ends of the earth but you can't escape your share of punishment.*

Bovill's holding up a volume that Helen recognizes as her leather-bound appointments book.

Hawkins stands up to protest: "That item was seized in the respondent's absence, and by force."

"Need I remind my learned friend that on the respondent's wedding day, she gave up her legal identity, including rights of property?"

He purses his lips. "Wives have always been allowed to hold certain personal possessions, of no great monetary value."

"My Lord," Bovill appeals, "the book was found within a cherry-wood writing desk, which, as part of the house's furnishings, can be considered the chattels of the petitioner."

Judge Wilde nods. *He just wants to hear what's in it*, Helen realizes. All these distinguished men, agog like boys outside a circus tent.

Bovill reads various short entries, giving them a grim emphasis. "*Scene with H, put a veto on my going out.* 'H' can be none other than the petitioner, Admiral Henry Codrington," he remarks. "*To V. P.* This can be taken to refer to the Victoria Press, the place of business of Miss Faithfull on Great Coram Street. *To T. S., And. there, unsatisfactory.* Which clearly stands for: a visit to Miss Faithfull's residencc at Taviton Street—Colonel Anderson there—and an unsatisfactory meeting."

Helen curses herself for making these brief jottings.

"Thus we see that the respondent's missing witness—Miss Emily Faithfull—has played a shameful role in the Anderson intrigue, as go-between, accessory, in short as panderess!"

The word thrills the crowd.

Hawkins stands up to make a token protest about initials proving nothing. Helen rests her veiled, hot face on her hand.

"Now we come to a vital clue on September the twenty-first," Bovill goes on. "*E. F. has letter from Scotland. Miserable night.* While the misery of the respondent's night might of course have been caused by some minor ailment," he concedes, turning sardonic, "I think it more likely that this refers to the news of Anderson's engagement, passed on by their guilty abettor, Miss Faithfull."

A new witness is stepping into the box, a stranger with spotty cheeks. "John Crocker," he answers nervously. "Cabman at Southampton Mews."

"But on this occasion, weren't you employed to make private enquiries?"

"Yes, sir, I watched Mrs. Codrington from the eighteenth till the twenty-fourth of September," he says, checking his little memorandum book.

So Harry did set a spy on her. Who knew the old man had so much go in him? Helen listens to the tedious detailing of Crocker's long days outside the house, waiting for her to show herself, the trips to Whiteley's on which he trailed her. *As if I were some princess.*

Bovill leads Crocker on to Monday the twenty-fourth.

"She came out of her house alone, in a hurry, and took a cab to Number 24, Pall Mall. Or rather, the cab drew up outside Number 28, but she sent the driver to knock on the door of Number 24" says Crocker scrupulously. "A gentleman with blond whiskers came out and got into the cab with her. As I was standing some thirty yards down the street, I didn't see his face well enough to identify him, but his colouring and regimentals matched that of the photograph of Colonel Anderson supplied to me by the petitioner the previous day. I then followed their cab to the Grosvenor Hotel, where they went inside."

Helen closes her eyes, remembering the shabby room, the harshness of cigarette smoke in her throat. One never knows, at the time, that this is the last time.

"I waited till about midnight, when the two emerged and took a cab to Eccleston Square. Mrs. Codrington alighted from it about four doors from her house, then walked the rest of the way."

I'm done for. Helen subsides a little on her bench. There's nothing theatrical about this fellow's testimony, nothing that rings false. It's as plain as day.

Hawkins cross-examines, but to little purpose. He sneeringly enquires the rate of pay for *spy-work*—nine shillings a day, it emerges, rather less than Helen would have thought—and asks about the man's long-standing family connection with Mrs. Watson.

"Before the night of the hotel, I did offer to resign," Crocker volunteers. "It seemed low to spy on a lady when she wasn't up to any mischief that I could see. But Mrs. Watson kept assuring me it was an honourable business, because the lady was no better than she should be."

Sporadic laughter from the crowd.

"As so often occurs," Hawkins tells the jury with majestic scorn, "a detective is brought in to 'discover' only what will confirm the prejudice of his paymasters."

Yes, yes, thinks Helen, *but this doesn't make the Grosvenor Hotel go away.* She wonders, now, if she'd been just a little more careful, a little more discreet, could she have saved herself even on the brink of disaster? She seems to have acted like a boy pushing his tin soldier inch by inch towards the edge of the table, just to see what will happen.

It's Bovill's turn again. "I would like to enter into evidence something found with the appointment book," he says, almost pleasurably. "A folded strip of paper containing what have been identified as fragments of moss and heather, marked *Yours ever, A.*"

Helen's veil is suddenly sticking to her wet face.

"While, as my learned friend has been at some pains to emphasize, initials are subject to interpretation, I would put it to the gentlemen of the jury that in this particular case, *A.* can only mean the co-respondent, Colonel David Anderson."

She heaves silently. *Fragments of moss and heather.* From that hill above Valetta, that afternoon kissing in the bushes. The fragments are hers, hers alone, nobody's but hers. And yet they'll be filed away somewhere in the bowels of this medieval building, by faceless men, and she'll never get them back.

"And last but by no means least," says Bovill, "a letter—perhaps a draft or copy—found in the respondent's desk, which will remove any remaining doubts as to the nature of the relations between the respondent and the co-respondent."

People sit up straight, shush each other as Bovill starts to read.

Sunday, September 23

It has taken me two days to compose this letter.

Surely, before you formed an engagement you were bound in all honour to tell me of the changed state of your heart . . .

As he recites her words with monkish precision, Helen tries to shut her ears. She's on the hillside above the harbour, sun warming the heather and moss under her skirts, salty breeze in her hair.

"Although the letter contains no names, nor even initials," concludes Bovill, "to men of the world such as yourselves, gentlemen of the jury, it will clarify that for two years, Mrs. Codrington and Colonel Anderson have been on terms of declared, illicit affection. And although the letter contains no evidence of carnal *actions*, as such, you will bear in mind that when a married woman so abjectly surrenders her heart, it is a very short step indeed to the surrender of her person."

A skinny man hops up and turns out to be Dr. Swabey, for the co-respondent. Helen's neck prickles. "My Lord, I submit that this letter does in no wise tell against my client, Colonel Anderson," he says squeakily. "No proof has been offered that it was written to, posted to, or received by him, or that it has any bearing on his character at all."

A wintry smile from Judge Wilde. "The learned counsel is quite right in point of law, but not in point of common sense. The jury are free to interpret the letter in such a way as to conclude that Mrs. Codrington committed adultery with your client."

Swabey's mouth opens and shuts. "Even if they do," he maintains, "my duty is to create a reasonable doubt as to whether my client committed adultery with Mrs. Codrington."

A gale of laughter goes up, and Swabey's frown deepens.

"Very well, Doctor," says the judge, deadpan. "Gentlemen of the jury, if you find it plausible that a woman may have carnal relations with a man without him having such relations with her, then I direct you, in considering Colonel Anderson's guilt or otherwise, not to take this letter into consideration."

More hilarity, which the men of law pretend to ignore.

~

Few comes to her at Eccleston Square in the evening.

"I do hope you and Mr. Hawkins realized that Mrs. Watson's testimony was a heap of rubbish?" she demands.

The old man sighs. "Many of her stories did have the ring of yellow-jacket fiction, but they'll still have had their effect on the jury. As it happens, what interested Hawkins most was her emphasis on your powers of imagination."

Helen is open-mouthed. "You mean—when the creature claimed I deluded myself into thinking that every man I met was in love with me?"

"Mmm. Hawkins believes this could work to your advantage, if he were to reshape your defence somewhat along those lines."

Helen lets herself lean back into the sofa's padded embrace. "I'm entirely bewildered."

"Please don't take offence, Mrs. Codrington. Desperate times, desperate measures, eh?"

She stares him down.

"Hawkins says, what if he were to present you as an unhappy woman whose fancy has a tendency to run away with her? A woman who in fact has never gone further than the mildest coquetting, but who in her dreams is entangled in the most lurid intrigues?"

"Few, this is bilge, and offensive to boot."

The elderly solicitor holds up his hand. "Of course, but have the goodness to hear me out. In this way your gaddings about in Malta, your so-called confession to Mrs. Watson, even your appointments book and your letter to Anderson could all be explained away as mere . . . fantasy."

"Madness," she corrects him.

"There's a recent precedent," he tells her with dry enthusiasm. "A Mrs. Robinson: her husband's counsel produced a very frank diary in which she recorded her adultery with a hydropathic physician—but her side claimed that she'd made it all up, being afflicted with erotomania brought on by measures to prevent conception! The jurymen preferred to believe her unbalanced rather than immoral, so Mr. Robinson was denied his divorce."

"What cretins!"

Few shrugs. "Englishmen are reluctant to knock ladies off their pedestals."

"If Hawkins proves me mentally unhinged," Helen snaps, "am I right in thinking my husband could have me confined in a private asylum for the rest of my days?"

"Oh, come, the chance of such an eventuality—"

"Why risk it? And why humiliate me still further?" The words burst out of her. "I'd rather every paper in the country called me a harlot than a pathetic lunatic who only *imagines* that men desire her."

The look Few gives her is long and chilly. "That's your prerogative, Mrs. Codrington."

"Besides, I was under the impression that in order to block this divorce, you don't need to prove that I'm blameless, but only that Harry's somehow culpable."

"That's true."

"Well, then!"

"That's become exceedingly difficult in the absence of our chief witness." Few tugs at his collar. "I wish you'd never brought your unreliable friend to my office in the first place."

"Believe me," growls Helen, "I feel the same way."

"By the by. A solicitor of my acquaintance has heard a rumour that Miss Faithfull's still in London."

She blinks at him.

"In male disguise, if you can believe it."

"I can't," says Helen with disdain. That's just the kind of thing they like to invent about *strong-minded women.* Going uncorseted is one thing, but trousers? "For all her strong views on certain subjects, Mr. Few, she's an utterly conventional woman."

After the solicitor has left, Helen sits up by the dying fire, eating some old ham she found in the pantry. (Mrs. Nichols, unsurprisingly, has not returned to the house after her performance in court, and her room is bare.) Tomorrow, Helen supposes, she'll have to start sending a corner boy to fetch her meals from an inn. And do something with the rotting silver fish in the bowl. How fast a life comes undone. When the trial is over she must hire a new maid-of-all-work, but more urgently, she must get hold of some clean linen. How has she been reduced to this?

She goes up to bed, and sits reading *The Small House at Allingham* to bore herself to sleep.

XII

Evidence

(proof; knowledge on which to base belief; oral testimony, writings and tangible objects admissible in a court of law)

Each person in a dwelling should, if possible, have a room as sacred from intrusion as the house is to the family.

Anonymous,
How to Behave (1865)

That Monday evening, Harry and William stand smoking in an alley outside Bird's chambers, as the sun's yolk trickles down between the roofs of Gray's Inn. Harry sucks the harsh tobacco deep into his lungs. "How the years fall away."

"Hm?"

"When we were boys. You taught me how to fill a pipe when I was just eleven, I believe. Mama was incensed."

His brother grins. "Cigarettes are so much easier."

"Oh Will," says Harry, releasing a long plume of smoke, "this has been the longest day of my fifty-six years."

"I dare say it went well, though, as such things are reckoned?"

"Well, yes, inasmuch as the most appalling proofs of my cuckoldry were exposed to the public view," says Harry grimly. Cuckoldry's an old-fashioned word; what name should his shame go by, nowadays? "That's the perversity of the process," he goes on. "To be quit of Helen, I'm obliged to offer myself as a laughing stock to every newspaper reader in Britain."

William claps him on the shoulder. "When a tar needs an amputation, what does the surgeon tell him?"

"*Sharp and sore's soonest 'oer,*" quotes Harry, managing a half-grin. They smoke on in silence. "I'm awfully grateful you could be here," he remarks.

William waves that away. "You've had to rely on strangers too much already."

Harry registers the implicit criticism.

"By the way. This Mrs. Watson of yours. Do you place full credit in her stories?"

"What, the dress, and the confession, and all that weeping at each other's feet?" Harry scratches his whiskers. "I don't—not Helen's style—and I have the distinct impression Bird and Bovill don't either."

"Well, perhaps the good lady was stretching a point," murmurs William. "Fibbing in the service of a greater truth, as it were. Is she, ah, happy in her home?"

Harry's eyebrows contract. "Perfectly."

"Oh, I'm not insinuating anything on your side, dear fellow," says William with a chuckle. "It's just that she seems very warm in your defence. These older, childless females . . ."

"She lacks occupation, that's all; she's taken me up as a cause."

"Better than joining that crew on Langham Place, I suppose! They don't seem to grasp that women have a business already: marriage. Spinsters should be considered as so many bankrupts who've failed at it," remarks William.

The very thought of Fido Faithfull makes Harry's heartburn flare up. "Tomorrow Bovill's main task is to clear my name of the charge of rape." He speaks the word aloud to try to harden his ears to it. "How long is this whole wretched business going to drag on?"

"Difficult to say." William speaks lightly, as if speculating about a cricket match. "The lower orders have a custom known as besom divorce, I believe. Delightfully simple: if you don't like each other, after a year, you simply set a broom aslant in your door, then jump backwards over it."

Harry manages a smile.

"But I dare say court cases are always long in proportion to the names involved."

"The names?" repeats Harry, with a huge yawn. Funny how tiring it is to sit as still as a gargoyle all day in a crowded room.

"Well, if you were a brickie who'd staved his wife's head in, say, they'd have found you guilty in half an hour." William chuckles. "And remember these lawmen charge by the day: they'll spin it out as long as your pocketbook will bear."

Yes, of course; until the moment the decree absolute is in his hands,

Harry's liable for every penny his wife spends, whether on bonbons or on dresses (*stained, about the size of the upper phalange of a finger*) or on defaming her husband. Harry's funding every word spoken in court, on both sides; it's like some absurd command performance. But if he wins, at least Helen will become liable for the fees of her expensive lawyers . . .

"Actually," remarks William, "what struck me today wasn't so much the long-windedness, as the dirty-mindedness. All those over-educated fellows vying with each other to invent euphemisms for *the act in question.*"

Harry nods.

"Did you ever go to the Judge and Jury, opposite Covent Garden?"

"What is it, an inn?"

"A sort of mock court," William tells him, "where you're entertained with some gross indecencies over your cigar and rum."

Harry fixes him with a look. "Can you imagine me in such an establishment?"

William grins. "I suppose not, Brother Temperance."

"Besides, on today's evidence, the institution hardly needs to be parodied," he mutters.

They smoke for another minute in silence, then go into the chambers.

Bird looks up to acknowledge each of them with a nod.

Bovill is in full flow. "I still believe she could be charged with contempt, as she so clearly decamped in order to evade the subpoena."

"But what I can't follow—forgive my stupidity, gentlemen," says Mrs. Watson, "is why we need to find the creature at all. Shouldn't we rather rejoice that her failure to testify to those audacious slurs on the admiral's character proves her a coward as well as a liar?"

The solicitor sighs, absent-mindedly crumpling his lapel. "Any jury is a microcosm of the public, madam, and the public is not logical. Rumours and allegations linger like bad odours."

"Or rather," contributes Bovill, "they stick like mud in a carpet, until they're beaten out!"

"There's a wild one going round at the Rag Club," mentions William, "that my brother's smuggled this Faithfull woman out of the country—or worse."

Harry stares at him, injured that he hasn't heard this before.

Bird shakes his head. "The paradox is that unless Mrs. Codrington's counsel produce their missing witness, we can't actually disprove her affidavit."

"It's patently absurd," Harry bursts out. "If you knew Miss Faithfull—she's simply not the kind of woman one would dream—" Remembering the presence of Mrs. Watson, who's another of those women whom no man would attempt to molest, he decides to drop that line of argument. "I swear, I never went into that room when my wife and Miss Faithfull were sleeping there, except on a couple of occasions, to see to the fire."

"What on earth for?"

All heads turn to the general.

"I mean to say," says William, addressing his brother, "that's the maid's job, isn't it?"

Harry feels his cheeks heat up. "I had acceded to separate rooms, at Helen's request, but I didn't take that to mean I wasn't allowed to address a few remarks to her, on domestic affairs."

"Ah, so the fire was an excuse," Bird murmurs.

"I might have sat on the edge of their bed once or twice, in the course of conversation," snaps Harry. "But I defy Fido—Miss Faithfull," he corrects himself awkwardly, "to look me in the eye and say I ever tried to lay a hand on her."

"Could she have formed a personal grudge against you, Admiral?" asks Bovill.

"On what basis? When she was living with our family, I considered her a friend." It sounds weak, to his own ears; yet again, he's coming across as an idiot.

"Ah, but she was little more than a girl in those days," remarks Bovill. "Perhaps, now that she's become a strong-minded reformeress, she disapproves of our sex on principle?"

"Gentlemen, forgive my interrupting, but I believe you're in danger of overlooking the obvious," says Mrs. Watson. "From all I've heard, and my own encounter with this person, she is Mrs. Codrington's gull. Her tool. Perhaps the appalling story of the, ah, attempt, is entirely your wife's invention, Admiral, and Miss Faithfull only parrots it."

Harry stares at her.

"None knows better than I, after all," says Mrs. Watson, eyes on the carpet, "how Helen can take advantage of the strongest sentiments of female friendship."

"I believe she's hit on the truth," Harry murmurs to his brother.

"Well, whatever the woman's convoluted motives," says Bovill irritably, "if we can only find her and drag her into the witness box, I'll make mincemeat of her."

"We don't need an address to send her a message; wherever she may be, she'll be reading the English papers," observes the solicitor. "Is there anything we could offer her by way of a lure?" After a second, "Or a threat?"

"I've already called her a panderess," Bovill points out. "What arrows are left in our quiver?"

"Apprentices beaten and starved, at this famous press of hers?" suggests William facetiously. "Men-friends? Some by-blow, fostered back in Surrey?—begging your pardon, Mrs. Watson."

"No need," she murmurs. "I hardly know how to put this, gentlemen, but—"

"Go on," Bird tells her.

Mrs. Watson puts her hand to her cheek. "First I must exonerate myself from any imputation of coarseness . . . Due to pastoral duties and extensive travel, I have more experience of the underbelly of society than perhaps a gentlewoman ought."

"Speak freely, do," says Harry, hiding his irritation.

"Well. Let me just intimate," looking down at her hands, "that a sinister construction *could* be put on the behaviour of a woman who, night after night, for months, usurps a husband's place in his wife's bed."

Nobody says a word. Harry feels a painful jab in his chest. He takes a breath. "You don't mean—"

Mrs. Watson's fingers are over her face. "Don't make me say a word more."

It's his brother who breaks the silence. "By Jove, you're on to something, Mrs. Watson. That might just fly."

Bovill is nodding eagerly. "I could certainly drop a few hints along those lines, intimating that I'll shout it to the four winds if Miss Faithfull doesn't come to court at once."

"This is ridiculous," says Harry, almost to himself.

"The knack will be, to say it without saying it; anything explicit could rebound in our faces," the barrister goes on. "Admiral, are you by any chance familiar with the story of 'The Purloined Letter'?"

Harry scowls at him. "I'm not a lover of fiction."

"Very instructive, Mr. Poe's stories, from the legal point of view. A government minister, aiming to gain power over a certain royal personage, has stolen a letter from her," Bovill tells them all. "The thing is, he doesn't show it to her husband and destroy her honour, because his—the minister's—power lies in the possession and not the use of the letter—rather, in its permanent *potential* for use."

"But I never thought of such bizarre possibilities." The words explode from Harry. "Are we to believe, or to expect an English jury to believe, that as well as indulging in relations with two different men, my wife would—" His throat locks.

William shrugs. "Really bad women can move from vice to vice, like butterflies in a flowerbed."

"She was brought up in India *and* Italy," Bird points out. He pats Harry's wrist. "But don't torment yourself, Admiral: no one in this room is claiming that any such debaucheries really occurred."

His chest refuses to unknot.

"Why don't you let Bovill hint tomorrow that you *might* have had such suspicions—so the Wednesday newspapers, by repeating it, will scare Miss Faithfull into taking the first boat back to London to defend herself?"

There's to be no end to the shame poured on Harry's head, then; no end to the lewd laughter prompted by the name Codrington, which his ancestors—all descended from a spear-carrier of Henry the Fifth's—passed down to him unstained. When Sir Edward was accused of exceeding his orders in starting the battle of Navarino, Harry remembers, he'd sat down calmly to draw up a narrative of proceedings that would clear his name. The truth was shield enough for all those bluff generations. Sir Edward's son has the misfortune to live in modern times, when, it seems, it takes lies to set one free.

After a long moment, he nods. "If you all think it worth trying."

"Very good," says the solicitor soothingly.

Bovill is musing aloud. "If someone had only written something down at the time Miss Faithfull was living at Eccleston Square . . . It wouldn't even need to be read aloud: the very fact of such suspicions having been consigned to paper would tell against her. I don't suppose you kept a diary, Admiral?" he asks in a curious tone, head on one side.

"I never have, apart from a ship's log."

"Or a letter to some trusted associate on the subject of your wife and her bosom friend?" suggests Mrs. Watson. "If you'd even confided your fears in me, in Malta . . ."

"You can't testify twice, madam," Bird reminds her quietly.

Harry's finally catching on. He knows what answer the faces turned towards him require. "Well, I dare say it's possible I did jot something down at the time, and have forgotten. I could look through my papers," he concedes, his stomach leaden.

"Anything at all," says Bird. "A brief memorandum, for instance, signed and dated and sealed . . . I'm sure it would have been sealed, as you wouldn't have wanted a servant to read it."

"Of course, the admiral might very properly have consigned such a document to the trusted hands of, say, his brother," says Bovill with a twinkle.

"Mm, that would be much the best," says Bird, "as the general, unlike the admiral, could appear as a witness and testify to the circumstances of its composition."

"Certainly," says William.

"If I wrote anything down, I very well might have given such a thing to my brother," says Harry woodenly.

Mrs. Watson rewards him with a dazzling smile.

~

In his bedroom at the Rag Club, Harry takes a few pages of notepaper from the back of his writing box. "These are rather yellow. Could they pass for seven years old?"

"They say *Vice-Admiral Henry J. Codrington*, though," William points out. "You were only a captain in '57, weren't you?"

Harry grunts at his own stupidity and screws up the pages.

"Plain paper will do. Here's some in the drawer."

To put the task off for a moment, Harry pours more brandy for his brother.

"Have another tot yourself, won't you?"

He shakes his head. "It doesn't suit my constitution. Clouds my head." Silence fills the room, like stale air. "I don't like dragging you into this, Will . . ."

"Stuff and nonsense. Besides," his brother adds, pragmatic, "I won't be testifying to anything but the fact of receiving a sealed envelope from your hands, which will be perfectly true."

"The perjury's all mine, then," says Harry grimly.

"Buck up. You won't be in the witness box. Just write this memorandum whatsit, and Bovill will see to the rest."

"These sleights of hand revolt me. What Father would have thought—" Harry breaks off, his voice shaking.

"Oh, to the devil with our sainted father." William's red about the cheekbones; it must be the brandy. "You've always carried him about like some idol, a figure of awe and reproach. But to my mind, his career would have benefitted from a sprinkling of diplomacy."

"You can spout such things—his heir, his favourite?"

"That old theme?" His brother rolls his eyes. "I tell you, he loved us all the same. The morning he got your letter after Acre, he wept, Jane says, wept into his porridge, out of pride in his young chip-off-the-old-block. I'm sure he's looking down from a better place, now, hoping you win your divorce, even at the cost of a little sleight of hand."

Harry sits, mulling all this over, while William drains his glass. Could his brother be right? He doubts it; his conscience is in a queasy state.

He takes a piece of plain stationery and smooths it out on the desk. "Something we hadn't considered yet," he murmurs. "Will an English jury understand a glancing allusion to this sort of vice?"

"Oh, the more up-to-snuff men will be delighted to explain it to the others, when they're locked up in their room," says William with a snort of amusement. "Anyone who's read Baudelaire, or—what's that old poem about the two lords' wives that still goes the rounds? *They ask no joys beyond each other's smock . . .*"

Harry winces, and returns his gaze to the blank page. "It's all nonsense, though."

"No doubt," William assures him. "My own dear wife insists on sleeping with her friends, whenever they visit."

"What I mean is, Fido—the woman—did stir up some trouble at one time, took Helen's side. I'd go so far as *alienation of affections*, even, if we're to use legal jargon," Harry makes himself say. This is like picking a scab, but he can't stop. "These all-engrossing passions of theirs can be damned inconvenient, can even come between man and wife, I don't deny that. But to go beyond, and fancy a monster behind every bush—"

"Yes, yes. It's after midnight," William reminds him, tapping the page.

"I'll begin in a moment." He stares at the paper, the subtle nap of it. "I know I've been mistaken before. After all, I thought Helen quite used up by motherhood," he says, hot-faced. "She seemed—to be frank, Will, she was as unresponsive to me as a dead fish."

A grimace from his brother.

"I assumed that all she wanted from men was flattery—and how wrong I was! Which makes me wonder, now, if it's theoretically—if it's within the realm of possibility that I might have been so blind as to miss other horrors going on under my very nose, in the very next room . . ."

"Enough! You may sit up all night trying to spook yourself," says William, standing up and stretching, "but I want my bed."

Harry stares at the page till his eyes unfocus. "What shall I put?"

"Bovill says in all likelihood it won't even be read," William tells him. "Just make a start and some suitably stern expressions will come to you. Goodnight."

Harry puts the pen down and wipes his sweating hands.

"What's the matter now?"

"It's my first attempt at forgery, after all," he says, trying for a jocular tone.

"It's not forgery when you're signing your own name," William tells him, making for the door.

~

On the second day of the petitioner's case, Bovill wears an air of mild cheer. "I will now dispose of the respondent's countercharges—libels, rather—against the good name of the petitioner. Specifically, her claim that *if* the adultery occurred, her husband conduced to it by neglect and cruelty. Now, a foreigner with a less than perfect grasp of the subtleties of British law might call this a strange defence from a woman who maintains her complete innocence." His tone's neutral, but he waits for the laugh. "But leaving that rather obvious point aside, let us consider how the petitioner is said to have mistreated his wife so badly that she was obliged to flee into another gentleman's arms. Oh, excuse me," he tells the jury, "I mean, of course, into the arms of not less than two other gentlemen."

This causes waves of mirth.

Harry's eyelids keep sagging. How embarrassing it would be if he were to doze off during proceedings of such importance to him. But he barely slept last night, in his narrow bed at the club, and when he did he was tormented by dreams of Helen. Not the snappish woman he shared a house with until just two weeks ago, but a dancing Helen in the glittering gauzes of an odalisque.

"Two of our witnesses—Mrs. Nichols and Mrs. Watson—have attested to the petitioner's exemplary treatment of his wife," Bovill reminds the jury. "He found her extravagance, her tantrums, and her flightiness distressing, but he bore with them all. Far from neglecting her, he maintained perfect trust in her honour while she was flitting all over the island with various officers. Even before their departure for Malta in 1857, when she demanded a separate bedroom, he had at no point insisted on his marital rights. What husband in this courtroom—in the country!—could match such forbearance?"

I sound like a doormat, thinks Harry, head down. *Or a eunuch.*

His barrister's tone turns outraged. "The respondent's counsel may accuse the petitioner, with the grim hindsight a courtroom offers, of uxoriousness—but what is that but husbandly love so perfect it borders on excess? They may even argue that he must have guessed the true role that Mildmay and Anderson played in his wife's life—but the truth is that this veteran of

Her Majesty's wars is of such an upright character that he can barely comprehend duplicity in his fellow man, let alone in the softer sex."

Harry wants to groan aloud. Some myopic Quixote; a feeble-minded Christian soldier. Is it really vital to his case to strip him of every vestige of manliness?

"Beset by official cares, reluctant to suspect any real ill of the mother of his children," Bovill goes on, "the petitioner nonetheless did share his concerns with others, notably the Watsons but also—very properly—his wife's widowed father, Mr. Christopher Webb Smith. If I may read the crucial sentence from a letter that venerable merchant of Florence sent his son-in-law in November of 1863, that is, last year—" Bovill clears his throat.

I can only express my hope that my daughter will alter her conduct and avoid disgracing her husband, children, and family, in time to save herself from ruin.

"The jury should note," says Bovill, holding up one finger, "that Mr. Smith, like the admiral, showed no awareness that Helen Codrington was *already ruined.* Thus the petitioner, like his father-in-law, was deeply troubled, but did in no sense condone, connive—in the popular phrase *turn a blind eye*—rather, he was blinded by the highest sentiments of familial affection. Only on the couple's return to London in August of this year did the petitioner, now released from the cares of his post, have leisure to consider his wife's behaviour more closely. It was the unhappy accident of their child's illness, which prompted the admiral to send his wife a telegram at Miss Faithfull's house on September the sixteenth—a telegram her response revealed to him that she never received—which caused him to face the dreadful possibility that she had in actual fact been unfaithful to him."

Where were Helen and Anderson the night of the telegram? Harry wonders. In some dubious hotel, while Nell lay white-hot and straining for breath at Eccleston Square? Even after all the evidence is presented, so much of his wife's hidden life will remain opaque to him.

Bovill consults his notes. "I will now address the most outrageous countercharge, that of cruelty, and in particular the claim, in Mr. Few's affidavit, that in October 1856 the admiral attempted the virtue of Miss Emily Faithfull. In that lady's conspicuous absence, I propose to my learned friend that it would be better for all concerned if that particular claim were withdrawn forthwith."

Harry's ears prick up at this. If the charge is withdrawn, there'll be no need for anyone to mention the memorandum he sealed up, with shaking hands, at half-past twelve last night.

Hawkins rises, suave as ever. "I thank my learned friend for the suggestion, but I decline. I would be delighted if he were to drop any of the even more disgusting charges made against my own client."

This little bit of repartee amuses the audience. *Damn these lawmen*, Harry thinks: *it's all a game to them.*

Bovill resumes mildly. "Well, then. In that case—my client has asked me not only to deny the charge in the most unequivocal terms, but also to make the jury fully aware of the poisonous role Miss Faithfull has played in his marriage as far back as that same year, 1856. The petitioner had by then harboured her at Eccleston Square, in the bosom of his family, at his personal expense, for over two years. And how did she repay him? On his return from the Crimea, the petitioner found that his wife's passionate feelings for this person were causing her to shrink away from her husband."

Hawkins, on his feet, blinking. "*Causing?* What proof of causality does my learned friend intend to offer us?"

"Very well: let me say instead that the friendship and the withdrawal were simultaneous and proportional," says Bovill crisply. "The respondent generally slept with her friend, claiming that Miss Faithfull was subject to asthma and needed aid in the night." He pauses significantly, as if to let those words ring hollow. "When the marriage reached a point of crisis the following year, and my client called in his brother and Mrs. Codrington's parents for advice, they fully concurred with him that Miss Faithfull should be dismissed from the house."

This causes a stir. Harry chews his lip.

"At which point, he entrusted to paper his thoughts on her role in the crisis, and his reasons for banishing her—which document was sealed up and placed by him in the hands of his brother."

There's a moment's silence. Then Hawkins rears up again. "I know nothing of such a document, and nor does the respondent. I object to any statement being made respecting its contents, unless it can be proved that the respondent was present and was cognizant."

"She was not cognizant," says Bovill silkily, "but the document has every bearing on the issue of her character."

"What is its nature, may I ask? Is it a statement of facts?"

Harry's sweating into his shirt, as if he's on deck in tropical waters.

Bovill hesitates. "At this time—"

"Is it addressed to his brother?"

"It is not addressed to General Codrington."

"To what party is it addressed, then?" demands Hawkins.

"To no particular party except perhaps to the petitioner himself. But in that it is not a record of events, so much as reflections, feelings—suspicions, even," says Bovill, producing the word with a sinister gentleness "—perhaps it can best be described simply as a letter."

Hawkins holds his opponent's gaze for a long moment. "Is this sealed letter in court?"

"It is," says Bovill.

A frisson goes through the packed chamber. Harry's hands are wet; he clamps them between his legs.

"I mention it to illuminate the testimony of my final witness: I now call General William Codrington."

After a few preliminary questions about Harry's treatment of his wife—"considerate in every way," William says, more than once—Bovill asks about the marital crisis of 1857. "The sealed letter: do you have it in your custody?"

William pulls out of his pocket a white folded paper, heavy with black wax. Harry flinches at the sight of it.

Bovill pauses, and makes no move to take it. "Do you recognize the seal?"

"It's my brother's. Admiral Codrington's."

"Has it been opened or tampered with?"

"No, it remains in the state in which he entrusted it to me."

Every eye in this courtroom is trying to bore through the paper, Harry thinks. He risks a glance over his shoulder at the staring faces. Their vulgarity, their desperate greed. There's a lady at the back with a black lace veil, like those mantillas the Catholics wear on Malta. *Wait a moment.*

"Do you know its contents?" Bovill is asking the general.

"I don't."

Could it be? He moves his neck to get a better look at the veiled lady. There: a strand of red hair, below the hem of the lace.

"What did the petitioner give you to understand that it contained?"

William answers with a guarded discomfort. "An explanation of his reasons for ordering Miss Emily Faithfull to leave his house."

Helen. It has to be. Has she sat here all morning, and yesterday too? The gall of her! Yes, he might have guessed that a woman who pores over intriguing messages from strangers in the *Telegraph* could hardly resist watching her own terrible story re-enacted. Like Hamlet among the players.

"May I ask, my Lord," demands Hawkins, on his feet again, "whether the petitioner's counsel mean to open this document about which they've been making such a deep and dark mystery?"

Harry, rigid, turns his eyes back to the white square of paper, the black wax that bears the Codrington arms. Everything depends on the next few moments.

"I will leave it to my learned friend to have the seal broken or not as he pleases," says Bovill with a courteous gesture.

Hawkins clearly wasn't expecting that; he leans down to consult with the aged solicitor. Then he draws himself up to his full height. "I must observe that this whole proceeding smacks of pettifoggery and chicanery."

Harry registers with a prickle of pleasure that Helen's barrister is losing his temper. But will that make the man open the letter or not?

"If this document contained anything to support the petitioner's attack on Miss Faithfull's character," barks Hawkins, "surely my learned friend would have opened and read it aloud already."

"I wouldn't dream of taking such a step without my learned friend's consent," says Bovill. He holds Hawkins's gaze, raises one eyebrow.

There's a long moment in which no one speaks; the longest so far in this case, thinks Harry.

"I neither assent nor dissent to the opening of the seals," says Hawkins warily. "It's for my learned friend to attempt to enter the document in evidence, that is *if* and *only if* he can prove my client is directly connected with it."

Judge Wilde intervenes brusquely. "If the letter's contents are germane, by all means let the seals be broken."

Harry looks back at Helen, through the sea of heads. Of course it's her; he should have known her at first glance, for all the layers of black lace. She's frozen like marble. What's that play in which the statue of the wife comes to life?

"If my learned friend declines—I do not choose to take such a step at this time, my lord," Bovill tells the judge.

William puts the thing back in his jacket pocket. Harry's hands are shaking, between his knees, like some small captured animal.

"Then," says Hawkins, as quick as a snake, "I move to strike the whole tangential discussion from the record."

What difference would that make, Harry wonders? How can the jury unhear what they've heard?

Judge Wilde frowns in indecision, then says, "No, the transaction is part of the *regestae*, and no fact bearing upon the case should be concealed from the court."

Bovill gives Harry the smallest of smiles. "Gentlemen of the jury, in conclusion. We of the petitioner's counsel have shown how the latent germs of corruption that Helen Codrington displayed as a young bride gradually ripened into criminality of the most sordid kind. We need shock and weary you no longer, although a French novelist would no doubt delight in showing in endless, repulsive detail how immediately Mrs. Codrington fascinated, how inevitably she injured, all those drawn into her web—whether confidantes, paramours, or, above all, her long-deluded and now heartbroken husband."

Harry's learning to recognize his twisted image in a succession of cracked mirrors. When this whole thing is over, when the stacks of newspapers are wrappers for tea-leaves or turnip peelings, which Harry Codrington will linger? The hero of a tragedy, the butt of a farce? The battle-coarsened rapist, or Old Pantalone, the dotard who wears the horns he deserves?

It seemed such a simple decision, when he said it in Bird's chambers, during that first interview: *I want a divorce.* But it's himself Harry seems to be divorcing. Will he ever get back that firm sense of who he is, like a pebble in his palm?

When he turns his head sharply, to ease his aching neck, he notices Helen's elderly solicitor slipping out. Few stops to speak to his client; she adjusts her veil and follows him out. The door is closed softly behind them, and Bovill is still spelling out the nefarious details of Helen Jane Smith Codrington's career. *You're missing the grand climax*, Harry tells his wife in his head.

"I urge you," Bovill addresses the jury, "to acknowledge the terrible facts of this marriage, though they may contradict the polite, fashionable fiction of feminine innocence. I urge you to release, as from the coils of a serpent, one of the most honest, valiant servants our sovereign has ever had."

Bird turns to beam at Harry. But instead of any surge of pride, or even relief, Harry feels only a flatness.

In the brief recess, he stands in Westminster Hall, keeping one eye out for Helen, but there's no sign of her.

William takes him out for a turn around Parliament Square in the smoky October air. To the left of Westminster Bridge stretches the muddy chaos of London's most ambitious construction project. Having squeezed houses, streets and railway lines into every square inch of the city, the developers now mean to build on the Thames: fill a broad slice of water with mud and sewers and call it the Victoria Embankment. It would be hard to explain to a South Sea Islander. Harry thinks of himself as a progressive thinker, but in this case he can't help wishing they'd left the river alone.

"This city still stinks," observes William.

Harry nods. "Though the Board of Works are boasting they've found a salmon in the river."

"What, a single fish?"

"Mm, but alive. A sign of hope for the new age of sanitation, they're calling it."

William lets out a sardonic laugh. "You may as well have this back," he says, holding out the packet with the black seal.

Harry finds himself strangely reluctant, but pockets it. "I was sure, at one point, that Hawkins would insist on its being opened."

"No, it was just as Bovill predicted: no counsel will risk a document being read unless he knows exactly what it contains."

Exhaustion passes over Harry's head like a wave. "Was it worth the fuss, do you think?"

"Hard to tell, yet," says his brother, smoothing his glistening white beard. "It'll be in all the papers tomorrow, and just might flush this Faithfull woman from her nest in time to be examined."

Somehow, Harry doesn't believe it. Fido, in whatever corner of Europe she's hidden herself, on whatever ship steaming towards Philadelphia or Shanghai, seems as remote as a character from a fairy tale.

"At the very least," says William briskly, "it'll have splashed her with a bucketful of filth, and Helen too. The jury might have already decided not to credit a word either woman's ever said!"

Going back into the courtroom, Harry expects to find Hawkins already on his feet, outlining the case for the respondent. But both barristers are standing below the judge, deep in consultation. "What's afoot?" whispers Harry in Bird's ear.

The solicitor's puffy with irritation. "They've had the nerve to apply for an adjournment."

"An adjournment?"

"A delay of several weeks. On the spurious grounds that our original petition contained no reference to one of the acts of adultery having taken place in the lane behind the Watsons' house! Hawkins claimed he couldn't possibly rebut it without sending his agent back to Valetta."

"Surely one sordid location among so many is neither here nor there?"

"Not in the eyes of the law," says Bird through his teeth. "Opposing counsel claim the credibility of our witness hangs on it."

"Can't we withdraw that particular allegation, then?"

"It's out of our hands; we knew nothing about the whole confession story in the first place."

Harry silently curses Mrs. Watson.

Judge Wilde clears his throat and addresses the court. "As an adjournment would represent more distress, delay, and expense to both parties, I am going to suggest that the petitioner's advisers consider whether they might abandon the charges against the respondent with reference to Lieutenant Mildmay, and rely solely upon the charges against her and the co-respondent, Colonel Anderson."

This causes a stir in the audience.

"Should we?" Harry mutters to Bird. "I suppose we'd still have ample proof about the two of them, especially at the Grosvenor Hotel . . ."

"And throw away most of Mrs. Nichols's evidence, and all of Mrs. Watson's?" Bird's tone puts Harry in his place, as an ignorant layman. "By no means." He's shaking his head at Bovill, who nods and turns back to the judge.

"Well, then," says Judge Wilde. "There are times when the wheels of justice must grind slowly in order to grind thoroughly. I have no alternative but to adjourn this trial for two weeks, to resume on October twenty-third."

Harry's reeling. He'd hoped this nightmare might be over in another three days, or four. The fire put out. Sails set for a calmer harbour.

As the crowd disperses, Bird reaches up to put his hand on Harry's shoulder, a familiarity that makes him recoil a little. "Don't be downcast, Admiral. A delay will allow all our evidence to linger in the jury's minds, and no doubt our men can dig up some more dirt in Malta, too. Besides, that small commotion wasn't really about Mrs. Watson's lane."

"How do you mean?"

Bird taps his florid nose. "Just a pretext on their part, don't you know. Hawkins and Few must be desperate for time to track down their lost witness, especially since we produced our *sealed letter.* And now both sides will have agents combing the ports for news of Miss Faithfull, chances are we'll sniff her out."

XIII

Sabotage

(destruction of property to hinder a particular group; action aimed at weakening an enemy through subversion, obstruction, or disruption)

If our women, whom hitherto we have regarded in a certain sense sacred to the home life, come swaggering out into the streets like noisy brawlers in a rude crowd, they must forgo their privileges of respect and protection for that liberty which includes self-assertive competition, rough words, and rougher shouldering aside.

Montague Cookson, "The Sacred Sex,"
Saturday Review (May 13, 1871)

Miss Bennett sits by a moribund fire. She should ring for the girl to bring in more coals—though it's only mid-October, the afternoon is bitter—but somehow she doesn't dare.

She's been here a week and a half. (She hadn't the momentum to get as far as France or Italy; she knew she could lose herself in the less fashionable quarters of Pimlico just as easily.) A week and a half of solitary meals on trays, afternoons watching the dying fire, her lungs creaking like unoiled hinges. She broods over the possibility that the girl will have noticed something. Only this morning she remembered that her handkerchiefs are monogrammed: why would a Miss Bennett's handkerchiefs say *E. F.?* At any moment, the landlady might march in to demand an explanation. What decent woman takes lodgings under an assumed name?

Fido got it out of *Pride and Prejudice*, not that she resembles any of those bright girls with their futures sparkling before them. Well, maybe what's-her-name, the one who played the piano too long and bored the guests.

Her dreams have never been so lurid. Last night she was setting type, working so fast her hands blurred. She felt a tug; she looked down to see that she was wearing a voluminous white satin gown, and one of its flounces was caught up in the machinery of the Wharfedale press. Slowly, inexorably, Fido was being pulled from her desk, dragged nearer and nearer the hungry cylinders of the machine. Then she was in the bowels of the press, rolled quite flat, covered with red-inked words. The strange thing is, what was distressing her in the dream, what made her scream and keep screaming without a sound, was not pain, but the fact that she couldn't read the words.

After ten days in this rented room, she's finding it hard to get out of bed before nine. She speaks to no one, has no business, receives no post. In all her adult life, Fido's never been in such a state of isolation. She feels obscurely guilty about leaving her most responsible clicker, Wilfred Head, in sole charge of the press at such a busy time, not to mention dropping the new *Victoria Magazine* entirely into Emily Davies's hands—but a sort of helplessness has paralyzed her. Since a few days into what she's come to think of as her confinement, when she went out for air and happened to glimpse a placard advertising *Shocking Revelations on First Day of Codrington Trial*, she's read no papers, for fear of what she'll find there. Perhaps this is cowardice. Very likely. Fido has suspended all her principles on assuming the name Bennett.

If the trial began on the eighth . . . surely it must be over and done with by now? But to find out, she'll have to buy a newspaper, and the thought makes her sick to her stomach.

Her limbs have tightened from lack of exercise. This must be what it feels like to be one of those elegant invalids, cooped up and cosseted all over Mayfair and Belgravia. Fido's afraid to so much as walk in a park because she might run into someone who recognizes her. This city of almost three million souls is smaller than one might think. Accidental meetings happen all the time. (On the last day of August, for instance, on Farringdon Street. Two tangled fates wandered apart for seven years, then converged without warning.)

Fido broods, too, on the original accident, a full decade ago: the day she glimpsed Helen Codrington for the first time, crying by the shore in Kent. Was there a choice, at that moment? Fido could always have walked by, she supposes; pretended not to notice the tears streaking that small, lovely face; said nothing, not even a "May I be of any assistance?" But no, it's simply not in Fido to be so cold, not even nowadays when the world of business has toughened her, and certainly not back then, as a girl of nineteen. So perhaps it's our nature that makes our fate. Inescapable.

And even to save herself from complications, would Fido really want to be the kind of person who walked on past a distraught stranger, fearing to involve herself, averting her face? A dull, utilitarian life that would be. A life without risk.

A tap at the door, and she jumps.

"Miss Bennett?"

"Come in."

"Telegram for you," says the girl, handing it to her.

Alone again, Fido strains to breathe, waits for her pulse to slow. The only person who has her address—for emergencies—is Bridget Mulcahy at the press. *Please come at once. B. M.*

~

SHE TAKES A CAB TO BLOOMSBURY, and finds the press in a state of apocalypse. Great Coram Street is littered with hacking, sobbing typos. Miss Jennings, the deaf girl, is standing frozen on a curb, with streaming eyes. "What on earth has happened?" Fido asks another hand, who goes into a coughing fit at the sight of the proprietor. The girl beside her speaks up hoarsely. The word sounds like *dying*.

"I beg your pardon?"

"Cayenne, I said. Cayenne powder, madam, all over the floor."

The poisonous stuff is not just on the floorboards, Fido finds when she makes her way inside—handkerchief pressed to her face—but in the machines too, scattered among the type itself. What a simple technique, but how effective. Her throat makes a harsh whoop. She catches sight of some red paint daubed on a wall: *Something Stinks*, it says.

"Have the police been called?" she asks a red-faced Mr. Head.

"Of course," he says shortly.

She coughs and wheezes, then finds her way to her office, where Bridget Mulcahy, face swathed in a scarf like some harem girl, is mopping the floor.

"Miss Faithfull," she cries out. A cold breeze whistles in the window.

Fido collapses into a chair, shivering under her greatcoat. "We are veterans of this kind of sabotage, Miss Mulcahy, aren't we?" She means her tone to be encouraging, but it comes out piteous.

"'Tisn't sabotage this is, but war." The woman's brogue has strengthened in the crisis. "Those misfortunate hands who tripped in here first thing this morning—their throats are scalded."

"I blame myself," Fido mutters.

"That's nonsense, madam."

"I ought to have been here. I am the target." She makes herself go on. "This attack is not simply directed against the cause of female employment, for once. That graffiti on the wall—"

"The men should have scrubbed it off by now," scolds Bridget Mulcahy.

Fido shakes her head. "You know as well as I do that it refers to my name having been dragged into this divorce."

Miss Mulcahy's face remains blank. "I already told the peelers, I believe Kettle may be involved."

"Our Mr. Kettle? Our clicker?" asks Fido, startled.

"He ever so fortuitously sent in his notice yesterday morning. And no window was smashed, which means the brutes must have had the key!"

Fido drops her face into her hands. After a long minute, she tries to gather her forces; she straightens up. Her lips taste of harsh spice. Is it possible—Kettle letting their enemies in? She suspected him of fiddling the accounts, but no worse. She's beginning to distrust her ability to take the measure of people.

No matter how she flees from the grasp of the Codrington case, it finds her and drags her down. What good has it done her to go to such lengths to defy the court's summons? Without ever entering the witness box, she's been judged and sentenced in every household in London. Her knuckles are between her teeth now: the metallic tang of blood.

~

By the time the press has been cleaned up, all the hands seen by a doctor, and other small but urgent matters of business settled, Fido hasn't the heart to go back to Pimlico and take up her pretence of being Miss Bennett. She sends a boy to collect her things from the lodgings instead, and walks home to Taviton Street.

It's only a few minutes from the press, but today it takes her a quarter of an hour. She stumbles along in a daze through the sharp October afternoon.

Letting herself into the house with her own key, she startles Johnson in the hall. Wide-eyed, long-faced, the maid stands staring as if at an apparition.

Fido can't summon the energy for any sort of explanation. Besides, what good is it to have servants if you have to explain yourself to them? "I'll be in my study," she says instead, hoarsely.

"Yes, madam."

She coughs up a lot of yellow-brown stuff into a basin, and drinks two glasses of water. On her desk, a perfect stack: unread copies of the *Times*. She shudders at the sight. And then decides to get it over with, because this day could hardly get any worse.

The first report, which she finds in the edition of the ninth, gives her a vertiginous feeling as she reads about all these colourful characters: the reckless Mrs. Codrington, the sorrowful admiral, the audacious, interchangeable Mildmay and Anderson. And here comes the wife's friend, this enigmatic Miss Faithfull. (She's described as Helen's *companion*, as if she was some kind of toady working for bed and board during the three years she spent at Eccleston Square.) Fido cringes at the references to meetings between Helen and Anderson in her own house. How could she have been taken in by Helen's rigmarole about breaking with him gradually? *According to Mr. Bovill, the co-respondent's missing witness—Miss Emily Faithfull—played a shameful role in the intrigue, as go-between, accessory, in short, as panderess.* She tries, and fails, not to think of her parents and brothers and sisters reading this.

But it's when she finds, in the report of the tenth of October, that Few's affidavit about the attempted rape was not withdrawn, that she starts to tremble. The admiral's barrister mocks the very idea of his client's molesting a young woman *not reputed to be of conspicuous beauty.* Fido wipes her eyes—*vanity, vanity*, she scolds herself—and forces herself to read on. *What shadow Miss Faithfull's flight casts on the veracity of her tale, I will leave to the gentlemen of the jury to decide.*

Her eyes scurry through the columns, hunting for her name. There's worse: Here comes a peculiarly distorted version of the summer of 1857, when she left Eccleston Square. *Miss Faithfull's poisonous role . . . his wife's passionate feelings for this person were causing her to shrink away from her husband. He entrusted to paper his thoughts on Miss Faithfull's role in the crisis, and his reasons for banishing her—which document was sealed up and placed by him in the hands of his brother.* There follows a lot of legal bickering about the status and relevance of this *sealed letter.*

Fido rubs her aching forehead. She's never heard of this document. When Harry suggested she go home to Surrey . . . she remembers the conversation as cordial, if awkward. Why would he have sat down to write a memorandum about it? Surely he'd remember what had been in his own mind, without having to commit it to paper?

A kind of proof, then. A proof of what? Slowly, cumbersomely, her mind grinds the husk off the seed.

Her eye moves up the column again. *His wife's passionate feelings for this person were causing her to shrink away from her husband.* Fido stares at that sentence, reads it again, and once more.

Oh, good God.

A proof of a suspicion, only. No one has named that suspicion, in court or in the newspaper. (Not the kind of thing anyone wants to spell out, even in these tell-all times.) A word to the wise. Those who don't understand it won't even notice what they're missing; those who do, will comprehend the whole business in a moment. *Sealed up.*

Nauseated, she holds to the edge of the desk as if she's in a rowboat, being pulled into the eye of a storm.

XIV

Contempt

(an intense feeling of disrespect and dislike;
a wilful disregard for authority; an act calculated to hinder
a court, punishable by fine or imprisonment)

A man who should be all head would be as monstrous an anomaly as a woman all heart . . . Men have no monopoly of working, nor women of weeping.

Emily Davies,
The Higher Education of Women (1866)

The following day Harry stands on Langham Place, looking at the brass plaque that says *Ladies' Reading Room.* It sounds so harmless, as if all the inhabitants do is sit around reading poetry or consulting French fashion plates.

A bespectacled little person answers the bell at last, and he expects the sight of a naval officer—six foot five and scowling—to make her falter. But she only tells him that he's early.

"You don't know my business, madam."

"Oh, I beg your pardon, I thought you must be here for the meeting."

"What meeting is that?"

"Why, the Social Science Association; we're to discuss the results of the Cambridge Locals. The girls did remarkably well, considering their lack of training in mathematics," she assures him in her whispery voice. "I do hope you stay, we expect the Earl of Shaftesbury and Mr. Fawcett too."

Harry brushes this off. "You are—if I may?"

"Miss Lewin, sir. Secretary of SPEW."

That means nothing to him. "I wish to speak to someone about Miss Faithfull."

"Ah yes, we've been hoping to hear from any friends of hers," says the secretary with an uneasy smile. "She left no forwarding address when she went off on her travels, which has caused no end of trouble."

Harry clears his throat. As if he gives tuppence for the inconveniencing of this gang of do-gooders! "Who's in charge here?"

Miss Lewin blinks at him.

He racks his memory. "Isn't there a Miss Parkes?"

"She's upstairs," the secretary admits, "but I'll have to enquire . . ."

When Harry's finally shown into the office, a surprisingly good-looking lady in a loose grey dress offers him a firm handshake. Even standing, she's half his size, but he recognizes her air of command, as surely as if he could count the stripes. "Thank you for seeing me," he says with unwilling courtesy.

"I recognized your name, of course," says Bessie Parkes.

"So does everybody in England, by now," he remarks with some bitterness.

"Do have a seat, Admiral. You have my sincere condolences—"

He inclines his head, oddly gratified, and pulls out the chair.

"—though I must also mention, you've set our work back by about ten years."

Harry speaks thickly. "I did not name your friend in my petition. It was she who chose to meddle on my wife's behalf, by embroiling herself in the case and telling the most appalling lie about me. Now I must insist on being told her whereabouts so that she can be served with a subpoena—"

She interrupts him quietly. "You may be surprised to learn how little formal connection Miss Faithfull has, these days, with this establishment."

His eyebrows go up.

"Although formerly a keen worker by our side, for some time she's gone more and more her own way," remarks Miss Parkes sorrowfully. "In my view, her interests lie more in commerce than in reform. She's recently founded her own magazine, quite independent of any of the society's endeavours, and I've been obliged to cancel the Victoria Press's contract to print the *English Woman's Journal*."

Harry's voice comes out full of gravel. "Do you suppose I give two figs who prints your journal?"

The tiny woman's look quells him. She rises as if to show him out.

"I beg your pardon, Miss Parkes. I'm under some strain," he says, clasping his hands to stop them from shaking.

"I understand." She sits back down, still cool. "I only mention these details to convince you that none of us here has the slightest idea where Miss

Faithfull has sequestered herself, since she didn't even have the courtesy to inform us of her departure."

It's not the words so much as the biting tone that convinces Harry. "I was expecting something rather different, when I came here today," he admits.

Miss Parkes flushes a little. "What, a devoted little clutch of hens?" She hesitates. "I imagine you know how it is, Admiral, to serve alongside a comrade of whom one's views have changed."

"I've sailed with men I'd gladly see tossed overboard."

A tiny smile from the lady. Harry's bemused to find himself enjoying this conversation. Apart from William, it seems as if Harry speaks to no adults these days except lawyers in his pay.

"There's an unsoundness in Emily Faithfull; a coarseness in the grain that I hoped might disappear, as she matured, but quite the contrary," she says, gazing into the middle distance. "May I speak quite frankly?"

"Please do."

Bessie Parkes licks her upper lip neatly, like a cat. "I could tell by your expression, as you came into the room, that you're not a believer in our Cause."

He huffs out a half-laugh. "You know—everyone knows, by now—the story of my marriage. Can you imagine it's inclined me to think your sex should be granted even more liberty? Freedom to earn your own money, while squandering that of your husbands? Freedom to roam where you will, abandon your children, leave your households in chaos?"

"Admiral—"

"You and your ilk are bomb-throwers in bonnets," he tells her. "You may fool yourselves that you only mean to redecorate a few rooms, but in the end you'll tear the whole building down."

Harry expects this provocation to put Bessie Parkes into a rage; he's quite looking forward to seeing her throw off the mask. But instead she looks away, and her elegant cheeks are hollow. "With regard to Miss Faithfull . . . For most of us, the Cause—the zeal for a new, and better relation between our sex and yours—has demanded the sacrifice of the pleasures of marriage and motherhood. And yes, I assure you, most of us are womanly enough to miss those pleasures."

He stares at her.

"But in some few cases, especially if the individuals lack any real religious faith, something . . . goes awry," says Bessie Parkes, her mouth twisting. "Spinsterhood is a sort of spiked armour that such women as Fido Faithfull wear with relish. What's been revealed in court about the lengths to which she's gone in thralldom to your wife—" She shivers.

"If you knew her hiding place," Harry asks, "I wonder would you tell me?"

A painful smile. "I must admit, I'm glad I don't."

Harry bows, and thanks her for her time.

~

THE NEXT DAY comes the first bad fog of October. The sky begins to darken at eleven that morning, and lights glimmer in windows. His cuffs are tinged with black by the afternoon.

A bell rings in his room—the latest innovation; the senior members are up in arms, complaining it makes them feel like footmen—and Harry goes downstairs, to find the head porter waiting for him in the marble hall, under the tapestry of Diana and Actaeon. "A lady insists on speaking to you, sir."

"I've left clear instructions—"

"Not your wife," the porter corrects him in a whisper. "This person wanted to come in, but I explained our strict rule against ladies, except on our annual Ladies' Day. She's waiting in a cab outside."

Could it be Mrs. Watson? "You might have let her stand inside, on such a day," snaps Harry.

"Mustn't set a precedent, Admiral."

Harry hurries out. The air's thickly yellow, almost green at the edges, and reeks of coal; it burns his lungs. Coatless, he's shuddering with cold by the time he looks in the cab window.

Fido looks back at him with her big brown eyes.

He straightens up in shock.

She clears her throat. "I understand you called at Langham Place, looking for me."

He finds himself helplessly matching her civil tone. "That's correct. I'm afraid I can't ask you into the club—"

"Rules," she says, nodding.

He throws a glance up and down Pall Mall. There's really nowhere a man and a woman of their class can go to speak to each other in private.

"Would you—will you join me?" She says it squeamishly.

Harry thinks how it would sound in court. *The petitioner and the hostile witness, glimpsed sitting close together in intimate tête-à-tête in a hansom . . .* But everything sounds sordid to him nowadays; his imagination is contaminated. He opens the door and gets in.

Their knees almost touch. Harry busies himself unfolding and tugging at the leather door, until they're at least partially enclosed.

"Why do you persecute me?" Fido bursts out.

Harry stares at her in the dim. "Well, I like that!"

"This *sealed letter* your brother produced in court," she says. "Have you been plotting my destruction, all these years?"

He leans his elbows on his knees, till his face is only inches from hers. "You're the one who accused me of behaving like some crazed ape."

A sob escapes from her throat. "I was a guest in your house; I was only a girl. Can you look in your heart and deny, deny that you at least tried . . ."

"It must be your lack of experience of my sex that deludes you as to the brutishness of our appetites." He leans away, to study her more scientifically. "The fact is, not in my wildest dreams, not even if delirious or demented would I ever consider carnal relations with you."

She turns away, curling into herself with mortification.

His breathing is heavy. He knows he's being cruel, but she deserves it, and it may do her good. After a moment, he says, more gently, "But I rather think you're sincere in your belief that something of the sort happened."

"Of course I'm sincere!"

"Then you're a sad dupe. The story has Helen's dirty fingerprints all over it."

Fido stares at him.

He's getting somewhere, now. "However did she manage to convince you?"

She speaks in a small, hoarse voice. "I know what you're doing. You're taking advantage of my confusion as to what took place."

"Why on earth would you be confused?"

"I'd taken a syrup, for my asthma . . ."

"Ah," Harry groans. He sees it all now. Such simple stuff out of which Helen weaves her schemes.

"When I woke up you were just going out the door," she insists. "Can you look me in the eyes and swear to me that you never got into the bed, even—"

"Of course I can," he roars. "And in return, I ask you to trust what you do remember: in all the years you shared my home, I never did you any harm, did I?"

Fido only blinks.

"Wake up! Hasn't the witch deceived you, over and over?"

After a long moment, Fido shakes her head. "I grant you, Helen does exaggerate, sometimes. She sees things as if by limelight—"

"She lies," he corrects her, flatly, "with a monomaniacal disdain for the truth. She makes things up like a child who hardly knows the difference."

"You're hardly a neutral judge of her character."

He lets out a sort of laugh. "You're in thrall to her. I was too, once, so I recognize the symptoms. You mistake her firework displays for true feeling. Believe me," Harry says hoarsely, "you'll recover in the end, and regret it took you so long."

The moment teeters. Then Fido speaks coolly. "To business. This document your brother waved about—exactly what does it contain, may I ask?"

He almost admires her for standing her ground. He feels a surge of improvisatory brilliance. "Oh, you needn't trouble yourself about that, Miss Faithfull," he says, reverting to the formal. "It's in your power to keep it permanently sealed."

"They're speculating and joking about me in every coffee-house in London," she says, gesturing so violently she slaps the pleated leather door.

"Speculations and jokes will blow away like chaff," Harry tells her. "If you appear as my witness on the twenty-third—"

"*Your* witness?" Fido's voice is shrill.

He manages a smile. "Now you're back in London, my wife's side will serve you with a subpoena and compel you to appear, on pain of being charged with contempt of court."

"I know that."

"But only your conscience can instruct you what to say. As two rational beings—let's put an end to all this awfulness, shall we?"

She doesn't answer.

"Tell the truth, and your reputation will be restored." He means it to have the ring of a sermon, but somehow it sounds more like Mephistopheles offering a bargain.

Not a word from the woman.

"Would you really testify for Helen, after the ruthless way she's treated you? To drop you the minute we left for Malta, then pick you up again on her return, like some handkerchief or umbrella—"

Another vehement shake of the head. "There, you don't know what you're talking about. There was a ridiculous misunderstanding, letters gone astray—"

Harry feels a vast impatience. "I always liked you, Fido, and considered you a sensible person," he tells her. "But when it comes to Helen you're a perfect idiot. Letters gone astray, indeed! I remember Helen slitting open one of yours, at the breakfast table in Valetta, and casting it aside with a snide remark about spinsters having too much time on their hands."

The cab is choked with silence. He waits. With this last detail he's broken her, he's sure of it: in a moment she'll start to weep, she'll beg his forgiveness . . .

Instead she tugs at the leather door, as a signal that the interview is over.

XV

Charge

(an accusation of wrongdoing;
a sudden attack; a price)

Friendships are not always lasting—particularly those that become inordinately violent, and where both parties, by their excessive intimacy, put themselves too much into each other's power.

Eliza Leslie,
Miss Leslie's Behavior Book (1853)

Helen lets her head roll back against the raised velvet edge of the sofa. "I've nothing more to say."

Few taps his fingertips on his knees, one of many tiny, irritating tics she's come to notice in her solicitor. "Mrs. Codrington—"

"It's bunkum," she bursts out. "Some conjuror's trick. Must I tell you for the thousandth time, I don't know what's in this *sealed letter*, and I don't care?"

"I believe you ought to care. You must have some idea what was going through your husband's mind—"

"That noble organ has always been opaque to me. How should I know what fantastical tosh Harry might have scribbled down on a piece of paper, seven years ago? The things I heard about myself, over those two endless days in court—" she's almost shouting "—do you think there's anything left that can make me blanch?"

The solicitor says nothing.

"In the end, they didn't open the wretched document, did they? So let's consider the subject closed."

Helen's eyes are clamped shut. She knows that's not how trials work. She may not be an expert in the law, but she's come to realize, already, that just as the hearing of a petition for divorce involves probing into every corner of the past, so the words said in court—every epithet, petty fact or grandiloquent piece of rhetoric—become in turn the object of enquiry, and are repeated ad nauseam in the popular press. Barristers quote and question each other and the witnesses; not a slip of the tongue goes unpunished. Nothing, once said, can be taken back, and no subject can be closed. It's an endless, sickening spiral of language.

"I raise the matter again for a particular reason," says Few quietly. "Miss Faithfull's back."

A jolt goes up Helen's spine, and her eyes open.

"Today I received a short note from her to apologize for her absence. She tells me she's ready to testify, when your case resumes on Tuesday."

Relief flows over her like a fur cloak against her shoulders. "Why, that's marvellous!"

"I hope so."

His guarded tone sets her teeth on edge. "Few," she says, puffing up her plaid-silk skirt, "you lack confidence; I'm surprised you've ever won a case."

His grizzled eyebrows go up. "Didn't you tell me you left Miss Faithfull's house under duress?"

"Ah, but she'll be true to me, though, now it's come to it."

"I thought she resented being press-ganged into appearing as your witness."

Helen laughs. "Men don't understand the first thing about friendship."

"Female friendship, you mean?"

"It's the only kind. The dry, straightforward, temporary alliances among your sex hardly count. Women can fly at each other like cats," she tells him, "and yet deep down, hidden, there's a bottomless well of love."

"I'll take your word for it, Mrs. Codrington."

When he's gone home, Helen goes from room to room of the dusty house, turning out the lamps. She makes it up one flight of stairs before the tears come rolling down her face.

She swabs a tear off her bodice before it can leave a mark on the silk. She sinks down, crouching on the thickly carpeted step. *Oh Fido.*

Helen should have known her friend was coming back. Ought never to have sneered at or abused her, to her plain and honest face or behind her sturdy back. Never should have dragged her into these treacherous waters in the first place. In four days' time the vicar's youngest daughter, a shining light of the Reform movement and renowned example of the heights a modern woman can reach, is going to step into the witness box and commit perjury—and all for the sake of Helen Codrington. For the sake of a most flawed, grubby specimen of humanity. *A worm*, thinks Helen with a sort of guilty relish.

Oh Fido, I never should have doubted your love.

XVI

Witness

(to see with one's own eyes;
to testify against, or for;
to be a mark, token, sign)

What so false as truth is,
False to thee?

Robert Browning,
"A Woman's Last Word" (1855)

On the evening of the twenty-second, Fido walks the polished boards of her bedroom. Tomorrow she'll wait till her name is called, then mount the steps to the box. She'll take her oath, hand on the Bible, and then—

What on earth is she going to say?

Each time she passes her mirror, out of the corner of her eye she glimpses her large, moonlike face. *Not reputed to be of any conspicuous beauty.* She doesn't turn to look at herself head-on: no need. *Not in my wildest dreams*, he said in the cab, *not even if delirious or demented.* Fido doesn't care so much about that; it's not as if she's ever wanted men to take that sort of interest in her. She can bear to be plain; she has other shining qualities. What's tormenting her is the sense that she's been a fool.

There was no attempted rape. Oh, Harry has attacked her savagely, with this ghastly, un-spelled-out story of the *sealed letter*—but he never laid a hand on her.

How could she have been taken in by Helen's lurid tale for one second? Leaving aside its intrinsic unlikelihood—the timing rings false. Why, if not to bolster her desperate legal defence by smearing her husband's character, would Helen have brought the thing up, that day in the teashop? *The unspeakable incident. Hidden away in the deepest folds of your memory.* Nonsense! And all that posturing, those delicate qualms: *I'd never ask you to testify, dearest. . . . If only I could take this cup from your lips . . .* Fido's hands have contracted into fists, now, and she's pacing faster; one board groans every time she puts her weight on it. Looking back, there were so many points when any woman of average intelligence should have smelled a rat. And Fido knows that she's more intelligent than the average woman—that is, when her brains aren't blurred by the proximity of Helen Codrington. *She deceives me over and over, and I let her, I open my arms to gather her lies like blossoms.*

Now she's begun admitting the sense of what Harry told her, she can't stop. Stitch by stitch, Fido is unpicking the woman's fraudulence. That pair of missing letters, for instance: the vilified Maltese post. How likely is it, really, that two different letters from the same sender, on two different mail-boats, would go astray in the crossing from Valetta to London? *Slitting open one of yours*, Harry said, *at the breakfast table in Valetta, and casting it aside with a snide remark about spinsters having too much time on their hands.* Yes, Fido can just imagine Helen in that little scene, a roll of those sapphire eyes. So the truth must be that Helen simply discarded her best friend, as soon as Fido was too far away to be of any immediate use. *After all the years I'd lived in her house, slept in her bed, tried to keep her life from flying into pieces!* Then when Helen ran into Fido again seven years later, on Farringdon Street—

Hold on. Her mind works slowly, a worm chewing up dirt, but it still does work.

Fido pulls the bell-cord, and waits for her maid to mount the stairs. Her throat is dry. "I'm sorry to trouble you so late, Johnson, but I believe some warm milk may help me sleep."

"No trouble at all."

The expressionless, ageing maid must know that tomorrow's the day her mistress is going to testify. The staff must all be familiar with every detail, from the specific—the colour of the yellow nankin stained dress—to the opaque—the *sealed letter* and what it may say about the relations between their mistress and an adulteress. It occurs to Fido that this is the measure of loyalty: Johnson could have made her nest-egg by now, simply by offering an interview to one of the weekly papers. *The Faithfull Connection: Behind the Scenes in Woman-ist's Bachelor Household.*

She forces herself on. "Also—I wonder if I could check your memory, a small point . . ."

"Certainly, madam."

Fido swallows. "The first time you met Mrs. Codrington—" The name's like a stain on the counterpane. "Do you happen to remember when that was?"

The maid's lined face has stiffened.

"Was it towards the beginning of September? The sixth, I believe?" Fido sighs; how can the maid be expected to remember? "She came to tea that day. As did a military gentleman." It's ridiculous; she finds she can't say Anderson's name.

Johnson shakes her head, suddenly decisive.

"Of course, you'd have had no reason to make note of the date," Fido mutters, partly to herself.

"It was before that, madam."

This is what she dreads to hear. "You first laid eyes on Mrs. Codrington *before* the day she came to tea?"

The maid's nodding. "At least a week before that—the end of August, it must have been—though I didn't know who she was then, of course. She came by in a cab with the same gentleman," says the maid with pointed hostility, "and asked for you."

Fido's pulse is painful in her chest. "You're quite sure?"

"Yes, madam, it stuck in my mind because they didn't leave their names, though I asked of course," says the maid. "She—Mrs. Codrington—she wanted to know was this the correct address for Miss Faithfull. I said you were at your steam printing office on Farringdon Street, and would she like to leave a card? But she didn't. She just drove off in a hurry. The two of them did, I mean."

Fido's hand is over her mouth.

"So I'll bring up the milk now?"

"Never mind that," she manages to say, turning away. Waiting for the door to shut.

It was a conspiracy from the beginning, then. Helen, learning from the maid that Fido was in the City that afternoon, hovered outside her office with Colonel Anderson so they could pretend to bump into her, quite by chance. How beautifully it all worked out—Fido's asthma attack on the Underground, their visit to the press, the whole flurry of newfound intimacy . . . And Fido, in her sparking soap-bubble of self-delusion, attributed the whole thing to providence!

Perhaps there is no providence, no fate, no grand plan, she thinks now. Perhaps we dig our own traps and lie down in them.

Her cheeks are encased in her cold fingers. *Oh Helen, what wrong did I ever do you? Haven't I loved you with all my being, tried to save you, suffered untold humiliations for you?*

But no, it occurs to her that she's looking at it from the wrong angle. The mortifying truth is that Fido's irrelevant: a convenient messenger, go-between, mouthpiece. *Some handkerchief or umbrella.* In Helen's tangled melodrama, Fido's is only a walk-on part. That's what leaves her sick and dizzy now; that's why this little lie about Farringdon Street hurts more than all the other, graver ones. The joke is that Helen is probably not guilty of any malice towards Fido. She's dealt her a mortal blow, but carelessly, as one might drop a book.

Does that make it better? No, worse. *I'd rather count*, Fido decides, lifting her face.

She heaves a long breath, and squares her shoulders. She pads over to the dresser. In the jewellery box she finds the velvet choker, and she holds it taut in her fingers and marvels that she was ever charmed by such trash. With her thumbnails, she starts stripping off every dull bead, every last fragment of shell.

Knowledge like honey in her mouth: *I can destroy her. I can do it tomorrow.*

~

Fido, hovering at the back of the court, looks around the packed rows. Will she have to stand for hours? She's not sure she has the strength, after a sleepless night. But just then a gentleman stands to offer her his small portion of the bench, and she accepts with a grateful nod.

She's wearing her usual business costume of long-sleeved bodice and ankle-length skirt. (At first light, she put on her best dress—plum velvet, over a stiffened petticoat—then told herself it was rank hypocrisy and took it off again.) Nobody casts her a glance; her name may be somewhat famous, but her face, not at all. That will be different by the end of the day: everyone in this crammed courtroom will have memorized her features. (Please, no photograph in the papers!)

The tallest of the barristers rises. "I rejoice, gentlemen," he tells the jury, "that the moment has finally come to argue the case of my much persecuted client."

Hawkins, for the respondent: that's how the papers describe him, Fido remembers.

"I regret that the adjournment was necessary. But I have the fullest confidence that despite all the arguments prejudicial to Helen Codrington you heard two weeks ago, you will have held your judgement in righteous suspense, remembering that your verdict is one of moral life or death for the lady. This is a tragic story," Hawkins goes on sonorously, "of an ill-matched couple who, by British law, I trust you will find, must remain married for the rest of their days and make the best of it. Such a verdict will teach a valuable lesson to husbands, that if they choose to live more or less apart from their wives, they cannot, at some future period of their own convenience, shake off the yoke they have come to find heavy."

Fido's eyes seek out Harry, sitting beside his lawyers. In profile, he's a wooden figurehead, weathered by storms.

"The respondent is of a lively and artless disposition," admits Hawkins, "given to speaking in superlatives, and kicking against the chains of custom. Unwise, perhaps, in agreeing in her carefree girlhood to become the helpmeet of a sober naval officer in his middle years—unwise, I grant you, but never criminal."

A few snickers from the audience.

Hawkins looks graver. "Raised in the relaxed atmospheres of India and Italy, my client has foreign habits, such as letting gentlemen escort her at night, or conversing with them while sitting up in bed. These habits may arouse your English distaste, but it would be most unfair to judge them by English rules of propriety."

Does anyone believe a word this man is saying? Fido wonders.

"A web of malicious, salacious innuendo has been all my learned friend has offered to prove Mrs. Codrington's misconduct," remarks Hawkins. "For a couple to live separate lives, even with each other's full sanction, is dangerous, especially for the wife. A husband's frequent visits to another woman—in this case, Mrs. Watson," he adds darkly, "are generally assumed to be harmless, whereas a wife's friendship with another man is vulnerable to the most sordid suspicions."

Well, that much is true, Fido admits; there's nothing symmetrical in marriage. If Fido didn't know the truth—if Helen were any other woman in the world—she'd probably give her the benefit of the doubt.

"But the petitioner was fully aware of his wife's friendships," Hawkins points out, "and did nothing to curtail them. Regarding Lieutenant Mildmay: may I—need I—point out that my client would hardly have asked for him to be examined if she were conscious of the least guilt in her relations with him? Mildmay's declining to be interviewed may be due to a natural dread of publicity, or perhaps some lower motive: it is not impossible that he may feel some enmity towards her for refusing him her favours . . ."

Fido almost admires the light way the man drops in these outrageous suggestions.

"We have been told of wild conversations, private trysts and assignations," Hawkins sweeps on, "but all this testimony has been circumstantial and contradictory. We have heard inferences, not facts, from a shabby line-up of witnesses, including an embittered housekeeper, a footman discharged for a brutish attack on a fellow servant, and the most patently hostile of former friends, Emily Watson," says the barrister with a handsomely curled lip. "Much of this so-called evidence is obscene fantasy. My learned friend has asked you to believe, for instance, that a lady and gentleman would commit adultery in an upright position on a quay under full dazzling moonlight! Or on a cabin bench of no more than twelve inches in width, on a journey by gondola of no more than ten minutes!"

"Three would do," shouts someone from the gallery, which provokes roars of mirth.

Fido goes hot. Unspeakable things can all be spoken in this packed, stifling room: it's a little hell at the heart of the metropolis where a sort of alchemy turns everything to dirt.

After a brief hiatus as Judge Wilde orders the offender found and ejected from the court, he gives Hawkins a warning.

"The court must pardon my explicitness, my Lord," says Hawkins magnificently, "since it is the tool required to hack through the thickets of innuendo that threaten to ensnare my client."

Now he calls his witnesses one by one: another boatman who denies that the gondola got particularly out of trim on the nights when Mrs. Codrington was in it with either of her escorts; another former servant who insists that on Malta Mrs. Codrington usually had a maid sleeping in her room. Fido's not really listening, she's distracted by a kind of stage fright: when will she be called?

Turning to the London evidence, Hawkins admits that his client's meetings with Colonel Anderson—by sheer coincidence, on home leave this summer—did become covert, "but only because the petitioner began to display an unaccountable hostility to his wife continuing in England the independent life she'd formed in Malta," he says. "As for the so-called assignation at the Grosvenor Hotel, no witness from the hotel has been produced, nor any evidence that Colonel Anderson took a bed-chamber. He and Mrs. Codrington can hardly have committed the act in question in the coffee-room! My learned friend has performed a similar sleight of hand on the letter found in the respondent's desk," Hawkins rushes on. "There is no proof that she ever sent it; it might have been merely a private soliloquy—an outpouring of emotion. Its language, in either case, is not that of hardened adulteress to paramour, but that of a troubled lady to a platonic friend, on the eve of his rash marriage. As a missive from a married woman, I do not deny it is imprudent, but it contains in its sorrowful tone and high-minded wishes for the co-respondent's welfare much that is creditable, and nothing—*nothing*—to prove that she broke her marriage vows with him."

Hawkins pauses to sip from a glass of water. Fido feels a mad impulse to applaud.

"But I understand that some gentlemen of the jury may still be feeling swayed by the many petty and misleading anecdotes got up by the petitioner's agents and counsel," says Hawkins sternly. "This is why the respondent's counterclaim states that *if* you are led into the error of believing her guilty of misconduct, she wishes you to be made aware of grave neglect and cruelty on the part of her husband which *would* have conduced to that misconduct, *had* it occurred."

His grammar's getting strained, Fido notices. It must be difficult for a barrister to keep up the pretence that he believes his clients. Are lawyers liars by definition? Do liars, then, make good lawyers? She thinks of a world in which all careers will be open to women, and wonders—aware of the absurdity of the thought—whether Helen Codrington would make a good barrister.

"Firstly, neglect," says Hawkins crisply. "The petitioner's insensitivity to, and virtual abandonment of, his charming young bride began as soon as she followed him from Florence to England. She found herself expected to occupy every day with running his household, bearing his children, and nursing his dying father. I put it to you, gentlemen of the jury, that by ignoring his wife's needs for stimulus and amusement, the petitioner left her to seek these things alone, unguarded, exposed to the rumours of a malicious world."

His tone turns hushed. "Those were not the only needs of hers he neglected to fulfill. The last issue of the marriage was born in 1853: some four years later, her patience exhausted and her heart broken, the respondent finally requested the dignity of a room of her own." He pauses to allow the whole audience to register his meaning. "Since the petitioner, as we have been told, did enter his wife's room on occasion—the door not being locked—it may be presumed that it was by his own acquiescence, or even by his own wish, that marital relations did not resume at any point in the seven years that followed. I need hardly remind you, gentlemen, that it is for the spouse of the stronger sex, not the weaker, to demand the exercise of conjugal rights."

Fido watches the jury: the smug faces, the uneasy ones.

"To shed more light on this delicate subject I now call Captain Strickland of the Royal Navy."

Strickland turns out to be a hangdog, red-haired subordinate of Harry's from Malta.

"Did the respondent complain to you bitterly about not seeing her husband from one day to the next?" asks Hawkins.

"Ah, yes."

"Did the petitioner ever ask you how many children you had?"

A glum nod. "I told him two."

"His reply?"

"I believe he said, 'That's quite enough. Follow my example and have no more.'"

This starts a scandalized ripple in the crowd.

"Did you think he meant simple abstinence," asks Hawkins grimly, "or—I beg the court's indulgence—the use of devices to thwart conception?"

"I don't recall what I thought, exactly," mutters Strickland, scratching his temple.

"Did the petitioner express any shame on the subject?"

"No, no. Pride, if anything."

"Pride!"

Bovill, muttering in Harry's ear, is offered the opportunity to cross-examine, but shakes his head.

It suddenly strikes Fido that the Codringtons are—or rather were—a thoroughly modern couple. Progressive, even, in some ways (even if in others they resemble some stomping crusader and his lecherous chatelaine). The discreet limitation of child-bearing, the separate friendships, the refusal to allow two unique characters to be assimilated into one—are these not ideals Fido and her friends at Langham Place have often invoked when discussing *a new relation between the sexes*?

The coincidence turns her stomach. Women like Helen taint the very notion of female independence. Is this what it all slides into in the end—grunting couplings on sofas?

Strickland gives way to a short, busy little man: a naval surgeon called Pickthorn.

Hawkins asks him, "Did they quarrel about the care of the children?"

"Indeed, yes," says Pickthorn, "and in particular Mrs. Watson's interference in their management. She—Mrs. Codrington—told me the admiral threatened to send the girls to England to live with his sister, Lady Bourchier."

The barrister raises his smooth eyebrows at that. "Now, turning to the matter of the bedrooms. What did Mrs. Codrington tell you on one occasion in 1862?"

"That when she attempted to go into the admiral's chamber, he'd put her out of the door, and hurt her in doing so."

"Hurt her," Hawkins repeats, eyes on the jury. "Did you confront the petitioner about this assault?"

"I thought it my duty, as the lady's physician. But he denied having used the least violence."

"In your experience, Dr. Pickthorn, what effects might it have on a woman to be thwarted of the normal outlets?"

"You mean—"

"Conjugal outlets."

"That depends on her constitution," says the doctor gravely. "If cool or sluggish, the answer may be, none. But if she's of a warm constitution, she will suffer from tension, broken sleep, digestive disorders, and emotional disruption."

"How would you characterize the respondent's constitution?"

"Very warm."

He wants her, Fido realizes. This little surgeon pants for her, and tells himself it's benevolence. It seems as if every man Helen meets is roused by her, in one way or another, and the sad joke is that Harry, once past the point of desiring her himself, couldn't see it.

"So if a man denied his wife her rights over a period of many years," asks Hawkins, "would that man be altogether blameless if her natural passion were to overflow and seek release elsewhere?"

"Not blameless at all."

Bovill has been huddled in whispered consultation with his client. Now he leaps out of his seat to cross-examine. "On the night of this so-called assault, Dr. Pickthorn," he barks, "would you be surprised to learn that the respondent had returned very late from a ball in a state of unnatural excitement brought on by dancing—and strong punch," he adds pointedly, "and that when she persisted in hanging over the petitioner's bed and making provoking comments unworthy of an English lady, he was obliged to very gently remove her from his room?"

The surgeon falters, and shrugs. "What seems gentle to a tall, muscular officer may not seem so to a delicate woman."

Bovill's mouth tightens. "In addition, are you aware of the view of many eminent medical authorities that virtuous women have no need for sensual outlets? That to many wives, the natural cessation of relations after the birth of several children is, if anything, a relief?"

"I am aware of that notion," says Pickthorn stoutly, "and I believe it to be ignorant cant."

Bovill's eyebrows shoot up.

"Are not men and women, for all their differences, made of the same stuff?"

Fido groans inwardly. He sounds like a supporter of the Cause.

As soon as the witness has been dismissed, Hawkins stands up again. "This court has often heard appalling accounts of the brutality of working men towards their wives, but educated gentlemen have their own refined forms of cruelty. They rarely strike with their fists," he says snidely over his shoulder in Harry's direction. "They only assail the tender feminine affections, only lacerate the heart!"

Helen's case is looking much stronger, Fido realizes with a start. The jury may well decide that Harry was at least partly to blame. What kind of life will Helen have won, in that case? No children, a reputation in tatters. But she'll still have her name, her income, a separate household.

Except that I haven't testified yet.

"The petitioner went further," says Hawkins with a flourish, "and revealed the true baseness of his character on October the eleventh, 1856. I now call Miss Emily Faithfull."

She barely hears her name over the roaring in her ears. She wants to run down the aisle, away from the buzzing hive of watchers.

As she steps up into the box, she feels giddy. She scans the crowd for Helen, but the only face she recognizes is—to her horror—her sister Esther's: meaty cheeks and a grave mouth. Fido averts her gaze. How kind, how scrupulously loyal of Esther to make a showing on behalf of the family. But Fido wishes her at the other end of the earth.

She puts her hand on the Book and takes the oath without a qualm. The letter of the truth doesn't matter to her anymore, only the spirit. Somehow she must find her way through the tangled forest.

Hawkins gives her a small, tight smile, as if to congratulate her for having overcome her feminine qualms at last. Fido steels herself against him.

Mechanically, she answers several questions about her proprietorship of the Victoria Press—meant to establish that she's a serious person, she supposes.

"Under what circumstances did you first become acquainted with the Codringtons?"

"In 1854," she says, then clears her throat. "In 1854 I was staying with—" no need to name her sister. "I was staying at Walmer in Kent when I met Mrs. Codrington."

"Ten years ago, you were what age?"

"Just nineteen."

"You'd always lived in a country parsonage, had been educated in very strict principles, and were altogether ignorant of the world?"

"I suppose so." Is that his angle? She waits, then goes on with the account she's prepared. "After Mrs. Codrington introduced me to her husband, I visited them at Eccleston Square, at their joint and repeated request. I stayed there on and off until 1857—not as Mrs. Codrington's companion, as was stated in a newspaper," she adds stiffly, "but as a friend."

"A trusted family friend," says Hawkins, nodding.

He believes I'm still Helen's witness; he thinks I'm her last, best chance.

"How did their marriage seem?"

Here it comes. "They were in the habit of quarrelling. In the very first days of my acquaintance with her—Mrs. Codrington—she admitted she was not happy. Sometimes they wouldn't speak to each other for a week."

"In the autumn of 1856," he asks, "what room were you occupying at Eccleston Square?"

"The large bedroom next to that of the Codringtons."

"You mean they slept together in one room?"

Fido can hardly believe she's spelling out these private details in a witness box. "Sometimes, at that point. It was the room designated as theirs," she says weakly.

"Had they shared it, during the months between the petitioner's return from the Crimea in August, and October of that year?"

"Really, at this distance of time, I can't remember remarking it." *Liar*; she was always aware of where Helen was: only an inch across the pillow or shut away behind the oak-panelled wall.

"When did Mrs. Codrington sleep with you in your room?"

"Whenever the admiral was away." Afraid of being caught out, Fido adds, "Also sometimes when he was home. I am subject to asthma, and sometimes need medical assistance . . ." *Isn't that what maids are for?* she asks herself, brutally, but Hawkins doesn't probe.

"Now, when Mrs. Codrington was not sleeping with him, where did the admiral spend the night?"

"In his own room."

"You're now referring to a third room, on the other side of yours?"

"No, I—" Oh heavens, she's got in a muddle already. "He'd sleep in that room—the room designated as theirs. While she was in the room beside it, with me."

To her ears that's no clearer, but Hawkins only says, "There is a communicating door between the two rooms?"

Fido nods.

"Answer in words, if you please."

"Yes." Of course, everything must show up on the record. Like speaking in stone.

Hawkins's tone is becoming that of a teller of ghost stories. "On nights when Mrs. Codrington was sharing your room, Miss Faithfull, was the door locked?"

"Shut fast, but not locked. Helen—the respondent—used sometimes to pass in and out between the two rooms." Then she wishes she hadn't added that detail. It conjures up visions of casual flittings in the dark.

"Did the petitioner ever come into the room when you and his wife were sharing it?"

She stiffens. "Occasionally he might walk in to address a remark to her, or poke the fire."

One eyebrow goes up. "Did you often have a fire in your bedroom?"

"A concession to my health; I'd had a fever, and my habitual asthma," she explains, absurdly apologetic. "The admiral can be . . . a rather fidgeting man; he didn't trust the maid to see to the fire." She ought to have said *the fires*; why would he single out the one in her bedroom, rather than those burning downstairs? It all sounds so peculiar, she can't help defending herself. "I didn't like it, and I told her—Mrs. Codrington—that I wished she wouldn't allow it. But she laughed and said that if the admiral liked to play the housemaid, what did she care?"

Hawkins nods twice, as if to stem her nervous flow of words. "Now for the night of the eleventh," he says portentously. "What time did you and Mrs. Codrington retire to bed?"

Her body's as rigid as a mummy's. "About ten, perhaps? I'd taken medicine," she says, getting the fact out brusquely. "I fell into a deep sleep."

"And woke up at what time?"

"I've no idea." She clears her throat, too loudly. "All I remember is that the fire was low and I saw a white figure leaving the room."

Hawkins frowns slightly. "No no, Miss Faithfull, take it from the beginning."

"I have done so," she says through clenched jaws.

He doesn't understand; he still thinks his star witness just needs a little encouragement. "First the petitioner came in through the communicating door?"

Fido shakes her head. "I woke, and saw a white figure going out the door, and presumed it was the admiral, as no one else was in the habit of coming in, and Mrs.—the respondent—said afterwards that it was he." She's gabbling. It's all the literal truth, so why does it feel like a lie?

Hawkins, frowning again, refers to his notes. "Was he in his nightshirt?"

"His dressing gown, I believe." That's not half as bad. "Really, it was all so very rapid that I could hardly tell what I saw; I was still drowsy from my medicine."

"Had he his trousers on?"

"I'm sure I can't say," she snaps.

"What else do you wish to tell the jury about the incident?"

"Nothing."

A long glare from the barrister. "Miss Faithfull, I feel sure it's from womanly compunction, rather than from any wish to perjure yourself, that you're holding back."

The word *perjure* makes her pulse thump loudly. She shakes her head. She keeps her eyes away from the part of the courtroom where her sister's sitting. How will Esther report all this to the Faithfulls?

"Need I remind you that you gave a drastically different account of this incident to the respondent's solicitor, Mr. Few, on September the twenty-ninth?"

Black spots in front of her eyes. "I'm aware of that," she says, almost stuttering, "and I'm relieved to have this opportunity to clear up any misapprehension."

"Misapprehension?" Hawkins's smooth voice cracks. "Madam, either you were lying in assenting to that affidavit, or you're lying now!"

The jury watches Fido, open-mouthed as fish. At the lawyers' table, Few sits staring up at her with mute fury. She looks at her hands. "No, I believe I told Mr. Few what I have just told you," she says, stammering a little, "but with some details added."

"Yes, including one significant detail," Hawkins storms, "namely that what woke you was—allow me to quote from the fourth paragraph—*The petitioner in his nightdress came into the room and got into the bed where Mrs. Codrington and Miss Faithfull were sleeping together, and attempted to have connection with Miss Faithfull, and was only prevented from accomplishing his purpose by the resistance of Miss Faithfull on waking up*."

The hum of talk among the audience deafens her. Her face feels as if it's crackling with flames. Faintly: "That was what Mrs. Codrington said."

"Speak up," advises the judge.

Fido raises her voice. "Just before my interview with Mr. Few, she—the respondent—told me that her husband had . . . behaved improperly to me on the night in question. She persuaded me that the drug I'd taken had erased my recollection of the incident."

Hawkins's eyes are bulging.

She hurries on. "It must be understood that it wasn't that I gave Mr. Few the whole account as from my own memory; he already had it from Mrs. Codrington, and I felt I was being asked only to support her evidence. Particulars were barely mentioned, and he put things delicately, to spare my feelings," she says desperately. "When he asked me whether the account was true, I gave him to understand that the answer was yes, because I sincerely believed what my friend had told me."

"Come, Miss Faithfull!" The barrister is almost shouting. "You're an educated person. And, may I add, a celebrated advocate for the competencies of women. You must know that when a lawyer asks you a question, he means you to answer on your own authority. Mr. Few passed you the affidavit to read—"

"He slid it across the desk," admits Fido, "but I wasn't able to read it through, not so as to know its contents. I was very much confused and agitated, and my breathing was troubled; also Mr. Few was talking the whole time, so I couldn't concentrate." *Women are idiots*, she thinks, *that's the burden of my testimony. Feathery creatures who couldn't be logical if their lives depended on it, who lack the capacity for the civil duties that would go with civil rights.*

"You formally assented to the document!"

"I didn't dissent from it," she says miserably, "but I do not recall saying that it was correct in all particulars. I deeply regret the trouble my ignorance of the law has caused," she rushes on, turning towards the grim judge. "I see now that I ought to have explicitly stated to Mr. Few that his client was my source. Later that day I had reservations, and asked for the affidavit back, but it was too late." She looks anywhere but at her sister sitting in the fifth row. "In a moment of weakness, I went abroad to avoid being summoned to repeat the story in this court."

Hawkins looks disgusted. "Well, Miss Faithfull. Although you were in a stupor at the time, do you now believe that the petitioner attacked you, just as the respondent related?"

He thinks me excessively scrupulous, Fido realizes. "No," she says into the silence, very clearly.

His eyes lock onto hers. "You must admit that what you do recall—waking up in a sudden terror, glimpsing his fleeing form—is not incompatible with attempted violation."

She takes a long breath. "I never said I was terrified, or that the person I saw was fleeing." She must go further, if she's to look herself in the eye in the mirror tomorrow morning. "It's my firm belief, now, that nothing happened that night."

"Nothing?" The barrister's Adam's apple is bulging.

"That the admiral came in while I was asleep, exchanged a few words with his wife, and walked back to his own room."

There's a silence, while Hawkins gathers his forces. "You realize, madam, that you're accusing your dearest friend of inventing the most appalling falsehood in order to pervert the just process of this court?"

Fido is mute. And then says thickly, "Perhaps she dreamed it," which raises a great whoop of laughter from the audience.

"Could it be, I wonder, that someone has threatened you in some way, to force you to change your story?"

Her skin crawls. She mustn't look over at Harry. *This is what happened*, Fido reminds herself desperately, but she's never felt more of a liar. "No," she insists, "having had time to think it all through, I've resolved to do my duty and tell the whole truth."

"I have one more suggestion," snarls Hawkins. "Perhaps the admiral's attempt on your virtue that night was successful?"

She reaches out blindly for the wooden edge of the witness box; holds onto it so she won't fall down.

"I put it to you that all this talk of drugged stupors and blanks in memory is a futile endeavour to deny the horror of what happened."

"Mr. Hawkins!"

"If the petitioner is guilty of adulterous rape, madam, no one will blame you for having fallen a helpless victim to his lust."

"I—"

He plunges on. "But if in a feeble attempt to save your reputation, you cover up his crime and thereby destroy my client—"

"There was no crime."

A single blink from Hawkins. Then he changes his tone again. "Ah, then perhaps you did not resist?" he asks.

So mildly, almost pleasantly, that at first she doesn't follow. She stares at him.

"Half-consented, in fact, to overtures from your friend's handsome husband, with whom you'd lived on the most intimate domestic terms for more than three years? Allowed connection to be achieved, there in the bed a matter of inches from his sleeping wife?"

"How dare—"

"Mr. Hawkins," the judge interrupts.

But the barrister is unstoppable. "And when she woke, you panicked in your guilt, and told her he'd tried to violate you—"

"No!" she roars.

For all the weeks she's spent dreading this day, Fido never imagined such punishment. Barristers are wolves. Hawkins has long since given up constructing a plausible argument, she realizes; he's merely trying to discredit her with the jury. *Just a little longer*, she tells herself, as if comforting a child.

"Nothing happened," she says in a choked voice. "If the court requires it, I am willing to submit to medical examination." *Not that; please, anything but that.*

After a long second, Hawkins steps away. "No further questions, my Lord."

Fido has pushed the gate open; she's on the top step before Bovill gets to his feet and she remembers she still has to be cross-examined by Harry's side. She fears she might burst into tears, but instead she sits down again.

"Do take a moment, Miss Faithfull. Would you care for a glass of water?"

"No, thank you," she whispers.

His voice is melodious. "By now you've realized that you were wrong to maintain a credulous attachment to a dangerous friend, wrong to trust the respondent against the evidence of your senses, wrong to attempt to evade a summons to this court. But on behalf of British justice, I'd like to thank you for coming forward so bravely today." A broad smile. "The gentlemen of the jury will, I'm sure, sympathize with your tale of duped innocence, and rejoice that you've seen the light in time to clear the petitioner's character and your own."

The kind tone weakens her. *Don't cry*, Fido tells herself. *Don't you dare.*

"I can only regret that in previous speeches I have said some harsh things of you, Miss Faithfull, and here, in open court, I wish to withdraw them all. My client has now come to a better understanding of the complexities of his household in the period 1854–1857," says Bovill, "and wishes me to clarify that your influence over his wife seems to him to have been rather beneficial than otherwise."

Here it is, the reward Harry offered her in the cab. But how will the jury swallow these volte-faces? *We all sound like liars, every one of us.*

"Would you agree that the petitioner treated you well while you lived at Eccleston Square?"

"With nothing but kindness and courtesy," says Fido mechanically.

"With regard to the so-called sealed letter which has provoked so much idle speculation," Bovill goes on, "I would like to specify that to the best of the petitioner's recollection, it contains a simple record of his view that you would be better off returning to your parents—and nothing at all to your detriment."

She should feel grateful: this is the key to the door of her cell. (But this will make no sense to the listening crowd: if the letter contained no terrible charges against her, why would Harry have written it at all, and put it into his brother's hands, and why did Bovill brandish it in court two weeks ago like a pistol loud enough to be heard across the country?) Hush, hush, Judas has received his silver. *Oh please let me go now.*

"Now, turning if I may to the co-respondent, Colonel Anderson. When did you make his acquaintance?"

Fido's heart starts to pound again. Harry and his lawyers must think that by the terms of their bargain she's about to tell all. And certainly, last night, while she was ripping apart the seashell choker, that was her plan: pay Helen back for everything. But now it's come to it, somehow—

She begins with a bland summary of social encounters with David Anderson. "I'm afraid I don't know the dates of his various calls; I keep no diary."

"Were they ever alone together in your house?" asks Bovill suggestively.

"Alone?" Fido repeats. Here's her chance; here's the line in the sand.

The barrister nods and waits.

She finds herself strangely unable—unwilling—to step over it.

"Shall I repeat the question, Miss Faithfull?"

She shakes her head. This isn't mercy; she feels nothing that tender for Helen Codrington anymore. "No," she says hoarsely.

"By *no* you mean that I need not repeat it?"

"I mean no, they were never alone together in my house." *I was there too; I was just outside the drawing-room, listening.*

The audience stirs and rustles. How many are cheering on the pretty, naughty lady, Fido wonders, and how many would rather see Helen punished? It's like a witch-ducking: the sleek copper head rises above the water, sinks again, rises, sinks.

The barrister's pouchy eyes narrow. "Do you recall any conversations with Mrs. Codrington on the subject of the co-respondent?"

If I say no, no one in this room will believe me. She pauses, choosing her words carefully. "I believe I told her that her friendship with the colonel had an imprudent air to it, and that I didn't like to be mixed up in it." There, that has a credible ring to it. It's true that Fido said that to Helen—among other things. *The truth, the partial truth, and everything but the truth.*

Bovill steps closer to the box. "Is that all you thought of your friend's behaviour? Nothing worse than *imprudent*?"

"As I said."

"You maintain you never, at any time, witnessed any impropriety between the two?"

What does it mean to witness? Outside the door, face pressed to the wood, shut out of the mystery. "Never," she says hoarsely.

Her hands are curling closed; she's dying for a cigarette. What Fido's done—refrained from doing, rather—may make no difference, of course. There are other witnesses, and they've been only too willing to give chapter and verse on Helen's crimes. But Fido won't take another step. Helen may very well fall—but Fido won't be the one to give her the final push. She'd rather leave it up to the court, to providence—or, if there's no such thing as providence, to chance. It's not loyalty that stays her hand, nor anything like forgiveness. Only a need to regain her balance, not to be like Helen. Only a reaching back to find herself, her real self, in the dank fog.

For a moment, it occurs to Fido that Bovill's going to strike back at his recalcitrant witness. He could call for the sealed letter to be brought into court again. She shudders at the thought. The black wax could be broken, the accusation released like a plague on the air. Fido's dropped her weapon, while Harry still holds his. She stares at the barrister, silently pleading.

Bovill lets out a brief sigh and glances towards his client. Harry gives an infinitesimal shake of the head, and the barrister pronounces the words that release her. "No further questions, my Lord."

XVII

Verdict

(from Anglo-Norman, "to speak the truth": the final and unanimous finding of a jury at the end of a trial)

Come, cheer up, my lads,
'Tis to glory we steer,
To add something more
To this wonderful year;
To honour we call you,
Not press you as slaves,
For who are as free
As we sons of the waves?

David Garrick,
"Heart of Oak" (1759)
anthem of the Royal Navy

Codrington v. Codrington & Anderson

The verdict was accordingly entered for the petitioner on all charges. Judge Wilde pronounced a decree nisi *and ordered the co-respondent (Colonel Anderson) to pay the petitioner's costs of £943. To the surprise of many present, Judge Wilde then took the unusual though not unprecedented step of ordering the petitioner to pay the costs of the respondent (Helen Jane Webb Smith, formerly Codrington) in the amount of £1,110, on the grounds that the petitioner had for many years suffered his wife to absent herself from his bed at night, and his company by day. As is customary, the Queen's proctor will be granted a period of not less than six months to look for any evidence of collusion between the divorcing spouses, in the absence of which Judge Wilde will then pronounce a* decree absolute.

~

THE LATE OCTOBER AFTERNOON IS COLD. Harry's been motionless in a wing chair for hours, near one of the six fireplaces in the Rag Club's famous coffee room. He's brooding over his daughters: what to tell them next week when he collects them from Mrs. Watson's house and takes them home to Eccleston Square. He's trying out lines in his head.

Mama did some very wrong things, and has gone away. Feeble, childish.

Your mother doesn't deserve to be a mother anymore. Unnecessarily cold.

It may be best to think of her as dead. Dead to us. No, Nan and Nell will start to shriek. He won't be able to bear it.

A divorce means that your Mama must go and live far, far away. In fact he has no idea what'll become of Helen: where she'll go, or what she'll do with herself. In his concluding interview with Bird, yesterday, Harry almost weakened and proposed making her some kind of allowance—but then he got hold of himself again.

Your mother . . . Need he say anything to them? The wrong words might be worse than none. Girls are quick to pick these things up without anything being spelled out. Should he perhaps simply bring them home in a cab, chatting about their zoetrope all the way, and make no reference to their missing mother, that day or ever again?

Two members come in and take a table behind him; he doesn't recognize their voices. It's the word *poker* that catches his attention. "In his nightshirt, poker at the ready," one is muttering. "Stiff as the proverbial!"

"Well, he was afraid the ladies would take a chill if he didn't rouse their flame," puts in the second man with a snigger. "When all the time the joke was on the ancient mariner, because they'd no need of his ministrations."

"Not those gels. Things were warm enough in the nuptial bed already—without him!"

Harry's hands form fists in his lap.

"The friend must be not just strong-minded, but strong-armed too, if she could beat off such a giant while she was doped to the gills," says the first man with a guffaw. "She was too many for the admiral. Oh yes, thank you, three lumps."

Drop it, Harry commands himself, as the two are served their coffee, a few feet behind him. He has no power to stop people having private conversations. He's become what the managers of great concerns call a household name.

But that first needling voice carries on, once the waiter's gone. "To my way of thinking, it was no more than the old buffer deserved."

"Oh really?"

"Well, for years before the wife started straying, he hadn't been much of a husband, by the sounds of it."

"She was bold as brass," objects the second.

"Still, he oughtn't to have stood for it, like the judge said. Stands to reason, she must have been thwarted in her normal appetites, to turn to the other thing."

What have I done? Harry asks himself. In those small, cramped chambers of Bird's, Mrs. Watson made up the most revolting rumour, and Harry agreed to spread it, and now the public takes it as gospel. Imaginary monsters walk the streets.

"Hm," says the second man, as if they're discussing a great question of the day, such as sewer construction or Irish tenant right. "But by all accounts she has more than the usual quota, when it comes to appetite."

"Notwithstanding. My wife's of a warm enough constitution, but you wouldn't catch her resorting to such folderols, not unless I'd left her in a very sad state of frustration!"

Harry can bear no more. He rears up so fast the chair skids, and spots appear before his eyes. He takes two steps, towers over the two men. "Do you know me, sir? Or you?"

One looks bewildered, the other, queasy. The one who hasn't guessed begins, "I don't believe I've had the honour . . ."

"My name is Henry John Codrington," he growls. *I loved my wife as best I could*, he wants to shout. *I was not a brute and she was not a freak.* "I don't know yours, but I can say with confidence that you're no gentlemen."

"Come, now, Admiral—"

"Everything all right?" The porter is at Harry's elbow.

Harry ignores him. "Such scurrilous indecency! You dare to sit here, soiling the name of a lady you've never met—" His head's a whirl of confusion. Can he really be defending Helen's honour—he, who to destroy that honour has squandered thousands of pounds and the long, impeccable patrimony of the Codrington name?

One of the men manages a half-smile. "We only repeat what's said in the papers."

"That's a worm's excuse."

The porter's put his hand on Harry's elbow. "Now, now, Admiral. No altercations in the club."

"In our fathers' day," says Harry, waving a finger in their nervous, smirking faces, "I'd have had you out. I'd have taken you by the throat and caned you like the curs you are."

"No altercations in the club," repeats the porter, leading him away.

XVIII

Feme Sole

(in law, an unmarried woman)

Rise! If the past detains you,
Her sunshine and storms forget;
No chains so unworthy to hold you
As those of vain regret:
Sad or bright, she is lifeless ever.
Cast her phantom arms away;
Nor look back, save to learn the lesson
Of a nobler strife To-day.

Adelaide Procter,
"Now" (1864)

NB—letters from applicants for employment being not infrequently sent to the Victoria Press, under the mistaken impression that its proprietor, Miss E. Faithfull, represents SPEW and is the right person to apply to for situations, it is thought advisable to explain the real state of the case here.

It was at one time contemplated by the society to establish a women's printing press, but the committee came to the conclusion that the undertaking would be more likely to succeed if left to private enterprise; accordingly, Miss Faithfull took up the project entirely under her own aegis and on her own behalf. The society wishes to clarify that it has no contractual or organizational connections with the Victoria Press. Miss Faithfull has not for the past four years had any share in the management of SPEW or the *English Woman's Journal*, and correspondence intended for her ought accordingly not to be addressed to the society's offices at 19 Langham Place.

It is hoped that with this clarification the subject may be considered closed.

Alexandra Magazine and English Woman's Journal,
Number 1 (Autumn 1864)

Langham Place
October 30, 1864

Dear Miss Faithfull,

I enclose the final draft of the first issue of the Victoria Magazine, and look forward to seeing the galleys as they come off the press.

As you cannot be unaware, however, your unexpected absence for several weeks caused me many difficulties with regard to readying this issue for publication. That task for additional reasons proved more onerous than I expected; I must tell you that I have found it well-nigh impossible to reach the high standards to which we both aspire, with the budget you have made available to me. I do appreciate that investment must grow gradually, but at present, without the funds to pay the best writers, I am doubtful of what real improvement is possible.

It is not without much hesitation that I have decided to withdraw as of next month from the challenge you so kindly offered me, that of shaping a periodical which I have no doubt will in time, under your own editorship or another's, become an important one, and an eloquent organ of our Cause.

Certain extraneous factors have, of course, played their part in my decision. We need not discuss them.

Believe me, Miss Faithfull, I mean no personal offence—will always have the highest respect for your work—and regret the necessities of the times.

Sincerely,
Emily Davies

~

FIDO LIES IN BED, curtains straining the pale yellow light. She's shocked to find herself wishing she'd never left Headley. But it does attract her, the novel idea of being an ordinary woman. A daughter at home, whose duties are limited to practising the piano and helping her mother clothe the village children.

Esther didn't stay to speak to Fido, after the trial. Fido caught a glimpse of her sister outside Westminster Hall, staggering along as if she were ill. How will she sum up that long day, when she returns to her husband, when she visits the Reverend and Mrs. Faithfull in their rectory?

Fido can't bring herself to care very much. How tired she is after six years of meetings in stifling rooms with dissatisfied faces; six years of dusty efforts to uplift her sex (who seem, as a rule, more interested in ribbons). She's spent all her strength, all her patience, all her sympathy. And what's come of the great projects she's joined in, to date? A couple of dozen girls who are setting type or keeping accounts instead of—or as a prelude to—having babies. Infinite numbers of words scattered on the wind. Not a single substantial law has changed.

I'm not that kind of woman, Helen said, when Fido had suggested she think of working as a proofreader. Only now does Fido register the full weight of the insult. Helen didn't mean that she lacked the capacity or talent, not at all. Her implication was that work is a humiliating recourse for those surplus females whom no man is willing to support.

Fido lies very flat in her bed. There's nothing left in her tank; she's used up all her reserves. *I could sell the press,* she thinks, darkly tempted, *or close it down. Go abroad: draw on my funds; the family would prefer it.* (Paris? Amsterdam? Rome?) Quite understandable; who could blame her after all that's happened?

She turns her head away from the window. She lies very still. In two more minutes, she tells herself, she'll get up and take a cold shower.

~

An hour later she's at the press on Great Coram Street, working through the backlog. She corrects proofs all morning, working too fast. She knows she's missing some errors, but never mind: the important thing is to press on.

How on earth is she to manage the *Victoria Magazine* now that Emily Davies has pulled out? Advance orders are not what she'd hoped for—not bad in London, but a dead failure in the countryside. She shouldn't have paid top rates for Tom Trollope's second-rate novel; next time she'll know better. She must be publisher, editor, sales agent, everything now. She'll be obliged to economize, and—under various names—write as much of the magazine herself as she can. Hm, where will she find some promising writers willing to contribute for practically nothing?

At intervals Fido sifts through her post, the letters that are there and those that are significantly absent. She reads the signs like a priestess deciphering entrails: counts friends, enemies, and of course fence-sitters who're waiting to see what becomes of the once mighty Fido Faithfull. She hasn't received an invitation to address the Social Science Association's conference this year—but on the other hand, they've made no move to cancel her contracts to publish their pamphlets and proceedings. Apart from Bessie Parkes, none of her customers has withdrawn any business yet, in fact.

Not so much as a note from Isa Craig, or Jessie Boucherett, or Sarah Lewin. Does this mean that the whole of the Reform Firm has gone along with Emily Davies and Bessie Parkes in casting Fido into the dark?

She won't let herself brood. She writes to no one to demand support. For now, she'll pay no calls, leave no cards, attend no occasions, in case she'll be snubbed. A temporary, strategic withdrawal. Bovill did all he could to cobble her reputation back together, by the time she got down from the witness box, she reminds herself. Fido will be meek, for a while, but she won't despair. Above all, for her own self-respect, she won't shut up shop.

Lunch is cold ham at her desk, as she works closely through the press's accounts. They're quite a bit worse than she feared. She stares into space for a few minutes, then comes to a decision and calls in the head clicker.

"I'm becoming aware of my failings, Mr. Head."

The young man puts his head on one side in polite enquiry.

"I'm tired of being cheated, and fobbed off. To keep the kind of close eye on the press's finances that I've neither the time nor the technical experience to do, I require a responsible manager. Will you take the job?"

"At an appropriate consideration," he says promptly.

"Of course. Also, I must tell you in confidence that the press is in desperate need of capital. I've decided—reluctantly—to sell off the steam press, as we really don't have enough newspaper work to require it." (And, incidentally, she never wants to walk down Farringdon Street again.)

"I wonder, Miss Faithfull, have you ever thought of taking on a partner?"

His tone makes her sit up a little straighter.

"My father has a sum of capital he intends to settle on me when a suitable opportunity arises," murmurs Mr. Head. "A thousand pounds."

Fido grins at him. "Such an investment would buy you a quarter of the business."

"A third, I think."

Her eyebrows jump.

"The last evaluation of the press came to three thousand pounds, didn't it?"

"Oh, but since then our reputation has grown considerably," she says, bluffing.

"Well." He pauses to let them both consider what's happened to her own reputation in recent weeks. "In consideration of my acting as manager, instead of a salary—shall we say a third share in the press, and an equal share in all profits?"

Is this young man her saviour, or a profiteer taking advantage of her weakness? No matter. There are no saviours. After a moment, Fido nods, and he extends his long cool hand for her to shake.

It will be strange, being on terms of equality with her subordinate, but Fido imagines she'll get used to it. People are more adaptable than they believe.

When Head's gone back to the press room, Fido sits looking around her office. The air still smells slightly of cayenne. History moves by fits and starts; certain battles must be fought again and again.

~

INSTEAD OF GOING HOME, she finds her feet taking her to Langham Place.

When she reaches Number 19, it occurs to her to knock, so no one can accuse her of rudeness. But she still has her key, so on second thoughts she lets herself in.

No one in the reading room, or the committee room; no one to greet her or bar her way. She taps on the door of various small offices, and the last she tries is Bessie Parkes's.

"Miss Faithfull." Bessie Parkes doesn't get up; she regards Fido tiredly across her orderly desk.

Fido finds she can't speak for a moment. Instead, she holds out the *Alexandra Magazine*, open to page eight. "I've come to insist you set the record straight." She takes a breath. "In this entirely gratuitous notice inserted in your new magazine, you distort the facts at every point. You claim I haven't had *any share in the management of SPEW* or the journal in four years—"

"You don't hold a position on either committee," Bessie Parkes reminds her.

"You know very well I've been at most meetings and involved in all the campaigns. I've set up branches of SPEW in Dublin and Edinburgh—run one of the employment registers—not to mention all those letters to the *Times* promoting our activities—" Fido is almost spluttering; she steadies her voice. "And if I haven't held a formal position, it's understood that's because I've been busy running the Victoria Press, which for all your feeble attempt to dissociate it from SPEW, is the one shining example, the great demonstration of women's capacity for skilled labour!"

A long sigh. "Is this conversation really necessary? What good do you imagine it can do?"

"Was it *necessary* to renounce me so publicly, to make a scapegoat of me?" roars Fido.

"Hardly a scapegoat," snaps Bessie Parkes. "You've brought notoriety on yourself as well as the Reform Firm: it's we who have a grievance. All the enamel's already been rubbed off your name, professional as well as personal. The SSA can hardly continue publishing with you, and if you brazen it out, no doubt the Queen will be obliged to withdraw her patronage from the press."

"I believe I've emerged from the recent unpleasantness with my name quite restored," says Fido, trying not to hear how unconvincing that sounds.

"Thinly whitewashed, rather," says Bessie Parkes, rolling her big doll eyes. "Judge Wilde was certainly merciful to you in his summing-up, in that he only made you sound like a cretin and turncoat. That's the wonder of it, really: that you managed to betray both your friend and the Cause."

Fido swallows. "I love the Cause, and you know it."

"No, I'm afraid I've given you up as a bad job, Miss Faithfull. For all your cleverness and energy, I see now that you have a certain screw loose which may some day—barring divine intervention—bring you to Millbank Gaol."

"It's not true," she insists. "I'm the same woman I've always been."

A shrug. "But now the mouths of the world are open, and can't be muffled."

"So the look of the thing is all you care about?"

Bessie Parkes flushes. "Keeping up appearances is an underrated virtue. If a working woman wears a clean, mended skirt without a petticoat under it, or turns a teacup so the crack won't show—you might call it hypocrisy, but I say she's doing her best, out of respect for society."

Something occurs to Fido. "This is what you did to Max Hays, two years ago, when you convinced yourself our falling subscriptions were her fault," she breathes, "and we sheep sat baaing in a circle and did nothing to stop you. What, are we to be purged one woman at a time, *and then there was one*?"

Bessie Parkes's face works oddly. "I will always think fondly of poor Max, and remember her in my prayers, but she's as unbalanced as you are. Those terrible, jealous scenes between her and Miss Cushman . . ."

Fido blinks at her.

"No, your type is a menace; I don't know whether you're mad or bad, but either way you can't be allowed to damage the firm."

"I've poured my lifeblood into it!"

"Then it's time you were stopped: you're infecting it."

Speechless, she moves towards the door. Then turns back. "The Cause needs all of us," Fido says, "flaws included. That includes you, I dare say. But you can't prevent me from carrying on my own share of the work, if not here then elsewhere."

"Please be sure to pick up all your possessions," says Bessie Parkes, turning back to her paperwork. Her voice quivers—only a little.

Blinded by tears, Fido feels her way to the desk that's been hers for the past six years, and starts filling her carpet bag with papers, pens, whatever her hands can find.

~

The first day in November, and Fido's in her study at Taviton Street, writing a piece about the three-year anniversary of Prince Albert's death for the *Victoria Magazine.* She still has the knack, she finds; still puts one word in front of another, though haltingly, like an invalid remembering how to walk.

She pauses and rereads what she's written so far. While gently urging the Queen to reduce the elaborate rituals of mourning that have paralyzed her court, it's important not to insult her. Can Fido broaden the message, somehow, so it applies not just to Victoria but also to any of her subjects who've ever suffered?

That dead stillness and passiveness which nature allows to a great sorrow. Ought *nature* to have a capital? No, Fido's suspicious of capitals, for instance in the case of Woman. *Rise up again and resume our daily burden*, she writes, then changes it to *burthen;* the archaic spelling takes the hard edges off the idea. She dips her pen in the ink. *Fulfilling unremittingly the duties of our station.* After *unremittingly* she adds *and at any personal sacrifice.* Had she better mention God? Providence, perhaps; it's a popular notion. She reads the line again.

Some of us, after a brief season of that dead stillness and passiveness which nature allows to a great sorrow, must rise up again and resume our daily burthen, fulfilling unremittingly and at any personal sacrifice the duties of that station, low or high, to which Providence has called us.

A knock at the front door. She lifts her head, waits for Johnson to come up.

It's not a card the maid brings, but a package. Not just any package. The brown paper cover slides off, and inside there's a stiff white packet. Fido recognizes it at once as the one that was brandished in court. The one that bears—like a gobbet of oily mud flung against a wall, it strikes her now—a thick black circle of wax, impressed with the dragon from the Codrington crest, and over it the family motto, *IEVV,* which means, she recalls with only a slight effort, *virtue cannot be conquered.*

A small slip of translucent paper sits on top: *With the compliments of Henry J. Codrington.* It's a set phrase, but not printed, she registers; the admiral wrote it out by hand. She imagines him at his desk this morning. Back at Eccleston Square, the girls reciting in their schoolroom, a leg of mutton on the boil? She sees him putting his affairs in order, posting bank drafts to the lawyers and the enquiry agent. Pausing, scrupulous, and deciding to send this particular document to Miss Faithfull, as some kind of acknowledgement. A signing off. *With the compliments of Henry J. Codrington.* She can't be mistaken about the hint of irony in the phrase. Is he offering a wry congratulation on all the equivocating she did in the witness box? On the twists and turns, the serpentine coilings with which she won her survival?

What's done is done, Fido tells herself yet again, her voice a bark in her echoing head.

She pictures Harry kneeling down beside the freshly blackened grate in his study, where there must be a small fire this morning, just enough flame to eat up the papers that he's consigning to it one by one. Yes, that would be characteristic of the admiral: to burn all traces of the whole episode. Not just of the trial, perhaps, but also of the woman who was once called his wife: every letter, every picture (the silver frames saved, though; perhaps there might be another wife to put in them someday, a thoroughly English one?).

And Helen, she wonders, where is Helen now? Not with a friend: she's got none left who would take her in. Not with a lover: they too have fallen away like grey leaves.

Oh my darling.

It's not exactly a sentiment that takes Fido unawares, at the thought of Helen adrift in the mean world; it's a sensation so physical it bends her over her desk, like a mantle of lead. How strange, she observes, her mind flailing to hold onto some command of the body that furls and gasps—how strange that even now, after the irrevocable events of the past two months, after blows and counter-blows so shaming that they should have atomized all the old attachments—how thoroughly strange to find a residue of what she can only call love. Spectral, ashy, white-hot.

Fido covers her mouth, makes herself draw a long hiss of breath between her fingers.

To business. Here it is, then, on the desk under her elbow, the simple pale packet over which the lawyers snapped like dogs. (What would it be worth to the *Times*, she wonders?) It bears no inscription, nothing but the oily black seal. Once she's read it she can burn it, Fido promises herself, and then the whole terrible tale will be over.

The minutes crawl by, and like some older, wiser, more craven Pandora, she can't bring herself to crack the seal. She reaches for the little silver knife with which she opens letters, and her fingers curl around its handle, but she makes no move to slit the paper. Fido's always thought of herself as a *femme de lettres*, text the element she breathes with ease, but recently she's come to know how dangerous words are, those black, razor-beaked birds whose feints and swoopings are entirely unpredictable.

But if she doesn't open this letter now, if she locks it away securely enough to thwart the spying eyes of the world—why, its hold on her will only tighten. By day and by night, she'll be aware of it in her safe, propped behind her cash box, beside the Last Will and Testament that leaves everything to be divided between her nephews and nieces because she has no one else in the world. Like some dark lamp it'll keep beaming out its malevolence.

Come, open the thing.

Then it occurs to Fido that she ought to burn it instead. Whatever it may say of her, whatever the insinuating theories or lurid threats a maddened husband might have written down seven years ago—it would only take a few seconds, this morning, for the document to char and curl to anonymous dust. Why should she make herself read it, after all? What possible good can it do her to fill her head with such words?

She thinks of what those words might be; she supplies terrible synonyms. But if she burns the thing, she'll never know, which—it strikes her now—may well prove to be worse. No, she can't bring herself to stand up and carry the letter three steps to the wan fire that lurks in the grate. It is as if the whole secret narrative of her life is contained in this thin envelope. *Oh, read it and be done with it!* Whatever the document may say—

Below, the door knocker thumps, and Fido flinches.

When Johnson comes in this time, she announces a Miss Smith.

Fido's forehead creases. "I don't believe I know a—"

"Helen Smith, she said to say," mutters the maid, looking away.

Fido slides the letter under a pile of books so fast the edge crumples. Her throat feels blocked. She has an impulse to say she's not at home—but that will only put the interview off, and besides, *you coward, you maggot, you pitiful excuse for a woman.* "I'll come to the drawing-room. No, on second thoughts, show her in here." Keeping it on a business footing.

"Here?" repeats Johnson.

"As I said."

Alone, she concentrates on steadying and silencing her breath.

When Helen walks into the study, Fido realizes that she was expecting a broken woman. Bruised, at least, if not repentant. But Helen is pearly-faced, today, dressed in scarlet and plum.

"You look very stylish," says Fido. It comes out as a gruff accusation. She's forgotten to offer her visitor a seat. She finds herself toying with her letter-opener, like some vacillating Macbeth; she puts it down.

"I'm going abroad," remarks Helen.

Of course. And yet it's a shock to hear.

"To what country?" Belgium, Fido wonders, perhaps Italy . . . Not Florence, no; the bitter old father won't open his doors to this prodigal.

"Does it matter?" asks Helen, head cocked almost playfully.

Fido clears her throat. "Not to me personally, no—"

"Nor to me," says Helen with a little shrug.

Her destination is that universal no-place, then, the demimonde. Every city has a twilight brigade of ladies with nothing to live on but cards and gentlemen. *Could I have saved her?* Fido wonders, with a stabbing sensation in her stomach. *If I'd been sharper, firmer, stronger?* She tries to summon the tone of the proprietor of the Victoria Press. "Your situation is indeed—"

But a laugh interrupts her, a small, peculiar laugh. "Whether forgiving me or judging me, Fido, the joke is that you've never understood me for a moment."

Fido stares.

"You've always thought me a sentimental Emma Bovary, when the truth is much simpler," Helen says as lightly as if they're discussing the weather. "I took my fun where I found it. If I couldn't bear marriage and motherhood without a little excitement, how was I worse than any creature in creation? We are daughters and sons of apes, after all."

Fido doesn't know how to begin to answer such philosophy. "We are . . . we are God's children," is all she can manage.

Helen leans her knuckles on the edge of Fido's desk. "Well, if God put the itch in me, God must answer for it, don't you think?"

Silence, a thick miasma filling up the room.

"But I haven't come for chit-chat," Helen adds in a brisker tone.

"What for, then?" Fido has to ask, after a moment.

"Money."

She's winded by the word. It's rarely spoken, in their circles; people prefer *means, emolument, resources.* "The admiral—surely, if you made a humble appeal, as the mother—"

"My capacity for humility aside," Helen interrupts her dryly, "in his view I'm no longer the mother of his children. I was a false start, don't you know, a fifteen-year error of accounting. I'm informed there are to be no visits, not even a last one."

Only now, and only for a split second, does Fido see a glitter of tears in those sea-blue eyes.

"Why do you ask me for money?" She's almost stuttering.

"Because I have none, except for what a few jewels have fetched," says Helen in a reasonable tone. "Until the day I die, I'll always be asking for my bread, one way or another."

"But why—" Fido tries again. "I thought—because I felt obliged to act as I did, in court—"

Helen flicks open her watch. "Much as it may console you for the two of us to confess, and recriminate, and fall on each other's bosoms in floods of tears—I'm afraid I can't spare the time today."

"All I meant was," says Fido, stiff-jawed, "why ask *me*?"

"Who better?" Helen considers her, across the desk. "You were the first, after all."

Fido stiffens. It's as if Helen has put her finger on some exquisitely sensitive scar.

"You haven't forgotten," says Helen, crossing her arms. "I'd bet you recall every single night of it, in fact, rather more clearly than I do."

Fido's throat has sealed up like wax.

Helen's smile has something terrible in it.

"We were so very young," Fido whispers.

Another sharp little laugh. "Oh, old enough to know what we were about."

"We've never spoken of it."

Helen shrugs. "There was no need, so I deferred to your squeamish sensibilities. But this appears to be the season for naming names."

Fido swallows hard. "After all you've put me through, will you now stoop to extortion?"

"The way I see it, my dear, it's much more simple than that," says Helen. "As you were first to induce me to break my vows—"

"No," Fido whispers. She can't bear the idea that there could be any likeness between herself and the men who stand like bloody flags in Helen's path. "It was . . . not at all the same thing." The silence stretches like a rope on the verge of snapping. "If we've never spoken of it, it's because words would only distort it. There are no . . ." She strains for breath. "The words don't fit."

Helen shrugs impatiently. "We took our pleasure like nature's other creatures, I dare say. And now it so happens that someone must pay up. Since you were the first to lay hands on me—long before those others—shouldn't you be that someone?" She waits. "Wouldn't you rather it were you, in a way?"

Tears are falling onto Fido's hands, her desk, her papers. She nods, speechless. Then she fumbles for her pen. "I can let you have a draft on my bank."

"I'd rather cash."

Fido goes to her safe and unlocks it. She lifts out her cash box, which is heavy with a full week's wages for the hands at the press. She hesitates for a moment but can't bear to start counting; she slides it across the desk.

Helen shovels it all into her bag: not just bank notes but gold sovereigns, silver crowns and half-crowns and florins and shillings, even. All she leaves is the copper.

Fido watches the rapid pink hands at work. She waits in silence. For what? Some recognition. Some release.

Helen snaps the clasp of her bag, and goes out the door.

Fido sits very still after her visitor has gone. She's looking down the long tunnel of her past. Kent, the weeping woman on the seashore, the first exchange of words. She wishes she could wish that it never happened. *Oh Helen, Helen, Helen*, the name like the wail of a gull. Love found and complicated and lost, found and destroyed again, and was there any way Fido could have shaped the story differently?

One last thing to do. She reaches under the books for the corner of the letter, and pulls it out. Against the black seal, the paper as white as the neck of a girl. What worse is there to fear, after all?

The seal cracks between Fido's fingers. The folded paper parts like water. The page is blank.

Author's Note

Emily Faithfull (1835–95), "Fido" to her intimates, was one of the leading members of the first-wave British women's movement. Her colleague at 19 Langham Place, Isa Craig, wrote a poem called "These Three," which celebrated Adelaide Procter as Faith, Bessie Parkes as Love, and Fido Faithfull as Hope. Here is the key verse about Fido:

Her clear eyes look far, as bent
On shining futures gathering in;
Nought seems too high for her intent,
Too hard for her to win.

But by the time this optimistic verse was published in *English Lyrics* (1870), things had changed utterly: Adelaide Procter was dead; Bessie Parkes had married a Frenchman she barely knew (their children would include the writer Hilaire Belloc) and effectively withdrawn from the movement; the HQ of the Reform Firm had shifted from Langham Place to Emily Davies's home; and Fido Faithfull was a pariah.

The Sealed Letter is a fiction, but based on the extensive reports on *Codrington v. Codrington* in the *Times* for July 30, August 1 and 2, and November 18, 19, 21, and 24, 1864, supplemented by the *Daily Telegraph*, *Spectator*, *Reynolds's Magazine*, and *Lloyds's Weekly London Newspaper.* Very closely based, in fact: for instance, the letter Helen sends Anderson protesting against his engagement, in this novel, is almost word for word the same as the one read aloud in court. What might seem like anachronistic allusions to the Bill Clinton impeachment, such as the stained dress, or the argument about whether a woman could have sex with a man without that man having sex with her, are real details from the Codrington trial. The only major change I have made is to compress the couple's legal wranglings of the period 1858 to 1866 into the novel's more dramatic time span of August to October 1864.

It is a matter of record that Emily "Fido" Faithfull, called as a witness by the wife, fled to avoid a subpoena, then returned to testify in the husband's favour. But why? Robert Browning certainly thought he knew, when he sent his spinster friend Isa Blagden the following tidbit on January 19, 1865:

> *One of the counsel in the case told an acquaintance of mine that the "sealed letter" contained a charge I shall be excused from even hinting to you—fear of the explosion of which, caused the shift of Miss Emily from one side to the other. As is invariably the case, people's mouths are opened, and tell you what "they knew long ago" though it seems* that *did not matter a bit so long as nobody else knew.*

Because the document was not opened in court or entered into the trial record, we are unlikely ever to know what was in it.

William E. Fredeman in "Emily Faithfull and the Victoria Press: An Experiment in Sociological Bibliography" (*Library,* 5th series, 29, no. 2 [June 1974]: 139–64) was the first to spell out Browning's sly hints about the "sealed letter"; he argues that Admiral Codrington must have used it to blackmail Faithfull into changing sides.

By contrast, James Stone's biography of his wife's great-great-aunt, *Emily Faithfull: Victorian Champion of Women's Rights* (1994), attributes her volte-face to her sense of betrayal that Helen had broken her promise not to drag her into court.

The first thorough reading of this complex case was an essay by Martha Vicinus ("Lesbian Perversity and Victorian Marriage: The 1864 Codrington Divorce Trial," *Journal of British Studies* 36 [1997]: 70–98, also included in her book, *Intimate Friends*). Based on exemplary research into all the participants as well as a close study of the newspaper coverage and legal documents, this brilliant analysis was invaluable to me in writing *The Sealed Letter*. Vicinus is not convinced by Stone's theory that Helen Codrington and her lawyer conned a naïve Faithfull into approving Few's affidavit. In this account, Faithfull emerges as an astute businesswoman who gave a brilliant performance in the witness box, drawing on Victorian preconceptions (for instance, about the naïve girl led astray by the older married woman) to get herself off the hook.

In creating my own "Fido," "Helen," and "Harry," and attempting to solve the ill-fitting jigsaw puzzle that is the Codrington case, I have borrowed ideas from these three historians and others.

Four years after testifying in the trial, Fido mulled over her experiences with Helen Codrington, more in sorrow than in anger, in a bestselling novel called *Change upon Change* (1868). The persona she adopts is that of a sober man called Wilfred, helplessly devoted and secretly engaged to his flighty cousin Tiny. "Women have so many natures," he concludes wistfully; "I think she loved me well with one." In the preface to the American edition of 1873 (renamed *A Reed Shaken in the Wind*), Fido admitted

> *I have seen with my own eyes the curious combination of intellectual power and instability of purpose portrayed in Tiny Harewood; I have watched with an aching heart the shifting weaknesses and faint struggles for redemption described in these pages.*

At least some of the Faithfull clan seem to have stood by Fido. At the time of the trial, she also had one loyal friend I have left out of the story, Emy Wilson (discussed in Martha Westwater's *The Wilson Sisters*).

I have simplified and compressed many events at Langham Place in the early 1860s, including the death throes of the *English Woman's Journal* and the founding of the *Victoria Magazine* and *Alexandra Magazine*. I have used quotations, paraphrases, incidents, and details from the papers of Bessie Parkes Belloc, her father Joseph Parkes, her daughter Marie Belloc Lowndes, and her colleagues Barbara Smith Bodichon, Emily Davies, and Adelaide Procter. Some of these papers are published, but most are held in manuscript at Girton College, Cambridge—the college for women that Davies founded in 1869. (When I did my PhD at Girton in the 1990s, I had no idea I would be returning one day to research a novel, and I want to thank archivist Kate Perry for her help and insights during my week-long visit in 2005.)

Though voluminous, the letters of the "Reform Firm" are often tantalizingly euphemistic. At points of crisis—such as the ousting of the fascinating Matilda "Max" Hays from the *Journal*, or Bessie Parkes's breaking off of relations with Fido—letters or entire sequences have been lost or (more likely) censored by heirs. For instance, the letter in which Parkes reports discovering Fido's involvement in the Codrington case is missing at least the first page. This means that much of my novel's depiction of relations among the women of Langham Place has to be guesswork. For factual accounts of these key years in British feminism I recommend Pam Hirsch's *Barbara Leigh Smith Bodichon: Feminist, Artist and Rebel*, Candida Ann Lacey's anthology, *Barbara Leigh Smith Bodichon and the Langham Place Group*, and Jane Rendall's essay on the *English Woman's Journal* in her *Equal or Different: Women's Politics 1800–1914*.

In her *Family Chronicle* for 1864, Emily Davies summed up the Codrington crisis as discreetly as possible:

> *Miss Faithfull was obliged, owing to some references to her in reports of a Divorce case, to withdraw for a time, from society, & I, & others, ceased to be associated with her.*

But Fido did very little withdrawing, in fact. For all Bessie Parkes's dark predictions, the Social Science Association did not take their custom away from the Victoria Press, and they resumed inviting Fido to address their annual conferences after a few years, in 1869. Nor did Queen Victoria ever withdraw her personal title of "Printer and Publisher in Ordinary to Her Majesty." Fido and William Wilfred Head legally partitioned the press in 1867, and it was not wound down until the early 1880s.

Despite having been cast out of Langham Place, Fido remained active—and does not seem to have been ostracized for very long—in the broader women's movement. She founded the Ladies' Work Society and the Victoria Discussion Society in 1869, and in 1874 the Industrial and Educational

Bureau for Women, to offer training, jobs, and emigration opportunities. In 1871 she was presented with a silver tea and coffee service by colleagues (including Lady Goldsmid of the SPEW committee), and Emily Davies resumed cautious dealings with her later in that decade. Fido continued to promote the Cause (including votes for women) in her *Victoria Magazine*, as well as in her cheaper weekly, *Women and Work* (1874–76), her *West London Express* (1877–78), and in her columns for the *Ladies Pictorial* in the 1880s and 1890s. Interestingly, she does not seem to have held a lasting grudge against Bessie Parkes, and often paid tribute to her in print.

Not content with being a campaigner, lecturer, publisher, editor, journalist, and novelist, Fido formed a small drama company that toured London and the provinces in 1875. Her reputation grew as a result of extensive U.S. speaking engagements, described in *Three Tours of America* (1884). In 1888 she received an inscribed portrait from the Queen in recognition of thirty years of work on behalf of her sex.

Nor was she lonely. After Fido's friend Emy Wilson got married in 1868, actress Kate Pattison acted as Fido's secretary and companion from 1869 to 1883. This long partnership was followed by one with interior decorator Charlotte Robinson. From 1884, Fido and Charlotte shared a quiet, thick-carpeted home in Manchester and ran a women's decor college and business that earned Charlotte an appointment as "Home Decorator to Her Majesty."

Despite her lifelong lung troubles, Fido remained a keen smoker: during her first U.S. tour in 1872–73, a Chicago journalist wrote that the "fat, famous and frolicsome Emily Faithfull smoke[s] like a Lake Michigan tug boat." She died of bronchitis in 1895, a few days after her sixtieth birthday. In her will she left a tactful but firm message for the Faithfulls:

> *I feel sure that any loving members of my family who may survive me will appreciate my desire that the few possessions I have should be retained for the exclusive use and as the absolute property of my beloved friend Charlotte Robinson as some little indication of my gratitude for the countless services for which I am indebted to her as well as for the affectionate tenderness and care which made the last few years of my life the happiest I ever spent.*

Fido destroyed almost all her private papers, except for some that she left to Charlotte to be passed on to her favourite nephew, Ferdinand Faithfull Begg, which have since disappeared.

But though she survived the Codrington case, both personally and professionally, it did cast a long shadow over her name; she remained vaguely associated with sex scandal. At least one obituary by a woman journalist (*Illustrated London News,* May 15, 1895) criticized her for having adopted a mannish style of dress—which by then carried sinister implications of what doctors were starting to call "inversion," "sex perversion," or "homosexuality." As James Stone documents in his biography, the death of this tireless maverick was followed by a conspiracy of silence on the part of her comrades, who wrote her out of the history of the first British women's movement.

As for Vice-Admiral Henry Codrington, he remarried—Catherine Compton, the widow of another admiral—in 1869, and ended up living two doors away from his brother William in Eaton Square. He never was sent on active service again; he received the titles of Admiral of the Fleet and Knight Commander of the Bath before he died in 1877, leaving £30,000 each to his two daughters. (Nan later became the mother of Denys Finch-Hatton, made famous as the hero of Isak Dinesen's *Out of Africa.*) Harry's sister Lady Bourchier published two volumes about the family, *Memoir of the Life of Admiral Sir Edward Codrington* (1873) and *Selections from the Letters of Sir Henry Codrington* (1880), classics of euphemism that manage to make almost no reference to Harry's first marriage.

From the day Helen Jane Webb Smith Codrington was divorced, nothing more is known of her. One genealogical website claims that she died just twelve years after the trial, in 1876.

~

In Britain from 1670 to 1852 there were fewer than two divorces a year (and men were the petitioners in all but four of them). After the Matrimonial Causes Act of 1857 this rose rapidly to several hundred a year, and despite legal and financial hindrances, women were the petitioners in almost half of the divorces and almost all the judicial separations. In 1923 the double standard was finally abolished: a wife could now ask for a divorce on the basis of a husband's adultery alone. (Interestingly, the double standard was a peculiarly English institution; in Scotland, women and men could both divorce for simple adultery as early as the sixteenth century.) The Guardianship of Infants Act, in 1925, finally gave father and mother an equal right to custody and established the welfare of the child as paramount. The Herbert Act of 1937 extended the grounds for divorce to include cruelty, desertion (three years), incurable insanity, and habitual drunkenness: the divorce rate doubled the following year. The 1969 Divorce Reform Act restated the three main "fault" grounds as adultery, desertion, and unreasonable behaviour (a broader concept than cruelty), and made it possible for a couple to obtain a divorce on the basis of incompatibility after simply living apart for two years.

In 1996 the Family Law Act tried to make divorce an even simpler, faster, and entirely "no fault" business, but met with opposition on several sides, and that section of the act was never implemented. In August 2006, calling in the *Independent* for a reform of British divorce law, Lord Justice Wall admitted, regretfully, that making divorce a "no fault" process will be difficult, as "people actually don't like not being able to blame someone."

Acknowledgements

I am grateful to my agent, Caroline Davidson, and editors, Ann Patty and Iris Tupholme, for asking all the right questions.